SHADOW OF THE MAGUS

SHADOW OF THE MAGUS

*STRANGER MAGICS,
BOOK THIRTEEN*

ASH FITZSIMMONS

Print Edition ISBN: 978-1-949861-33-4

Cover design by BespokeBookCovers.com

www.ashfitzsimmons.com

CHAPTER 1

Even after twenty-five years of practice, Frank's smile was imperfect. It wasn't for lack of diligence—he'd studied human facial expressions, trying to mimic the muscular movements and make them seem natural on his borrowed face. So much of our communication is physical, after all, and most of it is innate. A child blind from birth will still smile automatically. But smiles are weird things, particularly to one of a species for whom a flash of teeth has *quite* a different meaning, and Frank had never managed to produce an expression that checked all the boxes for "spontaneous expression of pleasure" instead of "prelude to attack."

Then again, he didn't need to. Though a master of controlled telepathy, he made no effort to prevent his happiness from broadcasting around the Away Team's conference room. Honestly, with the strong emotional coloring, his mood would have been evident even if he'd been poker-faced.

"We're going to miss you, man," said Ted Girard, helping himself to another pig in a blanket. He sported one of his favorite Hawaiian shirts that morning, a pale blue number dotted with pineapples, a wardrobe choice forgiving of the mustard stains he usually accrued at such parties. Sure, our boss was wizard enough to handle his own laundry, though he'd long ago reached the point of ambivalence toward fashion conventions. "But don't hurry back on our account," he insisted, pointing the cocktail sausage at Frank. "I'm not putting you on the travel schedule again until October—or would November be better? Got a project in the works with Giza for late autumn, and I was thinking you and Kitty could split the research," he said, aiming the sausage at me in turn as his gray ponytail swung and his blue eyes twinkled behind his glasses.

"October should be fine," Frank rumbled. If his expressions still needed work, his speech was more than passably good. While his accent had settled out in the Atlantic, a compromise between the American sounds he'd first heard and the English town where he'd spent most of his life, his deep voice made up for any linguistic sins. To his consternation, Frank had the sort of smooth bass that made heads turn, and he'd learned to recognize a flirtatious smile through *long* exposure.

"Okay, but you let me know if you want a longer leave. No questions asked," Ted assured him. "They're only young once. I mean, if Ione needs help—"

Somewhere along the way, Frank had acquired a passably convincing chuckle, and his red eyes, naked that morning without his usual dark glasses, crinkled. "Ione will be more than capable. I'm superfluous."

"How many did you say there were, again?" Mal Stowe asked, hovering near the perfect scones. By my count, Mal had already eaten five, but that was nothing unusual—he was a bottomless pit where pastries were concerned. Though in his mid-thirties, he'd lucked into his half-fae father's permanent dark-haired youthfulness and his lupine shifter mother's forgiving metabolism.

"Three," said Frank.

Mal's hand paused on its way back to the tray. "*Yikes.*"

"That's a small clutch. Her first was larger—the one that was cannibalized in the Gray Lands, you know?"

"Pleasant thought," he muttered.

Frank shrugged. "It happens. Anyway, three underfoot should be manageable. And Neve's brood are only two years old, so they should help keep the hatchlings entertained."

Antony Copeland, who'd been doctoring his coffee, straightened, pushed his graying blond hair from his eyes, and grinned. "You poor, optimistic fool. Come see me when they keep you up all night. I've got horror stories to share."

"Never heard of a hatchling with colic," he countered with a smug smile. "Allie was a *special* baby."

"Yeah, that's a word for it." He took a sip, and his face relaxed with the hit of caffeine and sugar. "I still can't get over the fact that you're going to be a father. Congrats, bud."

The news had come as a shock to us all. Over the last year, Frank had been slipping off to Faerie with greater regularity to visit Ione, the petite blue-green dragon who'd moved into his family's barn. We'd ribbed him about having a girlfriend at first—my little sister, Beth, had been merciless—but in time, Frank had admitted that there was something between them. Dragons might not pair-bond, but Frank had never been an ordinary dragon, and Ione obviously felt affection for him. They were two weird runts who'd found each other and still chatted daily by text, courtesy of Sam Rockwell, who hung out around the barn and didn't mind lending a thumb.

Frank hadn't dropped so much as a hint that Ione was ready to breed, but in retrospect, I understood why he'd returned to Glastonbury from a long weekend at the barn with scabbed-over bitemarks on his neck and chest that even his transformation bind hadn't been able to cover. Frank was the smallest of his brothers, and with a primed female in the area, instinct put the males in combat mode. I didn't know how he'd managed to win that one—maybe Sam or Joey Bolin had stepped in, or even Ros, with the power of the realm at her disposal—but the mating had been successful. One week ago, Frank had gone into Ted's office for a private word, but our leader's excited shouting had echoed across the subbasement. Soon, we were all privy to the secret: Ione had laid a clutch, and Frank had sired it.

This soon brought up the matter of parental leave. The only member of the Team to have ever needed it was Antony, who'd stepped aside for six months fourteen years before when Allie was born. Of the rest of us, Ted, Daphne Hopkins, Mal, and my sister Artur had never married, Lakshmi Gupta's boys were long grown, Bob Norge and his husband, Sylvester Hotchkiss, had never wanted kids, Marcus's son had lived to a ripe old age and died two millennia ago, and I...well, I'd been with Marcus for two years, but I'd taken precautions. No one had anticipated a request for leave from *Frank*, of all people, who seldom missed so much as a meeting. We'd feel the loss—Frank was clever, dependable, and in an emergency, two hundred thirty feet of muscle, claws, teeth, wings, and fire breath. Seldom did we ever need to break his bind, but when we did, the result was *terrifying*.

I'd never made a particular study of dragons, but considering what I'd gleaned from Frank over the years, I was surprised that he planned to be with Ione while she nested and for the hatchlings' first two months of life. She was in the barn, not the wilds of the Gray Lands, that strange third realm beyond the mortal realm and Faerie. It wasn't as if she needed protection from scavenging dragons. When I'd asked, Frank had admitted that theirs was an unusual arrangement. "I want to be involved in my children's lives," he'd said, his red eyes watching me over his computer's screen. "It's weird, I understand that, but I've seen Antony with Allie for so long, and...you know, Kitty, your father..."

He hadn't had to spell that out. I'd loved my dad fiercely before he died, and thanks to Hope Lozano, a gifted medium, I knew that he still checked in on Beth and me, just as Artur's long-deceased father looked in on her. Maybe that was slightly creepy, but our dads meant well.

Frank had sighed and propped his head on his fist.

"I've been around you for too long. Suppose something's rubbed off by now."

"Surely Ione doesn't mind having a helper," I'd replied.

"She wasn't certain at first. The impression I got from her is that a male's more likely to eat his young than protect them, but..." He'd flopped his free hand toward his loaded bookshelves and pots of ornamental succulents. "I'm not your average male, and so Ione's willing to take a chance that I won't cannibalize our children."

"So...we should expect you back in a few years, then?"

He'd snorted his amusement. "A few months is more like it. I'll stick around while Ione incubates the clutch, and maybe for a month or two after—they're due at the end of July or early August, so I won't miss much more than the summer," he'd explained. Seeing my bemusement, he'd patted his computer. "I don't envision myself staying there permanently, do you? By the time the hatchlings find their wings, I'll be dying to get back to Glastonbury. Don't get me wrong, I do love being with Ione," he'd hastened to add, "but living in the barn, day in, day out..."

I'd grinned. "Nothing to read?"

"Difficult to turn pages without thumbs, and claws are hell on a screen," he'd concurred.

In the days since the news leaked, we'd put together a TV and movie playlist for Frank, ready to go as long as someone created a projector, and had made offers to visit if he grew bored. The only person unhappy with the arrangement was Sylvester, our octogenarian unofficial Team chef, who once again aired his grievance as he emerged from the kitchenette with a tray of tiny ham sandwiches. "Do you know how long it's been since I baked for a proper baby shower?" he demanded as Frank helped himself to the plate of bacon. "*Years.* I have a lovely recipe for petit fours that I haven't brought out in ages—"

"They're fantastic," Bob agreed, his wild white hair bouncing as he nodded.

"And I could make them with little icing booties,"

Sylvester continued. "Just say the word, Frank, and I'll handle everything."

"That's very generous of you," he replied between thick slices of bacon, "but there's no need. The purpose of a shower is to get items for the baby, yes? You can't put a hatchling in a romper, and we won't need nappies or bottles or such."

"I do feel bad that we're not giving you anything," Daphne cut in.

She had a point. Frank was the only member of the Team without the first shred of magical talent, and most of us could have outfitted a nursery with an hour and a few inspirational photographs.

Together, we were an odd bunch of misfits hanging out in the subbasement of the Arcanum's international headquarters. Ted, a decently competent wizard of Canadian extraction, had set out to assemble a group of people with varying abilities in order to track down several millennia's worth of missing magical artifacts. The only other legitimate wizards in the group were Lakshmi, our Indian logistics expert and de facto den mother; Bob, a British former archivist; Daphne, a brilliant Jamaican-British wizard if not quite magus material; and Antony, a longtime American expat who was barely more talented than a witch but handled much of our tech needs. And then there were the rest of us, the ones whom the Arcanum either knew little about or barely tolerated: Maria Corelli, our Italian-born supervisory magus, whose drop of fae blood had been augmented to the point that she was now a faerie in all but name; Frank, our resident dragon, who'd turned out to be an excellent researcher; Mal, whose poor ability with magic was a minor blip beside his ability to shift into an oversized wolf in the blink of an eye; Marcus and Artur, time-displaced augmented quarter faeries whose age gave them a powerful boost; and me, another product of augmentation. Though I was technically witch-blooded—my mother was an American wizard, my biological father half fae—an unexpected encounter with my sister's magical sword had left me like Maria, intimately familiar with the wizard's playbook but unable to cast a single spell. Of course, now that I was fae for practical purposes, I could *enchant*, and far more effectively than I'd ever been able to cast, but if one were wise, one didn't blatantly show off fae abilities in a castle full of uneasy wizards. Though the current rulers of Faerie were half-blooded and thus far less psychopathic than their fully fae predecessors, many in the Arcanum still regarded the neighboring realm and its natives with a wary eye. It didn't help that while spellcraft was excellent for detailed magical constructions, enchantment could much more effectively make things go *boom*.

Daphne's dark eyes narrowed as she scowled in thought. "What about stuffed animals, something they can cuddle?"

"Too easily disemboweled," Frank replied. "I used to play with a sheep skull."

She scrunched her nose and stuck out her tongue. "That's *foul*."

"That's hatchlings for you," he countered, and bit into a fresh slice of bacon. "But thanks anyway. And for all of this," he added, nodding to Sylvester. "You shouldn't have gone to the trouble."

Sylvester waved him off. "It's no trouble, my boy. If you change your mind, now, the offer stands on the petit fours."

"We just wanted a proper send-off for you," said Ted, reaching up to clap Frank on the shoulder. "And I'll say it once more—we're going to miss you, friend. Couldn't be happier for you, don't feel like you need to hurry back, but know that we can't wait to have you in the field again, eh?"

Frank smiled down at him, and while it wasn't a perfect smile, it was close enough.

That night, while I tended the sizzling stir fry, I thought of how happy Frank had seemed when he left us after breakfast. Maria had slipped away from a Council meeting early to catch the last of Sylvester's spread, and she'd done the transportation honors, opening an inter-realm gate from the conference room to the meadow beside the dragon barn. For once, Frank hadn't bothered to strip, instead snagging a last sausage ball before taking a running leap at the gate. His clothing had shredded to confetti with the breaking of his transformation bind and his instantaneous return to full size, and he'd spread his wings and shaken himself to knock the last of the scraps of cloth off his iridescent white scales.

"Feel better?" Ted had called from our side of the gate.

Much, Frank had thought in reply, then dipped his massive head and lumbered toward the waiting eggs.

As I pushed the bits of chicken and vegetables around our modified wok—like almost everything in the kitchen, it was made of copper, a concession to the annoying fae contact allergy to iron—Marcus looked after the frying eggrolls. "Time?" he asked, turning the latest golden-brown batch in the skillet.

I gauged the color of the meat. "Two minutes, give or take."

"Perfect."

I tried not to let him see me smile as he extracted the eggrolls and carefully patted them dry. Though he still had a long way to go to match Sylvester's complex desserts and dainty cakes, he'd developed a knack for the kitchen. We'd learned through practice to share space and appliances, and I'd come to appreciate our nearly nightly ritual, a way to wind down after hours in the subbasement. I didn't mind cooking for the rest of our flatmates, as neither of my sisters was much use around food. Beth, sixteen, could reliably bake a frozen pizza, while Artur, whose training had skewed martial instead of culinary, could enchant food that was edible, if not exactly palatable. Even Maria, who was like a sister to me, preferred her kitchen adventures to come in microwave form. I didn't care. Cooking for four—or five, given Maria's frequent presence at our table—was as easy as cooking for two, and I enjoyed doing it with my partner.

It felt like home, really.

Granted, it wasn't a *traditional* domestic setup. I was Beth's official guardian due to our mother's incarceration, and Artur stayed with us because she had no other family. Maria kept her single flat but wasn't above passing out on our couch. As for Marcus...well, he still had his own bedroom, but it had become more of a place to store his clothing. Things had grown comfortable between the two of us—we seemed to fit, like pieces taken from different puzzles that somehow linked together. Had we been any other couple, I might have started hinting about a ring, but while I was ready to take our relationship to the next level, I didn't know if Marcus would ever reach that point.

It wasn't just that his first marriage had ended horrifically, his wife running off with his cousin and leaving him asleep in a wall for twenty-two centuries. That alone might have been enough to make anyone wary of matrimony, but then there were the complications Marcus had discovered on waking. He was functionally half fae now, immortal, and heir to one of the faerie courts—not a promising combination for someone hoping for marital vows. Few faeries stay together for long, as "until death" means something quite different once you get beyond the typical human lifespan. While I, too, had experienced the agony of having my fae blood augmented, I'd never so much as selected a court. If I followed my late (and certainly not missed) biological father and chose Coileán's court, then by birthright, I'd be a lady, as my father been a lord before me. Nobility came in two flavors among the fae: the high lords and ladies, children of a king or queen, and the regular variety, those who either were more distantly related to a monarch or had been elevated from among the general populace. Myrddin had been an absolute asshole, but his title in that court would have passed to Artur and me, had either of us ever tried to claim it. On the other hand, if I chose to join Marcus in Val's court, the odds were decent that I'd be elevated in my own right, since Val had practically fostered me. (Technically, I could have opted for the third court as well, Eleanor's, though I had no connection there.) But court politics were a matter I'd hoped to avoid, and so there we remained, two of Ted's infamous Away Team square pegs, squatting on Arcanum turf and trying to dodge the many bits of steel hiding around the castle.

There was no rush. I was only twenty-six, and I wasn't aging. My biological clock had come to a standstill, paused at the peak of youth—which, let's face it, wasn't a bad place to be. I certainly wasn't complaining. Still, considering the personality and relationship dynamics of the Team, I was surprised to find *Frank*, the runty, misfit dragon, beating me to parenthood.

Not that I would have shared those thoughts with Marcus. I loved him, and I knew he loved me—and I also understood that he needed time to work himself out. Those who knew us best remained optimistic. Maria insisted it was a matter of when, not if, with us, and Artur swore that he showed all the signs of a man besotted. Hell, even Marcus's *mother* had given her blessing to the relationship, which was a fine thing for me to have, as Caecilia had been dead for centuries. I took comfort in the fact that she liked what she saw of me, though I couldn't exactly ask her for tips on getting through to her son. Hope, my only friend with the ability to speak to the dead, hadn't left the Gray Lands in nearly a year.

Unlike me, Hope had found married bliss with her childhood sweetheart, Arik. I couldn't have been happier for her, and he'd seemed just as smitten with her as she was with him on their long wedding day, which had begun at dawn and hadn't wound down until the sky had lightened the next morning. Arik was the new king of the Gray Lands—or Conota, as they called it—and their wedding had been properly spectacular, a pageant far beyond the typical ceremonies. They'd invited Arik's peers from the other two realms—the Three, Faerie's kings and queen, and the Arcanum's grand magus—plus the entire Team to the festivities, though it was understood that few from outside the Gray Lands would attend. Toula Pavli and the Three wished them well, but as there's no magic useable to us in that realm, anyone who entered would have been at Arik's mercy—not the best position in which heads of rival magical factions could find themselves. Instead, I'd gone with Marcus, Artur, Beth, Maria, Frank, and Ted, as my boss never met a party he didn't enjoy, plus Carey and Zeb Jones from the Minor Arcanum. Arik had given us his native tongue and offered to work up a version of Frank's transformation bind, broken due to lack of magic, but Frank had declined—and I suppose the assembled lords and ladies had thought twice about starting trouble with a dragon curled up beside the outdoor seating pavilions, sunning himself in that realm's single patch of cloudless sky and showing a flash of teeth to anyone who ventured too close. If there was one thing at which Frank innately succeeded, it was reptilian menace.

Still, Hope hadn't left that realm in months, and so if Marcus's mother had changed her mind about my fitness for her son, I had no way of knowing. His *father*, however, made no secret of his feelings on the matter. Maria confided on occasion that Val made a habit of cornering her when she visited for dinner and asking if there'd been any signs of progress. The king was nosy but well-meaning, and I wasn't offended that he'd taken an interest.

But no matter how many people I might have in my corner, no matter how often I considered Hope's happiness with the tiniest twinge of jealousy, I wasn't going to rush Marcus. He was strong, but there was a brittle quality to that strength—a quality all too familiar to me. There was no need to back him against a wall and demand a date certain. I could be patient.

Of course, that didn't mean I couldn't drop hints.

Marcus caught me smiling to myself as I finished the stir fry. "What's on your mind?" he asked, sending the leftover hot oil into the ether as he tucked an unruly clump of brown hair behind one ear.

"Oh, nothing. Just thinking about what a baby dragon would look like in a onesie."

He chuckled at the notion. "Perhaps one with the phrases on. 'Mummy's Little Man-Eater'?"

"Ooh, better. They make onesies with attached tutus. Like, picture something all in pink, tulle skirt, silk rosettes, maybe some glitter…"

"On baby Frank."

The mental image was enough to make me laugh aloud—a winged lizard the size of a pony, waddling around like an overgrown toddler ballerina. "It'd be a pain to get the bloodstains out. You know hatchlings have to be messy eaters."

From the den, where Artur was reading with a beer, came a pronounced snort.

"Come on, you know it'd be cute," I called into the next room, but I dropped the matter when the front door opened and Beth, her blonde hair matted and brown with sweat, wearily shuffled in. "Hey, there," I said, stepping out of the kitchen to greet her with a dishtowel over my shoulder. "How was practice?"

She slumped onto the nearest open chair and groaned. "Brutal. Did you get takeout?"

"Homemade. Hungry?"

"Starving." Beth turned to Artur, who had put her book aside, and said, "Would I be a major disappointment if I begged off from sparring tonight?"

"No," Artur replied, and sipped her beer. "You should be resting, anyway. Are you hurt?"

"Banged up," she admitted, lifting her sweat-stained T-shirt to reveal a darkening bruise on her ribcage. "Shield failed at the wrong moment, and I got a bolt to the chest."

Artur peered at it, then offered a firm nod. "Nothing lethal. Let Marcus address it after we eat."

"Or *before*," he said as he joined us. "There's no sense in prolonging the pain. Bathe," he told Beth, "find any other sore spots, and then we'll see to it. Does anything feel broken?"

She took a deep breath without wincing, then muttered, "Nah. I'm okay—"

"*Bathe*. You're dripping on the furniture," Artur ordered.

With a put-upon grunt, Beth pushed herself from the chair and crossed the flat to her bedroom.

Once the shower started, Artur looked up at Marcus, her face unreadable. "Pain is an effective teacher, you realize. Sharpens the memory."

"That may be, but it's cruel to make her suffer through dinner." He perched on the arm of Beth's vacated chair and cocked an eyebrow. "And *you* are giving her the night off? No chastisement?"

I, too, was surprised. My half sisters' relationship, which had begun as Beth's overwhelming hero worship of Artur, had evolved over their nearly two years together into something far closer to familial. That said, the lessons in swordplay that Artur had started giving Beth as an incentive for her good behavior had become standing appointments, delayed only if Artur was away with the Team. Even on nights before tests, Artur dragged Beth out to spar, working her until the kid was red and drenched. The lessons had made Beth stronger, but they'd also improved her time management skills. More importantly, they'd given her a much-needed boost of confidence. Artur saw as well as I did how badly Beth wanted to make *someone* proud—like me, my little sister had never been good enough for our mother. Though Artur's praise was seldom effusive, it was given consistently, and with time and many painful bouts, Beth had begun to lower her interpersonal defenses. I was just grateful that she'd lost much of her old anger and made high marks. She'd even found a few friends in her year, girls whose names came up around the table but whose faces were seldom seen anywhere near the flat. Beth couldn't help it that her family was known to be weird.

"Maria told me how Beth is spending her last hours of instruction this month," Artur told Marcus. "Six weeks until the Games, you know. Maria is drilling anyone interested in single combat. I decided that doubling Beth's lessons would be unwise until Maria is finished with her."

She had a point. Maria hadn't been made a magus for her looks and charm—she'd had her first spellcraft training at the hands of a former grand magus, and she'd never slowed down. As she, like Marcus and me, had suffered through augmentation, Maria could no longer coax a spell from the tip of a wand, but she knew and taught the techniques…and if any of her upper-level charges' spells went awry, she could enchant a shield as easily as breathing. Not for nothing did Toula put Maria among the referee magi during the Games, whose job it was to keep the casualties to an acceptable minimum.

Judging by my kid sister's appearance that night, Maria was punching her students' weak spots—a smart tactic overall, though painful in the moment. Beth was no slouch, but she wasn't going to be a magus anytime soon, and so she couldn't simply rely on the strength of her bolts to carry her through the competition. I tried to be encouraging about her talent whenever she recounted a difficult session of practical magic—God knows that *I* was useless in that class, a witch-blood barely able to work a dragonscale wand at the time—but the only person in the flat who expected Beth to win her year at combat was Artur, who didn't understand the purpose of silver and bronze medals. To her credit, Artur had brought Beth along in ways that her Arcanum education never would have. Sure, they sparred with blunted swords and shields, but some nights, whenever Beth got too cocky about her performance, Artur would make her create at least part of her gear with magic. Extra casting practice was always a helpful thing, but casting under pressure, with Artur's *highly* accurate sword coming at her, had done wonders for Beth's shields.

When Beth limped out, shower-pink, wrapped in a fluffy bathrobe, and wearing a towel turban, she only made it halfway across the kitchen before Marcus intercepted her and returned her to her room. "I got the spells started," I heard her protest from behind the cracked door. "See? It's working."

Any further complaint came out as a yelp. "If that rib isn't broken," Marcus said, "it's close. You'll be soft all week with a healing spell like that. Be still, now, let me work."

I glanced at Artur, who continued to nurse her beer. My elder sister looked quite a bit like me—we shared Myrddin's white-blonde hair, though my eyes were green to her blue—but she'd mastered an aura of stoic competence that I had yet to match. "Beth wants to improve," she murmured. "To be independent. Perhaps we should refrain from tending her injuries for a time, give her a chance to develop her healing spells."

"Maybe after the Games," I replied, keeping my voice down. "Look, I get it, she wants to be all grown-up and competent, but I guarantee you that everyone else in her year who did time with Maria today is being patched up by someone tonight."

"It wounds her pride."

"Fine. I'm more concerned about the wounds to her *body*. She's a sixth-year, not a magus."

Artur sipped and stared at Beth's bedroom door. "Could Maria heal at her age?"

"Maria was a freak of nature," I said, waving the water glasses to the tap. "She won single combat overall as a *first-*

year. If Beth's charting her progress by Maria's yardstick, then I need to talk some sense into that kid."

My sister shrugged. "She has goals."

"Yeah, impossible ones."

"The harder the goal, the harder she will work."

I thought of my mother's disapproving frown and quickly pushed the image back into the pit from which it had arisen. "Sure, but let's not push her toward inevitable failure, okay?"

By the time Marcus had finished his ministrations, the table was laid, Artur had a fresh beer, and Beth seemed to be walking more easily. "How's your homework?" I asked as she eagerly attacked the stir fry. "Do you have much reading tonight?"

Beth rolled her dark eyes. "It's under control."

"That wasn't an answer."

She huffed and grabbed the rice. "Not bad. Like, maybe an hour. Of course, *some* schools are on summer break already…"

"Yeah, and the Arc 1 kids won't be nearly as prepared as y'all," I said, giving her shoulder a squeeze. "It's good for you."

"You're not the one with the reading," she muttered, but tucked in. "Is Frank gone?"

"This morning," Marcus replied. "The breakfast send-off was a success."

"That's good. So, when can I go over?"

I had to bite my tongue to keep from laughing aloud. Barely two years before, the idea of Beth setting foot in Faerie, let alone volunteering for the trip, would have been ludicrous. But she and I had come a long way together, and in truth, we had Mom's incarceration to thank for it. The sister who had loathed me had almost become a friend—a friend whose homework I still had to check, sure, but more than just a flatmate. She no longer hated my boyfriend on principle, she could be in the same room as Val without looking like she was about to faint, and after spending enough evening study sessions on my office couch, she'd managed to make friends with Frank, who tolerated her antics as one would the playful growls of an excitable puppy.

Then again, Frank had done his share of office babysitting when Allie Copeland was small and, from the stories I'd been told, into anything that wasn't locked away and quite a few things that were. Mal had been her favorite playmate back in the day, but then he could shift into an oversized wolf at will, and he hadn't been above giving pony rides. But Frank, who enjoyed the odd battle with foam weaponry, had been a close second. That he could put up with Beth's antics really shouldn't have surprised me.

"Any field trips are up to Frank," I told her between bites of golden eggroll. "This is time for him and Ione, yeah?"

"I guess." She drenched her mound of rice with soy sauce, then paused, fork halfway to her mouth, and peered at me. "He *is* coming back, right? He's not going to stay there once the eggs hatch?"

I glanced at Marcus and Artur and saw my concern mirrored in their faces. "He plans to be back this fall."

"But what if he decides not to leave his kids? I mean, would *you* walk out on your kids after a couple of months?"

I could only shrug. "Dragons are different, you know that. He's playing this by ear, but I can't imagine that he'll *never* be back," I said, trying to sound confident. "They'll be grown in five years, anyway."

"If he wants to raise his children, no one here will blame him," Marcus added. "Ted knows that the assignments may require shuffling."

Beth ate in silence for a moment, brows furrowed, then said, "What if they all came over here? Put them in the courtyard, plenty of room to wander around—"

"Remember that part about *flight?*" I pointed out. "Not

to mention an installation full of freaked-out wizards…"

"It's *Frank*."

"Yeah. And most of this castle knows him as the big albino in the subbasement. It's not like he walks around starting fires."

"I've seen him at full size," Beth replied. "He's not *that* scary."

Marcus met my eyes across the table. "Mm. I didn't check her head, but do you suppose she's concussed?"

"Jerk," Beth muttered.

He snatched her eggroll from her plate and bit it in half, grinning as she punched him in the arm. Beside me, Artur sighed and continued to eat, and I shook my head and did likewise, grateful for another family dinner. Maybe Beth wouldn't win her event at the Games. Maybe Frank wouldn't return to the Team for years. But that night, there was laughter and warmth, and Marcus levitating Beth's plate out of her reach as she climbed onto her chair to jump for it, and that was good enough for a Monday.

CHAPTER 2

Our first week without Frank in the subbasement was, if anything, quiet. Having been designated the distributor of updates from the barn, I received two status reports from Sam and a few photos to share. "Ione's handling it like a champ," he told me in one video call, panning the camera around the barn to reveal the bulk of the blue dragon curled atop her straw nest. "And Frank's outside seeing about lunch."

I was grateful that he didn't feel the need to video *that* moment. Unbound, Frank had a mouth full of massive, serrated teeth, and the flock of sheep penned nearby didn't stand a chance. "How's he getting them inside?"

The video shifted a few feet to the right as Sam peeked out the barn door, an opening wide enough to let a jumbo jet pass with room to spare. "Looks like he's beheading them. Carefully. He drove dinner in here live last night, but Ione doesn't want to risk too much movement around the eggs." Turning the camera around to himself, Sam grinned. "It's sweet, really," he said, lowering his voice. "From everything we've gathered, females typically fast during incubation, aside from the occasional water break. Our closet romantic here doesn't want his lady getting hangry." A bright flash lit his cheek from offscreen, and he looked that way and listened to what sounded like static on my end of the line. "Ros says hello and not to worry," he told me. "She's keeping an eye on them. Not that she'd do anything else, you know how she pries..." The static picked up again, and Sam feigned a fearful cringe. "I'm kidding, I'm *kidding*," he insisted, and laughed as a clod of what I sincerely hoped was dirt flew past his ear. "Sorry," he said into the camera. "Got to go make up to my girl. Bye."

Before Ros Bolin had become Faerie's nearly omniscient power behind the thrones, she'd been an unusually gifted witch-blood who'd settled in Faerie with her parents after toppling the murderous regime of Grand Magus Mulligan. When Georgie, the dragon in the barn next door, had laid a clutch, Ros had been on hand...and she'd hung out with the sixth egg, which hadn't hatched with the other five. That egg had been Frank, and since only Ros had been around when he hatched, he'd bonded to her. Sure, Frank's actual mother was in the picture, but Ros remained almost maternally protective of her former hatchling.

I was grateful that Frank didn't want for company. Aside from Ione, his mother, two brothers, three sisters, and five two-year-old nieces and nephews, Frank had regular visitors of the bipedal variety: Ros; her parents, Joey Bolin and Helen Carver, the original dragon rider and a former grand magus, respectively; and Sam, Ros's boyfriend of twenty-some years. For one of the most well-connected families in Faerie, they were surprisingly laid-back. Joey was a second-great-grandnephew to two of the Three, Eleanor and Coileán, but as he and Coileán were close friends as well, he'd accepted a place—and a title—in that court. He was also close to Coileán's augmented witch-blooded half brother, Aiden...who himself was half brother to Helen, Joey's wife and an incredibly talented wizard in her own right.

Faerie family trees were still difficult for me to fathom sometimes. For instance, the original Three—Mab, Oberon, and Titania—had left numerous fae, half-fae, and witch-blooded offspring scattered across the realms, and their children could be separated in age by centuries. Coileán, who'd inherited Titania's court, was almost eight hundred years Aiden's senior, while Val, who'd claimed Mab's, had more than two millennia on Toula. Eleanor, Oberon's heir, had nieces and nephews closer to her age than some of her siblings. This generational blending led to some odd results—I mean, Joey was both Aiden's second-great-grandnephew and brother-in-law—but then again, my sister Artur was more than fifteen hundred years my senior (and the basis for the freaking Arthurian canon), so I had little room to criticize.

The person at the barn in the strangest position had to be Sam, a half-fae Texan and one of Eleanor's many nephews. Once Ros inherited Faerie, Sam had opted to remain with her—she couldn't return to the mortal realm, and he'd left nothing there. Like all faeries, he couldn't come near animals in the mortal realm without gambling on an attack—a tough situation for a guy raised on a cattle ranch—but dragons were a different matter, and Joey, who superintended the enormous barn, had welcomed the help. Long before I made it to Faerie, Sam had moved into the Bolin–Carver guestroom, and then he'd built a place of his own. Their houses seemed to sprout from opposite ends of the barn like gabled outcroppings, near enough to be neighbors but sufficiently far to give both couples privacy. Ros was practically omniscient in the realm, but when she spent time with her beau, she didn't want an audience.

The best part of Sam's presence around the barn, at least from Frank's perspective, was his willingness to play transcriptionist. Much of Frank and Ione's relationship had grown from text messages, and Sam had served as their go-between, reading Frank's notes to Ione and taking dictation for her replies. For years, he'd done much the same for Frank and Ros, as she fried electronics and couldn't be understood over the phone, and so the role was a natural fit for him. In any case, I was glad that Frank had companionship, particularly if Ione became overprotective of her clutch.

Thus, when my phone rang around midnight eight days

after Frank left us, my first thought as I was startled awake was that Sam was on the line. On checking the screen, however, I frowned and blinked until the words I was seeing made sense. Tapping the screen, I mumbled, "Yolanda? Y'okay?"

"Sorry," said the voice on the other end, but judging by her tone, I sensed that she wasn't entirely apologetic for pulling me from sleep. "Are you awake?"

"More or less." I sat up and slid out of bed, trying not to disturb Marcus beside me. "What's going on?"

"I'm looking for backup. Got a wild one."

That pushed me over the line toward full consciousness. Yolanda Ford was the sole Fringe coordinator in the mortal realm, the daughter of two happily resettled refugees who had left the Fringe town in Faerie for Stanford and never looked back. Armed with a PhD in archaeology and a slight trace of fae blood, she'd proven to be a competent leader and an ally to the Team, not least because she and Mal were old schoolmates. Part of her duties as one of the few Fringers in the realm was to look for more of her kind—witches, lesser fae, and witch-bloods, people with a touch of magical ability in need of training and a community. But every so often, her leads went in a different direction, which was when she usually did the sensible thing and called in colleagues who could do more with magic than just make objects twitch.

"Where?" I asked, easing my bedroom door closed behind me.

"New York. Nothing verified by sight, but the signs are good, and I think our target is home. I'm in Peru. Can you come over?"

"That depends. Elevation?"

"Outskirts of Lima, you big baby. I'm practically at sea level."

"Excuse *me* for enjoying oxygen. Can you send me photos of the place so I can make a gate?"

"Incoming. Put on some real clothes, won't you?" she

added, and ended the call.

Ten minutes later, having slipped into jeans and a T-shirt and shaken Marcus awake to join me, I opened a gate into Yolanda's cluttered studio, a small space in a rundown block of flats filled with camping gear, computers, and several stacks of books that were probably long overdue. It was barely past seven p.m. in Peru, and Yolanda, sporting dirt-stained khakis and wearing her thick hair in a single braid wrapped around her head like a crown, leaned against her desk and chowed down on a bowl of instant ramen as she filled us in about the latest fish to be caught in Aiden's net.

While he might have been a high lord, Aiden was first and foremost the fae equivalent of a technomancer, having learned through decades of trial and error how to make magic and electronics play nicely together, or at least grudgingly cooperate. The discipline was rare among the Arcanum set for good reason: trying to cast around unshielded electronic components almost inevitably resulted in destroying them. But Aiden's great love was computers, and he'd worked out the techniques that almost no one else had the patience to master. He'd been assisting the Fringe for years, starting with making protected equipment and gradually progressing to software needs. His latest big project had been a magically aided program that scanned search engine data for particular terms and looked for user patterns. The computing power necessary to accomplish this was enormous—and I'd seen the windowless building on the edge of the Fringe settlement where the many servers were housed—but in its three years of operation, it had located several potential new Fringers. Admittedly, some hits had been false alarms, but the program had brought five witches into the fold.

"We've seen multiple pings over the last two weeks, all coming from an apartment building in Queens," Yolanda reported. "The search terms make me *very* suspicious."

"Not the usual?" I asked. Most of the witches picked

up by the system had been young and nervous, running searches about poltergeist activity and why strange things seemed to happen when they got upset.

"No." She put down her bowl and picked up a small notebook. "Repeated searches for *arcanum*, *wizard*, *magic*, and *bunker*, often in combination."

"Arc 1," Marcus muttered. "What else could it be?"

"My thoughts exactly. So tell me, why is a rando in New York looking for information about the Montana silo?"

I folded my arms. "What's the plan, then? How big is this building? Do you want to go door to door?"

"No need." She bent to her computer, though not without first snagging another bite of noodles. "Secondary scans came through. Our target has been making all of these searches from one ten-by-ten location, during roughly the same time period—my guess would be a home network after work. If we go now, we should be able to catch the target in the act."

"Pictures?"

"*Please*," she scoffed. "You know it."

I didn't understand the myriad ways in which Fringers hacked their way through problems, but I always kept a close eye on my computer whenever two or more of them were in the room. For most of the pickups on which Yolanda had requested my help, we'd found the target by using networked security cameras—simple enough to borrow for Fringe purposes, though the output was often grainy. But as we didn't need a professional photograph to direct a gate, we made do.

The pictures Yolanda showed us that night were of a short corridor off a staircase that might have last been spruced up fifty years before, all cheap tile and peeling paint. An empty glass box on the wall seemed to have been intended for a fire extinguisher at some point. The overhead lighting was dim, and I could imagine the dead bugs shriveling in the dusty fixtures. "Charming," I said, and glanced at Marcus. "Want to get this, or should I?"

"No trouble," he said, keeping his eyes on the pictures, then casually waved at the empty space to his left. An intra-realm gate ripped open at his will, and with it came the smell of the distant apartment building, an unappetizing combination of Chinese takeout, summer-ripe garbage, and industrial floor cleaner. With a grimace, he started across, and I closed the lightning-rimmed hole behind Yolanda.

"There," she murmured, pointing to the door at the far-right end of the hallway, and approached with her usual caution as the neighbors in the facing apartment yelled at each other behind their closed green door. "Number 401," she said, stopping by the rubber welcome mat, which still bore a crust of winter salt and sand. "Ready?"

Marcus and I nodded, and with a quick, deep breath, Yolanda knocked.

Ten seconds later, the door opened to a surprised young woman in pink leggings and an oversized T-shirt. "Oh," she said, her gray eyes scanning each of us in turn. "You, uh…you aren't bringing my order from Curry Kitchen, are you?"

I gave her a quick examination. She seemed to be about my age, give or take a few years—somewhere south of thirty, though I couldn't be more exact. Her hair was thick and textured like Yolanda's, but she wore it as a gold-highlighted mane of dark corkscrew curls, which fell over her face as she cocked her head in query. Her complexion lay between Yolanda's and mine, a color deeper than a mere tan that suggested ancestry from a region where rickets was never a problem. She was pretty but superficially normal—no wand in hand, no sudden shield, nothing that would suggest she was anything but mundane.

"Not delivery, I'm afraid," said Yolanda. "We're here to answer your questions and ask a few of our own—and no, we're not Mormons," she added as the woman's mouth started to open. "I've seen your search history."

That took her aback. "I haven't done anything wrong—"

"Didn't say you had."

Her eyes narrowed. "You're...FBI?"

Yolanda tossed her head back toward me. "No, but she's Arcanum. May we come in?"

The last was true—technically—but seeing the shock on the stranger's face, I decided not to quibble with Yolanda over my organizational affiliations. The woman stared at us uncertainly for another moment, then stepped away from the door, her empty hands raised in front of her chest as if to ward us off. "Look, whoever you are, I don't want any trouble—"

"We're not here for that." Yolanda closed the door, smiled, and gestured toward the nest of afghans and papers that the woman had constructed on her sagging couch. Her computer sat on the particleboard coffee table, silently broadcasting her secrets to the Fringe, beside a half-empty bottle of Sam Adams. "Have a seat. Really, we didn't come here to hurt you. You've got questions, yeah?"

Slowly, not taking her eyes off us, she sat.

"I'm Yolanda," the coordinator said, keeping her tone light and non-threatening. "My colleagues here are Kitty and Marcus. And you would be..."

She nervously licked her lips. "Quinn."

"Quinn," Yolanda repeated. "Nice to meet you. I'm from the Fringe, and I promise, you'll be alive and safe when your dinner gets here."

"You've been searching for answers online," I said, taking in the cluttered bookshelves and cheap furniture. To my relief, there was no string diagram of conspiracy tacked to the off-white wall. "You have questions about...magic? The Arcanum? You seem to have heard the name."

Quinn hesitated a moment longer, then nodded.

"Let me guess," Yolanda interjected, "craziness seems to follow you, yeah? Maybe you stub your toe and the dishes rattle, or you get angry and something catches fire.

Maybe you're aware of colors in the air that no one else seems to notice. Any of that sound familiar?"

While there was still fear in her expression, I could see relief bubbling toward the surface. "Oh, my God, *yes*," she began, "how did you—"

"You're not insane," said Marcus. "Whatever it sounds like to you, you're not insane."

She watched us from the safety of her afghans. "It happens to you, too?"

"Not so much anymore," he replied. "Training helps—with the outbursts, I mean. You'll always see magic."

"We can get you the training you need," I added. "So why don't you tell us what's going on, and let's see what we can do about it."

Before she could begin, someone pounded on the door, but Yolanda held up a hand to stay her. "Keep your seat. Folks, who wants to spot me?" Marcus produced a small wad of cash from midair, earning a gasp from Quinn, but Yolanda looked at the offering with disappointment. "Wrong currency, man. New York, remember?"

Since Marcus had moved in, I'd learned a wealth of profanity that my dry Latin classes never covered, such as the expletives he muttered under his breath as the bills' colors and portraits changed.

"Muchas gracias," said Yolanda, taking the money from him, then opened the door to a deliveryman in a sweaty off-white polo, casualty of the warm weather and, I presumed, the lack of elevators in Quinn's building. "Thank you. Prepaid?" He nodded, and she slipped him a pair of twenties. "Have a good night."

When she closed the door, Quinn protested, "You can't just tip him in fake money!"

"Who said it's fake?" Yolanda replied, carrying the bag to the couch.

"It's one of those gray skills we tend to learn along the way," I explained. "Not exactly legal, but if you know what you're doing, magic-made money can pass every forgery test. Go ahead, don't let your dinner get cold. We've all eaten."

She made no move to touch the food, instead pulling her knees to her chest and hugging them. After a long moment of silence, she mumbled, "You're right."

"About..." I prompted.

"The craziness. It's happening more regularly, and I can't control it."

Marcus leaned against her messy desk and crossed his arms. "Tell us about it. What's happened? When?"

Looking as if she dearly wanted a shell into which she could retreat, Quinn said, "Used to be little things. Lights would flicker, pens and pencils rolled around. It started ramping up in college—I'd get stressed, right, pull too many all-nighters, and then I'd snap at someone or have a crying jag, and shit would *shatter*. Windows, mirrors...my boyfriend's computer...I had a really bad night before this final from hell, and a car alarm started outside my building, and then the car just exploded. Looked like a bomb had gone off. NYPD had a detonation team out there for hours in case there was another bomb hidden nearby."

Marcus cut his eyes to me in query.

"This is going to sound like a dumb question," I said to Quinn, "but do you have any weird allergies?"

She frowned. "Pine pollen. I'm miserable around real Christmas trees. Oh, and mold, but"—she flopped one arm toward the discolored patches near the window—"that's why I live on antihistamines. Why?"

"No metal allergies?"

"I mean, cheap jewelry makes my skin turn green, but other than that, no."

I looked back at Marcus and nodded. "Okay. Based on what you're describing, I think the chances are good that you're a wizard."

Her bemused frown deepened. "*Witch*, you mean? And I can't believe I just asked that..."

"It's a lot to take in," I assured her, "but bear with me.

No, I meant wizard. It's a gender-neutral term for us. A witch is a wizard with less talent."

"About half of the Fringe are witches," Yolanda offered.

"But most wizards are affiliated with the Arcanum," I continued, seeing Quinn perk at the term. "Many live in its installations and work for the organization, but that's not mandatory. Basically, the Arcanum is there to teach wizards how to control their power, then to make sure that no one tries to take over the world. Staying off the mundane radar is key." Stepping closer to her, I said, "What you're telling us sounds like accidental releases of power. It can happen to anyone under stress, but there are techniques you can use to contain them."

The look that crossed her face was closer to relief than excitement. "*Good.* I can't trust myself with a job until I get this under control. A job in my field, I mean," she said, catching our glances toward her delivered dinner. "I haven't had any accidents yet at the campus bookstore. But I just finished my master's in art conservation, and the jobs I want are basically nothing but handling delicate items worth more than my life savings, so…you see the problem?"

I nodded. "Books of hours are flammable."

"God," she muttered, "you have no idea. I turned down internships because I was afraid of making something priceless explode."

"So who told you about the Arcanum?" Yolanda asked. "Unless NYU has started offering seminars in practical magic…"

"My grandpa." Slouching back against the couch cushions, Quinn said, "When my incidents started happening, he said I had talent. Started dropping hints about magic, and then he told me I needed to find an old missile silo in Montana, but he's ninety-five, and I think that last bit may be his mind slipping…" Her voice trailed off as the three of us shook our heads. "What, *seriously?*

There's a missile silo full of wizards?"

"That used to be the Arcanum's worldwide headquarters," I replied. "Relocated to England. Your grandpa's a wizard, then?"

She shrugged. "He said he wasn't. I'm the only one in the family with this delightful *talent*. But this Arcanum of yours…you really think you can fix me?"

"With study and practice, sure." I peered at her more closely. "If your grandpa isn't a wizard, then how the hell does he know about the Arcanum? We don't advertise."

Being lesser fae—she was slightly shy of quarter-blooded—Yolanda couldn't broadcast her thoughts, but the glance she shot me was an invitation to peek. *Could be in hiding. Conclave?*

The notion gave me pause. The Conclave, a separatist group with a disdain for new-blooded wizards and a grudge against the Arcanum's witch-blooded grand magus, had been forcibly disbanded almost three years before, after Toula broke a standoff at their compound in Alaska. I hadn't heard of any members unaccounted for, but I wouldn't have been surprised if Toula had decided to keep that information out of general circulation.

The other possibility was that he was a member of the Minor Arcanum, a confederation of wizards and witches who had no use for Arcanum bureaucracy. But if Quinn's grandfather was Minor Arcanum, then why hadn't he sent her to one of their members for basic training?

"Who's your family?" I asked Quinn. "What's your grandpa's surname?"

"Dellucci," she said. "I'm Quinn Dellucci, he's John. Why?"

I racked my brain but couldn't think of any Delluccis among the Arcanum members I'd known. "Tell you what, we should have a quick chat with him. Do you think he's still awake?"

Quinn's nose wrinkled. "Tuesday night is bridge night, and I don't bother him unless it's an emergency. He'll be up at dawn tomorrow, though—he's crazy like that. He's in Chicago, so he's an hour behind, but we could call him first thing."

I silently consulted Yolanda and Marcus, who nodded agreement. "That works for us. Why don't we meet you back here about eight in the morning, give everyone a chance to sleep and shower? We'll go to Chicago, have a talk with your grandfather, and then we can take you to Arcanum HQ for testing."

"They'll get you sorted," Marcus assured her. "For now, your dinner is waiting."

"Not much of an appetite, all of a sudden," Quinn mumbled. "You guys are serious? This isn't all some big prank?"

In response, Marcus waved open a gate back to Yolanda's place. "We're quite serious. See you in the morning," he said, and led the way out.

I was last to go, and I smiled even as Quinn gawked from the couch. "Everything is going to be okay. Try to get some rest," I told her, and sealed the gate while she watched in shocked silence.

Lucky for us, Quinn didn't flee overnight.

Her dinner remained untouched in its bag on the table, and judging by the shadows beneath her eyes, she hadn't slept in the interim. Personally, I was much more eager to face the day than I'd been the night before—I'd gone home, left Ted a message about why Marcus and I would be out of the office, fallen back into bed, and had time for a late rise, a leisurely brunch, and a word with the grand magus before picking up Yolanda and returning to New York. When we knocked, Quinn still looked stunned, but at least she didn't try to mace us, which I took to be a positive sign.

"You're expected at Glastonbury later today," Marcus informed her as she scarfed down a granola bar. "The plan is to do a preliminary examination, wand-test you, and determine how much of a threat you currently are to yourself and your surroundings."

She chased her breakfast with a swig of black coffee. "Considering that I'm becoming more accident-prone by the month…"

"You will have the training you need," he assured her, and muttered, "Probably far more pleasant than mine."

"Special case," I explained as Quinn's expression shifted toward apprehension. "However bad your accidents are, they're nothing like his. But first, let's have a talk with your grandpa. Does he know we're coming?"

She finished her coffee in one long gulp and wiped her mouth with the back of her hand. "I kind of got the impression that surprise might be the better option today."

"Your call. Do you have any pictures of his house?"

"No, and uh…that's another thing," she said, rubbing her elbow. "He lives in an assisted-living community. Lots of people around. He's got his own apartment, but we have to sign in, and visiting hours aren't supposed to start until eight—"

"Leave that to them," Yolanda interrupted, and shifted her computer bag on her shoulder. "Shall we?"

While I could have looked inside Quinn's thoughts, I left the delicate work to Marcus. Though he only had one more year of practice than I did, his far greater base strength made enchantment so much easier for him. My intrusions into mundane minds still had all the finesse of a whack with a blunt instrument, whereas Marcus could manage the trick with almost surgical precision, in and out with the subject barely aware of the breach. Considering the circumstances, I was happy to step back and let him do the fine digging.

When he opened a gate, it led into a small parking lot beside a high-rise tower overlooking the water—Lake Michigan, I assumed. The building was tidy, designed with clean lines and large windows, and judging by the lush flowerbeds visible beyond the few parked sedans, the management company paid their landscapers well. Traffic was heavy but moving on the six-lane road adjoining the parking lot, and I imagined that Chicago's morning rush was already in full swing.

"Quickly," Marcus said, and we slipped through before we could be detected—not always an easy feat when one is traveling by gate.

"The front door's around that way," Quinn whispered once the gate was gone. "Follow the sidewalk toward the lake. There's a check-in desk in the lobby—"

"And there's bound to be cameras all over the place," said Yolanda. "Why didn't we just go to his apartment, again?"

"I'd rather he not die of fright," Marcus replied, and beckoned us close together. "Stay by me. This glamour doesn't have a wide radius."

She looked doubtful. "It'll fool the cameras? You're sure of that?"

"Field tested, and that's all I'll tell you on the subject," he said, smirking. "Come on."

Walking in a tight huddle, we waited outside the automatic glass doors—Marcus's glamour was effective enough to hide us from the sensors—then followed a staff member into the building and past the security desk. I quickly examined the facility as Quinn, pointing the way, guided us toward her grandfather's apartment: neutral colors, tasteful paintings, occasional potted trees, and vinyl floors designed to look like dark wood. There were no rugs beyond the oriental-style carpet in the lobby sitting room—a concession to wheelchairs and walkers, I imagined—and while the place smelled clean, it lacked the institutional odor of disinfectant. The residents, I gathered, were well-to-do, the sort of clientele who might no longer drive but had a preference as to Mercedes or BMW.

We rode an elevator up five floors, then rounded a corner past a potted palm and headed for the end of the hallway. Some of the apartment doors had been decorated with seasonal wreaths of fake flowers or quirkier décor, such as a pair of painted wooden flip-flops welcoming visitors to the lake house. Our destination had no such adornment, nothing beyond the resident's brass nameplate: *Dr. John Dellucci.*

"He's a doctor?" I whispered, surprised. The Arcanum had an abysmal record of sending its members to medical school.

Quinn nodded. "Cardiologist. He didn't give it up until he was eighty, when Grams had a bad stroke. After she died, he sold their house in Evanston and moved here."

"I'm sorry to hear that."

She offered me a brief, polite smile. "I was fifteen. It's been a while, but thanks."

Yolanda scanned the hallway and nodded to a camera near the molding. "We've got eyes, folks."

I focused my will into a thin bolt, and the camera fell off the wall, landing with its lens facing away from us. "Better?"

"Should buy us a few minutes," she replied, then nudged Quinn as the glamour of invisibility fell away. "Going to knock?"

Quinn did the honors, and we stepped back to give her breathing room. A few seconds later, I could hear shuffling and the clank of a turning bolt, and the door cracked opened to reveal a pasty, elderly man with a head of wispy white hair, watery gray eyes behind thick glasses, a Black Watch plaid bathrobe, and an old-style wooden cane.

"Quinnie!" he cried, his broad smile showing slightly yellowed teeth. "What on earth are you doing…" His voice faded as he saw the three of us standing behind her. "Uh…is everyone okay, honey?"

Yolanda stepped forward. "Dr. Dellucci, my name is Yolanda Ford, and we're here because your granddaughter seems to be a wizard. May we come in? This probably isn't the best conversation to have in the hallway."

He stiffened, and I tried to look non-threatening—not incredibly difficult, considering that I'm all of five-six and far from a bruiser. "We mean you no harm," I murmured. "We want to help Quinn, and we're trying to get a sense of her background. She said you're the one who told her about the Arcanum."

The old man regarded us warily. "You're Arcanum, then?"

"They are," Yolanda replied, pointing to Marcus and me. "I'm Fringe. That's where most of the witches end up."

And lesser fae, but I knew why Yolanda hadn't mentioned it. If Dr. Dellucci was a wizard, then the last thing he'd want would be to confront three faeries while in his pajamas.

Though he seemed uncertain, after a moment, he stepped aside and widened the door opening. "Inside, then. I'm not supposed to have guests this early, you know. How'd you get in here?"

"Magic, I think," said Quinn.

He grunted and locked the door behind us. "Sit down. Coffee's on."

A short entrance hall terminated in a sitting room, in which a burgundy leather recliner faced a wide-screen television mounted on the wall. The matching couch sat against a window with an impressive lake view, and the end tables held a few framed photographs of smiling people in various decades' fashions. One in particular caught my eye: a sunburned, brown-haired man with a younger version of Dr. Dellucci's features standing with his arm around a beautiful black woman in a turquoise bathing suit, the two frozen in laughter. The resemblance between mother and daughter was strong enough that I could confidently make the connection between the young couple in the photo and Quinn, who seemed far less pleased with life at that moment.

Our host headed for the kitchenette off the sitting

room and its adjoining dining room, demarcated only by a half wall and a change in flooring from vinyl to beige tile. "Can't think without my coffee," he said, opening a cabinet of mugs and plates. "Anyone else? Quinnie?"

"Please," she replied, sitting on the edge of the couch.

The rest of us declined, and when he emerged, we'd crowded onto the couch beside Quinn. He delivered Quinn's coffee, retrieved his own, then winced as he settled into his recliner and gave us a long, hard stare. "What do you people want from me?"

When Yolanda didn't make the first move, I took the initiative. "Just information. We were wondering how Quinn heard of the Arcanum."

He drank in silence, considering us over the rim of his mug, then sighed and put it on the adjacent table. "I'm not saying anything without some guarantees."

"What sort?"

"You don't hurt me, my kids, my grandkids…anyone in the family. Swear it."

"Will an ordinary agreement satisfy you, or would you prefer a magical oath?"

His brow furrowed, which told me that whatever he knew of the Arcanum, he didn't have a full wizard's education. "Magical oath?" he asked.

"It's a very old form of magic," I explained. "Almost like you bind yourself to whatever you're swearing to do. If you break your oath…" I made a face. "Not pleasant. We don't often use them, but if it'll prove to you that we're trying to help Quinn—"

"No, thank you. That won't be necessary. Just…you won't come after my family?"

"You and yours have nothing to fear," I insisted. "Not from us, and not from the Arcanum." When he kept quiet, I asked, "How do you know about us?"

Dr. Dellucci let out a long, slow breath, locked eyes with his granddaughter for a moment, then looked away. "Because I was born in the silo."

"You—"

"My parents moved in shortly after it opened," he continued, ignoring my attempted question. "I was the second baby born on the premises, actually—Karen Ellerby beat me by two weeks."

"You're a wizard?" Yolanda asked.

He shook his head and picked up his coffee again. "Dud."

I cringed in sympathy, having grown up far too close to that end of the magical spectrum. "No talent whatsoever?" I pressed.

"None. Never had the knack for it." He sipped and stared at the darkened television. "Maybe I would have figured it out eventually—who knows? But I didn't stay long enough to find out."

"What do you mean?"

He continued to avoid our eyes, but I saw his fingers clench around his mug. "My dad was a magus. So was his dad—Inner Council, both of them. Grand Magus Callahan appointed Grandfather, and Grand Magus Harrison appointed Dad when I was six. My aunt Amelia never married, and I was the first child and grandchild—you see where this is going?"

"Expectations were high," I said softly.

"Yeah. But I never had any of those little childhood incidents like the other kids—I never set anything on fire or made my toys move, nothing like that. Grandfather tried to provoke something out of me, but it never worked."

"Plenty of kids are late bloomers," I said, thinking of the half-truths my dad had used to reassure me. "The Arcanum doesn't make an official dud determination until you're twenty, you know?"

Dr. Dellucci shrugged. "Couldn't prove it by me. I didn't make it that far."

A chill prickled up my spine. "Did they send you away? Boarding school?"

His smile was more like a smirk, and quickly faded. "No." After another long sip of coffee, he said, "When I was four, my parents had another son, and he showed talent early. Had a tantrum when he was three and shattered a lamp on the other side of the room. I still couldn't do anything, but I was seven then, and I remember hearing about ten-year-olds getting wand-tested and starting magic classes. Guess I thought that once I had a stick in my hand, everything would make sense, and I'd be just like Dad. *God*," he said with a sigh, "I wanted to be like my old man. He'd leave our apartment every morning in his formal robe and chain, and Mom would cast the wrinkles out to make sure he looked his best, and he promised to let me come along one day…"

The coffee mug had run dry, and as he started to get up to refill it, Quinn stopped him and brought the pot from the kitchenette. Murmuring his thanks, he gazed into space for a moment, then resumed. "I was nine. Summer after third grade. I remember it being stinking hot on the surface, but there was a movie theater in the silo, and they showed so many cartoons for the kids on summer break, and I got to take my brother when Mom was busy…" He cleared his throat. "One Saturday morning in July, Mom got me up early, and I found my grandparents waiting at the kitchen table. They said they were going to take me to see the circus—it had come to a town about an hour away. I was so excited, especially because it was just going to be the three of us, not my baby brother. I got dressed and inhaled my breakfast, and Mom and Dad kissed me goodbye and told me to be good. My brother was crying because he wanted to go, too…"

He needed several sips of coffee before he could continue, and I knew I wasn't imagining the sheen in his eyes.

"Grandfather had borrowed one of the Arcanum cars, this big green Cadillac," he said. "He could do that as a magus, see? They put me in the back, and away we went.

And about half an hour into the trip, when I got antsy and asked how much farther we had to go, they told me the truth. I didn't belong in the silo because I couldn't use magic, and so my family had decided to send me to a new family, where I'd fit in."

"Shit," Yolanda muttered.

"I bawled. I told them I'd be good, begged them to take me home…I even tried to open the doors, but they wouldn't budge. Magic, I guess—we didn't have child safety locks back then. So they let me have my fit, and then Grandfather pulled over, took out his wand, and told me to go make something of myself." Dr. Dellucci paused, his pronounced knuckles almost white around his mug. "That's the last thing I remember, and it was decades before I got those memories back."

"Your memory—" Marcus began.

"Wiped. I don't know if there's a more technical term for it, but the first nine years of my life were a blank for a long time." He glanced toward the couch as if remembering his audience. "For years, my very first memory of anything after that point was the lobby of Children's Memorial here in Chicago. I was terrified and disoriented, and a nurse took me aside and knelt down and asked me where my mommy and daddy were, and I didn't know what to tell her. They must have looked around for a bit, and then they called the police and took my fingerprints, but I guess the silo kids weren't in any sort of database. A neurologist ran tests—I was perfectly healthy, just an amnesiac, and I was so frustrated because I knew I must have had parents once, but I couldn't even picture their faces. And when no one claimed me, the hospital wasn't sure what to do. I couldn't stay there forever, right? Long story short, one of my nurses took a liking to me. She and her husband wanted children but couldn't have any, and I needed a home." He put his mug aside once more, adding, "Probably worked out for the best for them. Mom was busy at the hospital, and Dad was a civil lawyer—I have no idea how they would have handled a newborn. At least they got to name me."

"You couldn't even remember your *name*?" I interjected.

He shook his head slowly, his shoulders slumped. "Grandfather took that from me, too, along with my birthdate and everything else. Officially, I was John Doe until I was adopted. We decided to keep the John part, but I became a Dellucci. And that was me for almost thirty-eight years. Mom and Dad doted when they weren't working, I went to Europe three times before college, got my degree, did the med school thing, married the love of my life, joined a great practice, and had five kids of my own. Stephanie wanted a big family," he said with a smile, then gestured to the framed pictures scattered around the room. "Three boys, two girls. Her dad was our fourth," he added, pointing to Quinn, who looked shell-shocked. "I mean, it bothered the hell out of me that I couldn't remember anything about where I'd come from and who I'd been before I was John Dellucci, but no therapist could ever fix the amnesia. I tried everything from hypnosis to acid, but nothing worked."

"Let me guess," I said. "It started coming back to you in March of 2013?"

His white eyebrows shot toward his receding hairline. "How did you—"

"This realm was temporarily sealed off from Faerie," Yolanda offered. "Magic dried up, and anything without a built-in backup supply fell apart. Wards, glamours...long-term memory erasure spells..."

"I'll be damned," he muttered. "You're right about the timing. I woke in a cold sweat early one morning, and it was *there*. All of it. Like someone had flipped a switch."

"What did Grams say when you told her?" Quinn asked.

Dr. Dellucci answered with a weak chuckle. "I never said a word. She'd have thought I was nuts—raised in a missile silo by wizards? You hear how insane that sounds? Besides, it's not like I could have proven it. No talent, remember?" he said, wiggling the fingers of one hand. "No, your Grams didn't need to know about that. Sure as hell didn't tell the kids, either."

He groped for his coffee mug and took a bolstering swig. "I put myself out there, in case they ever wanted to find me," he murmured. "Everything short of driving back to Montana—I didn't want to risk my car being hexed, and Stephanie would never have understood why I wanted to go to the middle of nowhere. I did a few of those at-home DNA tests, you know, spit in the tube and mail it in. All of the major family tree sites. Never got a match closer than a sixth cousin, but that's not surprising. I remember my dad saying we were an old-blooded family—guess there aren't too many wizards in the wild looking for long-long family online." He sipped again, once more casting his gaze toward the wall. "Not going to lie, it stung. I always hoped my little brother would try to find me—he was five when I was kicked out, so maybe he remembers something about me. Or *remembered*, perhaps. I have no idea whether he's still alive. Haven't spoken to him in eighty-six years."

"What they did to you is unconscionable," said Marcus, his fists clenched in his lap. "I'm truly sorry."

"Hey, not your fault, kid. But thanks." Looking back at his granddaughter, the old man said, "I would have taken this to my grave, but then you came along, Quinnie. Maybe you're not quite as talented as my brother, but you're probably close. I didn't know if it might go away if you didn't practice, but just in case…that's why I mentioned the Arcanum, sweetheart. I think you're a wizard, *these* folks seem to agree, and…who knows? Might be good for you."

"My accidents, you mean?" she mumbled. "I almost started a fire in the library at school over a stupid Latin final. This isn't *good* for me."

"Once you've figured it out, it might be. Magic can't be

all bad, right?"

"And if Latin is still a problem, we can help with that as well," Marcus added. "No need for fires."

"We're going to take Quinn to a facility in England," I told Dr. Dellucci. "They'll set her straight, and she can go on with her life. You don't need to worry about a thing." I hesitated, then asked, "Is there a message you'd like to send? I certainly don't know everyone in the installation, but I'm sure the grand magus could locate your little brother."

He mulled over the question for a moment, his lips moving as if he were carrying on a conversation with himself, then said, "If you don't mind, yes. That'd be much appreciated. Even if Jimmy doesn't want anything to do with me, I'll be able to say I tried, right?"

Pushing himself from his chair, he limped to the heavy mahogany sideboard and rooted in a drawer for a notepad and pen. As Quinn and Yolanda cleaned up the mugs, I watched Dr. Dellucci scrawl a quick letter, then cleared my throat to interrupt him. "Who are we looking for, again?"

He glanced up from his work, his face creased into a hopeful smile. "My brother's name is Jimmy. Tell him this is from Philip."

"Your surname, I mean."

"*Ah.*" He lightly smacked his forehead with the heel of his hand. "Mulligan. Philip Mulligan is my birth name."

I jumped and wheeled around at the sound of shattering porcelain and found Yolanda staring at us from the edge of the kitchenette, Dr. Dellucci's mug in coffee-stained pieces on the tile. "Sorry," she managed, "*what* did you say?"

"Philip Mulligan," he repeated, regarding her with concern. "Are you okay, there? You look like you've seen a ghost, young lady."

Finding no help forthcoming from Yolanda or Marcus, I drew closer to Dr. Dellucci and touched his arm. "I don't know how to tell you this," I began, "but your brother—"

His face fell. "He's dead, isn't he?"

I nodded.

"Did you know him?"

"I, uh…I know *of* him. He died before I was born."

"Must have been a pretty important fellow, then, eh?" He paused, searching our faces, then added, "Or is the word I'm looking for *notorious*?"

"Why don't you have a seat?" Yolanda said, stepping over the broken mug to help guide Dr. Dellucci back to his recliner. Sitting on the edge of the coffee table in front of him, she leaned forward and held his stare. "Be grateful that he never found you. Your brother was a mass-murdering psychopath."

"*Jimmy*?"

"Staged a coup, made himself grand magus, and wiped out hundreds of my people. My grandparents on both sides among them, and my dad's three sisters. He didn't have much use for those of us on the less talented end of the spectrum, see?"

His jaw began to tremble. "What happened?"

"He had an eleven-year reign of terror, and then he was executed." She reached across the divide between them and clasped her hands over his. "What they did to you was terrible, and I know it must have hurt to be abandoned for so long. But for your sake, and your children's sake, you should be thanking every lucky star in the sky."

Before Quinn could lose her nerve, I opened a gate back to Glastonbury in the middle of the sitting room. "I…I'm really very sorry to have to tell you like this," I said as Marcus waved the broken mug back together and placed it on the counter. "We'll take good care of Quinn, I promise."

We coaxed Quinn across, and I paused on the edge of the gate for one last look. The old man remained in his recliner, staring at me with a mixture of shock and deep sadness, and I resisted the urge to run back and hug him. "She'll be safe," I said, and closed the gate.

CHAPTER 3

Putting Quinn at ease was simpler said than done. The grand magus's bookshelf-lined office was well-lit and comfortable, an almost homey space with plush furniture and thick rugs, and she'd been awaiting our arrival with coffee and cookies. Toula herself was hardly a threat on first glimpse, the picture of a slightly edgy older sister: a black pixie cut with electric blue tips, deep blue eyes rimmed with dark liner, metallic purple fingernails, and the sort of slouchy wardrobe best described as "dorm casual." Still, Quinn looked like she was about to be sick as we coaxed her onto the couch.

"Whoo, boy," Toula muttered once I'd brought her up to speed. "You know, ideally, we'd introduce people to this organization without leading with wizards with kill counts…"

"Mulligan *was* Arcanum," Yolanda pointed out before biting a gingersnap in half.

"I'm not denying that, I'm just saying that this young woman is probably worried enough without throwing murder and execution into the mix. Well, play the cards you're dealt, right? Hi," she said, extending her hand to Quinn over the polished oak coffee table. "Toula Pavli. Grand Magus Pavli if you're feeling fancy, but don't worry about that for now."

Perhaps it was just reflex, but Quinn shook it. "Quinn Dellucci."

"Nice to meet you," said Toula, settling into a chair. "Please don't panic. No one in this room is going to bite."

She crossed her legs and briefly studied her unnerved company. "You have questions. Let's start with that."

Quinn cleared her throat and murmured her thanks when Yolanda pressed a fresh cup of coffee into her hands. "My, uh…my grandpa's brother…"

Toula waited until her voice faded, then said, "James Mulligan was a talented man with some definite ideas about how this organization and the larger magical community should operate. Unfortunately, those ideas resulted in mass murder about forty-five years ago. His son tried to follow in his footsteps after James was executed, but Russell was an incompetent little shit by comparison. He still almost cost us magic as we know it, and while he was on probation, mind you." She paused, then said, "This will come out eventually, so I suppose you should hear it from me. I executed Russell and his mother for treason and a variety of other crimes."

The liquid sloshed in Quinn's cup as she stiffened.

"Yes, *executed*," Toula continued. "That implies a government function, I know. What you need to understand is that the Arcanum has been the governing body for most of the wizard population for the last millennium. That's not hyperbole—by official reckoning, we hit the thousand-year mark next year. That means we've been keeping the magical community in line longer than many nations have existed."

"But—"

"But we don't get a seat at the UN? We don't send ambassadors around?" She shrugged. "We are everywhere and nowhere in this realm, hon. If we were in the open, you'd see one of two outcomes: either we'd be persecuted as monsters or we'd run the world. The majority of us understand that neither of those is ideal, so we stay underground." After Quinn had taken a bracing sip of coffee, Toula said, "Keeping ourselves and the world safe means policing ourselves. Some offenders can be rehabilitated, but there are outliers, the ones who are so strong and whose crimes are so bad that we can't afford to keep them locked away indefinitely. My father was one of them, and so were your granduncle and cousin."

Quinn's fingers wrapped more tightly around her cup. "How bad were they?" she mumbled.

"I don't have the exact tally in front of me, but James authorized more than six hundred deaths in a two-day period and kidnapped hundreds more witches. Your family would have been targets. We can discuss that later," she hastily added as Yolanda's mouth opened. "The important thing today is that he either didn't know where to find your grandfather or didn't bother to look, and now here you are."

I could hear the forced enthusiasm in Toula's tone, but if Quinn noticed, she gave no sign.

"You know," she continued, uncrossing and re-crossing her legs, "I always wondered what happened to the other Mulligan boy. The popular opinion was that he was long dead, but I didn't think that Reginald and Corina had it in them to kill their own kid. *Clarence* Mulligan, now, maybe, but not his son. Reginald had a softer streak."

Quinn's head tilted in query. "You knew about my grandpa before today?"

"I knew the rumors. It was one of those seldom-discussed secrets." Her mouth tightened into a thin line of distaste. "The Mulligans are an *old* clan, prominent here and in Ireland for generations. There's almost always been at least one Magus Mulligan on the Council since the sixteenth century. The British lines mostly...well, 'daughtered out' is an unfortunate phrase, but that's the truth of it. There are still Mulligan descendants on the Council, but you'd have to look up the family trees to know it."

"You did your research, hmm?" Marcus murmured.

She nodded. "Know your potential enemy, though that's really not fair—some of my favorite magi are Mulligan cousins. But I digress." Turning her attention back to Quinn, she said, "Duds are rare, but they happen regardless of a family's old blood or general level of talent. We don't see records of them in a family as prominent as yours because there's a long history of removing duds before they turn into blots on the family name. There's a bit of a gentlemen's agreement among the oldest families: if the dud disappears before formal testing, then there was never a dud to begin with." She paused, giving Quinn a chance to wrestle with yet another unpleasant thought, then said, "Witches are also undesirable, but they're more difficult to catch before maturity—some children really are slow starters and turn out just fine. The old families have ways of dealing with their witches, most of which involve sending them out into the world when they're grown and asking them not to return."

"Badger," I muttered.

"Badger's dad," Toula corrected. "Shadow alder wands are another trick—they dampen talent," she explained to Quinn. "Anyway, while witches are problematic, certain families don't want to take the risk of having a dud around, so their likely dud children disappear from the records at a young age. It's impossible to track most of them now— some could have been fostered out, some *were* killed—but the common notation in the books over the last couple of centuries has been that the child was sent to boarding school, and that's the last anyone hears about it. I'm glad your grandfather survived," she said. "What was done to him is atrocious, but in all honesty, he was safer in Chicago than he would have been in the silo with his family, especially once James made his power grab. I wouldn't have been surprised if he'd met his end in an 'unfortunate accident' if he'd stayed long enough to be outed as a dud."

Quinn looked sick at the news, and Toula tried to reassure her. "I swear, you're not in danger, certainly not from me. Now, what do you say we test you?" she asked, her voice brightening. "Come on, I could use a walk. Let's take the scenic route."

Toula grabbed a flat black case from one of her many bookshelves, and we followed her out of the executive suite and through the long corridors of the castle. While Toula was a fast walker, she took her time that afternoon, slowing every few yards as Quinn lagged to look out the windows at the massive ward bubble around the installation. I couldn't blame our newcomer—she'd been in multiple time zones already that day, and finding herself in a magically shielded castle had to be just one more shock on top of many.

As we descended a spiral staircase, Toula looked back and smiled at Quinn. "There'll be time to play tourist later. The priority now is to see what you can do with a wand, and we have to go to the practice rooms for that. Untrained wizards aren't known for their aim, so we always test somewhere protected and padded. You wouldn't give a kid a shotgun and ask her to try a little target shooting in a china shop, right?"

"Sounds wise," Quinn replied, her fingertips trailing along the old stone wall. "You must have tested well."

Toula briefly chuckled. "Not at all, but then I was testing with both hands tied behind my back, so to speak. Long story."

"Still, I mean, you're pretty strong," Quinn pressed.

"I am."

"Figures. They said you were in charge around here," she continued, cocking her thumb back toward Yolanda, Marcus, and me, "but you're, like, my age."

Again, Toula offered a little laugh. "Baby-faced, I assure you."

"Not *that* baby-faced. You can't be more than thirty."

She waited until we'd reached the landing and started down a hall of procurement offices, then said, "For reasons we need not discuss today, in a building full of freaks of nature, I'm an outlier. I was eighty-three in February."

Toula walked on for a few yards before pausing and

looking back at Quinn, who had stopped in her tracks and was gaping. "Magic is a funny thing, kid. Also, I'm not going to eat you, if that's what you were worried about."

Quinn blinked, then hurried to rejoin her. "Sorry, I didn't...I mean—"

"This is all new to you," Toula soothed, "and you barely know what continent you're on right now. No one's offended."

"But *you*—"

"Marveled at *Tron* on VHS." As a noisy crowd approached from the other end of the corridor, Toula grunted, waved open a gate to a practice room, and shepherded us through the shortcut before anyone could hail her. "Sorry about that," she said to Quinn as she sealed the hole. "Better if we don't have to explain you today, yeah?"

She raked her teeth over her lower lip. "I guess no one would be thrilled to know I exist."

"Well, yes and no." After glancing toward the door, which was still closed and locked, Toula said, "You have distant cousins here—your grandpa's grandfather was the younger and far more talented of two sons born in Arc 2, and he only moved to North America because he was recruited as a Council aide. The Mulligans here haven't produced any magi, but there are a few of them around. If you want to meet them, I'll point them out to you, but you might not want to go trumpeting your newfound family connections from the rafters just yet."

"Because of Grandpa's awful brother," she muttered.

"Not quite. The family is old, remember?"

"So you said..."

"Certain old-blooded families look with *disfavor* upon those of us with fewer wizards up the family tree," Toula explained. "My father was new-blooded—first wizard in his line, spontaneously talented. It happens. Your grandfather is old-blooded, but he's a dud, and that, for counting purposes, qualifies as a break in the line. I assume your grandmother and your parents aren't wizards, either."

Quinn shook her head. "If they are, they've hidden it well."

"Assume they aren't, then. That's like having two generations of mundanes before you, and for the obnoxious subset of this community that ranks other wizards like papered poodles at a dog show, it's a major strike against you. The Mulligan cousins here aren't the worst of the lot, but you might get a few snide comments when word spreads."

"Nothing new there," she replied with a smirk as she folded her arms. "The Delluccis are proud Chicago Italians, and my mother is a proud Haitian immigrant. I've been deflecting crap about my ancestry for as long as I can remember."

Toula grimaced. "Sorry to have to say it, but a thick skin never hurts around here. And with that welcoming pep talk, let's see what you can do with a wand, eh?"

She flicked two fingers, and a wooden table appeared by her side, just long enough to hold the black box she'd brought from her office. Unsnapping the steel clasps, she raised the lid to reveal a set of five wooden wands.

Quinn, who watched from a safe distance, continued to hug herself. "I, uh…I should tell you that I've never held a real wand before…"

"Neither have many of the kids we test," Toula replied, carefully dislodging one from its depression in the rich blue velvet. Another careless twitch of her fingers and a whispered word brought forth a dozen cubes from the ether, ranging in size from a matchbox to a compact car. "What I'm going to do is let you try these wands on those boxes, one at a time, until we find a good fit for you."

She peered at the stick in Toula's hand as if it might sprout fangs at any moment. "Do I pick a color or something?"

The grand magus laughed, flashing a genuine, toothy smile. "Hope you like shades of brown. No, these are samples of wands made with the most common wood and core combinations. The testing process is like trying on glasses—you want a wand that's not too weak or too strong, one that will help amplify and focus your power without overloading your casting, as it were. Here," she said, holding out the first wand, "give this one a go."

Quinn hesitantly took it from her and pointed it toward the cubes. "What's supposed to happen next?"

"Focus on trying to move one of them. Any you like."

"Remember the feeling you get when you have your accidents," I suggested. "It's like that, only controlled."

She still seemed uncertain, but her fingers tightened around the wand, and she gave it a test flick.

Nothing happened.

The second flick was more emphatic, a conductor's baton on a sharp cutoff.

Nothing.

With a frustrated huff, she rubbed the back of her neck and contemplated the cubes, then stretched out the wand toward a box the size of a microwave, gritted her teeth, and muttered, "Do something, *damn it.*"

The box exploded. Quinn screamed and dropped into a crouch, but there was no need—Toula's shields were strong and nearly instantaneous, and the fragments bounced off the bubble without embedding themselves in anyone. Hearing the tinkle of wood against the shield, Quinn uncovered her face, then stood and marveled at the magic around her. "What the…"

"Shield," Toula replied. "You'll learn soon enough. Let me switch that wand, okay?"

Quinn passed it back, and Toula pulled another from the case. "Sorry about the box," Quinn mumbled. "My accidents are getting worse—"

"Which is why you're here. Believe me, in the history of testing mishaps, that was nothing. Try again," she urged.

That time, the result came on the first attempt, and a cube the size of a loveseat rose several inches above the padded floor. "Good, *good*," said Toula. "Can you make it spin?"

She could, as it so happened, and along several axes. After asking her to lift progressively larger boxes and toss some smaller ones to the ceiling, Toula nodded and put the wand away. "Maple's an excellent fit for you," she told Quinn, snapping the box closed. "I'll have one brought from storage."

"So…I passed?"

"More than passed." Taking up the wand case, she cast the table and boxes back into atoms, then opened a gate to her office. "This way, if you will."

When we were seated again, Toula steepled her fingers and studied Quinn. "A maple wand is the sign of a solid talent. Children who test to maple often end up with magus-level abilities. You're not a child, of course, but considering your lack of training to this point, I'd say there's a good chance of you topping out at pine. That's a magus wand," she clarified. "I can't guarantee anything, but I've got a good sense of patterns by now. With that in mind, you need remedial training *immediately*. You said your 'accidents' are worsening?"

Quinn nodded.

"I don't mean to scare you, but with a talent like yours, it's possible that you could hurt or kill someone if you were sufficiently provoked."

"*Kill?*"

"Someday, once you're settled in, have a word with my nephew Seamus. For now, though…what's your schedule like? Are you in school? Working?"

"Just finished my master's at NYU," she replied, looking slightly stunned. "Uh…I don't have a permanent job yet, I wanted to fix myself before I got near anything fragile…"

"She's in conservation," I offered.

Toula frowned. "Trees?"

"Art and artifacts," Quinn clarified. "My specialization

was in manuscript restoration, but if I start fires and make things explode…you see the problem?"

Her eyes widened. "You have training in book preservation?" she asked eagerly. "Actual, legitimate classroom training?"

"And a couple of internships," said Quinn, bemused. "Why?"

The look of incredulity that the grand magus shot Marcus and me would have been intimidating if the Away Team hadn't been on the receiving end of many such looks, often accompanied by muttered profanity, over the years. "You didn't tell her about the Archives?"

"It didn't seem like the most important item on the agenda," Marcus replied.

"Fair enough," she conceded, and returned to Quinn, who was growing more perplexed by the moment. "This facility houses the largest repository in the world of rare magical books and items. Those two keep bringing them in," she added, pointing to Marcus and me. "We have a staff of conservators in the Archives, but much of their training is on the job. Having someone around with a formal background in art conservation would be *fantastic*. I mean, do you have any idea how many slowly rotting books we have in storage?"

"*Rotting?*" she echoed, her sudden tension on par with that of one who's just been told that there's a sack of kittens in the well.

"Slowly," Toula repeated. "Magic is useful for preservation, but I feel better when it's used in tandem with mundane methods. That incident that restored your grandfather's memory also broke every spell in the Archives, you know. I can't imagine how long it took to rebuild those protections." She sat back and drummed her fingers on the chair's arms. "I have a proposition for you, Quinn. Stay here for the next six months and let us train you—"

"I don't know if I can afford that," she interrupted.

"There's no charge. No rent, no tuition." She held out one palm and smirked as a stack of bills appeared. "Wizards, yeah? Once you're comfortable with your talent and have the rudiments down, you're free to go on your way, or you could stick around. In the meantime, I'd like to introduce you to Jude Duffy, the head of the Archives. He'd be delighted to hear about you, I'm sure."

For the first time since arriving in Glastonbury, Quinn revealed a genuine smile. "Could there be a job opening?"

"Almost certainly. What do you say? Let us help you stop those accidents of yours. Whatever you've got in your place in New York can be stored here for now. We should have some single flats in one or two of the towers…"

"Or you could stay with us," I offered, and was relieved to see Marcus nodding agreement. "It's the two of us and my two sisters at our place, but you could have your own room and bath, and three of us are in and out. You wouldn't be smothered."

"You could do a lot worse," Yolanda added.

I snorted. "Such flattery, Lonnie."

"Yeah, yeah, you nuts are okay. How about it?" she asked Quinn. "Can you break your lease?"

"Well, I only have a month and a half left on it, so…yeah. I think so." Her smile widened. "You wouldn't have any moving boxes around, would you?"

Marcus and I saw to Quinn's packing after escorting Yolanda back to Peru, pulling cardboard boxes and packing tape from the ether as she scrambled to put her belongings in reasonable order. I took on her bookshelves while she packed her kitchenette—there was no sense in exposing myself to that much stainless steel without an emergency—and by noon in New York, we'd sealed her life into stacks of brown boxes and a pair of suitcases. "Have you got everything you need until you have time to unpack?" Marcus asked as she dug into lunch, one last order from Curry Kitchen to make up for her abandoned dinner the night before.

"Over there," she replied, gesturing to the suitcases and a few small boxes with a samosa. "Is there a magical moving van?"

"Better." He put down his fork, considered the situation, then produced a clear plastic tub with a locking lid, half as large as the ones we used around the office to hold file folders, loose papers, and the occasional misplaced bag of granola. With a gesture, Quinn's cartons destined for storage shrank to the size of matchboxes and floated neatly into the tub, followed by her similarly miniaturized furniture. Even her bed, a mattress and box springs on a rickety frame, came down the hallway shrunken and intact.

I was impressed—it takes work to enchant anything iron-based into cooperating—but Quinn watched with her mouth open until the samosa dropped from her hand. "How..." she whispered.

"You'll know in time," he told her, which wasn't entirely false, and clicked the lid into place. "There, ready when you need it." He gave the tub a pat as he slid it across the counter toward Quinn.

"That...is *insane*," she said, marveling at the items in the tub. "You have any idea how much of a pain in the ass it was to lug all of that up here in the first place?"

"I can imagine."

"It's so tiny! I'll have to find tweezers to sort through my winter clothes!" She laughed at the absurdity of it all, then resumed her lunch. "I hate to ask after *that*, but is there a spell or something to patch the walls and clean up for the inspection? I left the Windex out"—she pointed to a small collection of cleaning products on the chipped range—"but if you have a faster method..."

It was no trouble. With lunch behind us, we freshened the old paint, buffed the scratches from the laminate floors, replaced the bent blinds, and left the window both sparkling clean and uncracked. "Damn," Quinn decreed as she considered the ceiling light, now with four working bulbs and free of insect corpses, "I might just get my deposit back. You guys are great."

"Will work for tikka masala," I replied, opening a gate to our flat. "We'll take your things across. Get settled with your landlord and give me a call—here's the number," I said, producing a scrap of paper and a pen.

By the time Quinn's astonished landlord took her keys and left her with several hundred dollars in crumpled twenties, Marcus and I had added a second level to our flat, accessible by means of an interior staircase that hadn't existed that morning. Artur, working from the comfort of the den with her computer and a drink, watched as we created a floor between our ceiling and the flat above us, a space that had no right to exist, and shored up the walls with copious amounts of magic. We partitioned the area off into a bedroom, bath, and bonus space, added a suite of furniture that was more than merely utilitarian, and tucked Quinn's belongings into her new closet. Standing back to take in the large window, the wooden floor, and the plush mattress we'd designed, I nodded to Marcus and cracked my knuckles. "Don't know about you, but I kind of like playing fairy godmother."

His brow wrinkled. "Meaning?"

"Don't tell me you haven't read 'Cinderella' yet."

"Uh…something about glass shoes?"

I patted his shoulder as he sighed. "We'll put it on the list, sweetie."

Leading the way down our new staircase—the faux-oriental runner had been my touch—Marcus grumped, "Someday, you and I will have a full day of conversation in which I understand every reference you make."

"You're doing *fine*."

"You're trying to be nice." Reaching the main level, he headed for the den, and Artur looked up as he neared. "'Cinderella.' Are you familiar with it?"

My sister's eyes—mine in shape, if not color—narrowed at the query. "Could you be more specific?"

"A children's story concerning glass shoes."

She made a face. "Sounds impractical. Why do you ask?"

"Don't worry about it," I interrupted. "You're both getting folk- and fairytale compendia for Christmas. And in the meantime, who wants to help me make dinner? New roomie will be calling soon."

Artur stood and wandered into the kitchen after me, watching as I rummaged in the fridge. "This new roommate, is she any kin of yours?"

"Nope."

"Time-displaced?"

"Nah."

"Does she realize she will be in the minority, then?"

I pulled two packages of chicken breasts from the freezer and defrosted them with a snap. "Let's break her in gently, okay? She's had enough shocks to the system for one day, especially with an uncontrolled talent. I'd rather not have to put out fires tonight."

"Mm. You haven't answered the important question."

"Which is?" I asked, dumping the meat into a glass dish.

"Saxon?"

I threw a dishtowel at Artur in reply.

Beth was surprised but not upset when she came home and found Quinn lurking awkwardly by the couch with a glass of chardonnay. I stood outside my sister's bathroom door while she stripped off her sweat-soaked clothes and quietly brought her up to speed. When I finished, the door cracked open, revealing one of Beth's brown eyes and a lock of salt-stiffened hair. "What does she know about you guys?" she asked through the gap.

"That we can do things with magic, and that we're

great at home renovation. Go easy on her for the next few days, eh? She seems nice, but she's overwhelmed."

"So...we're *not* inviting Hope over tonight?"

"Elizabeth Lucinda Stanhope." She giggled on the other side of the door, and I sighed. "Bathe, brat. You smell gross."

Beth was feeling generous that evening, and so she was a perfect darling at dinner, if flushed and damp from her shower. As we ate, she reported on her practice session with Maria, who was growing more merciless by the day as the Games neared, and about her classmates' injuries. "Charlie broke his ankle," she said, spearing her tater tots. "Zelda had her wand in her right hand, see"—she raised her laden fork above her head for demonstrative purposes—"and he focused his shield on his face and chest, right? But she came back with a bolt from her *left* hand, and he wasn't even trying to block it. Went down *hard.*"

Quinn's eyes widened. "Shit. He'll be in a cast for the rest of the summer."

"Nah. Dr. Powell came down and got the spells going. He's got a pass for tomorrow because it might still be soft, but he'll be fine by Friday."

"You just said he broke his ankle..."

Beth raised an eyebrow. "In a skirmish in a castle filled with wizards, remember? You want me to tell you the number of bones I've broken in practice, or would that be inappropriate for the table?"

Quinn turned to me, still stunned. "That's incredible. Can you, like, cure cancer?"

"No, but not for lack of trying," I replied. "Repairs are easy enough—bones, soft tissue, even organ regeneration to a point, though we can't stick amputated limbs back on. And the infirmary is good at treating symptoms. But actually curing diseases is still beyond us. The kids here get immunized, just like mundane kids."

Her mouth twitched. "Crystal healing isn't popular?"

"Yeah, *no*. Don't let Dr. Powell hear you suggest that."

Throughout the evening, Marcus and Artur were pleasant but vague about their pasts, while I explained Beth's presence as a family situation, and Quinn was polite enough not to pry. Beth crashed early that night, worn out by the extra practice, Artur went for a long run after dark, and Marcus slipped down to his office in the subbasement, having neglected his planned work that day. That left me alone with our guest, who hadn't the faintest idea of what time it was supposed to be. I settled her in the den with a cup of decaffeinated tea and dimmed the lights, hoping her body would be fooled, and kept her company from the recliner. Around eight, my phone beeped, and I found a message from Toula waiting for me. "You're going to begin work with Magus Popova at nine tomorrow morning," I told Quinn, who'd tucked her feet onto the couch and covered them with an afghan.

"Is that a good thing?"

"Sure," I said, trying to assuage her fear. "Anna Popova has been a magus for almost thirty years. She teaches upper-level practical magic, and she's a good instructor. Tough but patient. She's Russian, so sometimes her accent's a little difficult, but you'll catch on quickly. She was always nice to me when I was in school here."

"She knows I'm a total beginner, right?"

"Toula wouldn't assign you to just anyone. You're going to be fine."

Quinn finished her tea and put the cup on the floor. "Tell me about the guy at the Archives...Joel?"

"Jude."

She smirked. "You don't sound enthusiastic."

"I'm biased," I replied, and leaned back until my footrest shot up. "Jude's good at running the Archives, but in interpersonal terms, he's kind of a prick."

"Tightly wound?"

"Yeah. I mean, I get it—a good number of the Archives' holdings are dangerous if misused, and he's in charge of keeping things catalogued and safe. He thinks my group is nothing but a bunch of semiliterate cowboys."

"Why's that?"

"Because he stays inside all day, and we divide our time between Glastonbury and everywhere else. The Away Team hunts down misplaced artifacts," I explained. "Books, jewelry, old wands, whatever. If it's mentioned in the literature, we try to determine whether it exists, and if so, to bring it in for safekeeping." Smiling to myself, I added, "Yolanda calls us cowboys, too, but she's a trained archaeologist, and we don't have much patience for dusting dirt away with paintbrushes. Anyway, there's a grand total of one person on the Team who's ever been an archivist, so I'm sure Jude thinks we stumble over everything we retrieve by dumb luck."

She frowned as she considered that. "Seems like you'd do better working together."

"Agreed. My boss tried to get us all on good terms— Ted seldom meets a stranger. But Jude's a little standoffish, and Ted is a hugger, and you see where this is going?"

"Clearly." Glancing at her empty cup, she asked, "Do you have any more of that tea? It was good…*oh*."

"Just orange pekoe," I said as I enchanted a refill. "Nothing fancy."

"That's a useful trick." She gave it a test sip, then nodded. "Yup, perfect."

"That's the end result of a lot of practice and very bad tea." I waited until she put it aside, then said, "There's something else you should know about Jude."

"Yeah?"

"He's a Mulligan. A descendant," I clarified. "Jude *Duffy*, you know. I haven't asked him about it or anything—I was doing some research a couple of years ago and stumbled onto some of the family records. His branch stayed in Glastonbury, yours went to Canada. Anyway, he's old-blooded, which is another reason why he looks down his nose at the Team. We're a highly mixed bag."

"Mm. In other words, he's not going to want anything to do with me," she muttered.

"I never said that. Maybe lead with 'I have a master's in art conservation' instead of 'I just found out about good old Granduncle Jimmy.'" I paused, watching her digest that, then lowered my voice and murmured, "Tell you a secret?"

"Sure."

"Another reason that Jude isn't a fan of my folks is that he and Ted have this silent nerd rivalry going on. Neither will admit it, but they're in a race."

She hooked her elbow over the arm of the couch and leaned closer. "To do what?"

"Find the Grail."

"What...*the* Grail?" she asked, laughing in disbelief. "Don't tell me it exists—"

"We don't know. There're enough hints in the records to give anyone pause. Actually, there are *several* grails in the records, but a few are solid contenders: the Cairo Grail, the Antwerp Grail, the Broken Grail, the Carolingian Grail...cups fancy enough to be written about and supposedly possessing powers. One of those might be *the* Ur-Grail, the one that started all the legends. Now, I'm not sold on it," I continued, "and neither is the rest of the Team, but Ted's got his heart set on finding the damn thing, and apparently, so does Jude. Ted drags us on the occasional quest to far-flung places, Jude pores over books, but it's the same quixotic nonsense. Anyway, that should give you some idea of what you're dealing with when you get near the Archives." Grinning, I added, "Maybe don't lead with that little factoid, either, when you meet Jude."

Quinn fell silent and contemplatively finished her second cup of tea. When it was down to the dregs, she said, "It's a lot."

"I know."

"Like, this time yesterday, I lived in Queens, and now I'm a wizard in training, and…"

"It'll get easier," I insisted. "For now, want to go upstairs and finish decorating? Marcus and I left your room kind of neutral, so if you have color or curtain preferences, we could make that happen." I pushed myself from the recliner and stretched my back. "Nothing else productive is going to happen tonight. Marcus will be in the office until the wee hours, and who knows when Artur will get in? She does like her distance runs."

Quinn's eyes flicked toward the darkness outside our windows. "Kind of late for that, isn't it? Will she be okay?"

It was, I decided, far too soon to explain Artur to Quinn. "Oh my, yes," I replied, and steered her upstairs to distract her from her upended life with tile and carpet possibilities.

If Quinn had her doubts about her new situation, she put on a brave face the next morning and let me take her to Magus Popova's office. When she came home that night, however, she was practically ebullient. She'd made her first shield and cast her first bolt, earning praise from the magus, but just as exciting to her had been her visit to the Archives.

"Jude was really nice!" she said over ravioli. "*Super* friendly. He wants me to start apprenticing there as soon as Magus Popova thinks I'm safe."

"Already?" Marcus asked, frowning. "No vetting process? From what I've seen of his recruitment, Jude can be difficult to please…"

"You'd have thought he'd won the lottery when I told him about my program. He got excited and wanted to talk about my internships, and that was that." She helped herself to the salad. "He said that most of his people learn solely by apprenticeship, and that takes years. I've got the basics down, at least on the non-magical front, which could make me useful in far less time. In any case, he's not the weirdest person I've ever worked under, so"—she shrugged—"might as well give it a shot, yeah?"

She remained upbeat for the rest of the week, carefully read the assignments her tutor gave her over the weekend, and was chipper on Monday morning. That night, however, she seemed somewhat reserved, claiming fatigue, and retired early. On Tuesday, she slipped out early to have breakfast with Jude before her lessons began, which I took to be a positive sign—if Quinn could find something familiar in the castle, then perhaps she wouldn't be tempted to end her training prematurely. I went about my day, reading in my office and passing around the latest "egg watch" photo set from Sam, and I was just putting a pot of potatoes on to boil that night when Quinn came in.

"Hi, there!" I called, adjusting the gas as Marcus worked on the porkchops behind me. "Kitchen! Hope you're hungry for…"

The anxiety on her face stopped my greeting. "Hey," Quinn mumbled, watching us through the cutout window. "Um…can we talk?"

"Sure. What's on your mind?"

She paused, taking in the flat—Marcus and me in the kitchen, Artur in her usual spot in the den with her reading, and Maria, whom she'd met at Sunday dinner, setting the table for six. "So, uh…I've been talking to Magus Popova and Jude, you know…and, uh…"

"Yes?" I prompted.

"Who the hell *are* you guys?" she blurted. "They've been hinting, but I don't know about *what*, exactly, and—"

"Whoa, *whoa*," Maria interrupted, putting down her armload of plates. "Sit."

Quinn tentatively pulled out a chair from the kitchen table and waited, locking and unlocking her fingers.

With a quick gesture, Maria put a glass tumbler half-full of clear liquid on the table beside her. "Vodka. The good stuff, not the swill that will make you regret your life choices in the morning. Start with that, and we'll answer your questions."

She did as instructed, wincing slightly as the drink went down.

"Decent?" asked Maria.

Quinn nodded.

"Good. Right, then," she said, motioning for Artur to join us in the kitchen, "who wants to kick this off?"

Slowly, as concisely as possible, and with occasional breaks to check on the dinner in progress, we told her what she wanted to know. The mortal realm as one of three. Faerie and the court system. The Gray Lands and its odd form of magic, unusable to wizards or faeries. The Minor Arcanum and the Dark Company. Maria's upbringing as the next best thing to a princess in Faerie. My dad, gone too soon, and my years of parental neglect. The treasonous, murderous mother that Beth and I shared, incarcerated in the bowels of the castle. Marcus, buried alive until a chance search for a long-buried wand led us to him. Artur, asleep in the Gray Lands for more than a millennium and a half. The biological father she and I shared who'd tried to kill us both. The Team and its square pegs. We told her about the Mulligan coup, about the Fringe's "Unravelling," about the small band that had stayed in the mortal realm to find hiding Fringers and ultimately stopped a Gray Lands invasion, about the nasty but doomed alliance between Russell Mulligan and Coileán's daughter, Moyna, about Toula's assumption of power and the Conclave that had tried to break the Arcanum apart, about the new half-human king of the Gray Lands and his early attempts at peace and diplomacy.

We spoke throughout the meal—even Beth chimed in once she came home from practice—and late into the evening, condensing lessons in magical history, geography, and politics into one night of talk, all of it smoothed over with an endless supply of alcohol. As midnight neared,

Quinn, who by then had migrated to the couch, said, "I had Magus Popova take me back to Toula today. Wanted to know if there was anything on Grandpa in the records here—I thought there might be family photos or something that he'd want to have. She pulled them for me. You know what it said about him? 'Sent to boarding school.' That's it. One last entry in 1975, and then he disappears forever."

"It's terrible," I said, keeping my voice down. Beth had gone to bed under protest an hour before.

"It's like he *died*," Quinn continued, her eyes watering. "They didn't give a damn about him. And his brother, he had to know what happened, and he *still* killed all those people in the Fringe...people like Grandpa..."

"Abhorrent," Maria concurred.

She sat in silence for a moment, staring at the wall as the muscles in her jaw twitched, then said, "I'm glad there's nothing overtly tying us together. I'm a Dellucci, and I always will be. The Mulligans can all go to hell, as far as I'm concerned."

"That's understandable, but know that not all of your cousins are terrible," Maria replied. "Most are quietly middling wizards. If you want to meet them—"

"Not yet." She finished her last vodka in a long shot and slammed the glass onto the coffee table. "This place— this *family*—didn't think twice about what happened to Grandpa. No one even tried to find him. I'm not ready to make nice."

"There's no reason to rush," said Artur. "Bind up your wounds, mourn your dead, then face whatever's next."

"I guess." She stood, wobbling slightly, then found her balance and released her hold on the couch. "Thanks. I'm going to bed."

Artur began to rise. "Can you make it—"

"I'm not *that* tipsy." She demonstrated by walking an almost straight line toward the staircase, then paused and turned back. "It's just...you know...I'm related to *them*.

They did horrible things, and I—"

"Sleep," Maria interjected. "You can't fix the problems of the world tonight."

Quinn considered that, then shrugged and stumbled up to her room. We listened until her door slammed, and then I grimaced and picked up my glass. "Well, that was fun. Maria, stay as long as you like, but I'm done."

I collapsed into my own bed a few minutes later, and I'd almost dozed off when I felt Marcus's weight press into the mattress behind me. His arm snaked over my waist and pulled me closer, and I shifted into our customary spooning configuration. When the bed had ceased creaking, he murmured, "Kitty?"

"Mm?"

"I've been thinking."

"About what?"

"We should go on holiday."

Laughing in disbelief, I rolled over to face him in the darkness. "*Holiday*? With Quinn still settling in and Beth limping home every night? What brought this on?"

"As I said, I've been thinking. You've never taken me to Tennessee."

"Because I have nothing to show you there."

"Your father's farm," he replied. "You care deeply for your home, I know you do."

"I did," I admitted, "but Mom sold it years ago. It could be a strip mall by now, for all I know. Maybe it's a Walmart."

"I'd still like to see it. You've visited what's left of *my* city."

"Yeah, because Rome is a *destination*. There's nothing in Winston but farms and a Kroger."

"What's a Kroger?"

"Grocery store."

"Ah. You forgot the possible Walmart."

I sighed and snuggled against him. "Rather not think about that," I mumbled. "If the sunflower fields are, like, automotive parts and housewares these days, I don't want to know."

He held me silently for a time, then whispered, "What if I went through the gate first and scouted? Would that help?"

"We'll talk about it later, okay?"

Marcus kissed my forehead, and I soon fell asleep to the sound of his breathing.

Quinn was groggy in the morning but otherwise hardly the worse for wear, and when Marcus eliminated her hangover headache, her grateful smile suggested that she wasn't about to run screaming from the flat. When she cheerfully offered to pick up Indian takeout for dinner—as long as someone could point her in the direction of a restaurant— I thought the crisis of the summer had fizzled. Artur took her into town via the castle's semi-permanent shortcut, and they returned home burdened with bags, laughing at a group of crystal-laden American tourists who'd wandered into the curry shop after them and tried to phonetically sound out the menu. "We see a little of everything here," I told Quinn, taking her load from her. "And this smells fantastic. Thanks for springing for dinner, but you really didn't have to—"

"I insist," she said, rubbing the red impressions of the bags' handles out of her bare arms. "You're letting me crash here, so this is the least I can do."

"We *did* kind of upend your life," I pointed out.

She smirked, then plucked her wand off the counter where she'd left it, muttered, and produced a decent shield about four feet in diameter. "For the better, I think."

CHAPTER 4

The rest of the week was relatively uneventful—work, look after Beth's cuts and bumps from practice, rinse and repeat. On Friday, I considered going into town to see a movie, but Beth begged to go along, and since she was already dragging from Maria's torture sessions, I decided I could wait until the Saturday matinee, when she'd be rested enough that I wouldn't have to carry her home.

I felt like I'd only been asleep for minutes that night when bright light on the other side of my eyelids agitated me back to consciousness. "Beth?" I mumbled, blearily squinting in the direction of my bedroom door. "You okay?"

But the light wasn't coming from the den, as I'd assumed. Rather, as my vision cleared, I could make out a gate in my room—that was daylight I was seeing, and standing on the edge of the rift between the realms, her corona visible even against the background light, was a familiar blonde whose look of anguish made my stomach lurch. If Ros was upset, then the situation was dire...

Frank.

I bolted upright in bed, sleep forgotten. Ros had raised him from an egg—of course she'd be beside herself if something happened to him. And as she'd come to me herself rather than ask Sam to make the phone call she couldn't, whatever message she bore was nothing good.

"Is he okay?" I demanded, untangling myself from the blankets as Marcus grunted beside me.

"It's Ione," said Ros. "You two need to come over

now."

Some requests can't be denied. I shook Marcus awake, and we hurried across in our nightclothes, not even bothering to find our shoes.

Ros's gate had opened onto the dirt yard outside the dragon barn, and the sunlight suggested early afternoon. On arrival, I heard the agitated mental chatter of its occupants, some of whom seemed to be clustering near the massive sheep pen. I ran across the yard, skirting the occasional forgotten bone, and scrambled over the fence as I saw the white dragon at the heart of the disturbance. Frank could adeptly focus his thoughts into words, but that day, all I could make out was emotion: confusion, fear, but mostly panic.

It's seldom wise to get too close to a creature who can crush you with a mistimed tail swipe and is too preoccupied to notice you, but that was Frank, and I took the risk. "What's wrong?" I called, yelling as loudly as I could while I ran closer, darting between two of Neve's curious dragonets. "Frank, it's Kitty! What happened?"

His head rose, and one red eye fixed on Marcus and me as we neared. *She won't get up!*

The draconic horde parted to make a path, and Frank shifted enough to reveal a blue-green bulk beside him. Ione lay in the grass on her belly, though her head was almost sideways, one eye turned to the sun and the other to the dirt. The eye that I could see was open but unblinking. I jumped in front of her, insignificant beside her enormous head, and held my hands close to one of her nostrils. But I could feel no breath, nor did her side rise and fall.

As Frank called for Ione again and butted at her as if trying to rouse her from a deep sleep, Ros appeared to my left and pulled me back. "I don't know what happened," she murmured when Marcus joined us. "She stepped away from the nest to eat, she was chatting with Frank, and then…" She scowled, searching for the words. "It's like something *popped* in her. She collapsed, and…"

"Dead?" I whispered.

Ros nodded. "I couldn't save her. It was over in a matter of seconds, and the damage was catastrophic, and I…I didn't know, I *should* have known, but I didn't examine her too closely when she came here…"

Ros could broadcast her sentiments as well as any dragon, and her guilt was palpable.

"Who's with the eggs?" I asked.

"No one. They've all come out to see what's happened."

"Stay with Frank," I told Marcus. "I'm going to the barn."

Slipping past the milling dragons—and Sam and Joey, who were running from their houses to join Frank—I darted into the cavernous barn, a space that never failed to make me feel Lilliputian by comparison. When I squinted into the shadows, I spotted Ione's nest near the doors, many bales' worth of straw flattened in a thick ring around three cream-colored eggs nearly as tall as I was but considerably wider. The floor of the nest seemed warm, and I reached down to confirm. Pushing the straw back, I could make out the traces of enchantment heating the ground beneath the nest, which must have given Ione a little freedom to stretch her legs and eat a bite. Still, without her body heat around them, the eggs would cool all too soon.

I had to act fast. A moment's thought produced a warming enchantment above the eggs as well, though I erred on the side of temperate so as not to cook them. I was making the finishing tweaks when I heard a thought directed at me: *What are you doing?*

Turning, I almost shrieked when I found Neve's purple face a few feet away from my own. "I'm not hurting them," I hastily told her, "just trying to keep them toasty—"

Why?

The enquiry took me aback. "I don't think Frank's going to be in any condition to deal with this today—"

Yes, I know, their mother is dead. Her exhalation, though relatively gentle, felt like a hot gust. *Runt is…upset.*

I hadn't spent much time around Frank's siblings, but his sister's bemusement surprised me. "Of course he's upset! Ione just *died!*"

She continued to give me a red-eyed stare of incomprehension, and I reminded myself that while draconic intelligence was comparable to human, their thought processes didn't entirely align. "He loved her," I said, my back warming from the radiating enchantment. "Or liked her very much, at least. And since I can't make that mess out there any better, I'm doing what I can to look after the eggs until he can pull himself together."

But why?

"Because Frank is my friend," I replied, trying not to show annoyance in my thoughts, "and this clutch means a lot to him—"

The eggs will die. Their mother is dead.

"Not necessarily. We've got some temporary measures in place." I gestured toward my new enchantment. "Maybe we can build an incubator, if need be…" An idea popped into my mind. "Or you—you've sat a clutch before."

Me?

"Sure. Or maybe Georgie, she's experienced—"

I would never sit another female's clutch. Her response seemed as disgusted as if I'd suggested taking a refreshing drink from a public toilet.

"It's Frank's clutch, too."

Though I was no expert in the nuances of dragon faces, Neve's confusion was easy to read. *How can it be his?*

"He *is* the father, isn't he?"

So?

I sighed, praying for patience. "Never mind. I'm going to go check on your brother," I said, and hurried on my way.

When I returned to the sheep pen, Joey caught my arm and pulled me aside before I could get too close. "Give him space," he murmured, though I almost wished he would have shouted with the mental buzzing around me.

"I—"

"You are small and squishy," he insisted, "and he's in a *bad* place. Stay back."

While part of me wanted to comfort my friend, the wiser part reminded me that Joey knew dragons better than any other biped did, and I heeded his warning.

Ros, however, had no reason to fear grievous bodily harm, seeing as her physical form was temporary on a good day. "She's gone," I heard her say as Frank continued to nudge Ione's motionless form. "Frank, honey, she's gone. I'm sorry, I'm *so* sorry, but you're not going to bring—"

Why did you let this happen? he demanded, throwing his weight against Ione as if a shove would restore her to life.

"I didn't—"

Fix her! Bring her back! He paused in his futile attempts at resuscitation just long enough to stare her down. *Please, it's Ione, you've got to do something!*

Shoulders tense, arms folded protectively in front of her, Ros watched him continue his work and bit her lip. "I'm not infallible, you know that. And I don't know what happened."

You're the fucking realm! You know everything!

"I know that something happened in her head. That's all, I swear. Frank, believe me, if I had any idea this was coming, I—"

Save her. He paused again, his chest heaving with his exertion. *Kura saved Joey, right? And you saved Maria. Save her—*

"Frank—"

She's all I have. Please, he begged. *Please, Ros, for me...*

I couldn't see her face too clearly from where I stood, but the hitch in her voice was unmistakable. "There's nothing I can do," she managed to tell him before she vanished.

Ros! he called, renewed panic in his mind. *Come back! Please, Ros!*

"Overwhelmed," Sam muttered beside me. "She gets like this when she's feeling too much, happy, sad, angry, whatever."

"Shitty timing," I muttered back.

He snorted. "You know she can still hear you, right?"

"Your point?" Brushing past the men, I approached Frank, who'd collapsed beside Ione and was resting his head atop her body. "Hey," I said.

His eyes opened, then blinked in surprise. *Kitty? What are you doing—*

"Ros told us to come. Marcus is over there with the guys," I added, pointing to their huddle. It's next to impossible to hug a dragon, and since Ione's body was between us, I kept my distance. "I'm so sorry, Frank. This is sudden, I know, but if you want, I'll ask around and see if I can find someone to give you answers. Autopsy. It won't fix anything, but if it would give you peace…"

I held my breath, hoping Frank wouldn't take offense, but he seemed more dazed than anything. *Thank you. Yes, that…that might…* Suddenly, he raised his head in alarm. *The eggs!*

Marcus and I ran after him as he barreled past his siblings. By the time we reached the barn, Frank was snuffling around the nest, and he looked at me, perplexed. *What is this?*

"I…I wanted to keep them warm," I said, unsure of how to read him in that moment. "I'm sorry, I'll break it—"

No. Just a moment. Stepping carefully, he fit himself as best as he could into the hollow Ione had left behind, then covered the eggs with one wing. *Okay, now you can take it down.*

I did as he asked, watching as Frank coiled himself into

a tighter ring. "I'm sorry, I didn't mean to overstep," I told him in a rush. "With everything going on, I just wanted to be sure—"

Thank you. The thought was colored with deep sorrow, but there was true gratitude in it as well. *I appreciate it.*

"I'll go back and start making calls. Maybe Dr. Powell has a suggestion."

As Marcus opened a gate to our flat, Frank called my name. I turned and found one of his eyes fixed on me, seemingly alight in the sun falling through the barn doors.

I can't weep for her, he thought dully.

"Sure. I mean, I thought that dragons can't cry."

Exactly. And it feels wrong this time.

I hesitated, then stepped close and reached up to put my hand on his cheek. "We'll be back soon," I promised, and hurried home.

While Marcus alerted the rest of the Team, I called Toula, then Dr. Powell. They had no leads, and neither did Yolanda, but I hit pay dirt when I reached out to the Minor Arcanum. Fortunately, it was still afternoon in New Mexico, and the Joneses were willing to help. Having met both Frank and Ione, they sent their condolences, and Carey, who was the closest thing that organization had to a coordinator, made a few phone calls.

Three hours later, Marcus and I returned to Faerie with Pritam Bhat, a short, nervous man in his early thirties whom we'd retrieved from his upscale, if spartan, bachelor pad in Delhi. Carey, a sleepwalker, had pulled him into the dream space and told him in no uncertain terms that he was going with us, and Pritam had been wise enough not to argue.

"I respect Dr. Jones greatly, but on occasion, she scares me. I'll ask you not to repeat that," he'd told us as he packed a bag, his accent suggestive of a long stint in a British boarding school.

Back at the dragon barn, I prodded the newcomer toward Frank, who hadn't moved from his post. "This is Pritam," I told him. "On loan from the Minor Arcanum. He's a herpetologist."

I could see Pritam's Adam's apple bob as he took Frank in. Then again, there was a *lot* of him to consider.

Frank barely raised his head and studied Pritam in turn. *Herpetologist, you said?*

Pritam twitched at the mental contact, but he held his composure. "Yes. Doctorate and everything. But, ehm, I should caution you that I've never worked with anything larger than a Komodo dragon."

Dare I ask why you got close to one of those? he replied, a shadow of incredulity in the thought.

"I had an internship with a zoo, and they had a small group on hand," he explained, fiddling with the strap of his black nylon shoulder bag. "Two of the males got into it over a female, and the loser got a rather nasty bite out of the encounter. But otherwise, I don't make a habit of seeking out venomous lizards large enough to eat me." He paused, shuffling in the straw, then said, "They told me what happened to your mate. I'm sorry for your loss."

Frank's response, a wave of sadness, didn't need to be compressed into the structure of words to be understood.

"If you want, I'll do what I can with an autopsy. I'm flying blind," he stressed, "but if your structure is anything close to what I've studied, I should be able to draw some conclusions."

He nodded.

"Probably too much to ask, but you haven't got any books on dragon anatomy stashed around here, have you?"

"Actually, we have a little that might help," said Sam as he joined us. "There was a breeding program here about fourteen hundred years ago. The guy responsible wasn't a scientist by any means, but he was an obsessive amateur. Do you want to come in?" he asked, pointing to the retractable part of the barn wall that led into Ros's parents' kitchen. "We thought you might want to look at the materials before you begin, so they've been pulled. Most of the useful stuff is in a giant scroll, which is a pain, but it is what it is."

"I'll take what I can get," Pritam replied. "If it's no—"

The rest of that sentence turned into a yelp as Ros manifested. "At ease, Doc," she told him, then looked up at Frank. "I'll block her from view. This part should be private, I think."

Again, he merely nodded.

"Frank," she sighed, "I'm sorry. If there were anything I could do, you know I would."

I know.

"Are you hungry? You didn't eat lunch."

No.

Pritam cleared his throat. "I, ehm...perhaps I should begin reading for the autopsy..."

"Right this way," said Sam, and began to lead him toward the house.

Before they could cover more than a few feet, however, Frank thought, *Don't you mean necropsy?*

They stopped, and Pritam looked back at him. "Technically, yes. It's only an autopsy if it's a human performing it on another human. But...you know, under the circumstances, the other term seems wrong."

How so?

"Well, I've never done a necropsy on behalf of the next of kin."

Once he and Sam had ducked inside, Frank dipped his head toward me. *He'll do. Thank you.*

The postmortem analysis took two long days to complete. Ros erected a laboratory of sorts around Ione's corpse, tailoring it to Pritam's needs once Sam introduced them and assured Pritam that he wasn't about to be vaporized by the glowing woman. Before he made the first incision, Pritam read everything he could find on the subject of draconic anatomy, then propped open a few of his old textbooks, donned gloves, a gown, and rubber boots, and went to work. When he was too exhausted to see straight, he bedded down at Sam's place, catching a few hours of sleep and downing strong coffee before jumping back into his work.

I returned to check on Frank that day and happened to be loitering in the barn when Pritam entered to give his report. His notes were still in the handwritten preliminary stage, and he leafed through them for reference while he delivered the news.

"Cause of death was a ruptured cerebral aneurysm," he began, his eyes drifting between Frank and Ros, who stood by with her arms folded. "Massive, even at scale. I doubt she lived longer than a few minutes after it burst."

How did it happen?

Pritam tucked his papers under his arm and spread his hands as if holding a large ball. "An aneurysm is a bulging spot in a blood vessel. When a cerebral aneurysm ruptures, there's a good chance of immediate death. Some patients are never symptomatic—there's no indication of a problem until they drop. You said she registered pain?"

We were talking. She threw back her head and roared...

"A severe headache isn't an uncommon harbinger." He turned a page over and scanned the notes on the back. "But that was only the most acute of her maladies. Ione had several physical defects."

She was small, Frank protested, *but that's hardly a defect.*

"It might have been a sign of what else was going on with her," Pritam replied. "Now, remember that I lack a proper baseline. I'm drawing these conclusions from other reptile systems and that scroll, so it's possible that I'm mistaken—"

What did you find?

"Multiple heart problems. You have a four-chambered

heart, which is surprising—all known reptiles but crocodiles have only three. She had several suspected abnormalities, probably congenital. And there were structural oddities in her brain beyond the aneurysm. Honestly, I believe she was a time bomb. How old was she?"

Almost twenty-two. End of the summer.

"If I'm reading my materials correctly, then it's remarkable that she lasted as long as she did."

Ros interjected with a lifted finger. "Is it possible that she had the aneurysm when she came here two years ago?"

"Certainly," said Pritam.

She turned to Frank. "It wasn't bothering her. I didn't pay enough attention, and I never realized the danger she was in."

Could you have stopped it?

She mulled the question over for a long minute before speaking again. "I could have tried. Enchantment to shore up the area, maybe call someone like Pritam over to operate. We've got a couple of Fringers who had early-stage cancer before coming here, and they've been able to maintain stasis with magic alone, but…" Her voice faded. "Sweetie, I'm so sorry."

Their attention shifted back to Pritam when he accidentally dropped his papers in the straw and scrambled to collect them. "There is one thing I wanted to discuss," he said. "I took pictures during the process, and I have voice notes to be transcribed. If it's acceptable, I'll make a copy and leave it with the library here, in case someone else should need to be opened. Do you mind?"

While Frank and Pritam discussed the specifics, I glanced out the barn door in time to see the lab disappear. *He has his notes*, Ros silently reassured me. *I don't want Frank to have any chance of stumbling onto her butchered corpse.*

I didn't bother responding—dragons being masters of mental communication, I didn't want my comparatively clumsy thought to Ros to be intercepted—but that didn't mean I'd escaped notice. I'd barely started toward the door when I heard another voice in my mind: *Could we talk privately?*

Searching for the speaker, I turned and found a black dragon behind me. Georgie, Frank's mother, was no stranger—it would have been difficult to spend as much time as I had in Faerie and *not* make it out to the dragon barn. Still, she'd never taken me into her confidence, and the development concerned me.

"Sure," I said, and followed her deep into the recesses of the building, where she made her bed. As matriarch of the clan, Georgie could call dibs on whatever spot she liked, and the choice areas were in the rear, where the sunlight didn't penetrate as strongly. The other flattened areas around her surely belonged to her children—I couldn't say which, though I knew that Neve was closer to the front with her own growing brood—but everyone else was outside.

Flopping down with a huff and curling into a comfortable position, Georgie watched me take a seat on one of the many nearby bales, then thought, *It's about Frank.*

"I figured. He's kind of tough for me to read right now—how's he holding up?"

Not well, I think. The tip of her tail twitched against her bedding straw, a motion more heard than felt in the shadows. *There's a problem with the eggs. We've offered to dispose of them for him, but he won't let anyone near them.*

"I...um..." Flummoxed, I tried to come up with a response to *that*, eventually managing, "They're his children. If he wants to try the single father thing—"

A male can't sit a clutch, she protested.

"I don't know, he seems to be keeping them warm enough. And Joey and Sam are around if he needs the temperature of the floor adjusted—"

No...no, you misunderstand. What he's doing is unnatural. Ask his brothers if you don't believe me. Shifting her head slightly closer to me, she thought, *I never knew my father. My children will almost certainly never know theirs. If my other sons have children, they don't know of them. So for Frank to have anything to do with Ione's brood would have been highly unusual, you see?*

"Okay…"

For him to nest in Ione's place, though…that's not right.

Georgie was agitated—I could hear it in her thoughts—and so I tried not to worsen the mood. "Neve seemed reluctant, but could one of his other sisters be prevailed upon to take over? Or you?"

Her reaction was much as her daughter's had been. *Absolutely not. No one will sit another female's nest, particularly the nest of a stranger.*

"Ione wasn't family," I conceded, "but Frank is, and they're his brood, too."

She blinked slowly, her eyes dark red in the gloom. *Your ways are not our ways*, she finally replied. *Perhaps this would be acceptable to you—Val raised Maria and looked after you, so I suppose it could be done*, she mused. *But such a thing goes against all instinct for us. It's…* She struggled, her thoughts jumbled, then concluded, *No. Out of the question.*

I thought of the long night Frank and I had spent in the wilds of the Gray Lands, shot down and stranded, and how he'd tried to apologize for the mess I'd gotten us into: *I really am a failure. As a dragon. I'm an utter failure.*

"I realize that what Frank is doing is unusual," I said, "but from a physical standpoint, can he do it? As long as he keeps the eggs warm, won't they hatch? They'll bond to him, and if I know Frank at all, he won't let them starve."

Physically…yes, Georgie allowed. *I suppose the eggs could be incubated with enchantment, and I hatched even after my mother abandoned the nest. It's just…you know, it's not right.* Her tail picked up its thumping tempo. *Granted, this is Frank we're talking about, so I suppose some oddities are to be expected. I love him, but he's never been normal. I don't know what to do with him half the time.*

I kept my mind a careful blank. Frank had told me

plenty about his upbringing—the late hatch who'd bonded to teenage Ros because his mother had busied herself with his siblings and left him behind, the runt who never quite caught up to his brothers, the adult adrift after Ros's "promotion," whose loneliness and dissatisfaction had led him to Ted.

"He does things his way," I replied.

Georgie snorted. *Sometimes I wonder whether he would always have been as he is or whether Glastonbury warped him.*

Maybe it saved him, I wanted to retort, but I kept that thought to myself. Instead, I said, "He's wrecked right now. If you could give him some space and, you know, stop offering to kill the eggs, he'd probably feel better."

So said Joey, but I honestly think he'd recover from this more quickly if the eggs were no longer a distraction.

"He loved her," I said as the fae side of my temper threatened to flare. "Those are her children. If I were you, I wouldn't try to get anywhere near them."

I suppose, Georgie replied, and closed her eyes. *Work on him, won't you?*

Clearly, the conversation was over. I rose, shaken, and made my way toward the sunlight.

Marcus soon took Pritam home to rest—the man was a wizard, true, but not gifted with gates—but I lingered near the barn door, watching the enchanted sheep graze and periodically bud in two, and tried to make sense of the last days. I thought Frank had fallen asleep when I heard him in my head: *Don't you have something more exciting to be doing?*

"Work can wait," I replied, turning to find him watching me. "How're you doing?"

Honestly?

No more needed to be said. "You haven't eaten in two days. I'll egg-sit for a bit, let you grab a bite—or I could coax a few of the sheep in here, if you'd prefer. I deliver."

A quick flash of teeth was as close as he was going to

come to a smile while in his true form. *Appreciated, but I'm not hungry.*

"Could I tempt you with a few gallons of hot sauce?"

No appetite for it.

"Bacon, then. *Bacon* with hot sauce."

Really, I'm fine. His head rose and turned on his sinuous neck as he gave himself a once-over. *It's not like I'm wasting away.*

"But you can't sit there until the end of July. Ione got up and walked around, right?" I pressed. "And I'm not telling you to leave the nest unattended—I'll gladly watch it, and everyone else on the Team has offered to pitch in. Say the word, and you'll have relief from Glastonbury."

I felt his mind probing through my thoughts, but if he was looking for evidence of hyperbole, he came away disappointed. Ted had already made it known that anyone on egg duty was excused with his blessing.

I appreciate the offer. Truly. But these are our children, and they're all I have left of Ione, and I'll be damned if anything happens to them. He fixed me with a red-eyed stare. *Mom told you to help me come to my senses, I trust.*

"More or less."

The low growl that welled up within him wasn't aimed at me, but still, the hair on the back of my neck rose in warning. *They want to kill the eggs. If I give them an opening, they'll strike.*

"Not if we're here to help guard them."

You may be right, but I can't take that risk. Frank paused, and I could sense the turmoil in his mind. *Ione...she's the one dragon who's ever accepted my...eccentricities, I suppose. Or she was.* The thought was colored with fresh shades of despair. *She's gone. What am I supposed to do, Kitty? I'll do the right thing for our children, I swear it, but what am I to do without her here?*

I couldn't properly hug him, so I settled for wrapping my arms as far around his neck as they would reach. "Take a break and eat something. She wouldn't want you to starve."

You're persistent, I'll grant you that.

"Let us help you."

"He won't starve," said Ros, and I released Frank to find her standing nearby. "I'll see to it. Nor will the eggs come to harm," she told him. "Rest. I've got the watch." Frank did nothing to disguise his broadcasting doubts about the plan, but Ros was firm. "You haven't slept in two days. I couldn't save Ione, but I can damn sure promise you that nothing will touch those eggs. I've got this, bud," she said more gently. "Try to sleep, okay?"

After a long moment, he snorted and closed his eyes, and Ros shooed me on my way. *Tell the others back in Glastonbury that I'm granting the Team full access to Faerie for now. Come and go as you will. If anyone here starts to complain, I'll set them straight.*

"Can you talk some sense into his family?" I muttered.

She grimaced and cut her eyes to Frank's brothers, who were dozing in the dirt outside the barn. *I can perform wonders, not miracles.*

Over the next week, every member of the Team made at least one appearance in the barn, juggling visits around the realms' off-synch days. Antony showed up in the middle of Glastonbury's night once Frank woke late on Faerie's Monday afternoon with more movies and a custom-designed remote large enough to be operated with a claw (and thanks to Aiden's tinkering, sufficiently shielded from magic so as not to fry). Mal brought audiobooks for a change of pace. Ted and Lakshmi spent all evening Wednesday with Frank, scheduling trips and planning the details of the rest of the year's projects to keep him distracted. Even Daphne, busy as she was with an esoteric side paper, brought over a large, unlabeled bottle of a suspicious reddish-brown liquid. "Made by one of my cousins in Jamaica," she told him, holding the bottle to the light. "You don't want to know the Scoville units of the peppers in this sauce. I think it'll eat through concrete."

But still, Frank's appetite was nearly nonexistent, and he lived in a state of hypervigilance. Any approach by one of his kin that he deemed too close elicited rumbling growls of warning like thunder heralding a summer storm. Compounding his troubles, he was deeply grieving, though he seldom spoke of Ione after the first days. Once they spent time around Frank, Artur and Marcus confirmed what I had gathered from the shadow on his thoughts—and besides, I knew Frank well enough to know when he wasn't himself. Depressed but determined not to harm the clutch Ione had left behind, he left the nest only once or twice a day, just long enough to get a drink and blink in the sunlight, and only if Ros had manifested to guard the eggs in his absence. Frank's family might have had ideas about how best to deal with Ione's leavings, but they weren't foolish enough to cross the realm herself.

Even with his difficult situation, though, Frank appreciated visitors. I spent more time with him than most did, and it reassured me to sense him perk up with every opening gate. Aside from the unwanted agitation of his encroaching siblings, nesting was boring, and we could provide a diversion.

Of course, that didn't mean he didn't feel bad about the trips we were making. *You don't need to worry*, he told Ted at the end of his Thursday visit. *You're busy. I have roughly three years of movies here, and the eggs only take two months. Don't mess up your sleep schedule on my account.*

Ted, being Ted, responded with incredulity. "We look after each other. Right now, that means you're on the receiving end. It's no trouble."

Ted, I—

"It's no trouble at all," he insisted.

Frank paused, regrouped, and tried again. *I appreciate the support, but you should be aware that I may not be able to return to the office as soon as I'd planned—*

Our boss looked almost wounded. "So? Doesn't mean

we don't care."

Hatchlings are clingy. I won't even be able to leave their sight for a time—ask Ros if you want proof.

"Frank." He folded his arms above his paunch. "Those are your kids. You take as long as you need, and if *I* have anything to say about it, there will always be a place waiting for you. Got it?"

Thank you.

"Now, if you want to come back sooner rather than later, remember all the days that Antony brought Allie down when she was a little thing? The crying fits, the tantrums, Allie running up and down the halls and grinding crayons into the carpet…"

A flash of amusement colored his thought. *Good times.*

"Yeah, says the guy who introduced her to Nerf. And if she was down there, you *know* there was a fifty-fifty chance that Mal had wolfed out. Honestly, people," he said, shaking his head. "What I'm trying to say is that if we survived Hurricane Allie, then surely we could handle a few little dragons underfoot."

Frank snorted. *I'm not sure what you're imagining, but you have seen the size of these eggs, yes? There's nothing little about them. Envision a pony trying to perch on your shoulder. A pony with claws and poor fire control.*

"We *do* have fire extinguishers in the castle, you know," said Ted. I opened a gate home for him, and he pointed up at Frank before he departed. "Eat something, eh?"

The next morning—well, *our* next morning—at Frank's request, I brought Quinn over to meet him. Having heard about her peculiar circumstances and her residence in my flat, he was eager to make her acquaintance so as not to be out of the loop. *Come on*, he told me, *she's been cooped up in the castle for two weeks. She's due a field trip.*

For her part, Quinn was excited at the prospect of seeing the dragon barn, though she grilled me the night before until she was certain that she wouldn't say anything to worsen my friend's pain. Once we crossed, she briefly marveled at the starry night and the abundance of ambient magic in the realm, a rainbow-hued mist of potential visible to most of us with talent, then turned, saw the monstrosity of a barn behind her, and broke into a wide grin. "Oh, this is *nuts*," she whispered, and hurried along as I led the way. I couldn't blame her for her excitement—there was a certain dearth of dragons in the mortal realm, after all.

"Hey, Frank!" I called as I neared the open door. "Brought Quinn! Don't eat her, okay?"

But he was too excited to even acknowledge my pathetic attempt at humor. *They're talking!* he called back, the thought seeming to sparkle with joy.

"Already?" Enchanting a cluster of floating orbs to light my way, I jogged closer, Quinn momentarily forgotten.

They're halfway along. Can you hear them?

I stopped within arm's length of his coiled body and tried to sort through the mental chatter around me. The older dragons I recognized, but there was something new: softer voices, the telepathic peeping that heralded the early formation of consciousness. The developing dragons were calling out into the universe beyond their shells in nebulous proto-thoughts, now singly, now in chorus, forming the first clutch bonds.

"Oh, my God," I breathed, and beamed up at him. "Well done, Dad."

They're little chatterboxes. Started after sunset, and they've barely stopped since, he replied with pride, then noticed the newcomer standing alone near the door and raised his head higher. *You must be Quinn*, he thought.

She nodded and awkwardly raised a hand. "Uh…hi, yeah, I'm Quinn. Sorry, don't let me interfere…"

What interference? You were invited. Come closer, he urged, turning his head so that she wasn't walking straight toward a mouth full of deadly teeth. *NYU, yes?*

"Most recently."

I've read good things about their conservation program. It's a pity more of the archivists don't pursue proper studies in their field. Then again, I can't talk—everything I've learned for the gig in Glastonbury has been either on the job or self-taught.

"You're in good company," I pointed out.

Says you, Oxford, he retorted. *Quinn, don't tell me that Jude has made you sign anything binding yet. If you're planning to stick around, I'm sure that Ted will want to make a pitch. Have you had a chance yet to look at the Archives' holdings?*

"Not really," she admitted—and if the tension in her back and shoulders was any indication, she was slightly freaked by exactly how *much* dragon was within striking distance. "Jude showed me some of the artifacts, the jewelry and cups and such, but I haven't been able to dig into the manuscripts."

The illuminated collection rivals that of the Bodleian. The codices aren't as well known outside of the Arcanum as the Bod's are, naturally, but there are some fascinating volumes if you get a break. If Jude gives you a hard time, ask Ted.

"Will do," she said, and rubbed her elbow. "Did I, um, hear something about talking eggs?"

Want to see? Climb up my side, there—he indicated an easy spot with his snout—*and I'll give you a peek.*

If Quinn was nervous, she knew better than to decline. Within a minute, she'd made her ungainly ascent, and with orbs hovering overhead for illumination, Frank lifted his wing to show her the eggs. "*Whoa*," she said, kneeling atop his back. "They're *huge*! Boys or girls?"

A mystery. There's no way of knowing without scanning them, but there's really no need.

"And…that sound, kind of like static in my head…"

That's them. They're not great conversationalists yet, but they still have a month to go, he thought, spreading his wing over them once more. *But tell me about your program, now—do you specialize?*

As the two of them talked shop, I heard Ros's voice in my mind: *Can I borrow you? Join me outside.*

Slipping away, I exited the barn but found myself alone in the dark yard. "Uh, Ros?"

I don't need to manifest, I just don't want Frank to overhear. At least he's distracted with the new girl.

"What's wrong?" I murmured, watching as one of Neve's sons, out for a midnight snack, tossed a sheep into the air and swallowed it whole.

The eggs. The fetuses aren't right.

My guts knotted. "How so?"

I'm not positive, but there seem to be structural problems with all three of them.

"Whatever was wrong with Ione…you think it was genetic?"

Possibly.

"Can you fix them?"

Her hesitation was answer enough.

I've been working on them ever since Ione died, she told me. *Kura made some pre-birth modifications to me, so I'm using her memories, but they're not enough.*

"Dragons are different…"

It's not that. Some things are simple enough to tweak—the witch-blood situation, you know? I can amp up the fae side without much difficulty. Or if someone's injured, I can patch holes. Bodies seem to know how they go together, and they have default settings. But where there are problems this big, this early on… Though Ros didn't technically breathe, I heard the mental equivalent of a frustrated sigh. *Like I said, I'm working on them, but I don't know if it's going to be sufficient.*

I thought of Frank on the other side of the wall, protecting those eggs as if it were Ione herself in the middle of the nest. His joy at hearing their voices…

"Have you told him?" I muttered, scuffing the toe of my shoe in the dirt.

I can't do that to him. I can't. Not after I overlooked Ione.

"So why tell me, then?"

Because if the worst happens, I'm going to need someone with a clear head in the room, and that's not going to be Frank.

Having dug a little trench with my foot, I began filling it in again as I tried to lock my feelings down where Frank wouldn't notice. "How likely, would you say?"

Ros wouldn't answer me, which was worse than any guess she could have offered.

Somehow, I got Quinn home to Glastonbury without alerting Frank to my distress. He was too preoccupied with the eggs, I suppose, listening to them reaching out into the world and answering their half-formed thoughts. Keeping my façade intact, I sent Quinn on her way to meet Magus Popova, as she'd been scheduled for a ten-day training session at Arc 3—a working trip, sure, but Quinn was excited about the prospect of an overnight stay in the Alps. Once I was alone, however, I hurried into the subbasement, let myself into Marcus's office, and locked the door behind me. He watched from behind his desk, silent but concerned, then rose and joined me once I'd landed on the couch. "What is it, Kitty?" he asked softly.

Reaching for his mind, I replayed the morning's events, barely noticing until I finished that my face was wet.

He had no solution to offer, and we both knew that, but he could hold me, muffling the noise while I cried, and murmur reassurance that neither of us believed.

Pulling myself together, I wiped my eyes dry and found him regarding me as if expecting a second round. "I'm sorry," I said, "I shouldn't have dropped that on you."

"Why not? It sounds like Ros did just that."

"Yeah, and I can handle it, it's okay, I—"

"*Kitty*." He squeezed my hand until I looked into his dark eyes. "Your troubles are my troubles. Let me help." He hugged me again until my sniffling ceased, then whispered, "We could go to Winston until Ros fixes this. You, me…a possible Walmart…this majestic Kroger of which you speak…"

I would have laughed had my heart not ached.

CHAPTER 5

I didn't tell anyone besides Marcus. The risk of leak was simply too great. Artur should have been able to protect that knowledge from mental prying, but she might have told Beth, who had no such talent, and neither did the rest of the Team. As for Maria, she wouldn't be back from Arc 6 until the evening, and I didn't want to bother her. And so, though I felt sick to my stomach, I kept up appearances for the rest of the day, shutting myself into my office and pretending to read.

Worn out, I passed on dinner and went to bed early, reminding myself that stress baking would be a dead giveaway to my state of mind. Sleep would help, I decided—sleep always seemed to help—and I'd see things more clearly in the morning.

Unfortunately, my phone woke me around ten that night, and I groaned when I saw the caller. "Hey, Yolanda," I mumbled into the speaker, trying to sound conscious. "What's up?"

"Sorry to…wake you?" she asked bemusedly.

"Long day. Is something on fire?"

"No, but we need to do some sleuthing tonight. Do you have anyone available?"

By then, Marcus was sitting up beside me, and I grunted in the affirmative as I put the phone on speaker mode. "What's the rush?"

"Secured archaeological site. If we don't get in before morning, the mundies might find more than they've bargained for."

Last-minute calls for backup weren't unusual for the Team, and I counted any such call that didn't involve magical booby traps or explosives as an easy day. Too many ancient wizards had been scarily creative when it came to protecting their treasures.

"Hold that thought," I told her, climbing out of bed. Throwing on a robe, I knocked on Artur's door to rouse her, then huddled in the den with the others and put the phone on the coffee table. "Okay, Yolanda," I said, "start from the top."

"So I got a call from Ireland about an hour ago," she said as we leaned closer to the phone. "There's a couple of Minor Arcanum witches living in a little town near Galway."

I frowned. "Why would they be calling—"

"Oh, I wasn't the first contact. They reached out to some wizards in that group, someone got word to the Joneses, and Carey slipped them my number. Seems no one in the Minor Arcanum wants to touch this one with a ten-foot pole."

"Why not?" asked Artur.

"Archaeological dig, for one. Cameras, security guards...it's a hassle to break in. Maybe it's crazy, but in my field, we generally prefer that the random curious don't go traipsing through our sites on amateur treasure hunts," she said, earning a quick grin from Artur. "Two, from what I'm hearing, there's some heavy spellcraft at work. Look, I've got no quarrel with the Minors, but if there's large-scale magic at play, I'd much rather have someone classically trained on hand."

I glanced at my companions. "Uh...I can offer plenty of theory, but you remember that part about how I can't actually cast anymore? If you need someone to do delicate spell manipulation instead of enchanting the place to smithereens—"

"I don't know *what* I need," said Yolanda, "but I'd be grateful if the Team would help me tonight. Besides, Kitty, you've got more experience in this area than I do."

That gave me pause. "*You're* the actual archaeologist…"

"Yeah, but my training didn't cover shit like this. Like I said, it's an excavation in small-town Ireland. A sinkhole opened in a parking lot, and there were ruins underneath. Probably the crypt of an old church, maybe an abbey. Hard to say, and this isn't my region of expertise."

"They paved over a church?" Artur interrupted.

"Eh, not too surprising. Remember how they found Richard III's body beneath a parking lot? There's only so much land in the UK and Ireland, and cars have to park somewhere. Anyway, the witches who called me run a little restaurant or something near the site. Husband and wife, elderly from the sound of it. They've been doing catering for the field team. When they brought lunch by today, everyone was excited at this discovery, and the crew let the witches take a look."

"What'd they find?" I asked.

"Stone coffin. Sealed, probably lead-lined. It's not marked with a name, but there's a decent chance that whatever's in there hasn't turned to dust or soup quite yet. They've got experts flying in from London in the morning, and they'll probably move it and try to open it. Which could be a problem, as the witches report that it's *wrapped* in spells. They told me they're almost surprised that it's not glowing in the mundane spectrum, considering the light show it's putting off in the magical."

"And they have no idea what's inside?" I pressed.

"Nada. They don't even have the training to take a good guess about the spells' purpose. But in case there's something inside that coffin that shouldn't be released…"

"You think there could be something alive in there?"

She hesitated. "Having not laid eyes on it, I can't say, but if the witches aren't exaggerating…maybe."

Beside me, Marcus muttered, "*Fuck*, not again." Artur nodded, her jaw clenching.

"As I said," Yolanda continued, "you've got the

experience here, Kitty."

"I'm no expert," I protested.

"I don't know, you have a decent track record of opening ensorcelled coffins."

"It wasn't even a coffin! It was just a box!"

"Yeah, a box with a body inside."

Marcus pointedly cleared his throat. "Speaking as said body, perhaps we should get on with it. You have location photos?"

"Coming your way momentarily," Yolanda replied. "Rendezvous at our witches' place at twenty-three hundred hours local time?"

As soon as I hung up, I took Marcus's hand and squeezed it hard. "You don't have to come. Neither do you," I told Artur, "not if this hits too close to home. I'm a big girl, and I'll get Maria to go with me."

"Nonsense," my sister replied, pushing herself from the couch. With a casual flick of her hand, she was dressed and heading back to her room to collect her gear. "Are you informing Ted, or shall I?"

"We're calling Ted?" I asked.

She turned and raised an eyebrow. "He'll be insufferable if we don't, and I'd rather he not sulk for the rest of the summer."

"I'll phone him," said Marcus, squeezing my hand in turn before extracting himself from my grip. "And I'm going as well."

"Honey..." I began as he stood.

He stooped and kissed the top of my head. "It's a box in a car park. What's there to fear?"

If Yolanda was surprised by the size of our party, she didn't let on. What had begun as three had more than doubled—Maria was willing to assist, and unsurprisingly, Ted would have gone in his pajamas. As Marcus had found him working late with Daphne, she also tagged along, and she made a point of calling Bob. The eldest member of the Team and the only one of us with archivist training, Bob seldom went into the field, but he made an exception that night. "My mother was Irish," he reminded Maria as she opened the gate. "I'm fluent. If someone's alive in there, maybe I can be of use."

The pictures Yolanda had sent led us to the parlor of a tidy, if severely dated, bed and breakfast. The scent of rose potpourri couldn't quite mask the telltale odor of ammonia from the litterbox in the corner of the room, and the culprit, a fat black cat with golden eyes, arched his back and hissed from the safety of the kitchen as we sealed the gate behind us.

"Faeries," Yolanda muttered, conveniently ignoring the fact that she was a lesser blood herself, then introduced us to our hosts, Susan and Daniel O'Leary. Aside from Susan's bright pink bob, the pair looked like kindly grandparents, a little paunchy and out of style but friendly enough as they welcomed their gaggle of late-night houseguests. "Just waiting on one more," Yolanda told us, glancing at the antique mahogany clock on the floral-papered wall. "Should be here…*ah*."

A second gate admitted a tall, youthful man in a black T-shirt and jeans, carrying a computer bag over his right shoulder. He wore a black ski cap, a poor choice for July that did nothing to hide the blond ponytail falling halfway down his back.

Maria wasn't the only one of us taken aback at his arrival, but she was the first to speak. "Lord Aiden? What are you—"

"Lonnie said there'd be security cameras," he explained, cocking his head toward the coordinator. "Figured you wouldn't mind a hand."

She folded her arms. "Unless they're protected, I'm confident that I can hex a camera."

"But can you hex it without *destroying* it?" he countered. "That's the real trick, kid."

In faerie terms, Aiden was a kid himself, barely into his sixties, but watching him speak with the other members of the Team, I was struck by the discrepancy between what I knew of him and what my eyes were suggesting. Though he was about a decade older than Daphne, he seemed young enough to be her son.

The O'Learys soon brought out a sheet of printer paper and a pair of pens to give us an idea of the obstacles. "Security guards," said Daniel, drawing three Xs on the periphery of the site. "There's seldom anything to give them trouble, so if we're quick about it, we may get past them without raising an alarm."

"Speaking of which," Susan cut in, "there's cameras with the guards and inside. No periphery alarm, as far as I can tell, but definitely eyes on the place."

We took a moment to commit the map to memory, then headed out to the site, a set of barriers and portable buildings with a white security light at the center. The witches led us up a narrow alley, and we observed from the shadows as one of the guards stretched his legs and returned to his makeshift booth with his phone.

Aiden glanced back at Maria and me and whispered, "How about it, girls? Want the first shot?"

I heard Maria's voice in my head: *Preference?*

All yours, Magus.

She snorted, then cloaked herself in a glamour of near-invisibility, her passage toward the guard shack marked by a disturbance in the air subtler than a heat mirage. When she was within a few feet of her target, the guard slumped against the wall, unconscious, and Aiden shifted his grip on his bag. "Wait for my signal," he told us, and glamoured himself as Maria had done. I watched for a long moment, seeing little but light and shade, until Aiden reappeared. Unzipping his bag, he extracted a computer, which floated at the right height while his fingers raced across the screen and, if I wasn't mistaken, a keyboard that didn't quite exist. After a minute or two of work, he nodded, then waved for us to join him.

"The cameras are networked," he said quietly as we clustered around. The computer showed an eight-part split-screen view of night-grainy streets. "I've gained access, and they're recording loops for the next hour..." He paused as Maria unglamoured herself and approached. "Any problems?"

"None. They're out cold."

Her glamour work was solid—I hadn't even noticed her slip off to send the other guards to sleep.

"Great," said Aiden. "And now, for my next trick..." After a few taps, two little amber lights that had been glowing at the top and bottom of a post beyond the guard shack winked out. "Motion sensors," he told us. "If anything large enough to break both beams simultaneously comes through, it triggers a silent alarm and a camera trap."

The O'Learys looked stunned. "I'm so sorry," Susan began in a rush, "I had no idea they were there—"

"You weren't supposed to," he replied, and grinned as he put his computer away. "But since the motion sensors talk to the cameras, it wasn't tough to put them back into daytime mode."

"But how did you even—"

"Break in?" he finished. "Practice, luck, and let's just say that it's amazing what you can do when you can make magic and a machine work together. Been developing this with the Fringe for thirty years. So, where's this supposed coffin?"

With Daniel on point, we picked our way through the site. I called forth a pair of tiny white orbs and sent them floating near my feet to reveal obstacles before I could trip and face-plant, and the wizards in our group followed close behind. At the heart of the enclosure, the O'Learys pointed to a dingy canvas tent, then waited while Aiden did a sweep for additional security before leading us inside.

I squinted on seeing the box—the witches hadn't lied

about the spells around it—though calling it a coffin was an understatement. The artifact was roughly the size and shape of the tomb of a medieval aristocrat, albeit without the decorative carvings. Indeed, the stone was unmarked by a chiseled name or even the rusted remnant of a plaque. Maria, Daphne, and I approached and considered the tight mesh of spellcraft that surrounded the supposed tomb like a sleeve, a brilliant magical construction that almost seemed to hum with the power surging through it.

"Reminds me of the camouflage around Afallon," Daphne murmured. "In complexity, I mean. I don't recognize much of this architecture."

I gestured to three pockets of ambient magic in the weave. "Look at the flow. Active siphoning through these ports, then into the rest of the matrix."

Frowning, Maria puzzled over them. "Flow regulation?"

"Maybe, but I'm leaning toward reservoirs. The pools here are constantly refilling, see? In case of sudden loss of magic—"

"The spell holds," she concluded. "Yeah, I see it…but that's not the usual technique for running backup pockets. The installation wards…" She paused, studied the construction again, then stepped back and ran a hand through her dark hair. "This is more efficient than the wards."

"I agree," said Daphne. "Look at the stacks on this— it's barely sipping from the power available."

I slipped a step to my right as Bob and Ted joined us. "What's the verdict?" Bob asked.

"Unrecognized construction," said Maria. "Highly efficient, protected against loss of magic."

"Not something recently added?"

She sucked her teeth. "Difficult to say. Some of the techniques used here look to be at least eighteenth-century developments, but with the age of the site…do we have an estimate?" she asked the O'Learys.

"Tenth to twelfth century," Susan offered.

Maria's frown deepened as she gave the spell another glance. "Remarkable. Whoever built this was ahead of his or her time, assuming that someone didn't come along a few hundred years ago and ensorcell this box for the hell of it. But in any case, let's assume this predates the '13 closure."

Once again, I was grateful to have missed *that* bit of fun. For a terrifying few days back in 2013, Mab—with an assist from Coileán and Eleanor's half brother, Robin—had sealed the border between Faerie and the mortal realm. Without Faerie's outflow of magic, the mortal realm had quickly run dry, and spells and enchantments without backup pockets of raw magic built into their matrices had fallen apart.

Ted ran a fingertip along one of the channels. "What's it doing, anyway?"

"Honestly, I'm not sure. I...*think* this bit is for preservation," she said, pointing to a cluster of eight finely braided amplification stacks, "but the rest—"

"This could be forced sleep," Daphne interjected, indicating another portion of the construction. "Actually, I'm almost sure it is. It's a modified form of a diary spell."

On that count, at least, Daphne was our unquestioned expert. For someone like her who wrote treatises on theoretical magic for the fun of it, the diary of Simon Magus was a prize to be studied, and Daphne had considered it cover to cover...the scanned version, that is. The original was under high security in the Archives, access to its vellum pages restricted to only the most senior archivists and the magi. Daphne had sufficient clearance to see an electronic copy without a few of the most sensitive pages excised, but even she had never seen the book in person.

I cut my eyes to Marcus and Artur, who lingered at the back of our crowd. True, they had no reason to join us—neither could have read a spell if their lives depended on it—but I knew I wasn't imagining the tension in their faces.

"Well, here's the problem, as I see it," said Maria. "We could take this home with us and leave a duplicate, but I'd rather not move it until we see if there are spells beneath it. I don't want to set off a trap." Daphne and Ted nodded vehemently—I hadn't been on the notorious trip to Ethiopia that had almost cost Daphne an arm, but I'd heard the cautionary tales. "It would be better to open this here tonight. That way, if anything's going to explode, it won't be the castle. Now, to open it, we'll need to break the spells—"

"But we could model them first," Daphne finished. "I'm game if you are."

Useless for the moment, I moved away from the tomb to give them space. Modeling was a technical and time-consuming piece of spellcraft in which a wizard made a non-functional copy of a magical construction for later analysis. I'd seen Daphne do it before, and though Maria could no longer cast because of her fae augmentation, she understood the process and could check Daphne's model as she went. The pair worked quickly while the rest of us stood sentry, watching for signs of motion from the sleeping security guards. After a long twenty minutes, they'd finished their project, and Daphne collapsed the model into a palm-sized holding sphere Maria created for safekeeping.

"Right, then," said Maria, beckoning me back to her side. "Want to see what's inside this biscuit tin?"

"Biscuits, I'm hoping," I muttered, and placed my hands over the spell's channels. "Ready."

There are two ways to break a spell: either move the ensorcelled person or thing into an environment devoid of magic or shoot so much magic through the spell that it falls apart. For us, particularly since enchantment can make fireworks when improperly used in proximity to a spell, overloading was the simpler option. Maria and I forced a blast of power into the spell, and its glow brightened almost to solar levels before the channels crumbled with a soundless pop.

To no one's surprise, there wasn't a mass rush to pry off the lid once the tomb was exposed. In my line of work, unmarked boxes could be very good or horribly nasty, and the level of protection around the tomb suggested the latter. Still, the clock was running on Aiden's looping cameras, and I didn't want to stand around shuffling my feet all night. I held my palms over the edge of the tomb and willed the sealant to disappear, then looked to Maria. She nodded, and with a little burst of force, I sent the stone lid floating. It rose a few feet, then landed gently on the ground beside the tomb, intact.

Steeling my nerve, I called up a new orb, let it hover above me, and peered inside the box.

"Well?" Ted asked from behind me.

"It's not biscuits," I mumbled, too struck to say more.

A boy lay in repose at the bottom of the tomb, a crude pillow propping his head. He couldn't have been more than a teenager, I estimated, comparing his face to Beth's, and for a corpse, he was remarkably rosy. He wore a hooded brown robe, loosely cinched at his waist with a rope belt, and his hands were folded over his chest, clasping a wooden Celtic cross. On his feet, he wore simple leather slippers.

Balancing myself on the edge of the tomb, I leaned down until my fingers could graze his neck. As I'd suspected from his coloration, the body was warm, and I thought I felt the faintest of pulses beneath his jaw. "Got a live one," I announced.

"*Shit*," Maria hissed as I pulled myself upright again. "You're sure it's not embalming?"

"Feel him for yourself. He's warmer than the ambient temperature, and no embalming is *that* good."

While Maria made her own brief examination, I considered the boy again. He looked as if he were peacefully sleeping—there was no sign of distress or struggle. Then again, Marcus had seemed to be at peace, too, and his last moments of consciousness had been terrifying. Still, from what I could see of the boy in the orb's light, there were no visible wounds, no scratches or bruises that would suggest he had been forced into the tomb. He appeared to be human, unremarkable but for the style of his clothing and a white forelock in his black hair—and the thick web of spellcraft shrouding his body.

I moved aside to give the others a chance to see our find. Bob was still studying the body by the time Marcus and Artur took a turn, his brow knitting ever more deeply. "Is something wrong?" Ted asked him.

"I would think so, *yes*," Marcus snapped.

"Aside from the obvious."

Bob's thick white hair seemed to glow like a moonlit cloud as he leaned closer to my orb. "Nothing about this burial makes sense," he said, switching places with Artur for a better look.

"How so?" asked Yolanda.

"Start at the top. This would seem to be a monastic burial, yeah?" he replied. "Judging by the clothing."

Yolanda nodded. "Sure…"

"Then why isn't this fellow tonsured?"

She joined him at the edge of the tomb and drummed her fingers on its lip. "He's pretty young for a monk. Maybe he hadn't fully joined yet."

"Perhaps," Bob allowed, "but the burial would suggest otherwise. And what sort of tomb is this, anyway? A monk wouldn't have been given one this size, but the lack of ornamentation would indicate that this kid was no one special."

"If one disregards the spells," Artur pointed out.

"Precisely," said Bob. "If I'm not mistaken, someone dressed this young man like a monk, buried him alive, and did everything possible to keep him that way. *Why?*"

"Does anything suggest a date?" she asked him.

He made a face. "Difficult to say. Medieval monastic garb is tricky, and I'm no expert in archaic fashion. Tenth to twelfth century sounds reasonable." He glanced back and forth between Artur and Marcus. "I'll defer to someone more experienced in this area, but I think we'd best bring him back to Glastonbury before attempting to wake him. Can't imagine that it would be pleasant to come to in one's own tomb."

"Not at all, I should think," said Artur, and levitated the body with a quick gesticulation. "Kitty, put the lid on."

"Not yet," Aiden interjected, staying me with a raised finger. He squinted down into the tomb, and a badly disintegrated skeleton appeared in the empty spot, left with only a few scraps of brown cloth to cover the naked bones. "I'd hate to disappoint the archaeologists," he explained, and helped me replace the lid and reseal it.

By the time we finished, Artur had a gate open back to our flat. "I'm taking him home with us," she announced, and floated the body through the gate.

The rest of the Team and Yolanda hurried after her, and Aiden shooed me on. "I'll reset the security and check on the guards," he said. "Send a gate to the O'Learys' in ten minutes, eh?"

It's difficult to be quiet in the middle of the night when seven people and a possible non-corpse are endeavoring to move around a dark flat. We'd left the lights off so as not to wake Beth, but the bumping and jostling proved that to have been a poor choice. As Artur lowered the boy to the couch, Beth emerged from her room in her pajama shorts and tank top, flipped on the overheads, and blinked groggily at our company. "What...?" she managed, stopping in the kitchen and squinting at the scene before her.

"Found him in Ireland tonight," Maria told her. "There's no telling what sort of state he'll be in once we get the spells off."

"Is he…"

"Probably not dead. Buried alive." She paused, then barely nodded toward the kitchen table, and an oversized mug of coffee materialized on a placemat. Beth took the offering without hesitation and shuffled into the den for a closer inspection.

"You understand that whatever happens in here *stays* in here, yeah?" Maria told her.

"I'm not an idiot, Magus," she muttered, and shivered as the warm drink went down.

Ted stood over the couch and considered the boy, whose hands had become unlocked with his movement. One still clutched the cross, but the other trailed on the rug, and his robe had twisted beneath him—overall, a less dignified repose than the one he'd enjoyed moments before. "What's the plan?" Ted asked the room. "Break the spells? Call the grand magus? Let *her* break the spells?"

While the senior members of the Team and Yolanda debated whether we should wait for authorization or even dawn, I opened a gate for Aiden, who popped through on schedule and closed the hole behind him. "Don't think our innkeepers are going to get back to sleep tonight," he told me, then noticed the cluster around the couch. "Is he awake yet?"

"There's some debate about the proper timing," I replied.

He snorted. "Hell, he's been in the box for centuries. Go ahead and wake…no, wait a second. Do we fix his linguistic problem before or after we revive him?" he asked, giving voice to one of the issues I'd been contemplating for the last minutes.

"I speak Gaelige," Bob offered, "but I wasn't expecting *this*. The modern language is one matter, but if he speaks something closer to Middle Irish, we might have trouble. Perhaps there's an archivist with a better grasp—"

"Or we could just call my brother." Aiden pulled out

his phone and cocked his head. "I think he learned it in the thirteenth century—that's got to be closer, right?"

The notion of asking a faerie king for assistance, much less casually inviting him over in the middle of the night, would have been ludicrous to most wizards. Then again, one of the Team's members was himself a high lord, and our supervising magus was the next best thing to a high lady—indeed, most of us had at least a few people in Faerie on our lists of contacts.

"Sure," said Ted, "if you think he's available. It's…what, early afternoon over there?"

Aiden shrugged. "Yeah, and I haven't seen him all day. Let's find out what he's up to." Leaning against the back of the couch, he placed the call and looked down at the body in the glow of the electric lights. "Hi," he said, segueing into Fae. "I just went grave robbing with Yolanda and the Away Team, and we may have a live one. Can you come to Glastonbury?" His mouth twitched as he listened to the reply. "One moment. Kitty," he asked, putting the phone against his shoulder, "what's your apartment number?"

No one bothered enquiring as to why Coileán didn't request a gate, nor did anyone in the flat seem taken aback when he and Toula knocked a few minutes later, both sporting grungy loungewear. That the king and the grand magus were lovers was hardly a matter of public knowledge—it would be a scandal of the first order if word spread—but one didn't make the Team if one didn't learn when to be discreet.

Aiden greeted them at the door. "Sorry to interrupt the sleepover," he said in Fae.

Coileán arched an eyebrow, then pointed to Ted. "You do realize that he's fluent, yes?" he asked in kind.

"Oh, it's not just me," Ted interrupted, and chuckled as Aiden's mouth snapped closed. "Found this kid in a medieval tomb," he explained to the newcomers as Aiden flushed. "How's your Irish?"

"Well practiced," Coileán replied, and hurried to the couch with Toula to take a look. "Moon and stars," he murmured as he examined the boy. "He *reeks* of magic…"

"You should see the spells," said Toula. "This is insane. Have you made any alterations?" she asked, turning to Daphne.

"None," she replied. "Maria and I modeled the spells on the tomb—"

"There were *more*? Damn, how many spells does one kid need on him? And what the hell does this one even do?" she muttered, bending closer to look at the channels.

"We hadn't got that far," said Daphne. "What would you say the odds are that we've unearthed the Antichrist and will bring about Armageddon if we unbind him? Fifty-fifty?"

"Sounds reasonable. Right, before we do anything, I'm modeling this spell for study. Get comfortable, kids."

"And turn off the lights," said Marcus, who loitered by the kitchen. When we swiveled his way, he nodded fervently. "Trust me. Electricity is terrifying."

"Beth, get the candelabra from the closet, will you?" I asked, and joined Marcus as Toula's casting commenced. *Again, I really am sorry about that,* I thought, taking his hand.

He smiled faintly, but I could see the turmoil in his mind—concern for the boy, stomach-roiling fear, and anger and shame at himself for his acute anxiety. *You weren't trying to kill me of fright.*

I slid closer to him, and he wrapped his arm around my back. *You're entitled to not be okay, Marcus.*

It's humiliating.

And what would Dr. Wanda say, huh?

His thoughts darkened. *Artur isn't affected like I am.*

Trauma hits people differently, and you have no reason to be embarrassed, I countered. *Besides, you were wonderful with Artur when we woke her.*

After she was awake. Seeing that boy like this…

I tightened my grip on his hand. *You're doing just fine, and*

I'm proud of you. Remember that it's over—no one's ever going to do that to you again.

I hope, he replied, the thought colored with doubt.

As Toula finished her work, Beth arranged candles on the end tables and the floor, including the glittery, pumpkin-scented black pillars she'd insisted on buying the previous Halloween. We cut the lights, lit the candles, and moved toward the door at Toula's direction, putting the back of the couch between us and the supine boy. "I'm going to break this carefully," she said, "and since I can only imagine that he'll be disoriented when he wakes, maybe it would be best if we didn't overwhelm him, eh?"

"Agreed," Artur muttered, standing well out of the way.

Breaking the spell was a much quicker job than mapping it had been. As soon as she finished, Toula darted out of view, and Coileán took a seat on the coffee table between Beth's history textbook and a votive that promised to smell like the beach and made it only as far as overwhelming coconut. There was no motion for perhaps a minute, and then, with a sound like an endurance diver gasping at the surface, the boy awoke.

My knowledge of Gaelige being limited to terms in the "sláinte" family, I couldn't understand what Coileán said to him as he tried to jump off the couch, but the shushing noises interspersed among his words needed no interpretation. He spoke softly—from what little I could see with the back of the couch in the way, he seemed to be holding the boy down—and at a moderate, fluid pace, though I could still hear the boy's rapid breathing. I looked to Bob, who was frowning in thought as he listened, but I didn't disturb him.

Finally, the boy spoke to Coileán—an ordinary teenager's voice, verging on a mature plunge but pitched higher with fright. The king's eyebrows rose ever so slightly as he listened, and the two conversed for a brief moment more before Coileán slid his arm under the boy's shoulders and helped him sit up. As the boy closed his eyes and rubbed his forehead, Coileán stood and joined our huddle. "He's not Irish," he murmured.

Bob nodded. "That was my impression, too, but if he speaks an older form—"

"Oh, he does, and fluently, but his accent is all wrong. I'd say he's English…from somewhere in the north, perhaps. Are we thinking as far back as pre-unification?"

"Probably not," Bob replied, "but he could easily be pre-Conquest."

"Yeah, I didn't pick up on any trace of a Continental accent," said Coileán, "though I could be mistaken. Anyway, his name is English enough. Called himself Eadwig."

"Eddie?" Beth asked, surprised.

"*Eadwig*," he repeated. "Older version. There was a tenth-century king by that name, but I'm fairly sure *that's* not him."

Beside me, Artur grunted but otherwise held her tongue.

The boy finally looked over the back of the couch and stiffened when he saw our small crowd. My little sister smiled and waved, which didn't go far toward comforting him. He spoke again, and after answering him, Coileán told us, "He's asking where he is. What shall I say, Wessex?"

"Just a moment, let me try something," said Bob, and Coileán swept an arm in invitation as Bob stepped out of the pack. He spoke briefly to Eadwig, whose face registered comprehension, then surprise. "Old English," he quietly told us. "My accent's not great, but he understood me. He wants to know what he's doing in Wessex." Turning to Artur, he asked, "Want to give it a try? Rule out anything older?"

"As you like," she replied, and took her turn addressing the boy. His head tilted, and a little wrinkle formed between his brows. When he answered, it was aimed at

Bob. "Not one of my people," she reported.

"Yeah, he was asking for a translation," Bob added.

She muttered under her breath, and while I didn't catch most of it, *Saxons* featured prominently.

"Well, at least that narrows it," said Coileán, and resumed his conversation with Eadwig as he returned to the couch. The boy's eyes widened in apprehension, but Coileán took hold of his temples before he could scramble away. I barely saw the flash of magic, the ever-so-useful enchantment that would put a new language in his head, before the deed was done and Coileán released him. "Give it a moment," Coileán told him in English. "The strangeness passes. Do you understand me?"

He pressed himself into the pillows as if trying to escape. "Who *are* you?" he asked, his accent thick but not impenetrable. "What did you do to me? Please, where am I? Where is my family?" he begged, his voice cracking.

A flicker of uncertainty crossed the king's face. "Well, uh…that's sort of a complicated question…"

"Excuse me," Marcus interrupted, marching across the room, and Coileán stepped aside. "Hello," he said, settling onto the vacated place on the coffee table. "Eadwig, is it?"

The boy's dark head bobbed.

"Where is your home?"

"Near Jórvík."

Marcus looked over the couch for help, and Bob offered, "York."

"*Ah.* What is your king's name, do you know?"

His answer was prompt. "Æthelred. All of my life—"

"Bob?" Marcus asked again.

He raised a finger for patience as he consulted his phone. "Reigned from 978 to 1016, with a brief break at the end. That considerably narrows the time estimate on the site…"

"And considering that range, where did we find Eadwig?"

That answer was slightly longer in coming. "Let's say

Connacht."

Marcus turned his attention back to the boy. "What brought you from Jórvík to Connacht? Religion, I assume."

But Eadwig's face twisted in befuddlement. "Connacht?"

"Yes, we found you in a…"

He caught himself, and I could see the word *ruined* at the top of his thoughts. "A church," I offered. "Perhaps a monastery. We didn't know."

Eadwig cut his eyes to me. "Where is Connacht? I do not understand, I—"

"What's the last thing you remember?" Marcus murmured.

"Going to sleep," he replied immediately. "My older brother and both sisters have been sick, no one has slept well with their coughing, and we retired early, as soon as the animals were fed. I lay down beside my younger brothers, and…"

"And?" Marcus prompted when Eadwig's voice faded.

"And that's the last thing I know. What is this Connacht?"

I felt Marcus's touch at my mind and admitted him. *Do I tell him now?*

Your call.

Anxiety made his thought seem jagged. *I've not done this before—*

You handled Artur well!

But Myrddin did the hard part.

What did Maria tell you, then? I was out of the room when you came to.

Nothing pleasant. He retreated from me and faced Eadwig, whose confusion was only deepening with Marcus's hesitation. "If you go west from Jórvík until you reach the sea, there's an island on the other side."

"Yes…"

"And on the far western side of the island lies

Connacht. We found you entombed there."

The boy's eyes flew open wide. "Am I *dead*?"

"No, *no*," Marcus hastened to reassure him before he could fall off the couch. "You are very much alive. But, um…"

Again, I stepped into his faltering silence. "It seems you were buried alive," I told Eadwig as I headed for them. "When we found you, you were so deeply asleep that you seemed almost dead. Tell me," I said, regarding him over the back of the couch, "do you know anything about magic?"

His eyes were blue, I noticed, and prominent in his paling face. "Magic?" he whispered.

"You're not in trouble," I soothed. "You've seen it before, haven't you?"

Slowly, he nodded. "I…I can do a little. My priest can do more," he said, picking up speed. "Much more. He's been teaching me, helping me. I've hurt no one—"

"Whoa, there," I said before he could start babbling. "That's good, that…that's a start."

"By chance, have you heard of Ordo Lucis?" Marcus asked.

Eadwig frowned, and I told Marcus, "They never left Italy. There were other groups here at that time." I glanced back at our audience, but since no one seemed overly eager to break the bad news, I steeled myself and dove in. "This is going to be difficult for you, and I'm sorry," I said to the boy. "I'm not quite sure how best to tell you this, but, uh…*something* drastic happened. We don't know what or how or why. For now, what you need to understand is that you went to bed in Jórvík around the turn of the eleventh century, and we pulled you out of a tomb tonight in Connacht in the twenty-first century. You were asleep for around a thousand years, give or take a few decades."

He stared at me dumbly, mouth agape.

"Someone went to a lot of trouble to keep you asleep and alive," I continued while he was too stunned to ask questions. "The spells on you were unlike anything we've ever seen, and believe me when I say that collectively, this group has *seen* things," I added, pointing to the cluster by the door. "And there was a second layer of spells on the tomb itself. I don't know too much about the place where the tomb was kept—I assume they put you underground, since there's nothing left of the church on the surface— but someone took pains to hide and preserve you. This priest of yours, what sort of wizard was he?"

Eadwig didn't answer me. His eyes filled, his jaw began to tremble, and though I could tell that he was trying with all his might not to cry in front of a room full of strangers, he was losing that battle. Realizing that the bandage-ripping for which I'd aimed had come out more like a mallet to the head, I perched on the couch beside him and held his hand. "I'm really sorry, buddy. We'll get to the bottom of this, we just don't have all the answers yet—"

"My..." he started, then faltered, and made a second attempt. "My...family? Did you find them, too?"

From his look of desperate hope, I think he knew, even before he asked, what the answer would be. My heart broke for him as I shook my head, and I pulled him into a hug as he succumbed to his shock and grief.

As the boy sobbed, Marcus squeezed Eadwig's shoulder until he managed to look up. "It happened to me as well," Marcus said in a near whisper, then pointed over the back of the couch at Artur, who loitered on the edge of the pack. "And to her. You are not alone." His voice took on a gentler tone. "Your family are...farmers?"

Are, I noted, not *were*.

Eadwig mumbled in the affirmative.

"And your brothers and sisters—how many of you?"

He hiccupped. "Six. Osweald, me, Ecgwynn, Æthelberht, Eadgifu, and..."—he sniffed and swiped at his nose with his robe sleeve—"and Eadgar. This isn't right," he insisted. "My father isn't even a thegn. Why would someone take *me* to this Connacht?"

Before we could begin to speculate, Toula interrupted. "I need to check something on you," she told Eadwig. "This doesn't hurt at all."

He watched suspiciously as a ball of white mist materialized in front of his face, then shrank back into the pillows as it flared a brilliant green. Even Toula seemed surprised at the brightness of his aural signature. "*Damn*," she murmured, and made a splitting gesture with two fingers. The orb flattened into a lattice and separated into two smaller spheres, each a dark blue. With a low whistle, she tapped her quartz ring until they vanished.

Eadwig stared up at her, alarmed. "What...what was—"

"A spell to see what you are," she explained. "A green aural lattice means magically gifted, and *you*, my friend, are at the top of the heap. I took a look at your parents' lattices, but neither of them had any talent. What about your siblings? Anyone like you?"

"No, I alone have the gift."

She made a face. "Well, this may be for naught, then, but I'm going to run your signature against the ones I have saved and see if I can't find any distant family of yours. You don't have any children, right?"

"None."

"Unlikely to be a match, but I'll check. And while I'm dealing with that, you need to go elsewhere." Turning to Coileán, she asked, "Houseguest? Just until Bee has a chance to work with him?"

The corner of his mouth twitched. "You want me to babysit a wizard?"

"I want you to look after a child who has no immunity to modern pathogens until the doctor clears him," she retorted. "Pretty please? Don't make me come up with a clean room."

Eadwig looked to Marcus for an explanation. "This will sound insane," Marcus told him, "but there are tiny, invisible creatures in the air that cause sickness, too small to see. I swear to you, this is the truth—"

"And in the water, and the soil, and the food, and the list goes on," Toula added. "Go with Coileán until you're strong enough to return here. Up you go, now. Scoot."

Marcus pulled Eadwig to his feet and half-carried him toward the gate that Coileán had opened, a passage into one of the stone-walled corridors of his palace. At the edge, Aiden took the burden from him and helped Eadwig out of the realm. "Stay here for now," Coileán suggested to Marcus. "He's overwhelmed. I'll get him to that therapist of yours as soon as she's available, assuming he doesn't crash on me. Whatever bind was on him took a toll—he's probably going to be weak for days." Marcus started to protest, but Coileán cut him off. "Get some sleep, kid. All of you," he said, looking around the flat. "And Toula?"

She kissed him and nudged him on his way, then turned to the rest of us with a coy smile. "You didn't see that. Goodnight. Yolanda, let me take you home."

When they departed, Bob sank onto the vacated couch and watched as Ted and Daphne claimed seats around him. "Something's bothering me," he said.

"Just one thing?" asked Daphne. "Because I can think of a few—"

"How does he speak Irish?" Artur interjected.

Bob nodded. "Precisely. How does a teenager from eleventh-century Yorkshire become fluent in a language like that? What isn't he telling us?"

"I sensed no deceit," said Marcus, leaning against the wall as if his legs were poised to give way. "Confusion, dread, fear, but he spoke the truth."

"You'd know better than I would," he conceded. "But what I *do* know is that someone ensorcelled that child for a reason. Why?"

I headed for the kitchen. "Beats the heck out of me. But while we're contemplating the mysteries of the universe, who wants caffeine?"

CHAPTER 6

Unless one is invited or practically family, it's a terrible idea to open a gate directly into the home of one of the Three. The guards are twitchy about stunts like that, and their bosses are high on my list of people not to annoy. I could get away with it at Val's—hell, I still had a bedroom at his place, and he insisted that I could crash there whenever I needed a moment's privacy from our crowded flat—but since Coileán had custody of Eadwig, Marcus and I decided to err on the side of protocol, waiting until the sun was up again in Faerie and landing outside of the palace's main door.

As we'd anticipated, there was no trouble from that point. Most of Coileán's guards had suffered training at Val's hands—some of them for centuries—and since Marcus strongly took after their former captain, the welcome we received at the door was far warmer than mere politeness. One of the guards escorted us to the small dining room where Coileán was reading petitions and absently downing scrambled eggs. "*Ah*," he said when the guard drew his attention. "I was beginning to wonder when you'd be by. Come in, sit down. Coffee?"

A carafe and a pair of cups appeared on the table across from him, and as both of us were then functioning on little more than chemical stimulants, we accepted the invitation. "Apologies for intruding so early," Marcus began, but the king stopped him with a wave.

"I haven't even slept. Have we sufficiently recovered from our spot of tomb robbery, then?"

"Just your average Friday night," I replied, pouring. "And, uh…sorry about the *interruption*. I haven't spoken with the grand magus yet, but…"

He smirked and pushed his stack of papers aside. "She and I have survived worse. So, the kid." Leaning back in his chair, he fixed us with a weary gaze. "I knocked him out for an hour after he got here, just until Wanda's schedule opened. Nice lady," he added, glancing at Marcus. "Your father thinks highly of her. He actually made the call—wanted to be sure we could get Eadwig in."

He nodded. "Have you told—"

"Eleanor? I didn't have to—Ros spread the word. She's intrigued, naturally, but she's keeping her distance for now, as is Val. Anyway, I delivered him to Wanda, and I just picked him up about two hours ago. He was sound asleep, last I heard, and I've been told that's the best thing for him."

"Or you could get him drunk," Marcus offered.

"Wanda discouraged that, for some reason," he said dryly. "Can't imagine why." He picked up his coffee and sipped. "You should go out to the settlement and have a word with her."

"Would she talk with us?" I asked. "With therapist–patient confidentiality—"

"This may be a special case. Here." He waved, and a gate opened beside the table onto the green park at the heart of the Fringe settlement, its playground packed with children shouting in the morning sunlight. Our coffee cups shifted into plastic tumblers, and a third one appeared on the edge of the table. "Wanda had a long night. Can't hurt to bring her a pick-me-up, yeah?"

We took our leave, and Marcus led the way through the little town toward Wanda's office, a path that we'd both had ample occasion to walk. A few of the locals nodded or raised a hand in greeting as we passed, and though we reciprocated, we maintained our distance. While the Team was chummy with the Fringe, those Fringers who were active in the mortal realm were few and daring. The majority of their members never left Faerie, where they enjoyed a quiet existence within the low walls of their former refugee camp, a product of the Mulligan era. Few faeries were ever given access to the town, and those permitted to visit were viewed with unease by some residents. Then again, magically speaking, the Fringe were at the bottom of the barrel, outclassed even by young faeries and almost defenseless against attacks. Marcus and I might have been known quantities, but still, no one ventured too close.

Wanda Fitzgibbon had been a practicing psychologist since the 1980s, one of the surviving Fringers who had counseled the hundreds of evacuees through their early days after the Unravelling. Barely fae herself, she was a birdlike woman, short, gray-haired, and physically frozen somewhere in her sixties by the quirk of the realm that prevented aging. Though the morning was young, we found her in her office, a homey space with comfortable couches in vibrant primary colors and an assortment of potted plants in full bloom, and she admitted us with a tired smile. "Kind of early for cookies," she said as she closed the door and accepted Coileán's coffee. "Can I interest anyone in banana bread? It's still warm."

If one was smart, one never said no to Wanda's goodies.

"So," I began between bites, "we heard you met Eadwig."

She nodded, chewing slowly.

"What do we need to know?"

Wanda hesitated—confidentiality was expected in our sessions, after all—but after a moment's thought, she said, "Given the…well, I was going to say *unique* circumstances, but this makes three, now."

Marcus spread his hands and shrugged.

"I'm not complaining, dear," she told him. "But this being an unusual case, I suppose I could share a few findings." Sliding her breakfast to one side of her leather blotter, she folded her hands on her desk and watched us eat. "The first thing I did was take him to see Candice—Dr. Agnew," she clarified. "Her specialty's in pediatrics, and she gave him a full exam. He's healthy enough—some gingivitis, and he'll need an appointment with a dentist before long, but she said he didn't seem diseased. Physically normal, good shape, nothing worse than a little acne. She puts him at about fifteen or sixteen. I mean, he's short by the current metrics, but given his approximate date of birth, Candice wasn't surprised."

"How about mentally?" I asked.

Wanda let out a long breath. "As expected. Anxiety and depression, but my feeling is that those are acute symptoms. Nothing about our conversation made me suspect anything concerning—he doesn't seem psychotic or delusional. I didn't do any formal testing, mind you, but my overall impression is that he's an average teenager, probably of above-average intelligence, going through a crisis. He told you he's a wizard?"

"Yeah, and his aura proves it," I replied. "Something about a village priest?"

"That's what I gathered." She opened a notebook and scanned a dogeared page. "Okay, here's what I gleaned of his background. Third eldest of nine children, six surviving at his last memory. Born and raised in northern England in a farming family. He started having magical 'leaks' when he was about four—minor levitations and such—and his parents took him to the local priest, who said he'd work with him. Turns out the priest was also a wizard, recognized the talent in Eadwig, and gave him some rudimentary lessons. You'll have to ask him for specifics—I know about as much spellcraft as that Christmas cactus does," she added, pointing to the pink-blooming plant by the window. "But he said the priest had discussed getting him into the clergy as well to further his education and protect him. He hadn't made up his mind."

"Any idea on how he came to be in Ireland?" Marcus asked.

"No, none. He's as baffled as anyone…and distraught over the loss of his family and community, though I shouldn't have to explain that to you," she said gently. "But here's what's puzzling me about him."

"He speaks Irish," he replied.

She cocked a pair of finger guns in his direction. "Bingo."

"We were wondering the same thing," I offered. "Did he explain?"

"No, and when I asked him how he'd learned it, he was flummoxed—he didn't realize he was speaking it." She tapped her computer on, pulled up a few sites, and brought it over to show us. "I'm certainly not fluent in Middle Irish, but I found some written samples and asked him to read them. He gave me translations. Same with Old English. He could read the Latin alphabet and the runic alphabet. Speaking of Latin, he could read it easily in an insular script," she said, opening the appropriate page. "Again, I'm no expert, but what he was giving me matched the translations available."

I frowned as I considered the reproduced manuscript page. "That doesn't make sense. He's a farm boy from the turn of the millennium. How the hell is he so educated? Not only literate, but literate in three languages—"

"At least. I tested him on Old Norse, Old French, Old Norman, Middle High German, and Old Spanish, and he had some familiarity with all of them. Perhaps more, but I was running out of ideas. He has no idea how he knows what he knows," she said, putting the computer aside. "Last he remembers, his priest was teaching him basic Latin. When he got through entire pages, he was shocked. I quizzed him on some historical details, tried to get a sense of whether he was being honest with me, and from what I can tell, he's not lying, or he *thinks* he's not lying. But you're right—that sort of education is inconceivable for a boy of his era, age, and socioeconomic status."

"Anything beyond linguistics?" Marcus asked her.

Wanda shrugged. "I didn't give him a full battery by any means. He's in no state to do academic testing. But my gut tells me that he knows more than he thinks he does." She rose just long enough to retrieve her coffee from her desk and returned to her usual spot on the couch facing us—by habit, Marcus and I had taken seats on the couch she generally reserved for patients. "I attempted hypnosis to see if I could pull something from his memory that would explain how he got to Ireland. He was willing to try, and he went under fairly easily, but it's like a blank in there. He remembers going to bed, then waking up in your apartment." She paused, then said, "I asked him to envision a door behind which were his memories of going to Ireland. He did that for me, but the door wouldn't open."

Marcus rubbed his chin. "Magic, do you think? We recently came across a man whose memory was taken from him with a spell."

"I don't know, but I didn't see any evidence of an active bind, so I'm leaning toward trauma. Dissociative amnesia," she clarified. "I'd like to have him checked for brain damage, but it's possible that he experienced an event so traumatic that he's blocked it out. That's not a sure diagnosis, but it's the best I can do after last night. He was here until the wee hours." Wanda stifled a yawn against the back of her hand. "He's staying with Lord Coileán for now, right?"

"That's the plan," I replied.

"Mm." She stood and tugged at her shirt, which had already begun to wrinkle. "Well, if I were you, I'd encourage the king to send him back this way. One marathon session of therapy isn't going to cut it."

Beside me, Marcus mumbled his agreement.

"Speaking of which, are we still on for Wednesday?" she asked him. Marcus nodded, and Wanda smiled.

"Good. Looking forward to it, and I promise"—she yawned again—"I'll be awake by then. Lord Coileán said he was putting Eadwig to bed?"

"That's what we were told."

"Might just do likewise. I thank you for the coffee, but you two won't think me rude if I cut this short and crash, will you?"

We saw ourselves home to Glastonbury and passed the rest of our largely unproductive Saturday in front of the television, dozing and waiting for word from Faerie that Eadwig was in any condition for company. As the afternoon light shifted, Marcus joined me in the kitchen to begin dinner preparations. There was no rush—Artur had taken Beth into the courtyard to spar with their wooden swords, as after Beth's interrupted night's sleep, she would have scrubbed toilets with a toothbrush if it meant avoiding a painful practice session ahead of the Games signups on Monday.

"Perhaps we should introduce John Dellucci and Eadwig," said Marcus as he chopped a salad. "Amnesia must be frustrating. John might know of a technique that Wanda didn't try."

We were out of my usual poultry seasoning, and so I raided the spice rack for curry mixes. "Could be worth a shot. After Eadwig's medically cleared, of course—given John's age, I don't want to take a chance of exposing him to anything Eadwig might still be carrying."

"I thought Wanda said he wasn't ill."

"He could still be carrying something, just be unaffected. Let's keep him in quarantine in Faerie for a bit and make sure before we start bringing him around the aged or immunocompromised. I'd hate to do anything to hurt Quinn's grandpa…"

I was interrupted by a knock at the door, and I put the seasoning bottles aside to investigate while Marcus made quick work of an onion. After the events of the night before, I wasn't entirely shocked to find the grand magus waiting in the hall. "Kitty, hi," she said, though she didn't smile. "Glad I caught you. Are you home alone?"

"Just Marcus and me," I replied. "What's wrong?"

"Could you two come to my office, please? Now?"

I slipped back inside long enough to put the meat in the fridge, and then we followed Toula toward the executive wing of magi's offices and meeting rooms. It wasn't a quick walk—the castle had grown large and unwieldy over its centuries of construction—but since nervous energy seemed to radiate from Toula like heat from a broiler, I didn't suggest taking a shortcut.

Maria was already waiting for us in Toula's office, though her grim expression suggested she knew the purpose of our meeting. Toula locked and bolted the door, and then, feeding my growing unease, she cast a complex spell. The walls of the room flared in the magical spectrum as her protective wards engaged. Espionage within the upper echelons of the Arcanum had been a problem almost since the founding, if one trusted the magi's diaries in the Archives, but unlike many of her predecessors, Toula was talented enough to protect her privacy.

"We've got a problem," she said, sinking into a chair.

"I'd, uh…gathered that," I replied, trading uncertain glances with my partner. "If this is about last night, you know the Team's not going to say anything concerning your private life, and Yolanda's not suicidal—"

"Not *that*," she interrupted, motioning us toward the couch. "If I were going to call a secret meeting about my boyfriend, it sure as hell wouldn't be *here*." She leaned back in her chair and considered the plastered ceiling for a moment, then said, "I ran Eadwig's lattice against my database."

"He's not fae—" Marcus began.

"No. Not in the slightest, and I split it several generations back just to be certain. One hundred percent human, but a *massive* talent. He's a new-blooded freak of nature."

That time, I met Maria's eyes, though my search for reassurance was in vain. "Okay, so he's gifted," I said. "What if you have him tested and put into remedial tutoring? Quinn seems to be enjoying herself."

"See, that's the thing. I don't think he needs it."

Marcus's brow furrowed. "You saw him last night—he was as confused as the rest of us."

"I know, but…"

As Toula huffed in frustration, Maria picked up the thread, keeping her voice low. "We've been working on the models from the tomb and from Eadwig's personal bind all day," she told us. "It looks like Daphne will have to wait to do her own analysis. This is…"

"Big?" I ventured.

"Bad." She plopped the pair of holding spheres on the coffee table, and Toula opened them with a muttered word. The models contained within appeared above the table in miniature, slowly rotating. "We've made headway on these constructions, but not nearly enough to explain their full function. For now, though, look at the stacks and the amplifying elements—this is genius-level construction. What we're seeing shouldn't exist. These spells should have collapsed ages ago, *especially* once you factor in the '13 closure, but they're so well scaffolded…beautiful, really," she mused. "The wizard who designed them…"

"Are we any closer to an identity?" Marcus interjected.

"Getting warmer," his aunt muttered, playing with her ring. "As I was saying, I compared Eadwig's aura to my collection."

"Partial match?" I asked.

"*Full* match. Several of them." She made four taps on her ring and whispered a spell, and a projection appeared atop the models. Waving the models back into their spheres, she enlarged the new projection and focused on the components at its base.

A family tree, I realized, and an extensive one at that.

"Take a look at these names and tell me what they have in common," Toula instructed.

I slid to the edge of the cushion and peered at the circles, squares, and tiny text legends. "Saito Rei, Benedict McDougal, Veena Amavasya, Hans Haas, Arnold Lowe, Bianca Powell"—I hesitated as an uncomfortable surety wriggled in my stomach—"Hannah Parsons, and I think I know where this is going. They're all descended from the Magus," I explained to Marcus. "He had about a dozen children, and some of their descendants are still within the Arcanum." Turning back to Toula, I asked, "Eadwig's a cousin?"

She chuckled, but there was no mirth in the sound. "Here's the overlapping bit in all of these lattices," she said, gesticulating a green sphere into being, then flattening it. "And here's Eadwig's."

I saw the match even as she was sliding them atop each other. "But...I don't..."

"Eadwig," she said, waving the projections off, "is either Simon Magus or his brother. Or perhaps his first cousin," she allowed, "if he's a double-first cousin. We have no records on the Magus's ancestry, so your guess is as good as mine."

Flabbergasted, I stared at the place where the lattices had hung, but I finally managed, "That can't be..."

"Makes no sense, does it?" Toula propped her feet on the table and linked her hands behind her head. "Every record we have shows that Simon Magus lived into his eighties and had children and grandchildren. Eadwig's barely more than a kid himself. He hasn't mentioned a brother named Simon, has he?"

"No," said Marcus.

"Which brings up another matter that's always bothered me." She glanced around our little circle and arched an eyebrow. "Simon Magus was English, yeah? An old man by the time the Great War ended."

"So the records say," Maria replied.

"That war ended in 1062—officially," she amended. "So Simon probably grew up in pre-Norman England, right?"

I saw where she was heading. "If that's the case, then why did he have such a non-English name?"

"Exactly. In origin, it's Hebrew or Greek. What's our eleventh-century magus doing with a moniker like that?"

"Could have been a name he adopted later," I suggested. "Or maybe he was Norman—maybe he wasn't native to England. Then again, good luck finding records to prove—"

"I've got a source." Seeing our surprise, she smiled to herself. "The Arcanum doesn't have much on Simon before he started consolidating power, but the *Fringe* does. I had a fascinating talk with Badger and Seamus once about some information given to then by Grivam."

"The merrow king?" Marcus asked, perplexed. "What would he know of your Simon?"

"Plenty. Grivam's been around a while, and to hear those two tell it, he knew Simon *intimately*, if you catch my drift. Wait right there."

She rose and fetched her computer from her desk, and from the long bout of tapping that followed, I suspected she was accessing the Fringe's highly secure, multi-point-authenticated network. I almost had to question the Fringe's wisdom in giving Toula credentials—the last grand magus who'd had access to their files had been coerced into unlocking them and triggering the bloody Unravelling—but then again, Toula was no ordinary grand magus. Exceedingly talented, witch-blooded, and technically a high lady, she remained on good terms with what passed for the Fringe's brass, and she came and went in the settlement without question. Marcus's cousin, Seamus, had another such pass—sure, he was half fae, but he'd married a Fringe coordinator, helped save hundreds of lives during the Mulligan era, and stuck by Badger in the mortal realm while she held the Gray Lands at bay. Since moving to Faerie almost twenty-five years before, the two of them had made a niche for themselves as the settlement's tiny police force, seldom needed but available in a pinch.

"Right," said Toula, finding the file she sought. "So, per Grivam, he met Simon when Simon was a young man living in a coastal village, which rules out York but not greater Yorkshire. Still, I'm more inclined to think that village was probably in the southwest. They met during the merrow civil war, which, as far as the Arcanum knows, was mostly an Atlantic conflict. Grivam said he came ashore injured, so the odds of him making it through the Channel and into the North Sea aren't quite as good as of him simply hitting land somewhere in Devon or Cornwall," she explained. "But I digress. Simon was a young priest at the time, living alone but affiliated with one of the small arcana. Another arcanum tried to send a message by torching his village, Grivam saved his life, and Simon started his conquest. All that survived of his belongings was his diary." She read in silence for a moment, her eyes flicking over the screen. "Grivam also gave us our only contemporary description of Simon not from some fawning magus. An unparalleled talent and a self-taught polyglot, not a large man...and, fun fact, he got around. He married, but they both had dalliances. Simon actually carried on for a long time with a witch-blooded man. And you wonder why *that* bit got left out of your history classes, girls," she muttered. "But...yeah, here's what I was looking for. From Grivam's description, Simon exhibited poliosis. Dark hair with a white forelock, much like Badger."

"And Eadwig," Maria murmured.

She nodded. "It can be hereditary, so if Eadwig is his brother, both might have it. And there was one other thing," she added, grimacing. "Per Grivam, after the war, Simon was old and paranoid, and he decided to wage a one-man invasion of Faerie and kill Oberon and Titania in their sleep. Didn't work. Grivam warned them, they were waiting for Simon, and they tortured him for about five years. Titania castrated him before sending him back."

Marcus flinched.

"Exactly, bud," said Toula. "Grivam recalled that Simon gave up magic after that, changed his name, became a priest again, and died at a monastery in Ireland about two years later."

"Did he say *where* in Ireland?" I asked.

"No, and I wouldn't look to a merrow for accurate directions on land."

"Stop for a minute and think about this," Maria cut in. "Assume that Grivam told the truth, our records are accurate, and Simon Magus died in Ireland in 1072. Now there's Eadwig, who shares the Magus's aural lattice, lay in ensorcelled sleep for about a millennium, and has no memory of going to Ireland."

"And speaks several languages, per Wanda," I offered. "He doesn't remember learning them."

Toula nodded. "Bee got a report from a Fringe doc who says Eadwig is physically normal. So we've got old, castrated Simon and young, healthy Eadwig—what's the connection?"

We pondered the question in silence for a moment, but as the ticking of the wall clock grew distracting, I said, "Those spells on him and the tomb—they weren't just keeping him asleep, were they?"

"Doubtful," Maria replied. "We're still analyzing, but the sleep bind only appears to be a part of the matrix."

"Could there have been a memory wipe in there?"

She squinted at the ceiling. "It's possible, but I didn't recognize anything like that on the first pass. Still, it's worth consideration."

Toula concurred but drummed her fingers on the arm of her chair, unsettled. "Now, while Maria and I dissect the models, there's still the matter of what's to be done with the kid. You two spoke to Wanda?" she asked Marcus and me. "How's he holding up?"

"Distressed, naturally," Marcus told her. "Perhaps if we brought him here, put him around people...I've been where he is, and Artur—"

"Has a Saxon grudge to work out?" said Maria.

"Will get over it," I interjected. "Plus, there's Beth, and now Quinn. We could finish that upstairs room and put him in with her," I said to Marcus. "Let the newbies have the loft."

But the grand magus wasn't ready to release him to our custody. "Not just yet—Bee's working with the Fringe medics to get his vaccinations started, and she wants him to have his first shots before he returns to this realm. I mean, he'll be getting stuck for months to come, but there's no need to make Coileán keep him until he's fully immunized. Once we do take him in, though, I'd like to let Anna Popova have a crack at him. If he really doesn't know anything about magic, then she can tutor him and Quinn. If he does...well, then maybe he can explain how those spells on the tomb work and save me the study." She swung her feet off the table and sat up straighter. "Eventually, I want Grivam to meet him. Not until we start to get a handle on him, but sooner rather than later, I want to put them in the same room. Maybe Grivam knows something about Simon's brothers."

"Or maybe he'll recognize Eadwig," Maria murmured.

Toula grunted. "I hope not. Can you imagine what the Minor Arcanum would say if we actually had *Simon Magus* here? They'd be demanding a chance to go after him for genocide, and frankly, I wouldn't blame them." She rose with a soft sigh. "All right, kids, keep this quiet for now. I mean it," she insisted, staring at each of us in turn. "None of this leaves the room. Don't tell Ted yet, don't tell Beth, and *definitely* don't tell Eadwig when you see him. If he's hiding something from us, I don't want to tip our hand."

I stood to leave, but one last question popped into my

mind. "Have you talked to Ros? Eadwig's been over there for hours, so surely she has a read on him by now."

Her smile was grim. "Coileán beat me to it. She says he's human, a wizard, and scared, and that's all she's got."

That surprised me, as Ros was seldom known for her incuriosity. As the realm, she was aware of everything that went on within Faerie's borders—*privacy* was a relative concept there—and had access to a collective memory stretching eons into the past. Had she been asked, she could have recounted every moment of my time in that realm, down to the color of my socks and whether I'd flossed that morning. But even she couldn't see what wasn't there.

And if she was preoccupied with Frank's eggs, I mused, then perhaps she wasn't paying attention to Eadwig.

I was turning to go when Toula added, "There's one other thing. His amnesia isn't caused by a spell. Either he genuinely has no idea how he ended up in Ireland or something—some*one*—took those memories from him. Ros says there's nothing on him left to break, spell-wise. As far as she's concerned, he's a closed book."

We took the long way home, mulling over all the things Toula hadn't said.

If, by some miracle, Eadwig was Simon Magus, then the Arcanum wouldn't know what to do with itself in the wake of that revelation. In our standard texts on magical history, he was practically deified, the genius wizard who'd forged order from chaos with might, talent, and a fifty-year war spanning three continents. The Magus had built a shadow empire stretching from the Atlantic edge of Europe to the islands of Japan, from the taiga of Siberia to the beaches of South Africa. If he were indeed alive, then surely the Arcanum would be his by right—and surely he would lead it into a new golden age.

There would be casualties, of course. Growth seldom

comes without a little pain. And Toula, who'd become grand magus because there wasn't a wizard alive either bold or foolish enough to fight her in single combat, would have to go. Once that was accomplished, though, what sort of golden age could be ushered in by a boy who couldn't even remember how he'd ended up entombed alive? Maybe "Simon Magus" would lead the Arcanum, but it would be ordinary magi calling the shots—and I didn't think I was wrong to assume that the sort of magi who would happily oust Toula for a puppet grand magus would be the same sort who would have fallen in line behind James Mulligan.

And then there was the matter of the Minor Arcanum. In Arcanum-taught history classes, the Great War ended in 1062 after forty-eight years of magical skirmishes and lopsided negotiations. The Fringe version, informed by the Minor Arcanum—and, I suspected, Grivam—continued until July 3, 1064, when Simon, having discovered both the technique of sleepwalking and the magical population of the New World and Oceania, slaughtered the majority of them in their sleep. He had been the only known wizard able to cast in the dream space until Badger, his many-times great-granddaughter, accidentally discovered the knack. Considering how many lives he'd snuffed out in a matter of hours, if Simon were alive, then the Minor Arcanum—some of them the distant grandchildren of the wizards he'd murdered—would want to settle *that* nasty score.

But would the Arcanum turn over Simon Magus to face punishment? The idea was absurd…and since that was precisely what the Minor Arcanum would want, the two organizations would have at least a war of words. Sure, the Arcanum was stronger than its cousin, but that wasn't the point. In the last half-century, the magical community had forged diplomatic ties like never before— hell, Toula and the Three had received wedding invitations from the *Gray Lands*. No one with a grain of sense wanted to disturb that peace.

That didn't mean that I couldn't imagine a few who might do it anyway. Retake the Arcanum, destroy the rebellious Minor Arcanum, stamp out what remained of the Fringe in the mortal realm, either hire or destroy the Dark Company...the possibilities were bloody but tempting to the right sort of mind.

I was still troubled when we reached our flat, then surprised to smell baking chicken. "Where have you been?" asked Artur, who leaned against the kitchen counter with a bottle of beer. "I took the liberty of putting the meat in the oven," she added, gesturing toward the appliance, which remained low on her list of kitchen tools to master. "Pray to whatever gods you claim that it's not blackened."

I checked the meat, then dialed the temperature back from the smoking point. "Thanks. Where's Beth?"

"Washing off the sweat and ignominy of defeat." She took a swig and put the beer aside. "What are you two hiding?"

My sister had known of her fae heritage roughly as long as I had, but although I had a full Arcanum education to employ in making my enchantment as efficient as possible, she had fifteen centuries on me and a corresponding natural strength that I couldn't touch. My mental blocking was secure, but that evening, I didn't feel like testing it against Artur's rough touch. While it wasn't a good idea to flout orders from the grand magus, I decided that I could beg for forgiveness later.

"Beth can't know about this," I told Artur, walking closer to keep my voice low. "Or Quinn. Or the Team."

To her credit, she merely raised a white-blonde eyebrow. "Understood."

Quickly, Marcus and I shared Toula's findings. She listened in silence until we concluded, then took up her beer again and downed half of it. "It sounds as if this flat has become the official home for the wayward and temporally displaced," she said.

"Just until Toula figures out what's to be done with him," I replied.

"Mm. You're certain of that?"

"Come on, Artur, he's only a boy," Marcus protested. "*He's* not one of those who attacked your precious Afallon."

"He is of that blood," she muttered.

I stole her beer and helped myself to a swig. "Not necessarily. Could have Danish roots if he's from Yorkshire."

"Shall we test?"

"Yeah, good luck finding anyone on this island of pure Saxon lineage," I countered. "Remember that little invasion in 1066?"

She snorted and snatched her beer back. "Very well. If you insist, I'll try to tolerate him. Now, how would you like to break the news to Beth and Quinn that we're gaining an amnesiac flatmate?"

I shrugged and headed for the panty to inspect our rice options. "We'll deal with Quinn when she returns from Switzerland. As for Beth, why don't you tell her he's your new squire or something?"

"Great idea. And once I've done that, would you like me to use your head as target practice?"

Artur's threat was in jest, I hoped, but I put together a shield between us anyway as I dug through the boxes and plastic jars. "Love you, too, sis."

CHAPTER 7

The rest of the weekend passed in peace. Quinn sent me a message on Sunday with beautiful pictures of Arc 3's summertime vistas, which was unsurprising. Nearly every first-time visitor to that installation found herself on a balcony at some point, snapping photos of the Alps, particularly in the dead of winter. The installation wasn't known as "the chalet" for nothing, and in terms of scenic beauty, it was rivaled only by the Amazonian treehouse complex of Arc 6. Quinn seemed upbeat, writing that her lessons were going well, even though she was sore in places she hadn't known could be bruised. Magus Popova was an excellent tutor, but like all good combat instructors, she could be ruthless.

The news from Faerie was minimal and came from Aiden, of all people. "I'm sure you're concerned," he told Marcus in a call on Monday night, "and since your dad hasn't been snooping and I'm betting that you're disinclined to drop in, I thought I'd put your mind at ease. Eadwig's still a mess, but he's come out of his room to eat and go back to Wanda."

"He's adjusting?" Marcus asked, holding his phone between the two of us so that I could listen in.

"Eh, as well as can be expected. I got to explain flush toilets to him, and that's about the upper limit of the technology I want to expose him to at the moment. But Coileán showed him the library this morning, and I haven't seen the kid since, so he must still be playing in there. I hear he's coming your way once he's medically cleared."

"That's our understanding, yes. Has his memory returned at all?"

"Nope," said Aiden. "Nothing. He's trying to recall, but it's a blank. Maybe once he's less overwhelmed by the wonders of modern plumbing—"

"And copious use of magic?"

"Yeah, that, too," he replied, sounding almost sheepish. "Sorry, *this* Arcanum kid sometimes forgets that not everyone in the universe grew up in a silo full of wizards."

Burdened both with Ros's concerns for Ione's clutch and Toula's concerns about Eadwig, I decided to stay out of the dragon barn for a few days and let my roiling thoughts calm. The last thing I wanted was for Frank to start poking around, and as it was nearly impossible for me to hide my emotional state from him, I chose not to give him a reason. While the rest of the Team made visits, I stayed in my office, practicing my poker face and trying to catch up with the work I'd neglected over the last days. Overall, the week was slated to be quiet, with the biggest excitement being Monday's official signups for the Games. Beth had acquiesced to my nagging and agreed to throw her name in for the academic bowl, but she'd set her heart on winning her year in single combat, and I tried to be encouraging. My little sister was no prodigy, but she was a solidly talented wizard, made quicker on her feet through long hours with Artur in the courtyard, and she stood a better chance than I ever would have at her age.

Tuesday and Wednesday were blessedly calm, to the point that I finally finished the reports I'd intended to submit back in May. Aiden's daily updates were promising—Dr. Powell had been spotted in the palace, wearing a homemade clean suit and hood over her springy red hair and carrying a bag of syringes—and I slept well as my stress subsided. Marcus even began to joke again about running away to Tennessee, where our chances of finding medieval wizards were considerably lower.

And then Thursday hit like a meteor.

I'd decided to spend the morning working from home for a change of scenery. Ted didn't mind, and I appreciated the quiet once the rest of my flatmates departed for the day. Having turned to the task of compiling the overdue June report for the Council, I took a break in the kitchen, letting the coffeemaker produce a reliably decent pot instead of trusting magic and my questionable imagination. As the brewing slowed to a drip, my phone rang. Sam, I saw, with a twinge of pity. Faerie was almost half a day behind us, and as it was already ten a.m. in Glastonbury, *some* dragon was up past his bedtime.

"Hey, Sam," I began, "tell Frank to let you sleep—"

"Get Pritam," he interrupted, his voice quiet but tense. "I'm sorry, I don't have his number—"

Ice ran down my spine. "What happened?"

"Tell you when you get here. Bring him, please."

I didn't bother alerting the rest of the Team. A few texts to Delhi and about twenty minutes later, Pritam and I arrived outside the dragon barn in the dead of night. The wordless psychic distress calls battering into us like storm-tossed waves against a pier could only have one source.

Sam ran out to fetch us, an orb lighting his way. "Thanks," he said, turning our twosome into a small huddle. "Sorry for the short notice."

"What's wrong?" I demanded, wishing I could block out Frank's anguish.

He rubbed his face. "One of the eggs stopped talking. Ros says it's dead."

"Shit," I whispered. "Is he…"

"Coping as well as you'd imagine, or can't you hear?" He tossed his head toward the barn, adding, "Want to come in, Doc?"

I created orbs to avoid tripping over stray bones and scat—Neve's dragonets were a mess in multiple senses—and Pritam and I followed Sam through the wide door to the nest. By the time we arrived, Frank had his snout deep in the circle he'd made with his body, nudging the lifeless egg and silently panicking. Ros stood beside him, bathed in her own radiance, and from the looks of it, on the cusp of tears. "I'm sorry," she told him, hugging herself. "I did what I could. I'm trying, but I can't fix everything."

Several minutes passed before he finally raised his head and stared down at her. *What happened?*

Ros looked away before she delivered the blow. "The whole clutch has problems. I've been attempting to repair them, but it's like using my fingers to plug a dike with dozens of holes."

All of them? he asked, his fear crescendoing in my mind. *What problems?*

"Physical issues." Acknowledging the rest of us with a curt nod, she said, "I asked for Pritam to be brought over in case you want to know…well…how bad."

Frank turned to Pritam, who held up his hands. "Only if you want that," he told Frank. "I'm so sorry. If you would like, I'll do what examination I can, but—"

Please. He stood and stared down again at the three eggs, then gently pushed one from the middle of the nest and rolled it beneath his body toward Pritam. *If there's something I'm doing wrong, if I can help the others…*

"I'll need that scroll again," Pritam told Sam, "and privacy."

As Ros floated the egg out of the barn and Sam jogged off to find the scroll, I watched as Frank settled down, tightening the protective circle around his remaining children. When he lay his head on the straw and noticed me standing there, all I could do was shove my hands into my pockets. "I don't know what to say," I murmured. "Nothing comes to mind that'll make this any better."

His reply was formless sorrow, and so I pulled up a bale, keeping vigil with him until Ros returned and Pritam's gristly work was underway.

I didn't go home for nearly a full day. After warning the

rest of the Team that visiting hours were off, I turned on Frank's projector and searched through his library of movies and programs, but nothing seemed appropriate. We settled on a nature documentary series and watched birds do courtship dances and lions chase after baby wildebeests for hours. I offered to lure a few sheep into the barn, but Frank insisted he had no appetite and watched without comment as I produced a barely passable sandwich from the ether to silence my own stomach. Ros offered to take over—she and I had independently decided that Frank wasn't to be left unattended until the results came in—but I didn't want to add to her load. Manifestation took focus and resources that could be better spent trying to save the other eggs.

Pritam completed his analysis more quickly that time, and he brought his findings to the barn a few hours after sundown—early morning, according to my confused internal clock. "Let me preface this with the disclaimer that I am no expert as to your species, and there is virtually nothing in the records concerning fetal development," he said to Frank, whose unease broadcast for yards in all directions. "But drawing on what I *do* know, I'm confident that what I found was incompatible with life. Gross abnormalities. The skull appeared misshapen, the front limbs were entirely absent, and several major organs were growing outside the body. I can give you details, but that's the broad picture." He tucked his notebook under his arm and looked up at Frank. "You did nothing wrong, and there's nothing you could have done. Even if he had hatched, I can't imagine that he would have lived more than a day or two, and—"

He?

Pritam paused, then nodded. "The gonads were sufficiently developed to identify as testes. But please hear me when I say that you did not harm your son. Having seen his mother, and considering what, ehm…"—he gestured toward Ros, who had appeared for the occasion—"the lady told me about the other eggs, this may very well be a genetic issue. Now, I can't verify that—no one's ever tried to analyze a dragon genome—but there *is* a pattern."

And the others? Can you fix them? he asked, looking back and forth between Pritam and Ros.

"I'm doing my best," she said. "It's…a *lot*. But I'm doing everything in my power to keep them alive."

"And without internal imaging of the eggs, I can't say what I could or could not do," Pritam added. "I've worked with very young hatchlings, but never one in ovo. If someone could create an artificial environment to replace the egg—"

"Hell, I spent most of my prenatal time in a spellcraft construction," Ros interjected. "The Arcanum knows how to make an artificial womb. It can't be that much more difficult to make an egg substitute. But…"

But it's untried.

"That, and I have a grasp on the eggs for now in their current situation. Adding a complex spell to the calculus…"

Pritam, if you had worked on…him…sooner, could you have saved him?

He grimaced. "Honestly? No. I could have tried, but I don't see that attempt ending in success."

Then they remain where they are, thought Frank. Nodding to Pritam, he added, *Thank you for what you've done. Twice, now.*

"It's my sincere wish that there isn't a third," Pritam replied, nodding in turn. "My condolences to you on the loss of your son."

Two days later, midmorning Sunday, Quinn returned to the flat with her bag, a fresh set of bruises, and a beaming smile. "The chalet was awesome!" she said, dropping her gear onto her bed—I'd taken the liberty of freshening the sheets in anticipation of her arrival. "*So* gorgeous. I don't know how anyone gets any work done there with a view like that. Maybe that's why the practice rooms are windowless, huh?"

"More a matter of safety," I replied, enchanting plaster over the fresh drywall in the unfinished space next to her suite. "Windows inevitably mean flying glass, and there's already enough to worry about when wizards go at it without adding *that* to the mix."

"Good point." Grunting, she sank into the mattress and slid off her well-worn tennis shoes. "Anyway, Magus Popova kicked my ass, but my casting is getting much faster. She's really encouraging while she puts you back together, you know? Like, 'My arm's not supposed to bend that way, but you thought that was a good shield, so we're still friends.'"

I grinned and finished the baseboards. "Didn't I tell you that Toula wouldn't give you to just anyone? If Popova's pleased, you should be proud of yourself. Is she giving you a recovery day?"

"Two recovery weeks, actually."

"Huh?" I turned and frowned as she watched me through one of her bedroom doors. "Why so long?"

"The Games. She said she's busy with that and can't afford to divide her time until it's over, so I called Jude, and he's letting me hang out in the Archives for the duration."

I snorted. "Fun."

"Should be," she replied, ignoring my sarcasm. "He's going to show me around the collection, maybe let me help with a restoration. They just dug a book out of storage, and from what Jude was saying, it's in need of some love." She paused and cocked her head. "By the way, what are you doing? Is someone else moving in up here?"

"This afternoon, actually." I watched the floor until the smooth wooden planks of Quinn's room extended to the far wall. "He needs a place to stay, and we offered to take him in. I hope you don't mind sharing space up here."

"Not at all. Hey, I'm the one crashing in your apartment." She pushed herself off the bed and leaned against the door frame to watch as I cobbled together a second bathroom. "So, who is this guy?"

"One moment." I tiled the floor and walls in a somewhat institutional blue and white, then added a glass shower cubicle and a sink. Surely, I mused, he'd have mastered indoor plumbing after a few days in Faerie. "Do you want the long version or the short one?"

"Let's start with the short one."

"Okay. English teenager who was trapped in suspended animation from the late tenth or early eleventh century until the night after you left for Arc 3." Glancing over my shoulder, I found her staring at me, wide-eyed with incredulity, and chuckled. "Would you like the extended version now?"

Ten minutes later, once I'd finished the bathroom and recounted what I knew of Eadwig but for the puzzle in his aural lattice, Quinn whistled and shook her head. "Just wondering, but how many people have you guys buried alive, anyway? Like, is this a wizard thing I should know about?"

"No, it's definitely rare," I assured her. "So far, just Marcus and Eadwig. Artur was kept in the Gray Lands."

"That's, uh…less reassuring than I'd hoped, but oh well. Don't forget curtains," she added as I put a rug beside the new bed.

"On my list." I hung a set and resumed my decoration.

"And he's English, you said?"

"Born near York, he claims." I looked over and found Quinn grinning. "What?"

"That book I was telling you about, the one Jude is going to let me work with?" she said, her tempo picking up as she went on. "It's a magus's notebook, eighth century, written mostly in Old English. If Eadwig needs a distraction, maybe he could work on the translation for me while I tackle the preservation end of it."

"Not a bad idea," I replied, "but there's one problem: we can't let Eadwig out of the flat yet."

Her brow furrowed. "I thought you said he's getting his shots."

"Yeah, but he's going to need time to acclimate. I doubt he'll be ready for an audience for a while."

She took in the new room and smoothed the navy duvet while I hung a mirror and created a pair of simple lamps. "What if I brought the book back here?"

"Good luck getting it out of the Archives—"

"Not *physically*. Jude wants me to work on the translation, see, and he offered to have the pages scanned so I could do some of it from here. I get the scans, give them to Eadwig, problem solved."

I tested the lamps, which responded with a soft white glow. "That...*could* work. Let me make a quick call."

Quinn stood by bemusedly as I pulled out my phone and selected a number. "Lord Aiden? Hi, it's Kitty Connolly," I said in answer to his greeting. "This may be a dumb question, but at any point in the last week, has Eadwig seen a computer?"

To my surprise, Coileán delivered Eadwig to us straight from Faerie rather than dropping him off at Toula's office. That it was possible to make inter-realm gates into the installation was known; that the Three occasionally deigned to do so was a better-kept secret so as not to incite a panicked mob at the grand magus's doorstep. While Marcus took the boy up to his new room, the king pulled me aside and lowered his voice. "The kid's been pumped full of God-knows-what for a week. Bee says to expect...hang on." He pulled a scrap of paper from his pocket and scanned the list. "Aches, lethargy, low-grade fever, and possibly an upset stomach, especially while he adjusts to the local environment. Call her if you notice anything more severe, else, hit him with"—he squinted at a word and slowly sounded it out—"*paracetamol* and fluids."

"Tylenol," I offered.

"*Ah*." His last residence in the mortal realm having been the States, and having never been sick himself, Coileán could be forgiven for his unfamiliarity with the term. "You have Bee's number?"

"The whole Team has Dr. Powell's contact info handy. It's almost obligatory for fieldwork." I accepted her notes from him, then asked, "Is he...*okay*?"

"Define 'okay,'" Coileán muttered. "Is he seeing visions and listening to the voice in his head telling him to burn the house down? No. But he's depressed, quiet, assumedly mourning."

"Sounds about right."

"And I should caution you that he's been having nightmares. *Screaming* nightmares."

Making a mental note to warn Quinn when she returned from the Archives, I asked, "Does he say anything coherent in his sleep?"

"No, he just screams himself awake. I would have asked Ros for insight, but she's preoccupied right now. You can imagine why, I trust."

"Unfortunately. But the eggs are due to hatch in about two weeks," I told him. "If he's still having these nightmares by then, maybe we could bring him back over and let her snoop."

"Could do." He glanced around us, but we were alone—Artur had gone for a walk, and Beth was being abused in a practice room. "Toula said that you and Marcus know her suspicions."

I nodded.

"You haven't shared them?"

"Only with Artur," I admitted. "Beth knows nothing, and neither does our houseguest. A late-discovered wizard," I explained, omitting certain details of Quinn's background. "She's getting basic training this summer, and she knows only what she needs to know about Eadwig."

His eyes, already ancient, seemed suddenly older. "Good. Keep it that way."

The king took his leave, but I had no doubt as to where his thoughts lay. The last Arcanum coup had ended with the then–grand magus imprisoned for years, not to mention hundreds killed and hundreds more joining her in captivity. With Toula and Coileán being on far better than collegial terms, his concern for her safety was understandable—and if Coileán was concerned, I could only imagine how Val felt about the potential threat to his baby sister.

Climbing the stairs to the loft, I overheard Marcus giving Eadwig a guided tour of his new room: "Do *not* put anything into those holes. They connect to the castle's electrical system. These particular outlets were created with magic, so they are probably unstable—"

"Quinn's seem to be working, thank you very much," I interrupted, then tapped my knuckles against the open door as a late announcement of my presence. "The whole installation's power grid is an amalgamated nightmare, and it's best not to ask questions of the three wizards who keep it running—you won't understand seventy-five percent of what they say. But yeah, please don't stick anything in the electrical sockets that's not a plug."

Eadwig, still wearing the monastic robe in which we'd found him, glanced distrustfully at the nearest. "What are they?" he asked, his accent thick and strange to my ear.

"It's complicated," said Marcus, "but imagine there's lightning in the walls, and it makes the lamps burn." He demonstrated by flipping on one of the pair I'd made for the dresser. "See? And it cooks the food, powers the computers...oh, the television, you'll like that—"

"Hold it," I said, pressing a hand to his chest before he could drag Eadwig back downstairs. "Eadwig, how's the room? Did Marcus go over the shower? I don't want you scalding yourself."

While my sheepish boyfriend stepped aside, I showed our newcomer around the bathroom fixtures—all in copper, far easier for me to make than trying to wrangle steel into existence—and demonstrated the taps. He paid attention but seemed listless, and I gave him a closer inspection: blue eyes half open, cheeks flushed, shoulders slumped. "You feel like crap, don't you, hon?" I murmured. "Hold still, now."

He endured my ministrations as I pressed the back of my hand to his forehead. "I am trying to be strong," he mumbled. "Wanda says I should occupy my mind. But..."

"But you need a nap. You're running a fever." With a moment's concentration, I called a thermometer into existence and stuck it under his tongue. "Keep your mouth closed and leave that there. Are you hurting?"

Eadwig hesitated, then offered a little nod.

"I've got something to help with that. Be still for a moment more..."

His fever was too high for my liking, and so I ordered him to bed, then sent Marcus to raid my medicine cabinet. Maybe no self-respecting faerie would have kept bottles of painkillers and antacids around, but old habits die hard, and I held on to my blister packs and vials like a squirrel who knows his prize is a rock but can't bear to let it go. Having convinced Eadwig to swallow a pair of pills, I turned back his duvet, then gave him a careful once-over and created a simple pair of gray pajamas for him. "We'll deal with your wardrobe later," I said, drawing the curtains and the blackout set behind them. "Get some rest. You'll feel better this evening." Doing the quick mental math, I realized part of the problem. "Coileán brought you back in the middle of the night, didn't he? No wonder you're exhausted. Here, go change," I ordered, and shooed him into the bathroom.

When he emerged—his pants, at least, were on the correct way, though I helped him turn his shirt around—I bundled him into bed, added another blanket against chills, and dimmed the lights to a dull glow. "We'll be downstairs," I assured him. "Comfortable?"

I could just see his head bobbing, a dark shape against the white pillow. In that moment, he seemed all of about ten, a lost little boy in a borrowed bed.

"Don't worry," I said, "It's going to get easier. Let Marcus and Artur help you." As he burrowed deeper beneath the duvet, I added, "You're going to be stuck in this flat until Dr. Powell clears you. We'll show you the entertainment options once you're fully conscious, but for now, try to sleep." With that, and hearing no protest from the bed, I left him to his medicated nap.

When Eadwig awoke and crept downstairs, Quinn and Artur had returned and were sitting at the kitchen table, talking shop, while Marcus and I finished dinner preparations. Spotting our new addition skulking in the stairwell, Quinn went to her feet and waved, her curls bouncing. "Hi! You're up! How're we feeling, huh?"

"Better," he admitted, slinking toward the table.

"Good. Pull up a chair—you thirsty? How's your stomach?"

He winced as he flopped into a seat. "Unsettled."

"Stay there, I've got a trick. Do we have any ginger ale?" she asked, heading for the fridge.

I produced a cold bottle, which Quinn brought to the wary patient. He took a test sip, flinched at the carbonation, then considered the beverage for a few seconds before going back for more.

"My dad's cure-all," she explained, sliding back into her chair. "And hi, there, I'm Quinn."

"Artur," my sister added with forced politeness.

I poked my head out of the kitchen. "Quinn's new here, too. And Quinn, did you want to—"

"*Yes.*" Her enthusiasm seemed suspiciously high for the circumstances, but I reminded myself that archivists were a rare, strange breed, the sort of people who had firm opinions about vellum. "I understand that you can read," she said to Eadwig.

Putting the bottle aside, he surprised himself with a belch. "Yes. I…I do not remember learning all the words, but I can read many things…" Scowling, he propped an elbow on the table and rubbed his temple. "I am *trying* to remember, but nothing returns to me."

"It's okay," she said, reaching over to pat his shoulder. "There's no rush. My grandpa lost his memory, too, and I'm sure that has to be so frustrating."

His reply was a vigorous nod.

"And all of *this* can't be helping," she continued, twirling a finger to encompass the flat. "New place, new people…new century…"

"New language. Languages," he muttered. "The king gave me Fae as well."

Though Quinn had taken the lead on the consolation front, Artur wasn't entirely a stone. "They will make sense in time. After a fortnight, your mind will stop insisting that the words you hear are nonsense."

"She's right," Marcus called from the stove, where he was finishing the risotto, the product of several magical shortcuts. "You'll adapt."

"But in the meantime," said Quinn, leaning a few conspiratorial inches closer to Eadwig, "I've got this new project, and if you don't have any plans, I could use some help."

He watched warily as she rose and returned with a computer. Aiden assured me that Eadwig had seen the things, but *using* them was another matter, and the kid was eyeing the machine like it might spontaneously combust. Seeing his unease, Quinn smiled and angled her chair beside his as she tapped the computer on. "So, there's this book. I'm working on saving the actual object—it's had a rough few centuries, as you can see from these pictures," she added, scrolling through—"but we're going to stop the decay. The thing is, this book was forgotten for ages, and no one's ever made a translation. Part of it is in Latin, but, say, this page…"

Eadwig's eyebrows rose. "I see."

"*Yeah.* I had exactly one hour-long seminar in runology, which is just enough to let me state with confidence that I don't have the first clue as to what this says. Very helpful, let me tell you."

He chuckled, then peered at the screen more closely. "This…yes, I can read this. Do you want to know what it says?"

"Sure. Not right now," she clarified—the smell of roast chicken permeated the flat—"but if you wouldn't be opposed to writing down a translation, that would be a *major* help. Maybe after dinner, I could show you how to turn the pages on here?"

To my relief, his smile seemed genuine. "You have ink?"

Quinn cut her eyes to Artur. "Best guess, how badly am I going to blow his mind when I show him a ballpoint pen?"

"A what?" Eadwig began, but before Quinn could begin to explain, Beth shoved the door open, groaning like a starving zombie and shuffling almost as badly. She was a sight to behold that evening: crimson face, limp ponytail, darkening bruises on her bare legs, and a pale green T-shirt with dark patches of sweat spreading under her bra and arms and down her back.

"Oh, God, please tell me the food's ready," she muttered, kicking the door closed with her heel.

"Soon," said Artur. "Once you're clean."

"Come on," she whined, "I didn't even eat lunch! I've been in that stupid practice room all day, and I *hurt*, and I'm *hungry*, and I'm *thirsty*—"

"And you're kind of disgusting right now," Quinn chimed in.

Beth fixed her with a weary glower. "I didn't ask you."

"Can't fight facts," she replied, unrepentant. "In all seriousness, you stink. Do us a favor and hit the shower, okay?"

My little sister's grumbling was too low for me to make out in its entirety, but I could have sworn that I heard a few choice bits of profanity before it stopped short. Peeking out from the kitchen, I found the cause: Beth had noticed Eadwig at the table, and the two were silently staring at each other, he with wariness, she with surprise.

"Uh…hi," she told him, lifting a filthy hand. "When did you get here?"

Eadwig looked to Quinn and Artur for an answer, but he never had a chance. "Less talking, more bathing," Artur ordered, jutting her finger toward Beth's room. "*March.* I won't wait all night."

"But—"

I cut her off. "Please, Beth? Five minutes, tops."

With one of her patented dramatic sighs, Beth limped off to hose down. "We've got the Games in a week and a half," she said, looking back over her shoulder at Eadwig. "My friends and I have been fighting each other all freaking day. Have I mentioned that I'm starving?"

Artur rolled her eyes at Beth's theatrics. "Stop complaining or I'll eat your share."

Her door slammed, and I said to Eadwig, "That would be Beth. She's about your age…"

No one in the room spoke aloud, but Artur and Marcus's identical thoughts came at me within milliseconds of each other. Eadwig wasn't paying attention to me—he was staring at Beth's closed door, a look of comingled uncertainty and interest playing on his face.

They're teenagers, I replied. *It's harmless.*

Artur quietly snorted and glanced my way. *Perhaps it's for the best that Quinn sleeps between his room and the staircase, don't you agree?*

CHAPTER 8

"**H**ypothetically," said Marcus, spooning behind me three nights later, "how would you feel about Simon Magus taking an interest in your sister?"

"We don't know that he's Simon Magus," I mumbled into my pillow.

"But we can be confident that he's interested, whoever he is."

"He's just lonely." Hearing Marcus chuckle, I rolled over and strained to see him in the darkness. "*What?*"

"You are indeed clever, my sweetest, but you were never a sixteen-year-old boy with his eye on a pretty girl."

Though I didn't want to admit it, even to my boyfriend in the security of the bed that had become less *mine* and more *ours*, I shared his suspicions.

With a good dinner and a long sleep behind him, Eadwig had seemed almost a new man on Monday morning. Over breakfast, Quinn had given him a crash course in electronic books, and I'd produced several hundred sheets of paper and a pack of pens for his use. We'd soon arranged a workspace for him at the kitchen table, and Marcus had read from home that day so as to babysit our charge and fit him with a wardrobe more extensive than pajamas. By the time I'd rolled in that evening, dinner had been well underway, and Eadwig, finally looking the part of a shaggy-haired teenager instead of a monastic novice, had been showing Quinn his work to much applause.

He'd beamed when Beth had arrived, once again wet

and filthy from her exertions but also nursing a splinted arm. While Marcus had attended to her injury, she'd explained to Eadwig how it had come about, and he'd peppered her with questions: What sort of fighting did they do? How did one fight with magic? What was Marcus doing to her arm? They *allowed* women to fight?

The last enquiry had resulted in Eadwig being flung from his chair and pinned to the wall with a burst of enchantment while Artur had crossed her legs, sipped her beer, and ignored his cries for help, and he'd soon learned which sentiments it was safest not to express in her presence.

That night, once she was clean and on the mend, Beth had introduced Eadwig to the television, before which she might have remained planted for the rest of the evening had I not reminded her that her homework wouldn't complete itself. She'd compromised by lugging her books into the den and working from the couch, keeping one eye on the TV and the other on her studies, and pausing for frequent breaks to answer Eadwig's many questions. Behind closed doors, I'd laughed with Marcus at the familiarity of it all, and he'd half-jokingly apologized for treating me like his personal encyclopedia as we fell into bed.

I'd panicked Tuesday morning when I'd emerged and found no trace of Beth, but Quinn— who, bless her, had already started the coffee—had a lead. "I heard him sneak downstairs just before dawn," she'd reported. "Something about a roof?"

Hurrying up the tower steps and through the trapdoor, I'd discovered our missing duo sitting on a blanket on the tower's flat top, watching the sunrise. I'd cleared my throat to draw their attention, then reminded them that Eadwig wasn't supposed to leave the flat. "He's directly *above* the flat," Beth had protested. "A little fresh air's not going to kill him."

But that hadn't been the hill upon which either of them

wished to die, and with the best of the sunrise behind us, they'd followed me home, where Artur had been waiting with coffee and a quirked brow.

Once Beth was off to school, we'd said nothing further about the brief escape, and I'd switched out with Marcus to supervise Eadwig that day. The boy had worked diligently, making little sound but for the scratch of his pen and the occasional sigh, though he'd seemed grateful for a lunch break. "We're really not trying to hold you captive," I'd explained as I made us sandwiches. "And I know that Quinn appreciates your help, but if there's something you'd rather be doing—"

"Such as?" He'd propped his arms on the cutout kitchen window and watched with interest as I wrangled the cold cuts and cheese. "I have no home or family left, I do not remember what happened to me, and I am not meant to return to Wanda until…" His face had screwed up as he'd sought the word.

"Friday," I'd reminded him. "You'll see Dr. Powell in the afternoon and Wanda that night. Faerie's days don't always line up with ours, so we do what we can to make it convenient for everyone."

"More needles," he'd grumped. "And what is that?"

Having been slicing a tomato, I'd reminded myself that Eadwig had never seen one, much less a sandwich, and explained the ingredients as I assembled lunch. As we'd eaten, he'd hesitantly asked, "Might I watch Beth at her practice? If I finish the work Quinn needs—"

"I'd let you go if I could," I'd replied, "but Dr. Powell has to approve. Besides, those practices are dangerous. You saw Beth's arm, yeah? Spells go awry, and the walls are padded for a reason."

But if Eadwig couldn't leave the flat, Beth had seen no reason why the world couldn't come to him. Though she'd suffered a well-earned lecture from Artur later that night, Beth had blown off Games practice to go into town on an impromptu shopping spree. She'd returned with a tote bag full of odds and ends: a few sodas she preferred, sixteen varieties of candy, chips, magazines, a thick guidebook to the UK and Ireland, a nice notebook with a brown leather cover, and oddly, a letter opener shaped like a dagger, just because she fancied it. She and Eadwig had made themselves sick with sweets and played with the camera on her phone, and when I'd heard laughter from the den at midnight, I'd come out to find them flopped on the couch, giddy with the hour and cackling as Beth did her worst fake narration of an otherwise respectable nature documentary showing lions in the throes of passion.

She'd hurt Wednesday morning—no amount of caffeine could mask that—and while Eadwig had slept off the late night, Artur and I had taken her aside and given her a brief, frank lecture about the facts of life. "He *can't* leave the flat," I'd told her as she'd folded her arms and blearily glared. "I know you want to help him, but remember that he's a thousand years behind, and we'd all prefer that he not die of a cold."

When she'd begun to protest, Artur had cut her off with a curt, "Defy us at your peril, girl."

That had shut her up—I was a fair target for Beth's pushback, but as far as my little sister was concerned, Artur was a force to be obeyed, never mind that *I* was Beth's guardian and she and Artur weren't actually blood. While it was frustrating to be challenged, I wasn't above pulling out my big gun on occasion, and Beth was usually wise enough to listen.

By Wednesday night, when Marcus gave voice to my concerns, I was almost confident that he was correct, even if I didn't want to admit it. For the rest of the week, Eadwig worked hard during the day to translate for Quinn, but as soon as Beth came home, the two were inseparable. I didn't want to play the role of fun police—I was the bad cop often enough for reminding Beth to do her homework and not leave dishes in the sink—but I kept one ear on their conversations when they were in the den, and Quinn did the same when they moved upstairs. Their budding friendship was harmless, I told myself. He was alone in the world, she must have seemed exotic and exciting, and if he was eager to listen to her explain casting and the nuances of combat, then at least he wasn't dwelling on the people he'd lost. Maybe distraction wasn't the best way of managing grief, but in the short term, it worked.

And given the hours the two of them spent together, Beth was certainly distracting. Over the weekend, Eadwig watched her go with the eyes of a puppy left at home during an ice cream run every time she headed for another punishing session in the practice rooms. I felt bad for the guy—Quinn was spending most of her time with Jude in the Archives, Artur kept her own schedule, and Marcus and I were only so much entertainment—but there was nothing for it but to sit him down in front of the television and try to keep up with his stream of questions as he attempted to make sense of a world glimpsed in soundbites and snippets, a brilliantly colored broadcast devoid of context. When Beth came home, she took over, either talking with Eadwig as the TV played in the background or demonstrating wand basics. On Sunday night, though she'd acquired a stunning black eye and a sprained ankle that afternoon, I caught Beth up late again with Eadwig, teaching him the rules of checkers over a pair of purloined beers.

Despite her long nights and a rough few days of practice, Beth was almost cheery when she staggered out of bed Monday morning. "Games week!" she announced, helping herself to Quinn's formidable coffee. "I'm going to veg on the couch until noon, and then—"

"No, you're coming to academic practice this morning." Maria, who'd stopped by for an early bite ahead of the chaos of the Games, peeked through the cut-out kitchen window and grinned as Beth's face fell. "The worst pain you'll receive will be a headache. This is the *fun* practice session."

"Yes, Magus," she mumbled into her mug.

"Don't sound so enthusiastic about it," she teased. "Your sister was the academic champ of our year four times. You want to make a good showing, yeah?"

"Nerd," Beth muttered.

I yanked on her snarled hair as I passed, heading for the cereal, and she swatted me away, grumbling about her elders' lack of respect.

Watching from the safety of the table, Eadwig asked, "What is academic?"

"Academic bowl, the only event at the Games in which I don't have to be ready to shield at a moment's notice," Maria replied, pulling out the chair beside him. "There are four events: academic, technical casting, rapid casting, and single combat. The casting contests will begin Wednesday morning—two days from now," she added for his benefit—"but Beth's a sixth-year, and her group won't take the floor until afternoon, maybe evening for technical. Academic is all day Thursday while technical finishes, and single combat is the only event on Friday."

"I've been sweating my butt off for single combat," Beth added. "Academic is so I don't twiddle my thumbs for two days."

Eadwig's brow puckered. "Why not try the other events?"

"Because I'd rather not blow my chance at single with some freak catastrophic injury on Wednesday. Of course, I could get a major papercut during academic…"

"And you could also spontaneously combust, but I'm not concerned about the odds," Maria retorted. "Get dressed and down to practice. Mr. Hogarth is giving up his time for this, so you can do him the courtesy of being punctual." Seeing Beth's dour look, Maria gestured a chocolate croissant into existence as a peace offering, and Beth snatched it up and retreated to her room to make herself presentable.

I spent the morning in my office, cramming as much as

I could into our abbreviated week. By tradition, the Team took off work for the Games, and we weren't the only group within Arc 2 to do so. Some groups could get away with it by claiming it was a talent-scouting opportunity, particularly when the oldest students competed, but in truth, most of us enjoyed the competition itself. Ted had never pretended that the Games was anything more than a holiday for us, and if pressed, he used Allie, and more recently Beth, to justify our cheering section.

Shortly after two, Beth knocked and let herself in, and I put my computer aside as she plopped onto my office couch. "Hey, there. How was practice?" I asked. "Marcus is upstairs with Eadwig if you want to interrupt them."

"Maybe in a minute." She swung her legs onto the couch, resting her ankles on the armrest to keep her shoes from dirtying the fabric, and tucked an arm behind her head.

I waited, giving Beth a chance to take the lead, but when she refused to make the first move, it was my responsibility as the designated adult to pry. "Did something happen? Are you nervous about this week?"

"Nah."

I ran through her morning schedule, looking for potential traps, but nothing leapt out at me. "Did you have lunch with your year? I don't know what it is, but academic bowl practice always left me *starving*. Brain needs fat, right?"

She didn't return my smile. "Yeah, we got lunch."

"Town outing?"

"Dining hall."

That was it, I decided, remembering how the sight of the dining hall packed at all hours with students from the other six installations had worsened my pre-Games jitters. "Who's arrived? Arc 3? Arc 5?"

Beth sighed and stared at the ceiling. "The group from Arc 3 came in this morning, and they've got the practice rooms booked until dinner. Arc 5 takes over tonight, so they're mostly hanging out in the courtyard. Arc 4 got in around noon. They're sightseeing to deal with the jetlag."

I checked them off on my mental list: making the trip from Switzerland or Egypt wasn't too painful, though Mongolia was seven hours ahead. "What about the other three? No sign of Arc 7 yet?"

She snorted. "Oh, they're here. You haven't left the subbasement all morning, have you?"

"What've I missed?"

"Some of the younger ones have buddied up with the Arc 3 group and are messing around in the practice rooms, and some others tagged along with Arc 4's field trip, but the eighth-years and up have been day drinking in the courtyard since they got here."

Slightly scandalous, but not surprising. Arc 7, the lonely Outback installation, had a well-deserved reputation of sending the friendliest, most sociable, and hardest-partying delegation to the Games. "Are they sharing?"

"You know it. Half of Arc 5 is, like, horrified and staying away, but the rest of them are going to be too wasted to practice tonight if they keep going like they were at lunch." She paused to shift position, burrowing more deeply into the cushions. "Arc 6 is due in around dinner, or so I hear—one of the guys in my year has a Brazilian girlfriend, and he spent most of practice this morning messaging her. And Arc 1 got here around eleven."

I winced in sympathy. Montana to Glastonbury was never a fun trip, and if their chaperones had dragged them across by lunchtime, the students would have left home around four in the morning. "Guess they sleepwalked through lunch, huh?"

"Yeah, mostly. I saw a few hanging out with Arc 7."

"Now *that* is dedication to day drinking. I wouldn't worry about them as competitors—they'll be too jetlagged or hungover to cast a straight bolt."

"Yeah."

Beth fell silent, and I sensed that my initial conclusion

might have been misguided. "Did something happen at lunch?" I asked after a moment. "However good their casting is, you've worked yourself half to death. There's no reason to worry now—"

"My former classmates were at lunch. Breakfast. Whatever it was for them," she mumbled. She kept her eyes trained upward, pointedly not looking my way, and when I failed to press her for details, she gave them of her own accord. "Some of them were talking shit. I heard them when I walked by to return my dishes, and I started to stay something, but they were just watching me and snickering, so…"

"I'm sorry," I replied. "Thank you for not starting a brawl in the dining hall."

"Whatever."

She continued to scowl into space, and I took the risk. "Something about Mom?"

Beth nodded.

At that moment, and not for the first time since my sister moved in, I wished Wanda were closer than Faerie. Beth had seen a counselor during her two years in Glastonbury, but therapy had yet to resolve her complicated relationship with our mother. Raised an only child because Mom had done everything in her power to keep me out of Beth's life, my sister was never able to win Mom's approval, either as a wizard or as a daughter. Once Beth understood who and what our mother truly was, she'd turned her back on her, but some part of her still craved Mom's love. I understood—part of me, too, wished for a relationship with a loving mother—and so I did my best not to badmouth Mom too severely around Beth, even if my incubator *was* a murderous, unfaithful traitor. You can't choose your parents.

During Mom's pretrial incarceration, Beth, refusing to live with me and my blatantly fae boyfriend, had moved back to the silo with Daddy's cousins, where she'd endured a miserable eighth grade. Having once been popular among her classmates, she'd become an angry, withdrawn pariah, quick to lash out with words and fists when provoked. The next year had been easier, once we'd begun to reconcile and she'd moved into my flat, but Beth remained conflicted: part of her hated Mom, part of her longed to free Mom, and a third, irrational part of her blamed herself for Mom's downfall, as if Beth, by not being talented enough, had somehow forced Mom to join the Conclave and attack the Arcanum from the inside. Slowly, Beth's outlook had improved, but from the sound of it, the kids she'd left behind in Montana hadn't forgotten the sullen eighth grader with a treasonous magus for a mother.

"They don't know jack," I told Beth. "Bunch of petty little shits. Ignore them. You have friends here, right? Friends who know all about Mom and like you anyway." Finally, she looked at me, and I saw the sheen in her eyes. "Sweetie, don't let them get to you. Kick their asses on Friday. That'll shut them up." Lowering my voice to a conspiratorial register, I added, "If they keep bothering you, Mal wouldn't be above paying them a visit tonight. And if a giant wolf didn't work for some reason, I'm sure Artur could be convinced to smash some heads."

She swiped at her eyes and nose, and when she sat up, I joined her on the couch and hugged her. "You're going to do amazing things, I know it. They'll see."

Beth remained in my office until her face had lost its flush and her eyes were dry—returning to the flat on the cusp of tears would only have raised questions she didn't want to answer—and I subtly removed her mascara smears while she brushed her hair. "This stays between us," I assured her as she started to leave. "Have a good afternoon. Pizza tonight?"

My sister smiled, then surprised me with a last hug before she went on her way to Eadwig.

On Tuesday, to my shock, Artur offered to take a turn working from home so that Eadwig wouldn't be alone in the silent flat all day. After a week of tolerating his presence under our roof, she attempted to clear the air over breakfast. "It's nothing personal," she told him, spreading jam on her toast with unnecessary force. "I hate your people with an undying fire. Otherwise, you seem...unobjectionable."

"I thought you were born here," he replied, his face crinkled with bemusement.

"I was."

"My people are from Jórvík."

She sighed and released her grip on the table knife. "*Before* Jórvík, where did they come from?"

Eadwig shrugged helplessly. "My grandparents were from Jórvík, and their parents...I think."

"Before they came to this island. You're of the Saxons, are you not?"

"He's probably descended from the Angles, actually," Quinn offered, bringing her plate to the table. "You're thinking of the post-Roman Saxon push into England, yeah? Hey, pass the butter."

Artur slid her the dish, frowning. "What do you know of it?"

"A little. I actually did a term paper on the Germanic migration back in college. History of England—I needed a seminar," she explained. "Anyway, it wasn't just Saxons who moved west. They settled in the southeastern bits at first with the Jutes, but there was northerly migration from the Angles and Frisians. If he's from York"—she indicated Eadwig with the tip of the butter knife—"then he's probably not descended from the Saxons you're thinking of. A Germanic tribe, or maybe even Vikings, but a different group...and what, five hundred years later?"

"Roughly," Artur conceded.

Looking back and forth between them, Eadwig said, "I have no idea what you mean. If I've offended—"

"For crying out loud," Beth called from the kitchen, "*he* didn't attack your settlements! Could you stop looking at him like you're *this* close to turning him into a shish kebab?"

Artur took a bite of toast, mumbling something that might have been agreement.

Satisfied that Eadwig was in no immediate danger, Marcus and I left for the subbasement and the crucial meeting at which Ted would provide handouts as to the times we should be present to cheer on Allie and Beth and a strategy for maintaining our seating in the crowded bleachers. Having almost come to blows one year with a gang of Council aides who lacked respect for personal space, Ted took no chances. When the meeting had adjourned and we'd received our bleacher-squatting orders, I closed myself in my office to read, planning to slip off a few hours early and surprise Beth with her favorite Indian dinner. For a kid raised in rural Montana, she'd taken a fast liking to curry—and besides, I wanted to have something good on hand for her in case the Arc 1 kids gave her trouble again.

I was just weighing the hassle it would be to fight the overcrowded dining hall to grab lunch against the rumbling in my stomach when a gate blazed open on the other side of my desk. Yelping in surprise, I pushed my chair away and squinted at the lightning rim until I could make out Sam standing at the edge, holding a red fireball in the darkness. "Egg number two," was all he had to say before I was on my feet.

"Want me to call Pritam?"

"Can you do it from Faerie? I could use you here."

Once again, Pritam was willing to drop everything and come. I hung back as Frank slowly stood and nudged the silent egg from the nest until it rolled to a stop near the herpetologist. "I'll give you a full report," Pritam promised, then followed Sam and the hovering egg out of the barn.

Frank settled down, his body coiled more tightly than ever, and I took a seat on a bale near his head. Though it was difficult to see much in the night-dark barn, Frank seemed thinner to me, and I suspected he hadn't left the nest since the first egg died. "Bacon?" I offered. "Sheep?"

I'm not hungry.

"I could attempt that gut-melting curry you like, but I make no promises."

He shook his head and lowered it to the straw with a sigh.

I could feel the fear and desperation radiating from his mind. The clutch had been due around the end of July, so the last egg had only another two weeks at most. He was doing everything he could to protect it, and since she hadn't so much as manifested, I knew Ros had to be working overtime to keep the remaining egg alive. All Frank could do was wait and hope that one of his children would live long enough to be born.

"Birds or whales?" I asked.

Whales.

I queued up the documentary, and soon, his body was bathed with the bluish light of the screen as humpbacks swam and sang. A mother lifted her calf toward the surface to a triumphant symphonic swell, and I cut my eyes toward his, purple in the screen's glow and barely blinking.

Marcus offered to come, but I asked him to look after Beth instead. For a second time, I passed the silent, waiting hours with Frank, watching wolves and fish and giant pythons until the sun was high in Faerie and climbing toward noon. Pritam's face was grim when he returned with the results. "Much like his brother. Abnormalities incompatible with life," he said. His white dress shirt bore stains of fluids I didn't want to name. "This is not your fault," he stressed, meeting Frank's stare. "There is nothing you could have done for your sons."

As I opened a gate to take Pritam home, I overheard Frank pleading with the last egg. He used pure thought, but the essence, condensed to words, was simple: *You're almost there. Hold on, I'm here. I won't let anything happen to you.*

The Games, at least, were a distraction after that miserable Tuesday. Antony's daughter, Allie, came in second place in her year in technical casting, and from the look on Antony's face, one might have thought she'd won the whole tournament. We adjourned to the subbasement that evening for celebratory ice cream—including Madison, Allie's mother, who was a much more talented wizard than Antony could ever hope to be—and while the elder Copelands beamed with pride, Mal helped Allie sneak extra maraschino cherries behind their backs. Beth had been invited to the impromptu party, but she'd begged off, though whether she felt bad leaving Eadwig alone with Quinn or had a sudden case of nerves about her own competition the next day, I couldn't be sure. When we came home that night, she and Eadwig were asleep on the couch—on opposite ends, to my relief—with the credits of a movie still running on the TV.

Beth didn't set out to win the academic bowl, but she finished in the respectable top third of the pack, for which she had Artur to thank. Lessons in swordplay remained contingent upon Beth pulling decent marks, and the bribe had worked wonders for Beth's standing in her year. She went to bed early that night, and when I wandered out of my room before dawn on Friday morning, I found her dressed, restless, and already on her second cup of coffee. Maria stopped by around seven, staring down the barrel of a long day of refereeing, and as she refreshed the coffeepot, Beth looked up from her oatmeal and said, "It's not fair that Ed can't watch. He's missing all the fun stuck in here."

Eadwig, sitting beside her with his own bowl, deployed his passable impression of a sad puppy as Maria continued to watch the pair of them. After a few seconds, I heard her in my mind: _Ed? Is he Ed now?_

News to me, I replied.

"_Please_, Magus?" Beth wheedled. "I've been telling him all about it, and he could sit with the Team, and he wouldn't get in the way—"

"Dr. Powell would have a fit," Maria interrupted. "A crowd from all seven installations, new and exotic germs…"

"What if he wore a mask?"

She folded her arms. "A mask."

"Yeah, we could pretend he has the flu or something. A little facemask." Beth sped up as she warmed to her subject. "And there's so many people there, so no one's going to ask too many questions about him."

By then, Beth's sad eyes were almost as bad as Eadwig's, and Maria and I shared a silent look of our own. "Fine," Maria said with a sigh, "but _just_ for the competition. He wears a mask, he stays with the Team at all times, and Dr. Powell is _not_ to know of this. Capisci?"

Beth grinned, and I patted Maria's shoulder. "I'll keep an eye on him," I promised. "You just worry about the first-years' aim, eh?"

To be fair, if I'd been on semi-quarantine for three weeks, I'd have been excited about a field trip, too, even if it was just to the competition room.

Eadwig sat sandwiched between Bob and me midway up the bleachers, well clear of all but the most errant of the stray spells and positioned for a decent view of the whole floor. Well, _sat_ is too generous a term; he wiggled and half-stood every so often, trying to get a better look at one bout or another, and chattered to anyone willing to answer his questions. Having not seen Eadwig since he awoke, Bob took the lead on that front, quietly explaining the basics of spellcraft and segueing into Old English whenever he could. I couldn't follow their conversation, but judging by the tone of Eadwig's voice, muffled as it was by the white facemask, he seemed to be having a grand time.

The first-years were fun to watch—most were still klutzes with their wands, their spells were either weak or overkill, and someone inevitably got worked up with nerves and puked on the sidelines. Though they had little finesse to their fighting, the odds of catastrophic injury were low, and so those of us who'd been first-years once ourselves could chuckle at the lopsided bouts and not feel too terrible. While Eadwig watched raptly, Bob pointed out interesting pairs and offered a rundown of the rules of combat.

Marcus joined us as the second-years started, and the rest of the Team squeezed onto the bleachers in ones and twos over the next hour. Antony and Madison came together—Allie was giving combat her annual try, and the fourth-years would begin before the lunch break. Eadwig's interest in the competition didn't flag as the morning passed, and he joined us in cheering Allie on...though not for long, as she was eliminated in her second round. "That's okay, sweetie," Antony called as she limped back to the competitor bleachers, "good try!" Madison tugged him back into his seat before he could humiliate their daughter, but Antony was unrepentant and fiercely proud, pointing out to anyone in the vicinity who'd listen that his little girl almost won her year in technical two days before.

The competition broke for lunch after the fifth-years ended, but as we couldn't risk taking Eadwig to the dining hall, we hustled him into the subbasement and brought sandwiches to the conference room. The three Copelands arrived together, and though Allie seemed glum about her performance, Eadwig was at her side as soon as she sat down, peppering her with questions about her opponents, her casting techniques, and even her wand. After a time, she offered to let him hold her wand and give it a flick, but I jumped in to nix *that* disaster in the making. Allie used a birch wand, and having seen Eadwig's aura, I feared for the structural integrity of the subbasement if he tried to cast with it—overloaded wands led to fireworks or worse.

Beth had been with her classmates all morning, and I only saw her that afternoon when *Stanhope* appeared on the competitor projection, across from the name of a girl from Arc 6. Artur sat beside me in silence, staring at the floor with her fingers steepled, and nodded her satisfaction when Beth ended the bout in under a minute. Her opponent was helped from the floor with a bad ankle and a ripped sleeve, and I elbowed my stoic sister. "Nice job, Coach."

She accepted the praise with a faint smile and relaxed in her seat until Beth's name appeared on the active roster again. That time, her opponent was a boy from Arc 5, but just as before, Beth mopped the floor with him. She wasn't a flashy fighter—some of the sixth-years seemed to be all about big spells they could barely control—but she was quick and decisive with her bolts, the product of two years of Artur's tutelage. Artur couldn't teach Beth how to improve her spellcraft, but she'd given her an equally valuable lesson: how to think on her feet. Beth knew her craft as well as anyone her age, and by her third win, it was evident that she was anticipating attacks.

As a proud big sister who knew her little sister had a reputation to maintain, I kept my seat but cheered with the rest of the Team every time she helped an opponent off the mats. Eadwig, however, had no such limitations, and he was on his feet from the time the field narrowed to sixteen. Beth won her quarterfinal, then her semifinal, and by then, reputations be damned, I was screaming her name along with the rest of Arc 2 when she joined Maria in the middle of the room for the final round. If Antony had been proud of Allie, I was ecstatic for Beth—she'd never made it that far, *I* hadn't even been wizard enough to compete, and she was one bout away from advancing to fight against the seventh-years. Even Artur watched with a grim smile.

Beth's opponent was listed only as *Norton*, but since the Arc 1 pack was chanting for Jessa, it wasn't hard to put the two together. She was of average size, a brunette with a French braid, a nasty bruise on her cheek, and fresh friction rips at the knees of her green leggings. Then again, Beth wasn't exactly looking put together at the end of her tough semifinal. The two met at the center of the ring and shook hands at Maria's instruction, and I saw Jessa's mouth move. The distance would have made hearing her difficult, even if the room hadn't been reverberating with the cheers of the crowd, but there was no mistaking the resulting tension in my sister's face as they took their places.

What was that? I asked Maria.

She didn't so much as scan the crowd for me. *Tell you later*, she thought, then gripped Jessa's shoulder and muttered something I couldn't make out. Jessa looked sullen but nodded, and when the two girls were ready, Maria raised her hand, stepped out of the ring, and gave the signal to begin the fight.

Jessa led with a well-aimed bolt, but Beth's shield was strong, compressed into the size of a large buckler to thicken it against strikes. She maintained the shield with her left hand and shot with her wand in her right, and after a few parries, she had Jessa on the defensive and stepping back toward the edge of the ring. One of Beth's bolts pierced Jessa's shield and hit her wrist, and the girl screamed and dropped her wand as her bones fractured. Seeing my sister's victory almost complete, I clapped and chanted in time with the Arc 2 kids, my heart full to bursting with joy for Beth's triumph.

Jessa took one step backward, then another, ever closer to the edge of the ring. She was barely a foot from the edge when a bolt slammed into Beth from the direction of the competitor bleachers, striking her in the side. Unprepared and unshielded, Beth flew out of the ring and into the padded wall…and to my horror, she hit headfirst.

"*Beth!*" I screamed, seeing eleven-year-old Maria superimposed over her for a split-second before the real Maria started shouting for the medics. Beth wasn't moving, and Maria was yelling at the bleachers from whence the bolt had come, and there was red-faced Jessa, picking her wand off the mat and starting toward Beth…

I only noticed that Eadwig had escaped when I spotted him at the balcony railing. As Jessa took aim—*a bolt for good measure*, reasoned the tiny part of my mind that wasn't frantically praying for my sister to be okay—she was flung off her feet with a shriek and thrown into a wall on the right side of the room. She didn't lead with her head, and the din of the crowd was too loud to hear anything snap, but she crumpled to the mats and rolled on the floor, her useless right hand flopping toward her freshly broken left arm.

The room was too distracted to notice Eadwig clutching the railing and bellowing with rage.

Go to Beth. I'll handle him, came Marcus's voice, cutting through the chaos of my thoughts. In seconds, I found myself on the floor, running with the medics to help my sister. I looked back in time to see Marcus wrap his arms around Eadwig's neck and waist, will open a gate in the floor, and yank him through the hole that closed as quickly as it had formed.

I stood over Beth while a medic patted her cheeks. "Is she…"

"Breathing," she replied. "Unconscious, but she's alive." With a few flicks of her wand, she stabilized Beth against an invisible brace and floated her off the mats. "We need to take her to the infirmary—"

A gate opened near Beth's feet, and turning to identify the creator, I found Artur at my right hand. The medic nodded her thanks and floated Beth through, and Artur nudged me on. "I'll join you soon," she said. "Be with her."

It didn't take a faerie to sense the murder in Artur's

mind. Grabbing her arm, I dragged her out of the competition room before she could kill the ponytailed blonde on the bleachers to whom Maria was delivering a lecture at blistering volume.

CHAPTER 9

The midnight hour was almost upon us when Beth woke in the infirmary, her head swathed in bandages and her body wrapped with healing enchantment. Maria had made a panicked call home while Dr. Powell was running her preliminary assessment, and as soon as the doctor had her monitoring spells in place, Val had stepped in to do what he could. "A thought," he'd said to us on departure, after making Maria and me promise to call if the situation deteriorated. "Perhaps the damn combat contest should involve *helmets*?"

Maria intended to convey the message to Toula, but the grand magus was busy for much of the day with the fallout, and Maria reluctantly returned to her referee duties when the eighth-years began. It was quiet in the infirmary when Beth finally opened her eyes, and we were alone in the dimly lit ward.

"Hey, brat," I said, squeezing her hand. "Welcome back."

She squinted at me, then noticed the projection above her, a Beth-sized outline made of light, with color-coded spots and strands of injury. "What…"

"Some little Arc 1 bitch on the sidelines sneak-attacked you. Fortunately, you're hard-headed."

Reaching up, she brushed her fingers against the bandages, then seemed to recognize where she was. "I…what did I…"

"Hit the wall. The padded part, thank goodness. The bolt broke a few of your ribs, but Val should have you feeling nice and numb."

She took a deep breath to inflate her lungs, then released it as a sigh. "Yeah. I'm fine. Have the seventh-years started yet? Did I—"

I pinned her to the mattress as she tried to rise. "You won. That Jessa girl was in cahoots with your attacker—someone named Gail? The magi disqualified them both, and Toula's taken their wands for the next six months as punishment. That's the good news."

"What's the bad?"

"The Games ended hours ago, and you're on bed rest until Sunday. Doc's orders."

Beth stared at me while the facts settled in, and then her eyes began to fill.

"Honey, *you won*," I insisted. "I know you wanted to advance, and you would have, had you not been unconscious. I'm just grateful you're not in a coma or worse right now. But it's official, you won your year, and Artur wants you to know that she's *immensely* proud of you. As am I, if it matters," I joked. "The important thing now is for you to rest and heal."

She rubbed her eyes with her free hand, and I passed her the bedside tissue box. "Jessa warned me," she muttered as she dried the escaped tears.

"What did she say? I can't read lips that well."

"Just that I was going to lose, one way or another." Wadding the tissue in her fist, she added, "Called me a faerie-loving traitor."

"I'm sorry."

Anger flashed across her face. "*Don't* be. I'll take you over those idiots any day."

Touched though I was, I resisted the urge to hug my sister, given what Dr. Powell had told me of her injuries. "Well, if it makes you feel better, Jessa's spending the night in the silo infirmary. When she went after you, Eadwig kind of lost it."

Her eyebrows rose in alarm. "He didn't jump off the

balcony, did—"

"No, no, he's unhurt. But, uh…" I hesitated, trying to gauge how much I could tell Beth, then said, "I've seen his aura. You should know that he has a *ton* of talent."

"*Eadwig?*"

"Yeah. He's not some village witch. From what we've been able to put together—the Team and Quinn, mind you, I don't think anyone else noticed with the confusion—he got upset when you were hurt and sparked *hard*. As soon as Dr. Powell clears him, Toula's giving him to Magus Popova for emergency training. The kind of spell he pulled off, at his age, without a wand…" I whistled low. "He doesn't know his own strength."

"Is he okay? Scared?"

"Shaken, but more concerned about you." Beth's expression was unreadable in the low light, and I forced myself to ask the question replaying in my mind like an earworm I couldn't kill. "Honey…it's none of my business, I know that, but is there something going on between the two of you?"

She laughed aloud, then cried out and grabbed at her side as she breathed too deeply for even Val's enchantment to mask the pain in her ribs. "We're friends. He's lived here less than two weeks." As her incredulous chuckling subsided, she gazed past me with a curious expression, then glanced my way again, her eyes shrewd. "Why do you ask? Do you think he likes me like…*that?*"

"I have no idea, but if he were to make a move…you know, take things slowly. He's still at that point where he barely knows what planet he's on. Now, if you don't get some rest, Dr. Powell's going to kill us both," I said, reaching over the railing to straighten Beth's blankets. "Sleep and let the magic work. I'll be here if you need anything."

I was loath to touch the spare beds, given their steel frames, so I made a friendlier version beside Beth's and climbed in. She stretched her hand past her bed's railing, and I caught her fingers in my own and closed my eyes.

In the interest of calming my sister, I'd *slightly* minimized Eadwig's reaction to his unexpected burst of power. While I'd waited for her to regain consciousness, I'd heard bits and pieces from Quinn, who'd assumed the role of go-between for the infirmary and our flat. She'd been the only candidate for the position: I couldn't leave Beth's side, and Marcus and Artur had jointly taken on the task of keeping Eadwig under control, a job easier said than done.

So intent had Eadwig been on maiming Beth's attacker that he'd barely noticed when Marcus manhandled him through a hole in the floor. The shock of landing on Marcus's seldom-used bed had broken his concentration, and Marcus had had him pinned before he could escape. He'd only released Eadwig once the boy's eyes had lost their wild look and could focus on him…at which point Eadwig had hyperventilated and curled up on himself. Marcus had hoped that the outburst had shaken something loose in Eadwig's memory, but the kid had remained as much of an amnesiac as ever, just terrified at the attack he'd unleashed. "That wasn't *me*," he'd insisted, though the evidence strongly suggested otherwise. As worked up as Eadwig had been, Marcus had known he couldn't be left alone, and Artur had agreed to stick around as backup in case he flared again.

Unaware of his true power, Quinn had tried to reassure Eadwig that everything would be fine, telling him about her own flares and her work with Magus Popova to control them. He'd remained troubled, however, and she'd brought her concerns to me late Friday evening, once Marcus had finally convinced Eadwig to go to bed and stop asking to visit Beth. "The kid has *bad* nightmares," Quinn had told me while the monitoring projection above Beth's bed had pulsed in silence. "Almost every night. Have you not heard him?"

I'd shaken my head. "He hasn't mentioned anything about that to me."

"You guys must have insulated the floor well, then, since he wakes himself screaming. It's okay," she'd hastened to add, "I've been checking in on him."

"Does he remember what they're about?"

She'd shrugged. "He doesn't know. Says they feel almost like snatches of memory, but not *his* memory. He doesn't seem to remember details when he wakes, but I've caught him crying in his sleep twice. When does he see his therapist again?"

"Next week." I'd glanced at Beth, who hadn't so much as twitched during Quinn's visit. "Do me a favor and keep this between us. I don't want to embarrass him, but I might quietly mention those dreams to Wanda."

Dr. Powell cleared Beth to go home after lunchtime on Saturday—too late for her to attend the awards brunch, so Toula personally delivered her trophy to the infirmary instead. Though Eadwig seemed poised to ambush Beth in welcome at the door of our flat, I held him at bay. "She's on bed rest until morning," I explained, helping her back to her room, "and the more she can sleep, the quicker she'll heal. You see the enchantment around her? That ain't for show."

While Beth dozed all afternoon, held under by a little enchantment of my own, Eadwig remained close to her latched bedroom door, sitting at the kitchen table to continue his translation for Quinn while she read on her computer. I listened to them while I worked on dinner preparations—honestly, after the previous night, I needed the distraction of a chopping board—and I smiled to myself when I overheard Quinn try to walk Eadwig through the basics of typing. They put their work aside and cleared the table for dinner, but as soon as the meal was finished, they returned to their places, Quinn engrossed in her reading and Eadwig focusing his nervous energy on the task at hand.

I was mixing up brownies for Beth around nine that evening when I heard Eadwig ask Quinn what she was reading.

"Want to see?" Glancing through the cutout, I watched her turn her computer to face him. "So, there's this thousand-year-old diary in the Archives, and it's particularly important to the Arcanum for some reason. Jude didn't give me all the details," she admitted, "but in any case, they want to preserve it. The pages are vellum, and I played with some cutting-edge techniques in New York, so Jude's invited me to work with the preservation group and see what we can accomplish. I mean, for a book of that age, it's in *fantastic* shape, but he said it was protected by spells for most of that time. I was curious about the contents, so Jude got me a copy to slog through."

"What does the diary speak of?" he asked.

"Less personal stuff than I'd anticipated. It's mostly theoretical spellcraft—way above my level, and in Latin, to boot," she said, chuckling. "Tons of fun, let me tell you. Anyway, don't mention to Jude that I let you peek, okay? I'm not supposed to have access to this book. The real one is under heavy security, and even the scanned copies are protected. This copy isn't even complete. Jude said they removed a couple of pages from the scanned version that have caused trouble in the past. Nuts, huh? I've never worked on a book that had to be *redacted*. Go on, you can take a look," she urged him. "I won't tell."

My guts clenched. There was only one possible book on Quinn's computer, and I watched Eadwig's face in profile as he peered at the screen. He scrolled through the pages, front to back, then frowned as he reached the end. "There should be more," he murmured.

"Nope, just the two missing pages. Books like this have pages in multiples of four, see, because of how they're assembled—"

"No. More than two pages. There's *much* more…" He

pushed back from the table and rubbed his forehead, and Quinn put her arm around his shoulders.

"Are you okay?" she gently asked. "Remembering something?"

"I…I don't know, I…but the book, I know there is more…" He lifted his face to hers, brow creased, eyes blinking rapidly in agitation. "I'm sure of it. I do not know how I know, but I *know* this."

"Hold that thought," I interrupted from the kitchen. "Quinn, show me the first page of the document. The cover info, not the text." She flipped back, revealing the standard Archives cataloguing page: author, date, medium, subject matter, restrictions. *Simon Magus* stood out clearly near the top, confirming my suspicions.

Alarmed, she demanded, "Who're you calling?" as I pulled out my phone and dialed. "I swear, Jude gave me permission—"

"You're not in trouble," I assured her, and listened to the greeting on the other end. "Sorry to bother you this late, Grand Magus, but you need to come to my flat. *Now*."

From the sour look on his face and his forced-march pace through the Archives, I sensed that Jude Duffy had better things to do on a Saturday night than accompany his boss into the restricted section. Never an effusively overjoyed man—at least not around the Team—Jude was more prickly than usual, though I couldn't entirely fault him. Under ordinary circumstances, Jude was a fastidious dresser who preferred three-piece suits, kept his gold-rimmed glasses polished, and carefully styled his graying blond hair. That night, having been summoned from his flat on short notice, he'd come out in sweatpants and a ratty T-shirt, which did much to explain the furtive glances he'd shot around the abandoned Archives on arrival.

I had little sympathy, as the problem was of his own making. Jude's presence was superfluous—by virtue of her position, Toula had full access to the Archives—but when she gave him a courtesy call to inform him that she would be taking the diary out of storage and not to worry if any alarm sensors triggered, he refused to let her go without his supervision, blaming the fragility of the restricted items. True, Toula lacked the archivists' training in preservation techniques, but she had the grace not to remind Jude that she was the person responsible for returning the diary to the Arcanum in the first place, and she tolerated his presence as he grumped about the hour and her research that couldn't wait for Monday.

He'd had the sense not to ask why Quinn, Eadwig, and I were along for the ride—indeed, his only acknowledgement of us had been a nod to Quinn before we reached the door to the restricted section. "Authorized personnel only past this point," he said, keeping the three of us back while Toula worked on the door's several locks. "Sorry, Quinn, but I can't allow you in here—"

"They're with me," Toula interrupted.

Jude stiffened and glanced over his shoulder at her while she opened the final lock. "Grand Magus, with all due respect, they—"

"Are the reason I pulled you away from your football recaps. Let them pass."

Reluctantly, he stepped aside, and I resisted the urge to smirk at him as we followed Toula into the room. The Team had brought all manner of items back to the Archives, but once they were out of our custody, we seldom saw them again. I could only imagine that Jude feared we'd put our grubby hands all over his pristine storage room.

Though the restricted section was the size of a ballroom, its available floor space was closer to that of a large parlor. Lining the walls were locked cases of all sizes: glass-fronted bookcases of rare and delicate codices, honeycombed wooden cubbyholes for scrolls, long cabinets of ensorcelled weapons, and even a mahogany jewelry box, which would have seemed ordinary enough but for the layers of spells wrapped around it like a fine mesh. In the center of the room was a setup much like the well-appointed reading rooms in the castle library, a pair of wooden tables ringed with padded chairs and topped with lamps, foam blocks, book snakes, and a modest selection of pencils. A thick oriental rug in crimson and violet padded all but a foot-wide border of old wooden floorboards, a last bit of protection in case of clumsy archivists.

For safety's sake, the diary wasn't kept with the other books, but rather in a triple-locked steel chest built into the wall. Toula fiddled for a moment before she gained access, and then the door popped open with a hiss of air. Ignoring Jude's pained grimace, Toula carefully lifted the ancient diary from its climate-controlled chamber and carried it to the table. I prepared a foam landing spot, and she placed the book in its cradle. "You look like you're about to shit yourself, Jude," she murmured as she turned over the cover. "I read this on my *lap* the first time, and we're all still here and breathing, aren't we?"

He grunted. "You'll excuse me for saying so, but that was a stupid idea."

"I might have asked for your sage counsel, but I doubt you were out of grade school at the time. Eadwig, dear, you can come closer."

"*Eadwig?*" Jude muttered, but no one bothered to explain.

Quinn and I stood on the opposite side of the table, and I watched Eadwig's face as he considered the diary. I couldn't read him—his expression vacillated between intensity and trancelike blankness—but after perhaps a minute of silently contemplating the first page, he turned it and began leafing through the book.

"Hey, kid!" Jude yelped. "Stop that! You can't touch it!"

Toula threw out an arm to block him before Jude could

grab Eadwig. "It's all right," she muttered.

"No, it's not! That thing is priceless…"

The rest of his protestation ended in a shriek as Eadwig, moving like a sleepwalker, held a hand over the diary and made a few subtle twitches. The vellum pages popped free of their binding and rose into the air in a loose stack…and then, to my horror, they splintered into strips barely wider than a hair. Toula seemed frozen beside Eadwig—perhaps she, too, suddenly felt this might have been a bad idea—but Eadwig made another gesture, and the slivers of precious vellum rotated slightly before reassembling themselves into pages, and the pages into a book. With the diary restored, he flipped to the first page and stepped aside.

Jude almost shoved Toula over in his rush to inspect the damage, but after scanning the page, his mouth dropped in shock. Beside him, Toula read with saucer eyes, then broke into a manic grin. "*Fuck* me," she whispered. "There *is* more."

"How…" Jude croaked, then cleared his throat and stared at the newly revealed page again. "That's not possible. Every spell on that book broke during the '13 closure…"

"No spell necessary." She turned the page, her smile widening. "This is solid—feel it," she said, running her fingers down the vellum. "This…it's not even a palimpsest, the text is *there*, hidden in the vellum…" Her breath quickened as her eyes darted back and forth, reading the fresh text. "He must have ensorcelled the vellum so that the ink barely soaked in. Split it into strands, turn them all, and voilà, clean page. My God." While Jude fumbled to make coherent sounds, Toula checked to the end of the book, revealing writing-covered pages throughout. "You know what this means? The diary just doubled in size…"

"Or more?" Quinn asked, looking at Eadwig, who seemed to have woken from his trance and was watching the proceedings with a look of confusion and worry. "Do the pages turn like that again?"

"Four sets," he whispered.

"*Four.*" Toula raised her face toward Eadwig and spread her hands. "Do you have any idea what you've just done?"

"I...I don't know," he replied, his voice trembling. "I don't know anything—"

"How did you do that?" Jude demanded. "Who the hell *are* you?"

"I don't know," he repeated, stepping away from the diary. "I *knew*, but I...I don't know how..."

"We've studied that diary for decades, and..." He sputtered, momentarily speechless, then managed, "The *control* it took to do that, and wandless..."

"But I do not have control," Eadwig protested. "Yesterday, when I—"

His mouth snapped closed, but Jude was no fool, and the tumblers had already fallen. "That was you? The one who threw around the Arc 1 girl?"

Eadwig nodded.

"Where did you come from?"

Shrinking into himself, he looked to Toula for help, and she took the reins. "The Team found Eadwig entombed in Ireland," she told Jude. "By our best estimate, he was buried alive in the late tenth or early eleventh century. Other than that, we've got nothing. *He* doesn't even know how he got there."

I could read minds, but I didn't have to that night. Jude looked at Simon Magus's diary, then at the miserable, cowering boy who had unlocked it, and slowly covered his mouth.

"We don't know that," Toula murmured, stopping him before he could make a scene. "And need I remind you he's a kid?"

"Yes, but—"

"You will say nothing about this to anyone," she

interrupted, her voice steely. "Eadwig is still trying to work out how he wound up in Ireland. We don't need to complicate matters, got it?"

"Understood," Jude mumbled.

"Good. Go get a scanner."

As he scrambled for the door, I couldn't help but notice how badly his hands were shaking.

Around midnight, once Jude had made a careful scan of every new diary page and Eadwig had returned the book to its original configuration, Quinn and I took Eadwig home and sent him to bed. He walked up to his room without protest, lost in thought, and Quinn and I waited in the kitchen to give him a moment's privacy in the loft. She made a cup of tea while I finished Beth's aborted brownies—at least I hadn't put them in the oven before running out to the Archives. Considering the hour, I poured the mixture into a pan, willed the mass into a solid form with enchantment, and cut it into squares with a fingertip.

Stealing one of the warm brownies before I wrapped the plate, Quinn said, "So, are you going to tell me what's really going on with him, or do I not have clearance?"

"*I* barely have clearance. Tell you when I can."

"Eh, figured as much." She tasted my handiwork and nodded approval. "But for now, is he…okay? Safe?"

I thought of the awe on Jude's face and the way Eadwig had stood back from the diary as if it were poised to attack him. "Your guess is as good as mine."

With the kitchen tidied, I went to bed, grateful that Marcus was already asleep. Explaining what I'd seen that night would take more time and energy than I had, and I pushed it away to be the morning's problem.

Despite my fatigue, my internal clock wouldn't do me the courtesy of letting me sleep uninterrupted Sunday morning, and I woke at five-thirty as usual. Slipping free of

Marcus's arm, which had migrated around me during the night, I pulled on a robe and padded toward my bedroom door, which I'd left cracked in my haste to crash. If Beth was awake, I needed to check her injuries and the healing constructions around her; if she wasn't, then I suspected her empty stomach would rouse her soon enough.

Before I could open the door wider, I heard soft voices coming from the den and paused to spy through the gap. Beth was indeed awake, and she was making a breakfast of brownies on the couch with Eadwig.

The mature thing to do would have been to casually announce myself, but that was my baby sister sitting beside the boy with a magus's power, and so I held my breath and eavesdropped instead.

"I've never seen that book," he insisted. "*Never.* But when I saw it, I…" His hands snatched at the air as if he were trying to grab the words he needed. "I just knew how it worked. My priest never taught me magic like that—"

"Or what you did to Jessa?" Beth asked.

Vehemently, he shook his head. "How did I do those things?"

"I don't know," she said, patting his shoulder. "But the grand magus will figure it out. Now, it's way too early to be worrying about Simon Magus, so try these before Marcus wakes up and inhales them."

Eadwig selected a small brownie, took a test nibble, then shoved the rest down in two bites. I couldn't see his face from my position, but Beth's knowing grin made his reaction clear.

"What is this?" he mumbled through a full mouth.

"Brownie, heavy on the chocolate. Want another? I'll share."

He took her up on it, and she moved the platter out of easy reach on the coffee table. "Will you explain something to me?" he asked once his second brownie had disappeared.

"Sure, I'll try."

"That book—why it is so protected? It's kept in a locked box in a locked room, and the man with us tried to stop us from going in."

"Archivists are twitchy in general, so don't take that personally," she replied. "As for the book..." She winced as she leaned back into the pillows. "About a thousand years ago, a little while after you ended up in Ireland, there was this incredible wizard named Simon, and he joined all the groups of wizards into the Arcanum. First grand magus, so everyone around here calls him Simon Magus, see?"

Eadwig nodded.

"Well, that book you were messing with was his diary. He hid it when he died, and it didn't surface again until about fifty years ago. Grand Magus Pavli brought it back to us. Anyway, Simon Magus was brilliant, and there's supposedly all of these insane casting techniques and stuff in there, but I don't have permission yet to see for myself."

"Quinn has a copy," he replied. "If I sneaked upstairs and borrowed her computer—"

"Not worth the lecture we'd get in return." Propping her arm on the back of the couch, she asked, "What's your connection, do you think? Did you know anyone named Simon before?"

He sighed and reached for the brownies. "No. A strange name, that."

"Not really."

"Perhaps not *now*. I never met anyone called Simon." Biting his prize in half, he briefly chewed in silence, then said, "It makes no sense, Beth. How did I know about the hidden pages? How did I unlock them? This sort of magic, it was never taught to me."

"Unless you've forgotten something," she countered.

"Thank you for reminding me," he muttered, then groaned and flopped back into the cushion.

"Any hints yet?"

"None. I remember falling asleep, my siblings

coughing, and then I woke here. There's nothing in between, not even dreams, but…"

"But?" Beth prompted.

Eadwig finished the brownie before speaking again. "I feel as if there's something I am meant to be doing. I cannot say *what*, but there is something, and I've forgot."

"Is this a new development? Maybe your memory is coming—"

"No, no, I've felt this almost from the moment I woke. I feel it, but I cannot say—"

"On the tip of your tongue?"

He considered the phrase. "Close. It's frustrating, whatever it may be."

"Hey, now," she said, reaching for the platter in turn, "don't beat yourself up. It'll come to you. Until then, it's not like Kitty's going to kick you out."

"Her charity is appreciated, but—"

"But nothing. You should have seen Artur in her first months here, and I don't know what Marcus was like, but he had to have been a mess. You're in good company, okay?"

Chuckling, he followed her lead on the brownies. "And how did you come to be in the middle of this strange company?"

Beth smirked in reply. "Remember when I said my mom's in prison? Kitty's all I have."

"At least you have someone."

Her expression softened at his dejected tone. "You have us now," she said, resting her hand on his knee. "It's not the same, I get it, but you've got somewhere to land, Ed. Not family, but…we could be friends, yeah? You and me?"

"Friends," he repeated carefully, as if feeling the shape of the word in his mouth. "I'd like that."

"Good. And, uh…you know, I didn't really thank you for sticking up for me at the Games. Tough to say much when you're unconscious, but thanks for not letting her bash my head in any worse than it was."

"You're welcome," he said through a mouthful of brownie. "I'm sorry I did not stop her sooner—"

Good morning, beautiful, came Marcus's voice in my mind, startling me from my observations. *Is there a reason why you're being sneaky?*

I turned and found him sitting up in bed, his tanned chest bare and his dark hair mussed with sleep. *Because Simon freaking Magus may have a crush on Beth, and I'm the responsible adult here.*

An eyebrow rose. *This has something to do with the trip to the Archives last night, I trust?*

Want the long version or the synopsis?

He patted the mattress in invitation, and I slid back into bed to tell him everything. Once I'd brought him up to speed, he let out a long exhalation, then curled up next to me, our foreheads almost touching. "I've had a thought," he whispered.

"And what would that be?"

"You and I run away to Tennessee and let Artur supervise until Eadwig sorts himself out."

I pulled up the duvet to muffle my soft laughter. "She'd kill us."

"She would need to find us first. If there's a large Walmart, perhaps we could hide for days."

Scooting closer, I kissed him beneath the blankets and closed my eyes as his arm sought the curve of my waist. "I appreciate the sentiment, but this is no time for sightseeing."

We lay together, still and silent—and, I suspected, both of us straining to hear the conversation on the other side of the door.

"I should probably confiscate the brownies before they make themselves sick," I mumbled.

Marcus pushed the covers back, and I opened my eyes to see him staring at me. "You didn't tell me you made brownies," he whispered.

"They were for Beth."

"She doesn't need the whole pan," he replied, then willed his robe from across the room and stalked out into the morning to claim his prize.

CHAPTER 10

I waited until mid-afternoon Monday to visit Frank again, having spent Sunday keeping an eye on my convalescing sister and our concerning houseguest. After a few hours in the office and a late lunch, I slipped across to Faerie, where it was barely past midnight. As I'd expected, Frank was awake and rewatching nature documentaries—more for the pictures than the sound, I assumed, as the other dragons' rockslide snoring almost drowned out the narration.

Frank didn't need a long-winded explanation. *You're troubled*, he thought as I approached the nest. *Is everyone healthy?*

It being impossible to keep secrets from Ros while in Faerie, I decided not to pretend. *Has Ros mentioned our suspicions about Eadwig?*

His massive head tilted in bemusement. *Who's Eadwig?*

She really has been busy, hasn't she? I motioned a bale closer for a seat and told Frank about our bizarre find, including the boy's manipulation of the diary. *For obvious reasons, Toula has me on a gag order*, I concluded, *but Maria, Marcus, and Artur know, and I'd rather you be prepared before you go snooping around.*

I'll say nothing to the others, he assured me. *The Three are aware of this?*

Whatever Toula knows, Coileán probably knows, and Val and Eleanor are aware of the kid.

What's the plan, then?

I snorted and tucked one leg onto the bale. *Hell if I*

know. Toula needs to get Eadwig into training, but after seeing what he can do wandless, I don't think I'd give him to Popova. She's fantastic, but I'm concerned that he might be stronger already—

A sharp crack cut me off, and Frank raised his head in alarm. He lifted his wing to peer into the warm heart of the nest, then turned to me, excitement radiating off him like neon glowing in the darkness. *It's hatching!*

I cut the projector and threw a hundred tiny orbs into the air above him, giving him light to see but keeping my distance. A sudden flash beside me heralded Ros's manifestation, but when I glanced her way, I was surprised to see how weary she appeared. *Long night?* I asked.

Her lips tightened into a pale line. *It's not over yet.*

We waited for a few minutes while Frank gazed down at the hatching egg, neither of us speaking over the sleeping dragons. Suddenly, Frank looked back at us, his expression shifting toward too-familiar panic. *It stopped.*

Want me to give it a hand? I offered. *Maybe the shell's tough.*

With a nod, he stood and uncoiled himself, granting me passage into the nest. The oversized cream-colored egg rested alone on its side in the depression at the center, unspoiled but for a black crack in the shell that stretched one-third of the way from the tip. I climbed through the straw, then crouched beside the egg and tapped my knuckles against the fractured point. Something inside pressed back, and then the egg rocked beneath my hand. *Hold on, sweetie,* I thought, then carefully struck the area near the fissure until the shell spiderwebbed beneath my fist. The first pieces fell away, and I tugged at the other loosened chips to widen the hole until a little forked tongue tentatively flicked out, tasting the air. Laughter born of relief bubbled up from within me, and I continued to break the shell until the hatchling took over and forced itself free. I scrambled to stand back, taking care that the little thing didn't mistakenly imprint on me, and held my breath as it stumbled into the world.

The hatchling was the same shade of blue-green as

Ione had been, and though small for a newborn dragon—perhaps only the size of a young Great Dane—it was alive. It turned its head, experimenting with the freedom of the universe beyond the confines of the egg, then noticed Frank's head resting beside it and reacted with joy, its pure thought translated most simply as, *Mama!*

Frank rumbled and gently nuzzled the hatchling, his own thoughts unrestrained by the courtesy of words but recognizable as relief and happiness. But as the hatchling took its baby steps through the nest, I saw why Ros was less than thrilled. Where the hatchling's wings should have been was nothing but unbroken scales, and its front-left leg ended in a stump around the knee joint. Unbalanced, it wobbled and fell over with a squawk, and Frank gave it a quick check while it was on its back. *Female*, he announced, the thought colored with pride.

What's her name? I asked.

Aurora. The answer came without hesitation. *Joey marked up a baby name book with Mom's favorites, and Ione and I liked that one. Isn't she beautiful? She looks like her mother—* His thought ceased abruptly as he noticed what Ros and I had already seen. *Her wings. Where are her wings?* he demanded, looking to Ros for answers.

Her sigh spoke of exhaustion. *She never grew them*, she replied, folding her arms in tense protection over her chest. *I did the best I could, Frank. You have no idea how many times I almost lost her. She was only mildly better off than her brothers…the strongest of the three, but only by a hair.* Turning to me, she thought, *Bring Pritam, if he'll come.*

Steadying the hatchling with a helping claw, Frank nudged her upright, and her thoughts showed only happiness as she rubbed against his leg. His, however, were a jumble, relief and fear jockeying for prominence in his mind, and I saw myself out as he wrapped himself around her.

Pritam's apartment was empty, but he directed me to his office and met me with his bag packed. "I don't care how many limbs she's missing—she's alive," he said as I briefed him. "I don't think I could have taken another dead egg. Has she fed?"

By the time we returned, the answer to that was a bloody *yes*. We arrived outside the barn to find Aurora in the sheep pasture, her head inside the belly of an ewe that Frank had killed for her, making quick work of its bowels. "Do me a favor and tell her I'm not food, please," Pritam asked Frank, who stood guard in the darkness, then turned to me and said, "Light, if you can manage."

I beckoned toward the barn, and the orbs I'd created flew out like a swarm of oversized fireflies and hovered over the hatchling. Too busy gorging herself to notice, Aurora didn't so much as raise her head from her prize as Pritam climbed the fence and crept closer, taking care to stay out of her line of sight.

She won't eat you, Frank assured him.

"You say that, but she appears to be a very hungry little girl," he muttered. Taking his wand from his bag, he worked a visualization spell—I couldn't understand the words he used to focus his will, but the glowing contours of the construction were familiar enough for me to follow along with his progress. When he finished, a copy of Aurora had been rendered in lines of pale yellow light, a perfect likeness feeding on nothing several yards away from the original. A word from Pritam and a twist of his wand peeled away her scales and skin, then her musculature, leaving an upright skeleton like a Halloween decoration gone astray. Pritam stepped around a pile of sheep droppings to inspect his work, then turned to Frank and beckoned him closer.

"Look here and here," he said once Frank had fixed a giant eye on the projection. "Her shoulders and hips appear to be formed properly. See, she shifts her weight with smooth movement. Spine looks straight"—he brushed one hand through the insubstantial vertebrae— "and if you examine her skull, it appears normal to me…based on the limited information available, of course."

Understood, thought Frank.

"Now, considering her brothers, I would expect to see the wing joints here," Pritam continued, tracing circles around the area above her shoulders. "Another set of shoulders. But there's nothing. No bones, not even a hint of one. Is this a common issue?"

I've never seen it. Perhaps my siblings, they've covered more of Faerie than I have, but—

"But it's not a beneficial mutation. You hunt on the wing? Mate? I don't mean to be indelicate—"

Yes to both.

"So one would not expect her to thrive in the wild. And that leg…" He squatted beside the projection and studied the short limb. "Again, no malformed bones—she's simply missing everything below the knee."

What can we do?

Pritam stood, wincing as his own knees cracked. "A prosthetic might be possible. I've never fit one on a reptile, but that's not to say I *couldn't*. It would have to be switched fairly often, though—if I read the notes correctly, she'll be at full size in five years?"

If not before.

"And that's a weight-bearing prosthetic. I could design something, perhaps work with whatever medical staff you have in Glastonbury. A craft-augmented prosthetic would be the way to go. But as for her wings…" He grimaced and rubbed his neck. "I wouldn't know where to begin. You're talking about constructing something light and large enough for flight, without even a stump for an anchor. And if we add the muscles back"—he twisted his wand in the opposite direction—"yeah, this isn't good. I'm not completely certain, but I think she's missing her wing muscles."

"She is," said Ros, who'd watched the examination in silence. "It was either leave them there to serve no purpose or leave her leg muscles misshapen, and I thought walking would be better than nothing."

From what I could sense of Frank's emotions, fear was beginning to win. *She'll never fly? Is that what you're telling me?*

"I did everything I could. Which would you prefer, another dead egg or your daughter?"

He stiffened, staring down at Ros, then thought, *I'm sorry, I don't mean to be an ingrate—*

"But that's your kid. I get it, bud." Turning to Pritam, she said, "I think there's more. Check her heart. I held it together, but I don't think my fix was perfect."

Another twist of his wand switched the view from Aurora's musculature to her organs. Again, Pritam squatted beside the projection, frowning as he considered the inflating lungs and swelling stomach. "On preliminary inspection, I don't see any major issues aside from this," he said, pointing to a tiny hole in the hatchling's heart. "Don't panic," he told Frank. "It's not a death sentence. My brother was born with one, and it closed on its own. We can fix it, I'm sure of that. Personally, I've never done cardiac surgery, but if there is someone in the Arcanum who has worked with human patients…"

"We could talk to Dr. Powell," I offered. "She's not a specialist, but she's seen a little of everything come through Glastonbury."

"Good. I would feel much better if this were a team undertaking," Pritam replied. "And it's not something we need to do immediately. *Soon*, yes—let's give her a better examination in a few days. But she seems stable for now, and she obviously has an appetite…"

Aurora, who hadn't so much as noticed Pritam, finally raised her head from the carcass and flopped into the grass, satiated and sleepy in the way of all newborns.

Pritam beamed and dissolved the projection. "Oh, that little beauty needs a nap. Has anyone been taking baby pictures?"

I pulled out my phone, willed Aurora's face clean of

gore, and began snapping shots of the sleeping hatchling. "We'll take some more after she wakes," I assured Frank once I'd captured her from every angle. "Whenever you return to work, you're going to need something for your desk. You've seen Antony's collage, yeah?"

What, the shrine to Allie? He settled down beside Aurora, whose back legs had begun to twitch in her sleep. *Thank you again, Pritam. I don't know how to repay—*

"Nonsense," he replied, stowing his wand away. "Though I would love a baby picture whenever the final set is compiled. Give your doctor my contact information," he told me, "and we can coordinate a time to come over and examine the little one, yes?"

I sent it to Dr. Powell after Pritam dictated a message, then took him back to his office to close up for the day. When I returned to Faerie, Frank had an audience: Ros's parents and Sam had come out in their nightclothes to see the hatchling, who continued to nap beside her distraught father.

"You did nothing wrong," Joey insisted. "Remember that. She's here, she's eating…"

Helen nodded. "We'll work on the leg, don't you worry. How's she getting around?"

Poorly. I helped her outside, but she's trying to hop, and it's not working. His tail twitched in agitation. *A tripod dog is one thing, but a tripod dragon…*

"And the weight distribution, once she packs on a few hundred pounds…yeah." Sam, who'd wrapped an arm around Ros, bit his lip and considered the problem. "The good news is that it's not a bridge we have to cross tonight."

"This morning," Ros murmured.

"It ain't morning until the sun comes up, honey," he replied, giving her a squeeze. "But for now, she's alive, and that's what matters. Well done, Dad."

Well done, Ros, you mean.

"I'll share the credit," she said with a weary smile. "And

will you *please* eat something now? I'm worried about you…"

Sam released Ros as her back straightened. "Babe? Everything okay?"

"No." Not bothering with the limitations of a physical form, she walked through the wooden fence around the sheep pen and was waiting, hands on her hips, when Frank's brothers emerged from the barn. "Don't even think it," she snapped, glaring up at the pair. "Go back to bed."

Of the three males in his clutch, Frank was the smallest by a significant margin. Red Horus, first-hatched and largest, measured almost two hundred fifty feet from snout to tail tip, while Rego, black like their mother, came in at only about five feet smaller. Still, while Ros was a relatively tiny impediment in their path, both had the sense to keep their distance.

Frank rose and hastily tried to block Aurora from view, but it was too late, and the orbs I'd hung above her showed her uncles exactly what had hatched. I couldn't follow much of their brief conversation with Frank— neither human nor faerie minds are designed to process draconic pure thought—but Frank's reaction needed no translation. Curling himself around Aurora, he bared his teeth and growled, a sound that gave me a sudden, urgent desire to be anywhere but near its source.

"What's the problem?" Helen asked.

Ros cocked her head and continued to stare at the interlopers. "Would you like to tell them, or shall I?"

Horus took the lead. *The hatchling is defective. It won't survive—*

"Actually, she's in decent health," I interjected, forcing myself to step in front of Frank.

Having not spent decades passing as human, Frank's brothers didn't roll their eyes at me, but I felt Horus's annoyance in his thought. *Look at it! It will never fly…can it even walk?*

"More or less," said Ros. "And *she*, not *it*."

Get out of the way, thought Rego.

I called up the biggest shield I could muster, but Rego only took one step before Ros flung him head over heels into the recesses of the barn. "Try your luck?" she asked Horus, her voice dripping with feigned sweetness.

He held his ground. *The whole clutch was defective. You know that, we know that, <u>Runt</u> knows that. This has gone on long enough. Kill it and be done with it.*

Shadows behind him resolved into Obelia, Zafira, and Neve, Frank's sisters.

"Guys, look," said Joey, stepping out behind his glowing daughter, "I hear you, and I understand what instinct is telling you to do. But Aurora's not hurting anyone. There's plenty of food, plenty of space—"

It's wingless! Zafira interjected. *Allowing it to live would be cruel. Runt, please*, she thought, looking past us, *either do the right thing or allow us to do it for you. You can mate again. Protecting a defective, motherless hatchling is madness.*

Frank's only response was his warning growl.

"We're working on a solution for her leg," Joey began, but the other dragons were having none of it.

Stop being such an idiot, Neve thought at her little brother. *You don't know how to raise a hatchling—no male does. We're not going to do it for you. Do you think Ione would have raised <u>that</u>?*

You didn't know Ione like I did, Frank retorted.

At least Ione had basic sense. If that were my hatchling, I'd kill it.

Frank's response was unconstrained by words, but I couldn't miss the overwhelming sense of possession in it.

Still, Joey tried to mediate. "Let's all just calm down, and we can talk about this after breakfast, okay? Frank's had a long night—"

And you're coddling him, Obelia retorted as Rego, now slightly limping, joined their line. *It was bad enough that he practically moved into the nest with Ione, worse when he took her place. This has gone on far too long. Get rid of the last of that clutch and let him move past this nonsense. It's not right!* <u>*He's*</u> *not right*, she added, glaring at Frank. *So move aside, and—*

"Over my dead body," said Ros.

Exhausted though she might have been, Ros was the voice of the realm, and with that came power beyond my imagining. Standing well behind her, I couldn't see her face, but something in her tone and stance told me that an attempt to muscle past her would be suicidal.

From within the barn came a voice with which I was more familiar, one whose wordless thought carried with it the sharp edge of command. The other dragons looked uncertainly at each other, then slunk back into the darkness. A moment later, Georgie took their place at the open door. *Stand down, child*, she told Ros. *I won't hurt them.*

Dipping her chin in a curt nod, Ros stepped aside, as did Joey, leaving nothing between Frank and his mother but me and my shield. Georgie paused a few yards away on the other side of the fence and cocked her head. *You think I mean him ill?*

"I think it's been a long night already," I told her. "And recent conversation has put me somewhat on edge."

Ros knows my intentions are good.

"Yeah, well, I owe Frank my life. Why don't you stay over there, huh?"

A puff of warm air on my back made me turn around, and I found Frank's head inches from where I stood. *Thank you*, he whispered to my mind, then gently nudged me aside. I lowered the shield and slid out of the way, reluctant to leave him exposed but reassured by the show of force I'd seen from Ros, who watched in silence as Georgie neared her son.

Talk to them, Frank thought, aiming at his mother but keeping the conversation intelligible for the rest of us. *Please. They'll listen to you.*

Even with me out of the way, Georgie kept the fence between them. *They're not entirely wrong, Frank.*

His head rose and recoiled. *Mom!*

What sort of life will the hatchling have here? Even if she learns to walk, she'll never fly. Never leave the barn, never hunt anything more challenging than a sheep, never mate...

She's alive, and she's all I have of Ione. I won't let them kill her.

And how do you intend to manage that? I assume you'll sleep again, son.

"*I* don't sleep," said Ros.

Georgie glanced back at her, then turned her focus on Frank once more. *She's not infallible. The barn is a dangerous place for the hatchling.* She took a step closer, slowly blinking in the artificial light of the orbs. *If you want her to live, then take her away. Glastonbury.*

I can't just take her there! he protested. *You know how quickly she'll grow, and there's no place to hide her—*

You've managed. Have Toula bind her.

She just hatched! he thought, aghast. *I can't...and why would you suggest such a thing? You've always said you hated that experience. It should be her choice...*

And what choice would that be? Georgie retorted. *There's nothing here for her but a life spent sleeping with one eye open. Maybe you can give her something more over there.*

Frank made no effort to hide his anguish. *She has her cousins here. Her family. Please, Mom, talk to them, tell them not to hurt her.*

Son—

Don't you want her here? She's my daughter, don't you want her? When that garnered no response, he asked, *Don't you want me?*

Georgie remained silent.

Mom?

She sighed and retreated a pace. *I'm sorry, Frank.*

Mom, please, he begged, stretching closer to the fence as she moved away. *Just once, could you want me? Want us?*

I do want you here, she replied. *But we can't have that. Not if you want Aurora to live.*

I felt more than heard Frank's heartbreak. *Like always, yeah? It's them or me.*

At that, at least, Georgie paused in her departure. *I can't change who you are. And I know in my deepest core that you will be miserable if you try to keep her alive in this place. Go where you can be happy. Where she may have a chance.*

Where you don't have to look at us, he snapped back.

If Frank's thoughts were red with his pain and anger, Georgie's were the placid blue of a still lake. *That's not true. I want the best for you, and you won't find it here. You have always been my strongest son*, she added, a note of tenderness coloring the thought. *But your strength is unlike your brothers', and neither you nor I can protect the hatchling forever. Take her tonight, before she knows much of this place. If she doesn't remember her true form, then maybe she won't miss it.*

You don't even want to see her first? he thought bitterly. *She's still asleep. You're content to look from a distance?*

You will need to be strong for her, Georgie replied, then lumbered back into the barn.

Mom! MOM! he called, but she never turned around.

When I phoned Toula to tell her what had happened, she canceled her remaining afternoon meetings and hurried to Faerie in her semi-professional best. Aurora continued to sleep off her feast, having missed every threat from her aunts and uncles, and Toula stood over the unconscious hatchling, rubbing her chin as she thought. "Wow," she finally said, "I forget how small you guys start off."

She's petite, thought Frank, who'd opened his protective circle only upon Toula's arrival.

"Petite? Hell, she'd fit in the back of a pickup truck."

What do we do? She's so young…

"The spell takes relative age into account—that's not the problem. I'm just concerned about the ethics of putting a transformation bind on a newborn when it's not a life-and-death situation."

"You weren't here earlier," Helen muttered. "Do it, Pavli."

She looked up at Frank, then back at the sleeping hatchling, and softly exhaled. "Okay. I'll do my best for her. But let's take care of you first, Frank."

I was never quite certain of the etiquette when Frank's bind was going on or coming off. While nudity didn't seem to bother him, I erred on the side of prudishness and averted my eyes while Toula worked. I felt the bind take effect only by the sudden rush of wind behind me—the act of condensing a large being into a much smaller space brought with it a little turbulence—but Toula's reaction made me turn around, clothing be damned: "*Frank*, good God! Where's the rest of you?"

Even in human guise, there had always been a *lot* of Frank: he stood a little over six and a half feet tall, and while he didn't come across as a bodybuilder, he was solidly built, the sort of man one wouldn't mind seeing shirtless and wouldn't want to fight in a dark alley. The Frank I saw sprawled in the grass was a shell of himself, still muscular beneath his pale skin but without an ounce of fat to flesh himself out. His face in particular showed the ravages of his monthlong near-fast, his red eyes sunken above too-prominent cheekbones and an uncomfortably sharp jaw. Slowly, he eased himself upright until he could sit, then nodded his thanks when a T-shirt and a pair of jeans appeared around him.

"Here," I said, offering him a hand and bracing myself. His grip was strong as ever, but I had to do more than merely steady him to pull him to his bare feet. Frank stumbled and clutched at my shoulders, and I counterbalanced while he closed his eyes.

"Okay, there?" I asked.

"Dizzy," he croaked, his voice rough with disuse.

"No surprise," said Toula. "You must be starving. Want a burger or—"

"I'm fine." He released me and took a few test steps until his gait was even. "Aurora."

Though she seemed uncertain about Frank, Toula

crouched beside the hatchling and began to whisper. The spell exploded in the magical spectrum, no less powerful for her smaller body, and what remained when the spots cleared from my vision was a sleeping child about the size of a one-year-old, a girl as pale as her father but topped with a shock of bright blue hair. She lay sprawled almost on her stomach, her right arm tucked beneath her and her malformed left arm sticking out to the side.

"Big for a newborn," Sam murmured beside me.

"Yeah," Joey replied, "but consider how mature they are when they hatch. Dragons bypass the floppy phase."

"And we'll speed her along," said Toula, willing a diaper and soft white onesie onto Aurora. Pulling a pink blanket from the ether, she gently lifted the baby from the grass, cradling her head in the crook of her arm, and wrapped her before she could chill in the cool predawn. "Let's see, now," she said, and passed a hand over Aurora's head, turning her blue hair white-blonde like her father's. Pulling back the blanket enough to see Aurora's short arm, she whispered until the missing half of the limb appeared, complete with fingers that curled and clutched at the edge of the blanket in her sleep. "It's not a perfect fix," she told Frank, "and that hand will never be as strong or coordinated as her real one. It's more or less hard illusion, but then again, so is the rest of a transformation bind."

"Can you repair her heart?" he asked.

"I'd rather let Bee do it. And she very well may have to break the bind to work on it," she added, "but this should do the baby for now. Let's see about language skills…"

Aurora's little eyebrows furrowed while Toula implanted English and Fae into her mind, but she was a sound sleeper. With that task accomplished, Toula carried her to Frank, who warily watched their approach.

Toula's smile spoke more of reassurance than pleasure. "Have you ever held a baby?"

He had to think about the question. "Allie. Once."

"Thought so. She should be strong enough to hold her

own head up, but you're going to want to support it, just in case. Bend your arm like mine…good, that's it," she directed as Frank mirrored her pose. "Okay, I'm going to transfer her…"

She shifted the bundle into Frank's waiting arms, and he stared down at Aurora's transformed face, clean of blood but so different than it had been moments before.

"You don't have to hold her like a bomb, but don't drop her," said Toula, and looked around our small huddle. "Uh…suggestions, anyone?"

Ros and Sam could only shrug, and there was no help from Joey and Helen, who hadn't met their daughter until she was ten.

No expert herself, Toula clapped Frank on the shoulder and adjusted Aurora's blanket. "You'll figure it out. Ready to go?"

He tightened his grip on his daughter and carried her through the gate Toula provided. Glancing back at the barn before I followed them, I caught a glimpse of Georgie inside the doorway, silent and still.

Frank seemed lost as I accompanied him back to his flat, his eyes blank and unfocused, his steps as unsteady as a sleepwalker's. I found myself catching his elbow from time to time, and he reacted with quick, surprised jerks and flashes of embarrassment. "It's okay," I said as we climbed the stairs of his residential tower. "You've been away for two months, and you've been starving yourself. Take it slowly."

I'd never had occasion to visit Frank's flat. Like most in the castle, his could be unlocked with a facial-recognition spell—a plus, seeing as he'd had no way to bring a key with him to Faerie—and he let me open the door while he carried Aurora inside. I set about turning on the few lamps and opening the blinds to admit the afternoon sunlight, and when I finished, I found Frank standing in the middle of the spartan living room, his expression inscrutable but his mind radiating feelings of weariness, fear, and despair.

"Sit down before you fall over," I said, guiding him to the plush brown couch—bachelor furniture, homely but comfortable. The rest of the room was much the same: a wooden coffee table with a pair of water rings and a collection of nicks and scratches, mismatched end tables, a serviceable TV on the wall, a faded green rug tying the space together. I willed away two months' worth of dust, but otherwise, the place was clean. Inspecting the rest of the flat, I found a poorly stocked kitchen—Frank had never shown an interest in cooking—a bedroom containing a king-sized bed, a lamp, and a wardrobe, a spare room lined with loaded bookshelves and plastic boxes of odds and ends, and a surprisingly tidy bathroom, the counter bare but for Frank's dark glasses and a lone toothbrush in a ceramic holder.

I returned to the spare room, wondering what to do about a nursery for Aurora. She was already too large for a bassinette, and with the speed of draconic growth, she'd be out of a crib before long. Hearing footsteps behind me, I found Frank on the threshold, still clutching the baby. "You've got quite a library here," I said.

His mouth twitched into an approximation of a fleeting smile. "I'm meant to be a hoarder, am I not?"

"Stuffed the gold and jewels in your mattress, huh?"

"Who wants to sleep on *that*?" He sighed and leaned against the ecru wall. "What am I to do, Kitty? They're right, I don't know how to raise her—"

"No parent does. Come with me," I said, leading him to the bedroom next door. The crib was the product of a moment's thought, white with a motif of pink and purple ribbons, and I added a mobile of pastel stars and planets to the headboard. "This should do her for the time being," I said, patting the slatted side. "If you want to keep your library, we can make a room for Aurora—my flat's had a new loft ever since Quinn and Eadwig moved in. Just tell us what you want."

He frowned at the crib. "Why does she need that? To keep her contained?"

"So she doesn't fall out of bed during the night. Babies don't bounce," I reminded him.

"Why can't she sleep with me? There's room enough," he said, nodding to the neat, duvet-covered bed, devoid of anything approaching a decorative pillow.

I thought of Neve and her five dragonets, all crammed into a snoring pile, and tried to be gentle. "It's safest for her to sleep alone. No accidental squishing that way."

Though he seemed unconvinced, Frank eased Aurora down into her new crib, adjusting the blanket so that her face was clear. Her mouth opened, exposing her few baby teeth, but she didn't wake with the light jostling.

Unburdened, Frank lowered himself to the foot of the bed and stared at the wall, and I squeezed his shoulder. "Stay there, okay?" I murmured. "Did I see a coffeemaker in the kitchen?"

He nodded. "Grounds are in the pantry."

"Great. You wait here, and I'll put a pot on. Black, yeah?"

"Thanks."

My enchantment-made coffee leaving much to be desired, I took advantage of Frank's kitchen, and soon, the flat smelled like French roast. "Here you go," I whispered, carrying a steaming mug back into Frank's room while trying not to wake the baby. "This should help with the jetlag…"

But Frank was in no condition for a drink. He silently sobbed with his face in his hands, his too-thin back shaking as he muffled the noise.

I put the mug on the wooden floor, sat beside him, and rubbed his arm until he raised his head, revealing wet cheeks and bloodshot eyes. Before he could speak, I hugged him, expecting that he would awkwardly pat my back and break contact as usual. Instead, he clung to me with rib-cracking strength and wept on my shoulder, and I held on, trying to sort through the scraps projecting from his thoughts. Sorrow, of course—so much sorrow, for Aurora, for Ione, for his dead sons, for himself. The sharp pain of old wounds freshly ripped open. Loss in its multifaceted agony. Loneliness. Fear for his daughter. Guilt over what he'd done to her, guilt that she'd been born less than perfect.

And there, a flicker of comprehension: *This is why they hug. They offer strength.*

Frank had almost brought himself under control again when Aurora finally woke. She kicked at the blanket, then began wordlessly broadcasting her disorientation and distress. Frank and I jumped up and hurried to the crib, and he reached down to stroke the baby's face, speaking reassurance to her mind. I heard her confusion— hatchlings had no volume control to their thoughts—but she seemed more perplexed than afraid. She could hear the voice she identified as "Mama," but the face looming over her was different.

I'm here, Frank told her, guiding her thoughts toward words. *It's me. Daddy.*

Her little brow knit. *Mama?*

Daddy, he repeated. *You're safe, my dearest. Nothing can hurt you here.*

That was, I mused, perhaps a bit optimistic for a castle filled with wizards, but there was no sense in quibbling around a newborn. "Are you hungry?" I asked, leaning over the crib until her red eyes fixed on me.

Hungry, she confirmed, and turned her attention back to Frank. *Mama, hungry.*

"You know, we can worry about gender later," Frank muttered, and carefully lifted her from the crib. Holding her under her arms, he studied her while she squirmed, then pulled her to his shoulder and let her cheek rest atop it. As he steadied her, he patted her bottom, and Aurora voiced her discomfort. "Uh…Kitty?" he asked.

I sized up the remaining space in Frank's bedroom and created a piece of furniture approximating a changing table. "Let me preface this by saying that my experience with babies is about as minimal as yours," I said, and pointed to the padded tabletop. "Put her down on her back."

He did as instructed, and I unsnapped her clothing to see the condition down below. "Wet, I think. Hang on, I can do this…"

A stack of passable diapers manifested on the shelf beneath Aurora, and I unfolded one, hoping I'd gotten the parts right. "Okay, little miss," I told her, keeping my voice light, "let's get you dry, and then we'll see about something to eat."

Hungry, she insisted, and whined as I pulled back the tapes.

Diapers were supposed to have wipes, I recalled, and a host of creams and powders I couldn't name. Out of my depth, I switched the offending diaper, tossed it into the ether, and dressed Aurora again. "Here, Dad," I said, passing him the baby. "I'm going to call for reinforcements."

Frank held her close and stroked her back. "Really, I don't want to bother anyone—"

"You're exhausted, and you've got a newborn on your hands," I interrupted, yanking my phone from my pocket. "Hold tight. This shouldn't take long."

"**F**orget petit fours," said Sylvester when I opened the door for him and Bob. The two came loaded down with freezer bags of meat. "Half a tenderloin, several kilos of mince, and there was a special on mutton," he said, marching toward the kitchen, then noticed Frank sitting at the table with Aurora, both of them overwhelmed by the influx of people. "Welcome back! Congratulations! Have you got a blender?"

I sent Marcus home for ours, and soon, Sylvester was decanting a pinkish slurry of raw beef and whole milk into a large baby bottle. "There," he said, widening the hole in the nipple to accommodate the thick sludge. "That should hit the spot. Warm this, Kitty."

Frank regarded the bottle quizzically as I heated it in my hand, but Lakshmi came to the rescue. "Here, let me," she said, and cooed over Aurora as she propped the baby in her lap. "Oh, what a dear! Rodney, have you seen her?"

Her husband, a reedy, bespectacled man in a gray vest, drew closer and beamed. "Sweet lamb," he declared. "Frank, she's beautiful."

"You realize that's a bind you're seeing, yes?" he replied as Aurora gnawed at the nipple.

Rodney chuckled, then pointed to the den, where I'd convinced the television to play a slideshow of Aurora's baby pictures. "I saw the real thing, and I stand by my assessment."

Considering that Rodney's first encounter with Frank unbound had resulted in screaming, I was proud of his progress.

"Darling, do you suppose she'll take a bottle?" he continued, turning to Lakshmi. "Reptiles don't nurse."

"Aurora?" said Frank. She looked up from the problem of the bottle—teaching the hatchling her name had taken merely minutes. "Don't bite. Watch," he said, and mimed a sucking motion. When that garnered only confusion from her, he must have followed up with a mental tutorial, as her eyes suddenly widened at the first hit of food. Within seconds, she'd established a rhythm and was greedily downing her meal.

"Like this, you see," Lakshmi told Frank. "Support her head, make her comfortable, and if she won't latch, try shifting positions. Rohan would only nurse if I were standing, the little devil."

"That little devil is giving us our first grandchild, remember," said Rodney, nudging his wife in the arm.

"And he'll get what's coming to him," she replied with a fond smile. "Goodness, she's hungry. It's all right, pet, it won't escape," she said, adjusting Aurora on her lap. "There's more where that came from...yes?" she called into the kitchen.

"Prepping," Bob called back, having donned a white apron with *Sous Chef* stitched across the front—a complement to Sylvester's, which matched but for the *Chef* label. "We need more bottles. Artur," he called into the den between pulses of the whirring blender, "spare a hand?"

While she multiplied the empties on the counter, Marcus dropped a plate laden with bacon and sausage in front of Frank, followed by one of the dozen bottles of hot sauce in his refrigerator. "You're not leaving the table until that's gone. Eat."

"I'm fine," Frank protested.

"You look sickly," said Marcus, and Lakshmi and Rodney nodded their agreement. "Go on, eat."

"Might as well get on her schedule," remarked Madison, Antony's wife, who was barely restraining Allie from crowding the baby. "Eat when she gives you a chance, sleep when she lets you. Now, that's the biggest newborn I've ever seen"—Aurora had to weigh at least twenty pounds—"so maybe her stomach's large enough that she won't want a feed every few hours."

"Maybe in a week or two," Frank mumbled through sausage. "She ate before we left."

Madison grimaced in sympathy. "This will pass, dear. And once she's a little older, *this* one is available for babysitting purposes," she added, giving her daughter's braid a tug.

"Payback," Antony called from the couch.

By the time Lakshmi was demonstrating how to burp a baby, the rest of the Team had arrived, plus Beth. Ted brought Oreos and beer, Daphne lugged in several more bags of steak filched from the castle freezers, and Mal walked in with his phone's speaker engaged. "Hi!" he said as Frank took Aurora back from Lakshmi. "I called my grandmother for you."

The gesture was about more than passing on congratulations—Rohese Stowe had raised thirteen children. "First thing," she said over the speaker, "is she eating?"

"Under control," Lakshmi replied.

"Good. Dry?"

I made a face at the phone. "Last I checked, but someone who knows babies should probably stock the changing table…"

Madison rose and headed for Frank's bedroom, readying her wand as she went. "On it."

"Blankets? Bedding? Clothing? Has he got a proper bath?"

Lakshmi, who was never far from a notepad, had already pulled one and a golf pencil from the embroidered pocket of her orchid sari. "On the list…and bibs…burping cloths…teething rings…"

The experienced parents in earshot collectively winced.

While Rohese and Lakshmi planned, Madison returned, cocking her thumb over her shoulder toward the bedrooms. "You don't want a nursery?" she asked Frank. "Trust me, she's going to need her own storage. For such small people, they come with *tons* of accessories."

"High chair…" Lakshmi muttered.

"Car seat, maybe," added Rohese. "Oh, and what about one of those bouncers? She can't be walking yet…"

Beth tapped Marcus's shoulder. "Do you want to make a new room?"

"I'll supervise," Artur interjected, heading down the hall. "Loft?"

Madison hurried after her, with Marcus and Beth on her heels. "Same floor would be ideal," she said. "You don't want to do stairs in the night with a baby. What about the bathroom situation?"

"Dibs on decoration!" Daphne called, jogging to catch up.

As they worked, the rest of us coaxed Frank into the den, and he placed Aurora on the couch beside him. She rolled onto her knees and stopped, unsure of the mechanics of movement, then flopped onto her side and was soon asleep again, full and comfortable. While Lakshmi outfitted the flat with the necessary baby gear and Rohese calmly instructed Frank over the phone, Antony helped Madison carry an assortment of tiny clothes and blankets out of the new room and spread the bounty on the coffee table. Though he was plainly overwhelmed and exhausted, Frank paid attention to lessons on the care, feeding, cleaning, and dressing of an infant, took note of the bottles with which Sylvester and Bob had packed his freezer and the new bottle warmer, and was persuaded to examine and approve the new nursery, including Daphne's aesthetically improved versions of my crib and table. All the while, he kept his plate of meat close at hand, absently but steadily eating. Marcus refilled the platter twice before the impromptu shower wound down and the Team took their leave, the parents in particular stressing to Frank that he could call on them with any problems.

Last to go were Ted and me, as our boss had stuck around to give the place a final inspection and tidying. While I moved a few bottles into the fridge to thaw, Ted wrapped a blanket around Aurora and passed her to her father. "Didn't want her little arms and legs to get cold," he explained. "Her tummy feels warm enough…"

A look of dawning horror crossed Frank's face. "Fire. *Shit.* There's dark magic here, what if she—"

"Ahead of you," I said, and pointed to the smoke detectors that Madison and Artur had installed around the place. "Fire extinguishers in the nursery and under the bathroom and kitchen sinks."

"And if something gets out of hand, you've got a phone full of wizards, faeries, and whatnot to call for help," Ted added. "We mean it, you know that. Don't hesitate."

Sighing, Frank shifted Aurora's weight in his arms. "I'm sorry for the trouble today, I didn't mean—"

"What *trouble*? Did anyone look even slightly put upon?"

"I…everyone's busy…"

Ted gripped his arm and stared up at him over his glasses. "Frank. Look at me." When Frank glanced down, Ted insisted, "You're not a burden. The Team is a family, and this is what families do. Besides, I've made it a personal goal to be 'Uncle Ted' to as many of my colleagues' children as possible, and this is only my second chance, so, you know, I wasn't going to miss this homecoming party."

For the second time that day, Frank's eyes began to fill, and Ted, a hugger to the last, didn't disappoint. "Glad to have you back, friend. You're still on paternity leave, now, but if you wanted to bring the munchkin downstairs, I'm sure no one would mind."

"Her food's ready when you need it," I told Frank, "and Marcus stocked the rest of the fridge for you. Just a word of warning: he's never made a turkey that's exactly right, but he's improving. Maybe save that for last. Come on," I said, taking him by the elbow, "it looks like you could both do with a nap. Let me show you how the baby monitor works."

But there was no need. Frank placed Aurora in the middle of his bed and curled around her as well as he could. She roused slightly with the jostling of the mattress, but I overheard his wordless reassurance, or at least its contours: *Safe. Always safe.*

Ted cut the lights, and as Frank joined Aurora in sleep, we made a final pass through the nursery. Taking in Daphne's handiwork—if she hadn't been such a competent wizard, she would have made an excellent interior designer—Ted nodded approval, then pulled out his wand to add a last touch. With a mutter and a flick, a plush blue dragon appeared in the crib, its wings floppy and teeth covered. "In case the little one gets lonely," he whispered to me, and we quietly saw ourselves out.

CHAPTER 11

Though the Games were behind us, Magus Popova had earned a break, and that meant a week alone in the Greek isles. Under other circumstances, Quinn might have been disappointed for the extended respite, even with Popova's rigorous training, but she had the Archives to keep herself entertained. With Quinn having been involved, however tangentially, in revealing the rest of Simon Magus's diary, Jude had passed far beyond warming to her, and now enthusiastically welcomed her presence in the Archives. He'd set aside a cubicle for her, arranged for her to have a trainee archivist's credentials, and encouraged her more than ever to shadow him. Judging by her rapid flow of excited stories at dinner, Quinn was in nerd heaven.

Having spent the day deep in their restricted complex with her phone silenced, Quinn had missed the impromptu baby shower, but that knowledge did nothing to dampen her mood as she drew Eadwig back to the table after dinner and turned on her computer. Flashing her most persuasive smile, she showed him the screen and said, "Jude's letting me read a digital copy of the full diary. I mean, it's still got a couple of pages missing, but all the new stuff is here. How would you feel about giving me a hand?"

Eadwig considered the screen, his mouth tightening. "I know of nothing else hidden in that book, and without the book itself, I can't search. This is only a copy."

"Sorry, I wasn't clear." Zooming in on a half-page of text, she asked, "Notice anything odd?"

Curious, I left my as-yet-unmixed cake on the counter and read over Eadwig's shoulder. "*Ooh*," I said, "it's not all in Latin."

"Exactly. Jude says there's a sprinkling of Greek, but that bit right there looks like Old English," she replied, tapping at the screen to highlight the characters. "Would you like to guess how many archivists are fluent in that language?"

"A handful?"

"None." Quinn turned in her chair and smirked at my surprise. "I know, right?"

"Bob Norge is at least close to fluent," I told her.

"Yeah, Jude mentioned him, but he said that since Bob joined the Team, he doesn't really count. Anyway," she said to Eadwig, "Jude said that every European wizard of note from that period wrote in Latin, maybe with a little Greek mixed in for the really esoteric bits. As far as Old English goes, only a few hundred manuscripts have survived at all, and the only one in the Archives is that other magus's notebook I was working with. It's just not a language that warrants much study around here. Like, if someone needs to translate, it's done with a grammar book open. *Beowulf* is interesting but not exactly relevant, you know?"

Having read that one only in translation, I had to agree.

"But seeing as *someone* appears to have a working knowledge of Old English," she continued, grinning at Eadwig, "and since someone was so nice and helped me with my last manuscript…"

He made a show of cracking his knuckles. "I suppose my schedule could be somewhat open."

"Ah, yes, your very important TV schedule," she teased. "You know you can only watch so much of that before your brain melts out your ears, right?"

"She's kidding," I interjected as Eadwig's eyes widened in alarm. "*Right*, Quinn?"

"Oh, God, yes," she hastily replied, taken aback by his

reaction. "Sorry, my parents used to say that to me all the time…"

Eadwig's panic turned to a look of reproach. "There is a box in that room," he said, pointing to the kitchen, "that makes food hot by creating a light and spinning a plate around. How am I meant to know what's dangerous if nothing makes sense to begin with?"

Deciding that Eadwig's lesson in the mechanics of microwave ovens could wait for another day, I left them to their reading, though I wondered if I shouldn't cut the translation project short. We still didn't know with any certainty what connection Eadwig had to the diary or why a teenage boy would possess the secret to unlocking pages that the finest minds in the Arcanum had overlooked for decades. But seeing as Toula had instructed us not to share her concerns with him, I couldn't very well forbid him from helping Quinn—nor could I tell Toula that he was digging into the diary without possibly landing Quinn in massive trouble. When I went to bed, Eadwig was hard at work, sitting in front of Quinn's computer with a stack of paper and pens beside him.

To my annoyance, I woke around four the next morning. Marcus remained unconscious beside me, and so I rose in silence, trying not to disturb him. Technically, he could have managed for a few days without sleep—he was over two thousand years old, after all, and I'd seen him plow through without resting during a rough crunch week at work—but all the same, I hated to wake him. Pulling on my robe, I eased the door open and slipped into the den, then spotted Eadwig slumped over the kitchen table. The computer was dark and pushed back, his transcription pages shuffled off to the side, and he'd folded his arms on the placemat as a pillow.

I thought back to my uni days and the many times I'd taken just such a quick nap that had turned into a multi-hour snooze, and gently shook his shoulder. "Eadwig?" I whispered. "Do you want to go to bed?"

He bolted awake, mumbling incomprehensibly, then noticed me and seemed to remember where he was. "I'm sorry, I…how late…"

"It's getting close to dawn. Go on upstairs, your bed's got to be more comfortable than the table."

But he shook his head and rubbed his neck. "No, I need to continue. My reading—"

"Can wait until the sun's up. I know Quinn appreciates your help, but you don't have to work around the clock."

"This has nothing to do with Quinn." Continuing his neck massage, he looked up at me with a hopeful smile. "Is there coffee?"

By the time I had an oversized mug and the sugar bowl on the table, Eadwig had awakened Quinn's computer and was reviewing his notes. "What's the big rush?" I asked, pulling out the chair beside him. "Did you find something interesting?"

"Much. Theoretical musings, personal information…and this." He selected a sheet of paper from the stack and placed it on the table between us. "Here," he said, jabbing his finger at a long block of text. "Wait, I will show you the original…"

Eadwig's handwriting was tiny and almost perfectly straight, the letters angular and faint with the rapidity of his writing…which appeared to be in Old English. "This bothers me," he said, repositioning the computer to give me a better view. "I cannot tell you why."

The screen was likewise illegible to me, a scan of runes marching across the parchment. "What does it say?"

"Nothing clear. I haven't made the second translation," he said apologetically, "but I am not as comfortable with runes, and this part of the diary was slow for me."

"Faster than I'd have been."

My reward was a perfunctory smile before he returned his attention to the screen. "This passage occurs in about the middle of the diary. See this?" he asked, tapping a line of runes. "It says 'blodig calic.'"

"Meaning?"

"Bloody cup, I believe. Maybe chalice. The words..." He struggled briefly, then tapped the side of his head in frustration. "They're in here, and I understand them when I see them, but..."

"It'll come more naturally in time," I assured him. "I went through the same thing—could carry on a full conversation in Fae, but if you'd asked me to describe the nuances of words..." I patted his arm and scanned his translation, which, if unreadable to me, at least appeared in a Latinized script. "This bloody cup could be metaphorical. Maybe it's a reference to the Eucharist."

"No."

I was surprised by his confidence. "You're sure?"

He nodded. "Something is wrong with the cup. I don't know what or why, but I *know* it's a bad thing. The writing shows that."

"What do you mean?"

"Whenever the writer—Simon—had something private to note, he used my language instead of Latin," Eadwig explained. "And if it was particularly private, he used runes." He paused, a guilty expression flashing across his face. "This Simon, he had many, uh...women."

"So I've heard," I replied.

"And some men."

"Heard that, too. Did he go to runes for his affairs?"

"Not usually. But I don't understand—why use my language for his secret matters?"

I sipped my coffee and glanced again at the scanned page. "Simon died in the late eleventh century, probably about seventy years after you were buried," I explained. "He kept his base in England, but he traveled far abroad, and he had magi around him who spoke many languages. Everyone who could read and write either knew or learned Latin, but almost no one who wasn't born on this island would have been able to read your language, especially if he used runes. Simon put protective spells on the diary, we know that much, but maybe this was another line of defense against snoops."

"Ah." He considered the computer and his sheaf of papers, then downed the contents of his still-warm mug in three long gulps. "I should keep reading. Before I do, how do I make more of this drink?"

The responsible adult in me cautioned that Eadwig had less than a month's exposure to caffeine and should ease into the habit, but considering my end-of-term consumption back in the day, I had no room to talk.

"Come with me," I said, ushering him into the kitchen. "The machine doesn't bite. Just promise me that if your hands start shaking for no good reason, you'll have a glass of water."

For a brand-new parent, Frank seemed almost calm and well-rested when I checked in that morning. Then again, having a child who could tell him exactly what she wanted had to be helpful.

"She can't walk yet," he said, watching from the safety of the couch as Aurora scooted around the rug in an ungainly crawl, stopping every so often to headbutt her stuffed dragon. "Her balance isn't steady. And she doesn't trust the fake arm—I've seen it buckle twice when she put her full weight on it, so she's favoring her right side. Went in a circle there for a bit," he added, and drank his breakfast. I wasn't going to fight him for it—Frank took his coffee black, bitter, and strong enough to give the average man heart palpitations, and I'd learned through experience not to accept anything from him unless he swore it had been brewed at a strength approximating safe for human consumption.

"She's less than a day old," I pointed out. "For a newborn, that's pretty remarkab—oh, *easy*, there," I said as Aurora abandoned her attack on her toy in favor of my shin. "Hey, baby, you're going to give yourself a headache." I hoisted her off the floor and onto my lap, and then I made the rookie error of attempting to wipe a disturbingly reddish-brown streak from the corner of her mouth with a moistened thumb. Aurora didn't have many teeth, but her bite came without hesitation, and I yelped in pain.

"*No*," Frank snapped, prying her jaws open. "No biting. What did I tell you?"

Aurora's thoughts shifted from playful to confused and upset, and I ignored my throbbing hand to pull her against me before she cried. "It's okay, sweetie, you didn't mean it," I soothed. "I'm not angry."

She felt for my thoughts, saw the pain I was trying to hide, and looked to Frank for an explanation. *Mama?*

"Shit, Kitty, I'm sorry," he said, his face coloring as he examined my injured thumb. "Did she break the skin?"

It was red but not bleeding, and I played it off. "Nah. Kid's got good reflexes."

"It's how hatchings play with each other, there's teeth everywhere, I—"

"Frank, she's a *baby*. They all go through a biting phase. Isn't that right?" I said in a singsong voice, bouncing Aurora on my knee. "You just want to put everything in your mouth, don't you, cutie?" Remembering the teething rings we'd hidden in the freezer the day before, I beckoned the door open, and one flew into my hand. "Try this," I told Aurora, holding it up to her lips. She mouthed it tentatively, waited for a reprimand from her father, then chomped onto the plastic and managed to grasp the ring in her chubby hand on her third attempt.

I gave Aurora a pony ride on my lap while she grunted with delight over her new toy. "How're we holding up?"

Frank sighed. "She's alive, I'm alive, no scorch marks on the walls yet."

"She's eating?"

"Heartily. She'll want another bottle soon," he said, consulting the clock on the wall. "I thought we could use those for a few days, then transition her to real meat…"

"With *those* teeth? There's a reason that baby food is mostly purées." Turning Aurora to see her face, I said, "Sweetie, open your mouth for me, will you?" Once Frank reassured her, she did as I asked, showing off her tiny teeth and undisturbed gums. "Yeah, I wouldn't give her a raw steak just yet. We should ask Dr. Powell."

Distracted by the examination, Aurora dropped her teether, frowned, then thought, *Hungry.*

"Right on schedule," said Frank, pushing himself from the couch. "I'll get it—"

"Let me." He sank down again with gratitude in his eyes, and I balanced Aurora on my hip as I selected a bottle of meat slurry and warmed it with a burst of enchantment. She grabbed for it, her fingers still too uncoordinated to grip on the first try, and I carried her back to the couch for her feeding. "That's a girl," I murmured as she gulped down her breakfast. Glancing at Frank, who was supervising the proceedings, I said, "What if I called Pritam over today? Surely Dr. Powell could work her in."

"I don't want to bother them—"

"Okay, first, it's Dr. Powell's job, and second, Pritam would probably move in for research purposes if you invited him. You're not bothering anyone." He made no secret of his doubt, and I fought the urge to hug him again—not with a hungry hatchling and a bottle of reddish goop in my hands. "I know the last month was hell," I said softly, "but you're here now, and we're glad to have you."

When he spoke again, his voice was low. "I finally cried for her. Ione."

"Feel better?"

"No, but it felt right. An outlet. Stupid, I know," he muttered, "it's nothing but the bind—"

"That bind's been part of your life for a long time. If tears help, they're not stupid."

"Still unnatural." He watched as his daughter

contentedly suckled. "I grew up in my own body. What am I doing to her? If *this* is all she ever knows…"

"Talk to Artur," I suggested.

Frank huffed. "There's a slight difference between growing up in a body of the wrong sex and growing up in one of the wrong *species*."

"I know, but what's the better option here?" He said nothing, and as Aurora finished her meal, I suggested, "Why don't you wait a few weeks, get her heart straightened out, then maybe you could talk to your mom and—"

"I'm not putting my daughter at risk," he said, and took the empty bottle back to the kitchen. "If Mom wants to see us again, then she can damn well make the trip. And if she has to do so on her hands and knees, that'll be a good start."

"Understood." I burped Aurora over my shoulder and carried her to her father. "Let me call Pritam, okay? The sooner they start working on her, the better."

He took her from me and propped her against his chest, and one of her arms snaked around his neck as she peeked over his shoulder. "If they have time to see us," he replied, stroking Aurora's back through her T-shirt.

To no one's surprise but Frank's, Dr. Powell gladly cleared her morning appointments, and I escorted Pritam in while she was weighing Aurora. I'd tried to prepare the herpetologist for the situation at Arc 2, but he still did a double-take upon seeing the compressed version of Frank in the examination room. "Goodness," he said with a nervous laugh. "That…*is* a change. And, ehm…"

"Scrawny, I know. I lost a lot of weight," said Frank, answering his unspoken question. "A few weeks of dining hall cuisine should remedy that."

"And if not, you're coming back to see me," Dr. Powell cut in, then turned to Pritam, her bushy red curls bouncing as she extended her hand. "Dr. Bhat? Bee Powell. Pleasure."

"Pritam," he replied with a smile, and dropped his bag on a chair.

"Welcome to Glastonbury. Minor Arcanum, yes?"

"Indeed. Nice space you have," he said, turning to take in the infirmary. "Had you told me two months ago that I would be visiting an Arcanum compound to treat a dragon, I would have thought you mad," he added, chuckling. "Speaking of whom, how is the patient?"

"Squirmy. Yes, you're a squirmy girl, aren't you? Yes, you are," she said, reaching down to tickle Aurora's chin.

"*No biting!*" Frank yelled.

Dr. Powell flinched at his shout and retracted her hand, and Aurora, all wide-eyed innocence, kicked her legs and flicked her tongue at her.

"Sorry. Best to watch your fingers," he said, plucking Aurora from the scale. "Uh…where would you like her?"

"Table," said the doctor, giving them a bit of space as they passed. "Pritam, I've taken preliminary measurements, but with the bind as it is—"

"We can't be sure," he finished, peering at her computer. "And given our overall dearth of knowledge about the species…hm. Temperature is higher than I would expect."

"Warm-blooded," Frank offered.

"That, plus the internal combustion," said Dr. Powell, making passes over the baby with her wand. "I hope *someone's* nursery is outfitted with flame-retardant fabrics."

Pritam finished his scan and joined her at the examination table. "She seems large for a newborn…"

"Oh, certainly. That spell is working overtime—I'm surprised Toula knew what to do with her. Physically, I'd put her around a year, which, considering draconic growth patterns, isn't too surprising. Mentally, she seems more advanced than a year-old human, certainly in comprehension. Again, no great shock."

"You know something of dragons?"

She glanced up at him and grinned. "Spend enough time in Faerie, and you'll find yourself at the barn. My best friend sort of fostered this one," she said, nodding to Frank, "and I got the full report in real time. How is Ros, anyway?" she asked.

"Tired," said Frank. "She's the only reason Aurora lived to hatch, so…"

She whistled low. "Sam mentioned that. If you see them again before I do, tell them that Daisy and I haven't forgot dinner—she's been buried at work, and considering what Ros has been doing, we just haven't scheduled in a few months. Now, let's see if I can get past the bind…*ah*."

With a final tweak of the visualization spell, a projection of Aurora's true body appeared above her, stretching the length of the table and wiggling its legs and tail as Aurora perked, squealed, and reached for the glowing form. "Can we be still, dear?" Dr. Powell asked, smoothing Aurora's short hair. "We need to have a little look inside you."

Frank stepped into Aurora's line of sight, and her broadcasting thoughts warmed. "This won't hurt," he assured her, taking Dr. Powell's place at her head and pressing his hand against her scalp. She tried to butt against him, and he smiled sadly.

While Frank distracted his daughter and I provided a fresh teething ring, her medical team considered the projection, switching the views to see her systems individually and in combination. After a time, Dr. Powell tweaked the spell to show a second projection of Aurora's bound form, and she examined the two in tandem. Finally, as Aurora's stomach began to gurgle with mounting hunger, Dr. Powell drew Frank's attention to the pair of projections, both depicting the cardiovascular system within a ghostly outline of the patient. "Pritam's right, there's a small hole in her heart."

"Will it close on its own?"

She folded her arms and gave the projection another look, her mouth pursing in thought. "Let me preface this with the obvious: I'm no cardiologist, and this is not a human patient."

"Granted…"

"Considering the size and placement of the hole, if I had to decide, I would take a 'wait and see' approach. Bring her in every few weeks—maybe every week, considering how quickly she's going to grow—and reevaluate. But I can't give you anything more definite than that. Pritam?"

He shook his head. "This is far beyond my experience, too. That said, I don't believe she's in immediate danger. Her color seems healthy."

"Heartbeat is strong, respiration is good," Dr. Powell concurred. "I think we can afford to wait."

Frank, who continued to stroke Aurora's head, remained unconvinced. "What if you fixed it now? What's the harm?"

"The harm is that any surgery on a neonate is inherently risky," she replied. "Particularly *this* one, since Pritam and I would be doing a fair bit of guesswork. We'd have to do it with the bind off, and if something went wrong…" She cleared her throat. "Well, let's try to be positive about this. I say we give her a few weeks and see if her body will fix itself. If not, we'll go plan B."

"I agree," said Pritam. "Let her get stronger before we attempt something invasive. I mean…Bee, have you ever anesthetized an infant?"

"Only with magic. I'd rather not get into drugs, if we can avoid it." She patted Frank's arm and flashed a reassuring smile. "Bring her back in three days, eh? We'll get her sorted. By the way, what are you feeding her?"

Frank's response was cut short by a yelp from Pritam, who'd tried to touch Aurora's cheek and had received a bite instead. "Meat, mostly," Frank replied as Pritam sucked his injured finger. "And I think she's a bit peckish."

Having spent most of my morning with Frank, I decided to put off my appearance in the subbasement until the afternoon and headed to the flat for lunch. When I returned, however, I was surprised to find Eadwig working at the table alone, still in his pajamas. "Where's Beth?" I asked, going to the fridge to consider my options. "And have you eaten?"

"Artur took Beth to the courtyard some time ago," he replied, standing for a stretching break. "Beth did not seem entirely enthusiastic about it."

"*Ah.* Must be combat practice. Beth's on her summer school holiday, and I'm sure she'd rather sleep in. How early did they leave?"

"Shortly after you did."

I chuckled and pulled out the cold cuts. "Listen to experience: avoid Beth when they come back. She's going to be sore and in a *mood.* Sandwich?"

"Please." He leaned on the counter and watched as I hunted in the fridge for the multigrain loaf. "Quinn said to tell you that she's with Jude all day, and Marcus suggests…ehm…"—he plucked a scrap of paper from the table and sounded out the note—"fajitas?"

I could only imagine how Eadwig had spelled it. "That man has yet to meet a Tex-Mex dish he didn't like…and that would explain the flank steak defrosting in here. Yeah, we'll do fajitas for dinner." Taking a pair of plates from the cabinet, I asked, "How's your reading coming along?"

He rubbed at his eyes with the heels of his hands. "Frustrating."

"More runes?"

"That's one problem." He picked up his mug, took a sip, and grimaced. "Could you…"

A flicker of will was all it took to bring his drink back to scalding, and I reached for the mustard. "A touch on the esoteric side?"

Eadwig pondered the term, then nodded. "In places. But more basically, he wrote in code."

"Code?" I echoed. "What do you mean?"

"The further I read—the material that was written later—much of it is encoded. Coffee helps," he added, and took a long sip.

"Show me?"

"Sure." He pulled up a page on Quinn's computer, and I abandoned the sandwich fixings to read over his shoulder. "This passage here, for example," he said, drawing a red box around the middle of the page with his fingertip. "See the problem?"

"I'm not great with runes," I began, then squinted at the screen and realized that Eadwig wasn't directing me to futhorc. "Lowercase Greek. You can skip that part—Greek's one of the standard classical languages, and someone in the Archives can make that translation."

"It isn't Greek. Only the letters are."

"Come again?"

"A code, not Greek. See? Those are not real words." Eadwig shuffled through his papers until he produced a handwritten key linking the Greek characters to the futhorc runes…and then, oddly, to the Latin alphabet.

"Cheat sheet for you?" I asked, pointing to the last column.

He shook his head. "Necessary to keep my mind straight. Earlier in the diary, whenever he used runes, he wrote in my language. *This*, however, is written in Latin, or something close. Let me show you." He slipped an ink-covered scratch page to the top of the stack. "Look, here's one of the Greek lines in the code. Each of these characters corresponds to a known rune, which produces this," he said, pointing to a pair of lines near the bottom of the page. "But the runes are not my language—they are used to write an approximation of Latin words. Not all of the sounds are quite the same, but it's close enough that I can see what he did." The line below the Greek and the runes was legible to me, and Eadwig looked up to see my reaction to his work. "Your Simon must have been clever.

It's coming to me more easily as I practice, but this is slow translation."

"Shit," I muttered, and patted him on the back. "Good job. How the heck did you crack the code?"

Eadwig could only shrug. "The same way I found these pages—instinct. I saw it, I knew what he had done, but undoing it is not easy."

I quickly finished making our lunches and brought the plates to the table, and Eadwig cleared his papers away. "What was so important to Simon that he had to put it in code?" I asked. "Something more substantial than Arcanum gossip, I figure."

"Actually, some of it concerns Arcanum matters," he replied, and bit into his sandwich. "What do you call them—magi?"

"Yeah…"

"He didn't trust his. Thought some were plotting to kill him."

"No big surprise there," I replied. "Simon's magi were often the leaders of arcana he'd conquered. Kind of a consolation prize, see? And the Great War went on for fifty years, so I'm sure more than a few of them would have liked to see Simon out of a job by the end of it."

He chewed in contemplative silence, washing it down with his refreshed coffee. "He seemed to trust them less and less as the diary goes on."

"Paranoid, maybe. What else have you found?"

"More about the bloody cup," he said, and took another bite.

I waited impatiently for him to finish. "So, what is it? What does it do?"

It might have been my imagination, but I thought he seemed uneasy about the topic. "Simon wasn't certain. Or not yet—I haven't finished reading. He had theories."

"Such as…"

"It's a cup, he was sure of that, but he had heard conflicting information about its construction and its maker. Magical. He thought it would make its owner immortal."

At that, I pushed my lunch aside. "How?"

"He did not know. But he very much wanted to find it. He wrote all the stories in his diary—places it might be, people who might know of it."

"My God," I mumbled, slumping back against my chair. "Maybe Simon wasn't trying to conquer the world after all. He wanted to live forever."

"Oh, no, he most definitely wanted to conquer the world," said Eadwig. "Unless he lied to himself in his diary. His belief in the war seems unwavering, at least to the point I've read. But I think you're correct about the cup. Maybe he thought there was a way to defeat death with magic."

"If there is, then we still don't know of one, and we've had a thousand years to work on it. Magic can heal, but it can't stop death forever."

He gave me an odd, searching look. "And yet, *you* are immortal."

I wondered who had let that slip. Discussing that awkward fact around the Arcanum, even with the Team, always left me feeling as if I'd committed a faux pas—like I was a billionaire eating dinner with a group of people living paycheck to paycheck, casually dropping references to my yacht and my offshore holdings. I was raised a witch, unremarkable by Arcanum standards, but because I'd ignored the rule against touching unknown magical items, I'd accidentally stumbled onto quite a bit about myself that I was never meant to know...and in the process, I'd ended up more or less fae. While it was nice to never have to worry about aging, I still felt guilty bringing it up around my middle-aged and senior colleagues.

"How did you know about that?" I asked.

"Beth told me. You, Artur, and Marcus. I've said nothing about it to Quinn," he hastily added. "But it's a bloodline thing with you three, correct? You're not fully human."

"Yeah. And Quinn knows." I bit into my sandwich as a stalling tactic in case Eadwig had other uncomfortable questions to pose, but he took the hint and returned to his lunch.

When he was down to his chips, he looked at me until I met his stare, then murmured, "How do I know so much about the diary? The pages, the code…"

"We're still trying to figure that out," I replied.

While it was only a half-truth, Eadwig let the matter drop, and I rose to put on a fresh pot of coffee before I left him to his labors.

I'd been impressed by Eadwig's work, but Quinn was floored when she came home and heard the recap. "This is *incredible*," she said, riffling through his handwritten translation. "And you had to decode part of it?"

"I still am," he replied, massaging his wrist. "He used the same code throughout, and it's coming to me more quickly, but much of the last section is obscured. Tell Jude that the Greek is only used to hide Simon's thoughts."

"Will do, but why don't you put it aside for the night? You've done way more than I thought I was asking of you."

"I appreciate that, but I am making progress—"

"Shut it down, it's movie time!" Beth called from the den. "Ed, are you going to come hang out with me, or are you going to be boring?"

He looked at Quinn, who cocked her head toward the couch. "Go on. Dead dude's diary can wait, eh?"

"You're certain?"

She patted his head and lowered her voice. "Hard to believe, I know, but I was actually a teenager in the not-too-distant past. It's okay to have fun."

His smile took five years off his face, and he vaulted the back of the couch to plop onto the seat beside my sister. Marcus plied them with popcorn, that most exotic of treats, and they were still laughing at the television when the rest of the flat went to bed. Physical comedy worked, no matter one's century of birth.

But while I found Beth asleep on the couch at dawn, covered by an afghan and snoring, Eadwig had already resumed his translation work—and worryingly, he'd learned how to operate the coffeemaker. "Beth taught me last night," he whispered. "I did not want to disturb anyone."

"And I don't want you to get sick," I whispered back. "Pace yourself, bud."

He paid lip service to my concerns and returned to the task at hand, and I tiptoed around the kitchen until Artur emerged and shook Beth awake for another day of sparring.

At lunchtime, when Marcus and I stopped by the flat to check on Eadwig, we found him in his room, sitting cross-legged by the window and staring out at the town in the distance, a place where Dr. Powell had still forbidden him to go. "Is everything okay?" I asked, rapping twice on the door to announce our presence.

He twitched and spun around, startled to find us on the threshold. "You're back! When did you return?"

"Just now. Lost in your own head?" I teased.

With a nod, he stood and straightened his T-shirt. "The translation is finished."

Marcus's eyebrows rose. "That was fast. Fewer encoded sections at the end?"

"No, almost everything was encoded, but the process seems far simpler now." Crossing his arms, he chewed on his lip for a few seconds, then murmured, "Much of it was about the cup. I don't like it at all."

"The cup or the diary?" I asked.

"Both. They make my stomach twist." He hesitated again before adding, "I do not believe that Simon ever found it. Probably a good thing, considering the rest of his diary."

I shared a quick look with Marcus. "That bad, huh?"

"Near the end, he sounded almost mad. And he spoke of slaughter...so much death." The boy shivered and hugged himself more tightly. "I *hope* he never found the cup. If it truly does grant immortality, then he would be the last person I would want to locate it."

Marcus considered Eadwig for a moment, then thought, *If he's concerned, I can think of no greater expert on magical cups than Ted.*

You want to drag Ted into this? I replied.

You're opposed?

Do you remember what happened the last time Ted took us on a grail quest?

I watched a flash of memory flicker across his mind— me, cradled in his arms and screaming in pain as I clutched a sword I couldn't release. *Clearly*, he thought. *But if there is indeed a dangerous cup out there, Ted should know about it. Maybe it's already been located*, he mused. *We could put Eadwig at ease.*

Or we could get dragged out again on another wild goose chase, I countered, but I was already relenting. He had a point, though I was reluctant to expose the kid to the full force of Ted's enthusiasm.

"You should have a word with our boss," I told Eadwig, who'd waited awkwardly while Marcus and I debated. "Magical cups are his specialty."

"Quinn said the same of Jude," he replied. "Are there so many ensorcelled cups in existence?"

I pulled my phone from my pocket. "Niche field, and let's get Ted up here before Jude butts in."

A thirty-second explanation was all it took to lure Ted from his office, and within minutes, he was puffing on our welcome mat, out of breath but sporting a quasi-manic gleam in his blue eyes. He waited until I closed and locked the door behind him, then spotted Eadwig lurking by the kitchen table and beamed. "Did someone say 'Grail'?"

"Not exactly," I cautioned, following him to the table.

"Simon called it something else—"

"The blodig calic," Eadwig supplied.

Ted mulled that over as he took a seat. "Bloody chalice, sounds like. Not every bit of Old English got Normanized away. Right," he said, leaning toward Eadwig, "Kitty told me you got a ton of information out of the Magus's diary. I've been hearing rumors from the Archives since the weekend that something happened to that book, but they're a tight-lipped crowd. Were you planning on filling me in?" he asked, glancing my way.

"There were more pages hidden," Eadwig mumbled. "I know how to read them."

"*You* know something about the diary? How?"

"We don't know," I cut in, hoping the warning note in my voice would discourage Ted from prying. "Eadwig just does, and we're leaving it at that for the time being. But yeah, the diary's about four times longer than we thought it was. Simon was a crafty old bastard."

"And he had much to say about his blodig calic," said Eadwig, taking a glass of water from Marcus with a nod of gratitude. "What is this grail you were speaking of?"

Ted leaned back, adjusted his glasses, and clasped his hands across his stomach, which would have given him a professorial air had it not been for the bright hibiscus flowers printed on his shirt. "Well, now, a grail, in its most basic sense, is a vessel. The word probably comes from the Latin 'crater,' meaning a cup, bowl, depression"—Marcus offered a shrug of agreement—"and because Latin got funky when it went north, we end up with the Old French 'graal.' As long as there have been wizards, we've been casting spells on inanimate objects, so history is littered with magical cups and such. But when people talk about *the* Grail, they're usually referring to a warped version of a concept from early Christianity, the cup used at the Last Supper. You're familiar with—what am I saying," he muttered as Eadwig nodded, "you were trained by a priest, yeah?"

"Was the cup saved?" Eadwig asked. "I've heard of miraculous relics, but not that one."

"Because any so-called 'Holy Chalice' in existence today is almost certainly a later fake. I mean, come on, a group of wandering Jews rent a room for Passover and somehow get their hands on a cup made of at *least* semiprecious materials for the evening? Unlikely at best. But around the late twelfth century, there was a confluence in the literature of magical grails and *that* particular cup, giving rise to the 'san-graal'—the Holy Grail—so prevalent in the Arthurian canon. All of that is said by way of introduction—I don't for one minute believe that the Grail is holy. What I *do* believe, however, is that smoke usually points back to fire, and the Middle Ages are lousy with stories about powerful dishware."

"Artur never had any," I reminded him.

"Yeah, but these stories postdate her by centuries. *Something* appeared, maybe around the millennium, that gradually trickled into the literature. The magical community has done a decent job of keeping our toys out of mundane hands, so either someone screwed up on an epic scale or something *very* big happened, and what we see in these stories are the distorted echoes of that event." Fixing his stare on Eadwig, Ted asked, "Did Simon have something to say about it?"

The boy sighed, then took a long drink. "Much. He believed it was the key to immortality."

"Sounds about right. The stories often attribute mystical healing properties to the Grail. Anything more specific?"

"He never referred to it as holy," he replied, brow furrowed in thought. "Always bloody. He wasn't sure *why* blood was important to the cup, but his notes insist that it is."

"From a magical standpoint, blood's a powerful substance," I replied.

"Blood traces," Ted offered.

"And worse. Give enough blood to a powerful wizard, and she can do damage." I hesitated, then asked Eadwig, "Do the notes seem familiar to you? Have they sparked something in your memory?"

He rubbed his face and drank again. "Yes and no. I can't remember anything specific—nothing more than I did when I woke. But it's as though there is light behind me, and I can see shadows on the wall, and every so often, one of them moves in a way that I almost recognize. Does that make any sense? It doesn't, does it?"

"Sure, it does," Ted replied, clapping a comforting hand on Eadwig's thin shoulder. "No need to beat yourself up, son. If there's something locked in that head of yours, it'll shake loose eventually."

His brief smile spoke more of politeness than reassurance. "Whatever it is, the cup makes me nervous. Something is *wrong* with it, I know that. I just cannot say what that might be. But..." He dug through his papers for a clean sheet and a pen, then began to sketch a chalice. "This is the general impression I had from the notes. Gold, all of it, and this mark repeated around the cup." He doodled a nine-pointed star, peered at it, then added a decorative flourish to every third ray. "Do you know this sign?"

Ted shook his head. "Never seen that in my life. What is it?"

"I don't know. Kitty?"

"Nothing here," I said, watching over his shoulder as he drew in the details of the stem and base. Whatever other talents he possessed, Eadwig had a good eye and a steady hand. "Did Simon draw that?"

The tip of Eadwig's tongue protruded from the corner of his mouth as he finished. "He described it in some detail. Several accounts of the cup spoke of this sign. As I said," he continued, looking my way, "I don't believe that Simon ever found the cup. But maybe someone here has. The Archives contain more than books, yes?"

"Considerably more," Marcus confirmed. "Weapons, jewelry…that one pair of boots…"

It had been Mal that time who'd disregarded the no-contact rule and tried on the artifact, and thanks to the pockets of magic that had sustained the boots' spells through the '13 closure, Mal had soon found himself floating upside-down twenty feet above a forest floor, dangling by his ankles and flailing for anchoring limbs as he rose.

"They're bound to have cups," I told Eadwig. "We could talk to Jude and see about getting you into the storage rooms. I'm sure he'd let you take a peek if we said it ties back to the diary."

Ted's mouth tightened at the suggestion. "Do we *really* want to bring Jude in on this? If it's not in a book, he doesn't care." I gave him a hard look, and he raised his hands in surrender. "Okay, *okay*. If we have to make nice with that overblown librarian, fine. I just think that if we're on the verge of a major discovery concerning an ancient grail…you know, we could surprise him once we find it."

"Transparent," Marcus muttered.

At least Ted had the grace to look mildly abashed.

CHAPTER 12

The matter of whether Ted wanted to clue in his Grail-hunting rival proved to be moot, since Quinn told Jude about Eadwig's early translation findings on her own initiative. "He's *thrilled*," she relayed to him at dinner that night. "Can't thank you enough for all the work you've put into this project. He'd be up here tonight to thank you in person except for the quarantine—he has a tickle in his throat and doesn't want to spread it."

"That's wise of him," said Maria, who'd joined us that evening for a post-dinner diary update. To me, she added, *Look at the kids.*

Over the last days, Beth and Eadwig had quietly staked a claim to adjacent seats at the table, and I glanced their way in time to see her nudge him in the arm as he flushed with Quinn's praise. *They're getting along well*, I told her.

Uh-huh.

She's sixteen, she's allowed to be friendly with a boy.

Unless he's Simon Magus.

I popped a piece of chicken in my mouth and tried not to look at her so as to keep our conversation hidden from the others. *He's appalled by some of the things he found in the diary. If he were Simon, don't you think he'd be a little more supportive of himself?*

Maybe, thought Maria, *unless he's trying to hide it from us.*

Is this a private conversation?

My eyes shot to Artur, who raised an eyebrow in silent enquiry. *Want the recap?*

No need—you're not as quiet as you could be, she replied

with a hint of reproach. *And Maria, your suspicions are reasonable, but you haven't lived with him. The boy is nothing but that—a frightened boy, displaced and alone. He's clever, certainly, but if he were lying to us, we would have noticed something by now.*

It was Maria's turn to arch a brow. *What did you tell her?* she asked me.

Only what I would have learned anyway, Artur thought. *Beth knows nothing, nor does Quinn, and...* She paused while an unmarked glass bottle half-full of a nearly clear liquid flew from the refrigerator into Marcus's waiting hand. "Oh, not *that*."

"Really?" said Maria, watching him uncork it with undisguised disgust. "On top of barbeque?"

"It's good!" he protested, liberally dousing his plate with homemade garum, his condiment of choice.

Her nose wrinkled. "It's fish guts."

"So is fish sauce," he countered.

"And do you see me putting it on barbeque?"

He grunted and took a bite. "I can't help it that Pater never cultivated your palate."

Maria rolled her eyes and resumed our three-way conversation while she attacked her unadulterated plate. *Men. You sleep with that, Kitty?*

He knows to brush his teeth, I thought, smiling to myself. Marcus might have been Maria's distant ancestor, but the two of them sniped like siblings when they were in a mood. "Quinn, what's Jude going to do next week when Magus Popova steals you again?"

"He'll survive, I'm sure," she said. "Also, you should know that he's offered to help get me my own place. I think he's afraid that you folks are going to rub off on me."

"Nonsense," said Marcus. "We wouldn't poach from the Archives. Go to Jude, learn everything you can, and in a few years, we'll send Bob upstairs for an archivist-to-archivist chat about exciting career opportunities in the subbasement."

Quinn smirked and sipped her water. "Sounds an awful lot like poaching to me."

"Completely different, I assure you," he replied with an almost straight face. My boyfriend was many things, but a poker player wasn't one of them.

As if feeling my gaze on him, Marcus glanced my way and grinned. *Do you think Ted gives recruitment bonuses?*

Do you need one?

Well, if you and I are to explore the wonders of Tennessee, we should probably think about funding this trip...

Smooth, I thought. *Nice try, hon.*

Come on, what would it hurt? he pressed. *It needn't be a long trip. When did you last visit, anyway? Surely you're curious.*

I haven't visited. Mom took me right after Daddy's funeral, and I've never been back.

Perhaps sensing the shifting emotional coloration of my thoughts, he stopped pushing. *I'm sorry, I didn't mean to upset you—*

You didn't. I smiled reassurance. *But with two houseguests, don't you think it would be a teensy bit irresponsible to get out of town? Do you really want to leave Artur in charge?*

His eyes slid toward my sister, who was raiding the chicken platter. *She's experienced.*

Yeah, but I'd rather not come home to find her making everyone do training laps around the castle. The current threat of Saxon invasion is low.

A muffled snort from Artur told me I still needed to work on my volume. *We can manage without your oversight for a few days*, she cut in.

Another time. I promise, I told Marcus. *Once things are settled around here.*

Really, Kitty, I'm capable of keeping three people in line, Artur insisted.

With or without a sword?

You'd be surprised how much work a good crown does for you.

I eyed her over my water glass. *Well, excuse the hell out of me.*

That would be, "Excuse the hell out of me, Your Majesty."

Sure, I thought, taking a long drink. *Is that going to be your ace forever, then?*

She grinned back at me and barely shrugged.

Beth interrupted us with a pointed clearing of her throat. "You know how it's rude to whisper in company?" she said, staring at Artur, Maria, Marcus, and me in turn. "Same goes for friggin' *telepathy*."

Eadwig stiffened in surprise, and Quinn frowned and looked around the table. "Wait…what?"

"Snitch," I muttered, and reached for the broccoli.

That night, once Maria took her leave and the others dispersed—in Beth and Eadwig's case, to her room to play on her computer—I sat up with Quinn in the den, half a bottle of chardonnay between us on the coffee table, both of us tired after the day but still too wired to sleep.

She languidly swirled her wine in its stem, her free arm crooked atop the back of the couch, and smiled at me. "You guys have an impressive selection of booze around here."

"You're only tasting the successes. Replication through enchantment is an art, and some of our early attempts were, uh…"

"Vinegar?"

"At best." I grinned and sipped. "When all else fails, the castle cellar isn't *that* difficult to access."

Her smile widened. "*Oh?*"

"One of those little things we don't discuss around the grand magus." Tucking my legs onto the couch to better face Quinn, I asked, "How's it going, really? Are you happy here? Quietly cursing our names for ever bothering you?"

She thought briefly, drinking as she did. "I'm not going to lie, this—all of *this*," she said, twirling her glass to encompass the flat and the castle around us, "is a lot…but it's been great." She sped up as she warmed to her subject. "I mean, two months ago, I wasn't sure how I was going to keep food on the table because I couldn't go after the jobs I've wanted, since I was so afraid of, like, burning a museum down. And now…" She chuckled. "Jude's holding a fantastic job for me, and I'm learning honest-to-God magic. This isn't exactly what I saw myself doing after my last degree, but…"

"Not too terrible?"

"It's *amazing*." She put her wine on the table and reached for my free hand. "You guys have been so nice to let me crash here, and I have no idea how I'm going to pay you back—"

"Stop that. We're happy to have you," I replied, and lowered my voice. "Honestly, it's nice to have someone in the flat who grew up with the same movies I did. If Beth's out, you know what I get when I sing a Disney song? Blank stares."

"Eh, could be worse. People cover their ears and beg for a merciful death when I try to sing." With a quick nod toward Marcus's room, she asked, "How does that work, anyway? No offense, but that's so far beyond cradle robbing…"

"Technically, maybe," I admitted between sips, "but he got knocked out when he was twenty-three and woke up here three years ago. His father went the long way, now, but Marcus…he's more like the victim of an unfortunate time machine accident. Same with Artur."

"That's got to be tough."

I nodded. "They'll be playing catch-up for years. But I'm here for Artur, as long as she wants to stick around, and Marcus…well."

Quinn's eyebrows waggled.

Dropping my voice to a whisper, I leaned toward her and said, "Don't repeat this, but I think he's the one."

"Does *he* know that?" she replied in kind.

I could only shrug. "It's complicated. I just wish he'd

give me a sign."

"If you want to get married, you could always propose. That's what my mom did, and my dad was *so* relieved to have the pressure off."

"It's not that, it's—"

"His native culture's uber-patriarchal, and he'd take it poorly?" she guessed.

"*No.* I mean, yeah, patriarchy, but he's come a long way. It's, uh…" I sighed, frustrated at my inability to spit it out. "Faeries aren't known for monogamy, yeah?"

"News to me, but okay…"

"Oh…right. They're not. *We're* not," I amended. "Barring some accident, we're going to live a very long time, and he's the heir to a court, and as such, he's going to be…*desirable*. See what I'm getting at?"

She picked up her wine again, swirled it, and took a sip. "How long have you been together?"

"As a couple? Two years."

"Has he cheated?"

"No…"

"So, here's how I see it," she continued, shifting against the couch cushions. "My exposure to Faerie has been somewhat limited—"

"*Somewhat?*"

"Okay, the dragon barn, but it was cool enough. I take it the rest of the place is pretty neat, right? Palaces, maybe? Attractive people? Unicorns and shit?"

"Unicorns stay out in the woods," I replied, "but you're on the right track."

Her jaw sagged. "You have unicorns?" she asked, sounding wounded. "And you didn't tell me?"

"They're really not tame…"

"*Man*, I've got to get out more often," she muttered. "But as I was saying, your crown prince could be hanging out over there, getting fawned over and whatnot, but he's here, in an apartment with five other people, living with your *sisters*, and going out at odd hours in search of weirdos like me. Open your eyes, babe."

"I know," I said, "but, like, in a hundred years—"

"Who can say? Some relationships fail after six months, some go on forever. I mean, look at my grandpa. He still celebrates his anniversary, and Grams has been gone for thirteen years. Gets dressed up and takes her picture out to dinner at a steakhouse."

I thought of the white-haired old man shuffling into the restaurant with his cane, maybe sporting a tweed blazer and a bowtie, taking a seat at a table set for two and carefully positioning a framed photograph at the other place setting. "That's really sweet," I told Quinn.

"And kind of pitiful, but that's Grandpa for you. He's always been sentimental." She finished her wine, pulled the cork, and helped herself to another glass after topping up mine. "Can I tell you something?"

"Sure," I said, scooting closer on the couch.

"When I first got here and heard about...*him*"—it didn't take a mind reader to know she meant James Mulligan—"I was pretty freaked out."

"You hid it well," I offered.

"I tried. You know, you go through life, you think you're an okay sort of person, right, you tip well and you don't litter and you vote...and then you find out there's someone like him in the family. Not a distant cousin—that darkness is in *your* family. And you start to wonder if it's in you, too, if it's something hereditary like kinky hair or dimples or freaking magic..."

"Quinn," I said, reaching for her hand on the back of the couch, "you're not *evil*. It doesn't work like that."

"I like to think so. But I'm guessing he thought he wasn't evil, either," she replied, and chased it with wine. "Anyway, you were kind of down on Jude, and I was worried about that, too...I mean, him being a cousin and all...but he's really *nice*." Her smile returned as she spoke. "I haven't had a cross word from him, and he's been showing me around some of the more restricted rooms—

I'm sure I don't have the clearance, but he says he wants me to be up and running once I come on board full time. This is the grad student's dream, here—I'm not applying for a job, I'm being *wooed* to work with this incredible collection. A slightly crumbly collection, but I can help fix that. But the great thing is that I think I've actually found a mentor," she said, beaming. "Jude's the kind of person I've been trying to find ever since undergrad. Maybe he's a little prickly around you, but you should see his eyes light up when we talk about manuscripts. He's passionate about his work, and he wants me to be a part of it, and…" She put her glass down again and squeezed my free hand. "Really, I can't thank you guys enough for bringing me here. This is…*everything*."

"We're glad to have you," I replied. "But there's one matter that's been nagging me of late."

"Oh?"

"What have you told your parents? Do they still think you're in New York?"

Quinn tapped her temple and grinned. "Seems that someone had to drop out of an internship at the last minute at the British Museum, and my name was pulled from the waitlist. As far as they know, I'm living it up in London with some other museum employees. So unless they get a wild hair and fly over to visit me, I've got this one covered."

I hesitated, then asked, "Have you talked to your grandpa?"

Her smile dimmed. "Yeah. He says he's happy for me, but he's pretty broken up about his brother. Understandable. I mean, if my brother turned into an evil overlord, I'd be upset, too. Speaking of whom—"

"Evil overlords?" I joked.

"Nah. What can I tell my family in the long term? Grandpa knows, but my parents don't, and Evan's my only sibling…"

"There are rules, but the grand magus can fill you

in…what?" I asked as a mischievous look flashed across her face.

"Evan's a doctor with a condo in LA, and you saw my swanky 'starving student' accommodations. I just want to roll up at Christmas some year, whip out a wand, and literally make it rain dollars. Petty?"

"Slightly, but I get it." I finished my wine in a long gulp and smirked. "You *have* met my sister, the once and future king?"

The Team convened in our conference room shortly after nine Thursday morning—including, to our surprise, Frank, who arrived a few minutes early with Aurora strapped across his chest. "You're on leave!" Ted protested upon their arrival. "Go home, man, you don't need to bother with this today."

"If I go home, I'll keep pacing the flat, and that's bad for the rug," he replied, settling into his usual seat at the table. Aurora squealed as they sank, and Frank absently handed her the well-gnawed teething ring he'd attached to the baby harness, which she stuffed into her mouth with glee. "I love her dearly, but I'm bored out of my mind, and I've watched *far* too much television this summer. Someone, anyone, give me something to do."

Mal handed him a large cup of tea, while Antony, who'd just set up his computer in the spot beside Frank's, patted his lap and beckoned for the baby. "Take a load off. I think I remember how this works."

But Frank smiled wearily and shook his head. "Hatchlings are clingy at first. She won't let me leave her sight without complaining."

"You're not going anywhere," he pointed out, and reached for Aurora. "Hey, sweetheart, want to come sit with Uncle Antony and give you poor dad a break?"

"He's a friend, Aurie," Frank murmured in her ear. "Daddy's right here."

No.

Frank met Antony's eyes and shrugged. "Kids."

Aurora proved similarly reluctant to be handed to anyone else in the room, though she was happy to play with a cup of crushed ice while we discussed the fall schedule. She was gleefully picking handfuls out of the cup and dropping them on Frank and the floor when the conference room door slammed open.

We wheeled around to find Jude panting on the threshold, his hair mussed with the run downstairs and his blue eyes bright. "Where is he?" Jude demanded, focusing his attention on Ted.

Our boss straightened in his chair. "Going to have to be more specific, there. Are you okay?"

"The *boy*," he said, the last word a pointed whisper. "Where are you hiding him?"

I traded glances with Artur and Marcus, then cleared my throat and lifted a finger. "Our place," I told Jude. "In quasi-quarantine, remember? How are you feeling? Quinn mentioned something about a throat issue—"

"It's fine. You have to bring him in."

Of all the people in the castle from whom I might consider taking orders, Jude Duffy was near the bottom of the list, but I tried to be polite. "May I ask what this is about? He did that translation for you, and I think he's due a day of vegetation."

"You know damn well what this is about, Connolly. Quinn told me that Ted sneaked up there yesterday," he said, shooting a glare at my boss. "And if you people think for one moment that I'm going to sit back and twiddle my thumbs while you chase after the *Grail*, you're absolutely mad."

At that, Ted rose and motioned Jude down. "Whoa, there. The diary mentions a bloody cup, that's all, and Eadwig says he's got a bad feeling about it. It might be *a* grail, or it might be the big one. Nobody in here knows. Hell, the cup might be in one of your storage rooms already. But Kitty's right, let's give the kid a little space—"

"Easy for you to say! You've already had a private chat with him!"

"And you don't see me running off to grab my hiking boots, do you?" He considered Jude's flushed face for a moment, then turned to me. "Kid's been out of the house already, yeah? What if we slapped a facemask on him again and took him to see the Archives' dishware?"

The suggestion mollified Jude, and I hurried home to retrieve Eadwig. I found him and Beth on opposite sides of the kitchen table, my fifth-hand Monopoly set between them. From the smug look of satisfaction on my sister's face, all of those houses on the green properties belonged to her, and the dog token sitting on Bond Street to her opponent. Eadwig conceded defeat and combed his hair, and then, promising Beth to have him back for lunch, I took him to the Archives by gate.

The opening gate resulted in a few curious looks from the nearby patrons—in recent years, Glastonbury had seen it all—and a scowl from Jude, who waited in the dimly lit vestibule with Ted. To my surprise, Frank had tagged along, toting a black satchel, and he rocked slightly as Aurora bounced her feet and squirmed. "Is the light show really necessary?" Jude asked as I sealed the hole.

"Rapid delivery," Ted interjected before I could retort, and beckoned for Eadwig to join the huddle. "Thanks for coming, son. Did Kitty tell you what we're doing?"

He nodded. "You want me to look at your cups."

"*His* cups, technically." Ted nodded to Jude and cleared his throat, "Eadwig, this is—"

"Quinn's friend, yes. We have met." His eyes slightly crinkled, and I assumed he was smiling behind his mask. "Shall we?"

"Let's," said Jude, but he held up a hand when Frank started to move. "Not you."

"I beg your pardon?" he replied, his voice quiet but rumbling like a distant storm.

"No children. This collection is far too valuable."

He passed his hands over the baby carrier. "She's attached to me. How is she going to break anything?"

As Frank tensed, Ted gripped his arm to keep him from closing on Jude. "His daughter's mother died," Ted murmured. "She's all he has, and she's understandably clingy right now. Frank's doing the best he can to go back to work. Come on, it's not like you've never had a child in here."

Jude regarded the baby with distaste. "Under close supervision, and only when they're sufficiently mature to follow instructions. *That* one isn't even out of nappies."

One of Frank's eyebrows rose, barely clearing the dark lens of his glasses. "Want to check? She's trained."

Already? I asked.

He didn't flinch at the mental intrusion. *It took a few hours yesterday, but she understands the protocol.*

Hours?

Cut her some slack, she's a hatchling.

Aurora gurgled happily, and I felt Frank's thoughts bend toward her and become amorphous, losing the structure of words for a simple wash of love.

"Please, Jude," Ted cajoled. "Frank's one of my best. If we do need to track down this cup, he'll be a help. To us *both*," he insisted.

The pair were comically unmatched—Jude, reedy, middle aged, and sporting a white dress shirt beneath a charcoal vest, had almost a head on my chubby septuagenarian boss in his hula dancer–print shirt—but after a moment, Jude weakened under Ted's quiet stare. "If you insist," he snapped, and stalked deeper into the Archives. "Don't let her slobber on anything!"

Jude might have been peeved with Ted and Frank, but Eadwig was a different matter. I couldn't help but notice that Jude kept a respectful distance from the boy as he hustled us through the door-pocked stone corridors, occasionally looking back and smiling encouragement as he motioned for Eadwig to hurry along. After a few turns, we paused outside a door indistinguishable from the rest but for a small brass plaque at my eye level. Jude pressed his hand against a scanner panel set in the wall, and the barrier wards flared orange before they parted to allow us entry. "This way," he said, stepping back and sweeping one arm into the dim room, and Eadwig ventured inside.

When the door closed behind us, the lights came up, illuminating shelves jammed with plates, goblets, and serving vessels—a display that would put a fine jeweler's shop to shame. I slunk near the padded table in the middle of the room, twitchy with the warning tingle of so much silver in proximity to my bare arms, and watched as Eadwig unabashedly took in the riches ringing the walls. "Have a closer look, please," Jude said, beaming. "Aren't they lovely?"

Goaded on, Eadwig stepped up to one set of built-in glass shelves and considered a pair of ornate silver candelabra.

"Useful, those," said Jude, sliding in at Eadwig's left shoulder. "Do you see the spell? Barely above the surface of the metal—that's fine crafting, that is."

The boy nodded. "Preservation," he said, sounding almost entranced.

"Precisely. Candles put in those sockets will never burn down. Magic fuels the flames instead of wax. It's subtle but practical. A gift from Magus von Staufen to his mundane mistress, kept in her family for six generations until one of her descendants produced a new-blooded wizard, who returned the candelabra to our keeping. Touch it, if you like." Eyeing the rest of us over his shoulder, he glanced at me and faintly grimaced. "Maybe not you, eh?"

For the sake of cooperation, I held my tongue. While I hadn't made a public declaration of my unexpected augmentation, neither had I made a secret of it—and I didn't need long in Jude's presence to feel his disdain.

Sure, I could have blasted a hole through the wall without working up a sweat, but I was witch-blooded. To the pedigreed wizards of his ilk, I'd been pitiable but respectable when I was merely a magus's almost-dud daughter. A mongrel was a different matter altogether, and while Jude had never used the slur around me, I'd sensed it in his thoughts.

Want me to melt them? Frank whispered to my mind. *No trouble at all.*

I said nothing, but he patted my shoulder, and Aurora fixed me with a quizzical stare. *Friend*, he told her, broadcasting sufficiently to keep me in the conversation. *Kitty is a friend.*

She seemed suspicious until she dropped her teething ring and I retrieved it from the rug. *Friend*, I thought, brushing off the lint and handing it back. Aurora didn't smile—human facial expressions weren't in her limited repertoire—but I sensed her happiness at the toy's return...and her sense of recognition.

You came around the nest, Frank explained. *She knows what your mind sounds like.*

"And this cup," Jude continued, nudging Eadwig along the shelf, "was crafted in Greece in the early sixth century. Instantly aerates wine. I'd love to take that one to dinner, but alas, it's far too valuable to leave the room. This one, now, this is a trifle—it has an anti-tarnish spell on it. Moving on..."

What is this?

Eadwig jumped as if he'd been goosed, but Jude's shoulders merely stiffened at the question, and I glanced at Frank. From the side, I could peek behind his glasses, and what I saw there looked suspiciously like alarm, then self-castigation. Hatchlings broadcast everything until they learned to focus their thoughts, and while that was no issue in the subbasement, the average wizard wasn't accustomed to telepathy without strong spellcraft at play.

But Ted was far from average, and he answered

Aurora's query without pause. "Cups and plates, sweet girl," he said, turning from the showroom display to address her head-on. More than a foot shorter than Frank, he could look the baby in the eye as she sat in her carrier on her father's chest. "Expensive dishes that we keep safe here."

Why?

"Because they're not for eating on."

Why?

"You know," Jude interrupted, holding an ordinary porcelain teacup that glowed scarlet in the magical spectrum, "if she keeps that up, we'll have company soon, and I, for one, would rather not be forced to explain why there's a juvenile dragon in restricted storage. Mind putting a lid on it?"

That got our attention. "Sorry, what…" Ted began.

But Frank cut him off. "How did you know?" he murmured, one arm wrapping around Aurora as if he feared a bolt.

The archivist put the ensorcelled teacup back on its shelf and turned, faintly smirking. "You realize this is the repository for the writings of a thousand years of magi and grand magi, yes?"

"I would assume that the current occupants of those offices use a measure of password protection."

"Of course. But there are workarounds, and I was curious as to *what*, exactly, the grand magus was entrusting with the retrieval of priceless artifacts." He brushed a speck of lint from his sleeve, his expression never changing. "You're full of surprises, 'Mr. White.'"

Perhaps sensing her father's mood change, Aurora twisted beneath his arm, trying to see his face. *Daddy?*

"Shh," he soothed, tightening his grip. "It's all right, little one. Jude won't say a word."

"Rather confident, there," Ted muttered under his breath.

Ignoring his commentary, Frank simply slid his glasses

down his nose with one finger, denuding the inhumanly red eyes behind them, and held Jude's gaze. "Snooping through Toula's files, hmm? What else have you found, you little weasel?"

Jude didn't flinch. "I know she's still studying the spells worked on *him*," he replied, nodding to Eadwig. "And I know your daughter was born with certain defects. The grand magus's memorandum to herself in case she ever has to explain your presence in this installation. You haven't exactly been forthcoming about what's under the bind, you know."

Frank bristled. "Do anything to hurt my daughter, and you won't have a body left to find."

"Big words for the one of us here without talent."

"Surprising cheek for a man whose most prized possessions are paper. Want to put those fire-retardant spells to the test?"

"Oh," Jude retorted, "threats against the Archives now, too? I'm sure the grand magus would understand if I revoked your access credentials."

"You can try," he replied, shrugging. "Toula has my back."

"Maybe so, but what about the rest of the installation? If they knew what was in their midst—"

Whatever else Jude had meant to say came out as a startled croak, cut short by Frank's hand around his throat. Even with his bind in place, Frank was unusually strong, and he lifted Jude several inches off the ground and glowered as the smaller man kicked and clawed. When Jude's face had turned a concerning shade of red, Frank dropped him, and he gasped in a heap on the rug while the rest of us watched from a safe distance. "My daughter has a chance here," said Frank once Jude's coughs had slowed from a desperate hacking. "Ruin it for her, and I'll destroy you. That's your warning."

After Jude had recovered oxygen, if not his dignity, Ted coaxed him to the other side of the room and quietly tried to restore the peace while Eadwig continued his perusal of the treasures. "If Toula's made notes, then you probably know all about the rest of the baby's family," I heard Ted murmur. "She has health issues beyond her missing limbs. Bee's helping her here, but understand that it's been a *long* few weeks for him, okay? Do you need to go to the infirmary? Your neck's, uh...pretty red."

"I'm fine," Jude muttered. "But if you can't keep your people leashed—"

A low growl from Frank silenced *that* sentiment.

By the time Eadwig finished his circuit of the room, Jude had calmed and was pointedly ignoring everyone but the boy. "Nothing here is familiar?" he asked, his tone hinting at desperation. "None of these cups?"

Eadwig shook his head and folded his arms, but he didn't shrink under Jude's unblinking stare. "I'm sorry, but no. The blodig calic is not here."

"You know what that means," Ted interrupted, unable to hide his spreading grin. "*Grail quest.* Hey, now, none of that," he said as Frank and I groaned. "We actually have a grail in mind this time! And Simon Magus's notes!"

"This should be handled by the Archives," Jude protested, "not you lot. A matter this sensitive—"

"You should work together."

Ted and Jude turned to Eadwig, who raised a hand to stop their rebuttals. "The diary was unclear about all of the cup's details, but I know it is dangerous."

"How?" Jude asked.

He huffed in frustration. "I don't know that, I just...*know*. It's bad. You need to find it and destroy it."

"But if the Magus sought it—"

A knock at the door heralded the arrival of a pair of senior archivists, and Ted seized the opportunity. "Let's talk about this in private, eh?" he said to Jude. "You have an office around here, I trust."

Lips pursed, Jude stalked through the maze of corridors until we reached his spacious suite, an office half the size of the grand magus's but well appointed in the Archives' style: dark woods, plush rugs, and brass lamps. Unlike the Team, *he* had a window with southern exposure, framed by red and gold brocade curtains. As Jude slammed and locked the door behind us, Eadwig, as if magnetically attracted to Jude's bookcases, left the group to peer at the leather spines and protective boxes housed behind the latticed glass, all softly illuminated by lighting strips.

"Sit, if you want," Jude offered with a brusque wave toward the cream-colored couch and flanking wingback chairs.

Hungry.

I looked his way in time to see Frank give the seating a grimace in appraisal. "We'll be over here," he told Jude, reaching into his satchel for a bottle.

The archivist paused behind his desk and watched with naked disgust as Aurora chugged her pinkish-gray meal. Looking up from the baby, Frank smirked and cocked an eyebrow. "You expected her to eat strained peas?"

"Have you considered opaque bottles?" Jude asked, looking slightly queasy.

"They're in the wash." His smile was cold and toothy, and Jude hurried to take one of the white chairs, putting his back to the feeding hatchling.

With Aurora's disturbing bottle out of his sight, Jude seemed to recover himself and cleared his throat. "This should be an Archives-led initiative," he said, fixing Ted with a hard stare. "As I was saying, if the Magus has truly given us a lead on a grail, then my team needs to manage the recovery effort. This is far too important a matter to chance your people mucking it up."

"*Mucking?*" Ted echoed. "I'm sorry, how much fieldwork have you done? Plan to send your finest librarians on a quest, eh? How are you going to select them, best penmanship or greatest familiarity with the Dewey Decimal system?"

There was little Jude could say to refute him on that point. The archivists were known for preservation and research, not the sort of work that might result in blisters, and no one with an ounce of sense would send a group of them over the Team on a recovery initiative like that. "At least my people are all wizards," he retorted after a moment's sputtering. "I can trust—"

"Oh, yes," Ted interrupted, chuckling incredulously, "because wizards are the most *trustworthy* people in the universe. Scouts, all of us."

"I can trust them to follow directives," he replied, crossing his arms. "You don't have so much as a clear chain of command."

"Boss," I interjected, pointing to Ted. "And if the Council gets involved, Maria."

"Yeah, that's about right," Frank chimed in. "Put Toula at the top of the heap. See? Chain of command."

Jude ignored our contributions to the debate. "Half your people have divided loyalties at best," he told Ted. "This is too great a potential find to chance losing it to an agent of another power—"

"I trust the Team," said Ted. "Wholeheartedly. Not a one of them has ever let me down. And if Toula thought for a minute that any of them were a security risk to the Arcanum—"

"This would be the same woman who allows her brother free access to this installation?"

Ted cocked his head. "You doubt her allegiances?"

"I doubt her judgment in certain matters, as does everyone else in this organization with any measure of sense—"

A brief cry cut him short, and we turned as one to Eadwig, who backed away from Jude's bookcases so quickly that he tripped and fell over the rug. I caught him as he scrambled to his feet and felt him panting in my arms as he stared at one of the shelves, the blood draining from his face.

"All right, there?" Ted asked, stepping between Eadwig and the bookcase. "Son? Look at me, now, that's it, right here, focus…"

By the time Jude joined us, Eadwig had regained some of his composure, though he remained distraught. "What is *that*?" he demanded, jabbing one finger toward the offending shelf.

Frowning, Jude opened the glass door and began pointing to groups of books. "What, these?"

"The *drawing*."

He reached to the back of the middle shelf and extracted a framed piece of faded vellum, the red ink brownish behind the archival glass. "What about it?" he asked Eadwig, bringing it closer for the boy's inspection.

I studied it over Eadwig's shoulder. The drawing was nothing as far as manuscript illustration went, just a simple sketch of a goblet…a goblet, I realized, that bore a repeated motif of a curious sort of star, a nine-pointed figure with flourishes on three of the rays. "The diary description—"

"That is it. The sign of the blodig calic," Eadwig murmured, and looked up at Jude. "Where did you find this?"

The archivist's hands began to tremble, and glancing at Ted, I caught a similar gleam of excitement in his eyes. "*That*," said Jude, holding the frame close, "is the Antwerp Grail."

"The, uh…the best contender for a truly powerful grail," Ted added. "Said to grant immortality to the holder. I've tracked its journey across Europe and back, but it disappeared—"

"In 1702," Jude finished. "Antwerp. This drawing is much older, of course, taken from a book produced in a French monastery in the early twelfth century—"

"The Unfinished Testament. Stops halfway through

Galatians, and then there's a big spill of blue ink, and then *that* page, which someone excised ages ago."

"Came into Arcanum hands in the sixteenth century," said Jude, his voice speeding up in time with Ted's. "We only tied it to that codex in the late nineteenth. My great-grandfather used it for decoration in his study—"

"*Stop*," I ordered. "Eadwig, you're sure this is the cup from the diary?"

He nodded. "This is what your Simon Magus sought. But he didn't know what he was seeking. Not in truth," he insisted. Though he kept his eyes on Jude and Ted, he appeared to stare through them. "It brings immortality, yes, but at a terrible price."

"What do you mean?" asked Ted.

Eadwig could only sigh in frustration. "It's evil, I know that, but exactly how…" His face screwed up in thought, and then he brusquely shook his head. "Find it. Destroy it. If you have any idea of where it might be—"

"*Destroy* it?" Jude repeated, aghast. "If the Antwerp Grail is the key to immortality—"

"Nothing good comes of it!"

His eyes narrowed, and he leaned closer to Eadwig. "The cup, or immortality?" he murmured. "Because something tells me you have certain insider knowledge of both."

"I don't!" Eadwig insisted. "All I'm certain of is that *this* cup must be destroyed. It is cursed."

"In what sense?"

The boy threw up his hands. "I would tell you if I knew. But you say that came from an unfinished book?" he said, pointing to the drawing. "You don't know why it was never finished?"

"No," Jude admitted.

Eadwig lowered his voice. "And you are sure that the drawing was done in ink?"

Jude shuffled his feet, and Ted leaned away from the frame. "It, ehm…it was not a *typical* ink…"

As he stammered, Frank strode across the room, tucking Aurora's bottle back into his bag. "Allow me," he said, yanking the frame from Jude's hands, then held it out of the smaller man's reach as he ripped open the backing and extracted the vellum. Dropping the fragments of the frame onto a side table, he held the vellum close to his face and took a deep breath. The tip of his tongue flicked from between his lips, almost too quickly to notice.

"Blood," he announced, offering the vellum back to Jude. "Definitely blood."

Hungry.

"Patience," he soothed, bouncing the baby. "You know, Jude, maybe this is just the non-wizard talking, but I've yet to see anything good come of blood ink. The Unfinished Testament came from Savoy, yes? Abbey of St. Martin? Didn't that place burn?"

Ted, at least, seemed to follow his train of thought. "Maybe the fire…"

A scene played out in my mind's eye: catastrophe at the monastery and a dying monk too weak to move, desperate to reveal the cause of the disaster and forced to use the only ink substitute available to him to make a drawing.

A drawing later removed to hide the secret.

I looked from my suddenly uneasy boss to Eadwig, his expression obscured by his facemask but his rigid posture offering no doubt as to his feelings about the drawing. "I think Eadwig's had enough for one day," I said, and opened a gate to my flat.

"Wait!" Jude yelped. "I'm not finished—"

"You are for now," said Frank, and covered our retreat while I hustled the boy out of the Archives.

CHAPTER 13

Ted called a Team meeting for ten o'clock Friday morning, thereby ensuring that all could attend and be relatively awake. Artur and Marcus beat me to the office that day, as I stuck around the flat for a while after Quinn's departure for the Archives to talk to Eadwig. He was no happier about the cup—grail, calic, or whatever it was—than he'd been the day before, and I caught him rereading the decoded diary after breakfast as if hunting for deeper meaning between the lines of neat characters.

"Why don't you take a break?" I suggested when he returned to the coffeemaker for the third time that morning. "Watch some TV, read something written in the last hundred years."

He smiled faintly and refreshed his mug. "It's like an itch between my shoulders, Kitty. If only I could scratch it…" He took a sip, made a face, and added a generous dose of sugar. "How soon until I'm free to walk about?"

"Very soon," I promised him. "Dr. Powell wants to see you this afternoon, and she might clear you today."

"If I were to go to her now and look sad as I wait…"

I mussed his hair, and he pushed my hand away. "Nice try, kid. She's got a full schedule this morning. I've got to go pick up Pritam, and they're going to take a closer look at Aurora."

He leaned against the counter and sipped his sweetened coffee. "She seemed healthy yesterday."

"Heart defect," I explained. "They're monitoring it in case they have to do surgery. Dragons grow like weeds when they're young, and the concern is that her heart will grow too quickly for the hole to have time to fix itself. Of course," I added, "since neither of them has done surgery on a dragon, this is all dicey." I glanced toward Beth's closed bedroom door—I'd seen to it that she was awake, but after forty-five minutes of hearing the muffled sound of running water, I feared she'd fallen asleep in the shower. "As soon as Dr. Powell clears you, I'll get a car, and we'll take a little trip, okay? Let you see some of the area."

Eadwig hesitated, then softly asked, "Home? Jórvík?"

"Sure. Whenever you're ready," I told him, and slipped off to Delhi.

Frank was far from chipper as he sank into his seat at the conference room table, and Antony and Lakshmi traded knowing smiles. "Long night?" Lakshmi asked. "Was someone not keen on bedtime?"

"No, she's sleeping like a champ," he replied, accepting a cup of tea from Mal with a flash of mental gratitude. "Barely even kicks me."

Lakshmi's brow furrowed. "You're not putting her in her cot, then?"

"Tried that once. She wasn't a fan." He drank, unflinching even with the steam rising from the mug. "Little angel discovered fire this morning."

"Oh, *God*," Antony muttered. "Is everything—"

Frank pushed up his right sleeve, revealing a white bandage taped around his wrist and forearm and wrapped with spellcraft. "Bee saw to it. Not her first burn. Aurie ate too quickly and burped, and I was still holding the bottle in position. It's not that bad," he assured us as the expressions around the table shifted toward horror. "Numbed nicely. But, uh…it would be best if you didn't stand directly in front of her until she gets control."

Daphne stared at him, aghast. "And how long will that take?"

"No clue. I figured it out in a day or so, but I was grown. She's just a hatchling..." He cleared his throat and propped up his computer, avoiding our ring of wide eyes. "Anyway, Bee put her to sleep for examination purposes, so I suspect the infirmary will be in working condition when this meeting's over. What's the agenda?"

"Autumn scheduling," said Ted, "and if you need to be with them..."

"They assured me that two trained wizards can handle a four-day-old child," he replied, though he didn't sound convinced. "Anyway, as long as I'm there when she wakes, we won't have trouble. So, Giza?"

With the specter of little fire-breathing Aurora freaking out over her missing daddy hanging over the room, we quickly got down to business. At ten of eleven, as we wrapped up, Frank excused himself to retrieve his daughter, and the rest of us opened our calendars for spring planning—Bob and Antony had been busy in the Archives and wanted to pitch an excursion to a ruined fortress in the Urals after the snow melted. Antony had just brought up a slideshow of manuscript pages concerning the wizards who had lived there and the treasures they had supposedly hidden when my phone began to ring. Apologizing for the disturbance, I pulled it from my bag, intending to silence it until I saw that Frank was on the line.

"Fire in the infirmary?" I asked.

His response was deafening in its force. "She's gone! They're unconscious, and *she's gone!*"

Frank was still shouting into his phone when I ripped a gate open and ran through. My eyes fell on Pritam and Dr. Powell, both of whom were sprawled on the tile floor. The GP had a nasty gash in her forehead, possibly from the edge of the examination table, the paper atop which was wrinkled from a small body. Aurora's chart was still up on the magic-shielded infirmary computer, and the pair of wands near the doctors suggested that they'd been mid-examination when they'd passed out.

Knocked out, more likely, I surmised, seeing the fine mesh of spellcraft hanging just above their auras. As the rest of the Team piled into the infirmary, I overloaded the spells on the doctors and shook them awake. They came around slowly, both groggy and groaning from the injuries they'd sustained in the fall to the floor, and I dabbed at Dr. Powell's face to clean away the tacky blood.

"What happened?" Frank demanded as soon as they were sufficiently conscious to focus. "Where's my daughter?"

The emotional cocktail radiating from him, heavy on the panic, should have been cause for concern, but the doctors were still too dazed to show fear. "We had her on the table," Pritam mumbled, gesturing toward the papered surface above him. "Cardiovascular imaging. I was checking her valves, and Bee..."—he rubbed his temple and winced—"Bee collapsed, I heard her fall..."

"Hit from behind," she muttered. "I felt the spell slam into me, and that's the last I remember." She whispered a hand mirror into existence, checked her cut, then took the wet cloth from me and held it in place as she woozily stood. "Pritam, are you all right?"

"I'm not the one bleeding," he said, and looked back up at Frank. "I turned when I heard Bee, just before the bastard hit me, too. Didn't have time to shield. I only saw his face for a second—"

"*Who?*"

"I'm sorry, I don't know him..." Pritam paused, an odd expression crossing his face. "Ehm...what..."

But Frank was already running for the door, and I shrugged at Pritam. "Telepathy. Sorry, he normally asks before prying," I said, and hurried with the others to catch up before Frank killed someone.

This was easier said than done—Frank had a head start, a foot on me, and correspondingly longer legs—but I yelled his name until he slowed to a jog long enough to let

Daphne and me reach him. "Where are we—"

Archives, he thought, not wasting his breath. *Jude attacked them.*

"Jude?" Daphne panted. "Why would Jude—"

He knows about me. About Aurie. I swear, if he hurts her—

"I'll hold the wanker down for you. Kitty, get the bloody gate."

Still running, I opened a gate in the middle of the corridor, which dumped us into the lobby of the Archives. Frank paused for barely a second to get his bearings, then sprinted toward Jude's office, swatting aside startled archivists like swarming gnats. "Jude!" he bellowed. "*Jude!* You're *dead!* You're fucking dead—"

He slammed into an invisible barrier and bounced back, knocking Daphne and me off our feet as he tumbled atop us. "Sorry, man," said Marcus, who'd crossed the length of the hallway in a split-second and thrown together an impressively tough shield, which shimmered between us like the curve of a soap bubble.

Frank jumped to his feet, red-faced and shaking with adrenaline, and growled. *Move.*

"He *is* a wizard, remember," said Marcus. "Let's be clever. You've lost whatever surprise you might have had, and if he's lying in wait in there, he's got a wand—"

The rest of Marcus's plea for rationality ended in a groan as Frank, though blind to magic, managed to swipe an arm around the shield and toss Marcus against the stone wall. I knelt beside him and checked for head injuries while Frank ran onward, the rest of the Team doing their best to keep up and stop him from killing himself.

By the time I had Marcus numbed, off the floor, and down to Jude's office, Frank was well along in the process of tearing the place apart, punching the walls and bookcases in a frantic search for hidden doorways. Of Jude, there was no sign—nor, I noticed, was the picture of the Antwerp Grail back on its shelf. Once Frank had broken every piece of glass in the room, Ted managed to grab his bleeding arm and his attention. "Let's go to Toula, eh?" he said. "She's a pro with blood magic, she can run a trace from you to Aurie…"

But Frank brushed him off, stalked back to the hallway, and grabbed a frightened junior archivist by the lapels of his sport coat. "Where the *fuck* is Jude?" he demanded, hoisting the man off the floor.

He squealed and kicked his skinny legs for purchase. "I don't know! I haven't seen him, I swear!"

A thought occurred to me. "Quinn Dellucci. Where has Jude stashed her?"

"*Who?*"

With a sigh, I called a picture of Quinn to mind and forced it into the archivist's head. "Look familiar?"

Fortunately, his face registered recognition. "Trainee? McInnis Reading Room, there are carrels through the brass door off the right side—"

His usefulness exhausted, he landed in a heap on the rug, and Frank was off again, the rest of us only paces behind.

We paid the surprised readers no mind—Frank certainly made no effort to keep the noise down as he threw his shoulder into the door, which smashed against the wall with a clang like falling armor—and it took only a moment's search to locate Quinn, who was still pulling her headphones off and goggling up at Frank when I arrived at her windowless cubicle. "The hell?" she asked.

"Jude," he said, chest heaving. "Where is he?"

"Beats me," Quinn replied, draping the headphones around her neck. "He said hi to me first thing this morning, but that was hours ago. I've been reading papers on vellum preservation all day," she offered, nodding to the carrel computer. "Got his number, if you want me to call him—"

"He took Aurie."

Her gray eyes widened. "*Jude?* What are you talking about?"

"You heard me. Knocked out the doctors and grabbed her."

"It's true," I said, catching my breath behind him. "You're *sure* you don't know what he was doing today? He's not in his office."

"Where's his flat?" Antony asked.

"I…I don't know, I've never been…been by," Quinn stammered. "That doesn't make sense, why would he take—"

"Leverage, obviously," Frank snapped. "He's got a hostage now."

"But for *what*? Jude's been nothing but kind to me. I can't believe he would *kidnap* someone!"

"Believe it," Ted muttered, tapping his phone and raising it to his ear. "Hi, yes, Grand Magus? Sorry to bother you. We have a situation…" He paused, and as he listened, his expression darkened. "I see. On our way."

"What's happened?" Marcus asked as he hung up.

Ted tucked his phone into his pocket and regarded Frank over the top of his glasses. "Jude called. We're expected."

We would have been better accommodated in one of the Council's meeting rooms, but Toula wanted guaranteed privacy, and the spells on her office were the only wards she trusted. She was waiting with Maria when the ten of us and Quinn arrived, standing behind her desk with folded arms and tight lips. Maria perched on the arm of a chair, watching in silence as we filed in.

"Sit down, Frank," said Toula, pointing to the couch. Her tone suggested that it wasn't a request, and he didn't fight her. "Jesus," she muttered, catching sight of his battered and bloodied knuckles, "what have you been punching, scrap metal? Let me—"

He pulled his hands away from her before she could begin her ministrations. "It's fine. Where's Aurie?"

She and Maria shared a look, and then Toula took a seat on the coffee table opposite him. "I got off the phone with Jude just before Ted called up. Untraceable number to our system, though I'll ask Aiden and Vivi to see what they can do. Then again, if he's got two brain cells to rub together, and I'm sure he does, he's bought a burner or six to keep us busy."

"Toula, *where*—"

"She's safe. He swore that. Said he hit her with the same spell he used in the infirmary…"

Lakshmi answered the query before she could ask. "Sleeping spell. Bee and the herpetologist are conscious again. No serious harm done."

"Good. It's bad enough we've got an attack in the fucking castle, let alone against a member of the Minor Arcanum—"

"*My daughter*," Frank demanded.

Toula held up a hand for his patience. "I don't have details, and he was vague with me, but here's what I gleaned from him." She beckoned with two fingers, and a notepad from her desk flew across the room into her lap. "Okay. Baby's with Jude, unharmed. He's keeping her unconscious, he said, and asked me to pass this message: *I've decided to take you up on your recovery offer. The grail for the girl.*" She looked at Ted, whose face had begun to color from more than just the run. "Not this again, you two. What grail is he going on about this time?"

"We haven't got the damn grail!" Frank shouted. "He knows that! *He's* the one with the bloody drawing!"

The grand magus looked more perplexed by the moment. "What drawing?"

"The Antwerp Grail," said Ted, earning curious looks from Bob, Lakshmi, Antony, and Mal. "You know, the sketch at the back of the Unfinished Testament…"

"There's a sketch?"

"It's been in Jude's family for a while," he explained.

"It's drawn in fucking *blood*," Frank added. "And the

kid said it's bad news."

"The kid," Toula repeated, and turned her gaze on me. "Which kid would that be, hmm?"

My stomach knotted under her stare. "I can explain…"

"Oh, I'm listening," she said, crossing her arms more tightly.

But before I could answer her, Quinn cut in. "It's my fault," she told Toula. "Eadwig finished translating that diary, and I told Jude that Ted here had been by to chat with him, and last night, Eadwig told me that he'd had a trip to the Archives to look at cups, and Jude wasn't happy about something. I didn't get a chance to really talk to Jude today, but he seemed fine this morning—"

"Ted, Kitty, the boy, Aurie, and I went to look at cups with Jude yesterday," Frank interrupted. "Jude's been reading your private files, Toula. He knew about me—"

"I'm aware," she said.

"And…you did nothing?"

She shrugged. "Jude thinks he's rather clever, but he's so busy with the tidbits I let him see that he doesn't bother looking for the juicier information I keep elsewhere. Mostly offline, to tell the truth. I'm not a complete idiot."

I saw more than a few confused faces around the room, and Toula, after scanning the crowd, sighed and rubbed her forehead. "Right, then. I suppose we'll work better from the same page. I was hoping not to bring this up until we had proof one way or another, but, uh…there's a non-zero chance that Eadwig is Simon Magus."

"I'm sorry, *what?*" Daphne replied.

"You heard me. His aural signature is present deep within the lattice of every wizard in this organization who claims a blood tie to the Magus. I've cross-checked them all. Maria and I are *still* working through the spells on the tomb and around him—they're incredibly complex, unique pieces of spellcraft."

"But Simon was old when he died, right?" asked

Quinn, who looked stunned. "Eadwig's a teenager—"

"A polyglot with an incredible talent, the ability to cast without a wand, an intimate familiarity with the Magus's diary, and a *very* convenient hole in his memory," said Toula.

"He's a *kid*," she protested. "And you should hear him talk about that diary. He doesn't even like what he's read of Simon—"

Frank cut her off. "Wait, he still hasn't remembered how he wound up in Ireland? Or did I miss something? Kitty told me about him, but I, uh…"

"You've been distracted, I'm sure. And no, unless you people are holding out info," said Toula, twirling a finger at Artur, Marcus, Quinn, and me, "then he has no idea how he got there. He remembers going to bed in York, then waking here—wait, where are you going?"

Frank was halfway to the door before he looked back at the bemused grand magus. "The diary talks about the damn Antwerp Grail, right?"

"Yeah, sounds like it," said Ted.

"And there's a decent chance that this 'Eadwig' wrote the diary. I'm going to go refresh his memory."

"Simon Magus never found the grail," I called after him. "Eadwig didn't see anything in the diary to suggest that."

"Then tell me," he said, yanking open Toula's door, "exactly how an old man winds up a boy again if not for an immortality-granting cup."

Marcus, Artur, Quinn, and I beat Frank back to our place, but only through magical cheating.

"Game's over," I said, finding Beth and Eadwig hunched over the Monopoly board at the kitchen table as I stepped through the gate. "Frank's on his way, and we've got an emergency."

Judging by the mugs on the placemats, the two of them

were fortified by caffeine, but neither had bothered to change out of pajamas, and Beth still sported traces of the previous day's mascara. "Huh?" my sister asked, squinting up at us. "What's going on?"

"Kidnapping, for starters," said Toula, following us with Maria, Bob, and Lakshmi, the rest of the Team having run after Frank. "Eadwig, I need you to think *very* hard," she continued, standing over him. "Has anything jogged your memory of late? Even a hint of a memory might help."

"I…I'm sorry," he said, casting nervous glances at the small crowd in the kitchen. "I'm trying, but nothing has come to me…"

"Well, you might want to think faster," she replied. "Or at least put on some shoes. This could be a long day."

As Eadwig and Beth scrambled to their rooms to dress, Marcus and I tidied the kitchen, taking pains to move anything breakable out of Frank's immediate line of sight. Artur opened one of the den windows, letting fresh air in to displace the summer holiday fug of unwashed teenagers, coffee, and scrambled eggs—I found the evidence soaking in the sink—then moved Beth's computer into my bedroom for safety.

The flat was looking marginally more presentable, and the kids had just emerged with clothes on and hair brushed, when the front door shook with the blows from a pounding fist. Artur turned the bolt with a gesture, and Frank stormed in, his head swiveling until he located Eadwig half-hidden behind Marcus. "*You*," he said, marching across the room as the boy shrank away. "Tell me where the goddamned grail is and do it now."

Eadwig's eyes rounded with fear. "All I know is what's in the diary, that's—"

He yelped as Frank pinned him to the wall with a hand to his neck. "Wrong answer," said Frank. "Care to try again?"

"*Let him go*," Toula snapped, and Frank jerked at the

command. "He doesn't have your daughter. Let's work with him and figure this out, okay? Killing him isn't going to solve anything."

Frank glared at Eadwig for a moment longer before relaxing his hold. As the boy rubbed his neck, Toula motioned for him to follow her into the den, then pointed to the couch. "Lie down," she said in a gentler tone. "It's time to get to the bottom of this memory hole of yours."

Eadwig slid onto the couch and stared up at her, worry creasing his brow. "I swear to you, I've tried—"

"I know, it's okay." Taking a seat on the coffee table, she folded her hands and met his frightened eyes. "Dr. Wanda said she tried hypnosis on you. Do you remember that?"

"Vaguely. That day was a blur."

"I'm sure. I'd like to try it again, but since we can't get Wanda here, I'm going to call in a favor. Try to relax, huh?"

Relaxation didn't seem to be in the cards for Eadwig—not with Frank glowering by the window—but he remained still while she slipped into my room to make a phone call. Shortly thereafter, I heard the muffled crack of an opening gate from behind the door, and then Toula reemerged with Eleanor at her side.

"Well, now," said the queen, taking in the assembled, "I wasn't expecting to perform for such an audience…"

"*You're* a hypnotist, my lady?" Maria asked.

She wiggled one hand in a noncommittal gesture. "I took it up in the nineteenth century on a lark. Better than wasting my evenings at séances. Where's the subject…*oh*. Little tense, are we?" she asked, looking over the back of the couch at Eadwig.

"A little," he admitted.

"Nothing to worry about, dear," she replied with a smile. Taking Toula's seat on the table, she placed two fingertips on Eadwig's forehead, and after thirty seconds, his eyelids drooped closed. "Much more expedient than the old 'follow the pocket watch' method," she told us as we clustered around the den. "Eadwig, can you hear me?"

"Yes," he mumbled.

"Good. Now, there is a door in front of you. A perfectly ordinary door. Can you see it?"

A pause, then, "Yes."

"Excellent," she said, her voice like velvet. "Behind that door are all of your memories—everything you've ever seen, ever heard, ever felt. When I count down from five, I want you to open the door."

He said nothing.

"Five."

Silence.

"Four."

"*No.*"

"No?" Eleanor asked. "You won't open the door?"

"No."

"Why not?"

Eadwig's eyes moved beneath his twitching lids, and his breathing grew shallower. "I'm afraid."

"Of your memories?"

"Behind the door. Something bad is there."

"You can face it," she coaxed him. "We'll do it together."

"No."

Frowning, the queen looked up at Toula. "I can try to break through, but I make no guarantees. If he fights me, this could take time."

"Or we can do this my way," Frank interrupted, and pushed through the crowd to the couch. Standing behind the armrest at Eadwig's head, his dark glasses glinting in the sunlight, Frank placed his hands on Eadwig's temples and took a deep breath. A few seconds later, he thought, *I see the door.*

"Can you help him open it?" Eleanor asked.

I'll do it myself.

The draconic mental talent is nothing to sneeze at, an

innate ability to penetrate all but the toughest defenses. Marcus was good, Eleanor had mastered mind-to-mind communication with centuries of practice, but Frank was a natural, and he struck hard.

Eadwig *screamed*.

"Stop it, you're hurting him!" Beth yelled, but Artur grabbed her before she could attack.

Frank withdrew and stepped away from the couch as Eadwig's screams gave way to hyperventilation. "That should have done it," Frank began. "Give him a minute to wake, and—"

The boy bolted upright, his chest heaving, and stared around the room as if he were seeing it all for the first time. Physically, he seemed unharmed by the mental intrusion—at least he wasn't bleeding out the ears—but the look of horror on his face was enough to make my stomach flip. With a wordless cry, he jumped off the couch, slid past Eleanor, and broke into a run.

Beth didn't waste time with words. Breaking free from Artur's grasp, she sprinted toward Eadwig and intercepted him before he could reach the open window, then tackled him to the rug. The two wrestled for purchase, shouting at each other, but Artur's lessons had made Beth strong, and she soon had Eadwig pinned. "Look at me!" she ordered, holding his wrists to the floor. "*Look at me*! Damn it, Ed, *focus*!"

"Get off me!"

"No."

"Let me go, you must let me go—"

"*No*," she growled, adjusting her hold. "You're not jumping out any windows today, so why don't you look at me, huh?"

Slowly, ever so slowly, his eyes ceased their wild rolling, and his struggling limbs went limp beneath her. His breath still came in shuddering gasps, but the fight appeared to have gone out of him.

"It's okay," Beth murmured, not loosening her grip in

the slightest. "You're safe, Ed. It's just me."

"B-Beth?"

"That's right. What happened?"

He pulled himself together only long enough to whisper, "It was horrible," then started to weep beneath her.

Frank made no effort to hide his frustration with this development, but Toula firmly ordered him into the kitchen with Bob and Antony while Eadwig, finally free of Beth's hold, curled into a ball on the rug and shook with his sobbing. The grand magus patted his shoulder and murmured vague reassurance, and when that had no effect, she beckoned Lakshmi closer with a crooked finger and murmured, "Get Bee up here, won't you?"

The doctor arrived ten minutes later, bandaged but steady on her feet and carrying a supply bag, and found the situation only mildly improved. Eadwig had regained enough control to sit up, but he'd yet to leave the floor, instead putting his back to the wall beneath the window and pulling his knees to his chin. His eyes continued to leak as he stared into space.

"Well, then," said Dr. Powell, "I suppose this party means the quarantine is lifted."

Toula hurried toward her. "Honey, your *head*—"

"Superficial, I'm fine. What, ehm…" She paused, looking around the flat at the Team, the grand magus, the patient, and Eleanor, who offered a little wave. "Would someone care to fill me in?"

"Eadwig got his memory back," Marcus told her.

"*Ah.*" She gave the boy a longer moment's consideration, then asked Toula, "Something to take the edge off, yes?"

"If you'd be so kind."

Dr. Powell knelt in front of Eadwig and opened her kit. "Hi, there. Remember me?"

He sniffled but nodded.

"Splendid. Someone grab a glass of water, eh?" she

called toward the kitchen. "And this," she told Eadwig, pulling a pill bottle from the bag, "is going to relax you just a touch. Thank you," she said as I floated a cup toward her hand. "Here, swallow this whole." He did as she asked, and she flashed a professional smile. "Okay. You should start to feel a little better in a few minutes. Want a chair?"

"No," he mumbled.

"That's fine. Frank, dear, boring holes into the back of my head isn't going to help. If you want a tranq, too, Pritam is still in the infirmary. Any lead on the baby?"

"Unfortunately," said Toula, and murmured a quick explanation while Frank paced in the kitchen.

Dr. Powell's eyes squeezed shut. "*Shit.* He's got her in a sleep bind, not in full stasis?"

"He didn't mention stasis," Toula replied. "Said he hit her with the same thing he used on you two. Why?"

"Sleep doesn't stop growth. *Stasis* would hold her in place, but she's just unconscious, and she's growing like mad. She's put on two kilos since I saw her last, and God knows what that translates to with the bind off. How quickly can you get Jude what he wants?"

"I don't know. If Eadwig remembers anything, we might have a starting point…"

"Not good enough." As Frank popped his head around the corner, the doctor turned to him, her expression grave. "Pritam and I didn't have a chance to finish our exam, but we agreed on what we saw. We want to do surgery soon."

He stiffened. "The hole…"

"It hasn't changed, but at the rate she's growing, I'm afraid it will tax her system if we let this go much longer. And that's not the worst thing we're facing."

"What do you mean?" he asked, his voice taking on a shade of panic.

"As I said, she's in sleep, not stasis. A stasis bind slows body systems to almost nil—respiration, circulation, digestion, all the important things. Someone in stasis probably would never even void. But a sleep bind is just that—sleep. A proper bind will slow the internal workings, but nowhere near the level one would see with stasis." Dr. Powell hesitated, then said, "She'll be unconscious, insensate to discomfort unless it triggers something in her dreams, and she won't be able to wake. Meanwhile, her body will keep using the resources available to it…"

Frank's eyes widened as the ramifications hit home. "She'll starve."

"Or dehydrate. That's the more pressing concern. But given how quickly she's growing…" Grimacing, she turned to Toula and suggested, "Tell Jude it's a medical emergency. It's not *quite* that dire yet, but if he thinks her life's in danger, maybe he'll return her. I can't imagine that he's strong enough to pull off a stasis bind on his own—"

"*Ha*," said Ted, his arms folded tightly above his stomach. "He's got a lead on the Antwerp Grail. You really think he's going to give up his best hope of finding it?"

"I don't know," said the doctor, "he's always struck me as a reasonable man—"

"But he may have immortality on the line now."

"I beg your pardon," Eleanor interrupted, "but *what?*"

My boss sighed and pinched the bridge of his nose. "Are you familiar with the grail lore, my lady?"

"As much as the average medievalist, I suppose. Why, have you got one?"

"Plenty, but nothing that would qualify as the capital-G Grail. Not *yet*. But there are several contenders in the literature, references in diaries and hypotheses in monographs, and the so-called Antwerp Grail is the most likely of the bunch. *If* it still exists, which until now has been decidedly unproven. It was barely more than legend even when there were people who claimed to know its whereabouts. But Eadwig found a description of a grail in the extended edition of Simon Magus's diary that matches a drawing of the Antwerp Grail—distinctive markings, see—and that grail's rumored to give eternal life to anyone who drinks from it, and now Jude—"

"Is a fool."

We turned to Eadwig, whose eyes, though still red and puffy, had hardened. "The blodig calic is a trap," he continued. "An irresistible bait, and damnation to the one who would take it."

Frank could restrain himself no longer and marched back into the room. "You know where it is?"

"No," Eadwig muttered. "He..."—he paused and nervously licked his lips—"*I* never found it."

Toula stepped closer until she loomed over the curled-up boy. "Simon, I presume?"

"I don't know. His memories...they don't feel like mine, but they're in my head, they were behind the damn door..." He shuddered. "So many years of memories."

"You remember his life?" Toula murmured.

"Unfortunately," he said, looking up at her. "I remember being old, and all that came before. My God, it's *horrible*. Is that me? Is that truly me?" He laughed weakly, a sound far too close to the edge of hysteria for my comfort. "Tell me it's not. I...I beg you, tell me this is some trick, this is...this is a game, yes? Just a game. Very funny, you win. Take them back, now. Take the memories back."

"Eadwig—"

"*Take them*," he pleaded. "I don't want them, I'm not...I can't..." He started to cry again as the words tumbled out. "This isn't me. These aren't mine, these things...God have mercy, this isn't *me*..."

Toula cut her eyes to Dr. Powell. "Up the dosage?"

"Not unless you want him unconscious," she replied. "And who's Simon?"

She pointed to Eadwig, who had begun to rock. "His aural signature is present in the lattices of all of the Magus's known descendants."

Dr. Powell's jaw sagged. "What, *him*? How?"

"Still trying to figure that out."

"You tested mine?"

The grand magus nodded. "He's in there. A generation further back than in Arnold's and Badger's, but he's there."

"Bloody hell," she muttered, then nudged Toula out of the way and squatted in front of Eadwig. "It's all right, love," she soothed, and whispered a wad of tissues from the ether. "There, now, dry your eyes. May I see something?"

"They're not mine," he weakly insisted, but wiped his face.

"This won't hurt. Back to the couch with you," she ordered, and helped him off the floor. Once he had stretched out again, she pulled her wand from her waistband and began casting above his head, muttering and flicking until the floating outline of what appeared to be a brain hovered a few feet above his face. Flashes of color flared and died on its surface. "Closest I can come to an MRI without a machine," she explained, tucking her wand away.

"Impressive projection," the queen allowed. "How does it work?"

"Modified visualization spell. Slightly trickier than the usual version, but it should give us an idea. Close your eyes, Eadwig, and be still. Don't move, if you can help it." When he was motionless but for the rise and fall of his chest, Dr. Powell said, "I want you to think of a memory you know to be yours. Something from when you were a little boy, perhaps. It doesn't matter what, happy, sad, whatever. Just focus on something you know is true."

A new pattern of colors rippled across and within the projection—corresponding, I supposed, to the variety of structures involved in memory.

"Another," said the doctor. "One of your siblings. Your parents. Imagine the face, voice, smell. Hold it fast in your mind."

The colors shifted only a degree.

"Your home. Picture your home. What does it look like? Can you hear anything? Can you smell your mother's cooking?" She waited for a moment, then whispered and snapped her fingers. The visualization duplicated itself, though the second version was a still shot of the first—a frozen picture of Eadwig's memory in action.

"Very good," she told him, pushing the copy aside. "Now, think of one of *his* memories. Anything. Good or bad, it's all the same." The colors in the visualization shifted again, but more dramatically than before. "Right. Another, but this time, I want you to focus on a voice…"

After asking him to dredge up half a dozen of his new memories, she snapped again, making a second still shot of the visualization. "You can open your eyes now," she said, dissolving the main projection, and pulled the two pictures together while Eadwig sat up on the couch and frowned in confusion. "This is what his base memory retrieval looks like," she told the room, pointing to the first colored brain. "See the differences in activity when he pulls from the other set?"

"I…see different colors," Toula admitted, frowning at the pair. "Mind dumbing it down for those of us who didn't retain high school anatomy?"

"Eadwig's genuine memories are functioning like memories should. Look here and here," she said, poking to bright patches in the first picture. "Auditory and visual cortices fully engage with these memories—his recall is strong, and vivid sensory memory translates into activity in the parts of the brain that interpret those senses, you see?"

"Sure," said Toula.

"Now look at the other one. We still see some sensory cortical involvement, but it's *much* lower. The memories aren't as strong." Turning to Eadwig, she asked, "When you thought about those memories, what was it like? Normal, different?"

Briefly, he pondered the question. "I suppose…it's as if I'm seeing someone else's thoughts, but they feel sort of like mine. Like television, I guess, but *realer*. I'm in it, but…but it's odd. Does that make sense?"

"Sense enough." Returning her focus to Toula, she said, "You say that, at least on an aural level, he's Simon Magus."

"Either that or a full sibling with an intimate knowledge of the complex spells worked on the Magus's diary."

"That would seem to be an easy use of Occam's Razor," Dr. Powell muttered, and pursed her lips in thought. "But how the hell could he have de-aged himself? It's almost like he's been…I don't know, *rewound*. That's not possible."

"Maybe, maybe not. Maria and I are still analyzing the spells on him and the tomb—"

"Don't bother," Eadwig interrupted. "I can answer that for you."

The grand magus arched a brow. "And?"

"And," he said, "to put it bluntly, he…well, I…fucked up."

CHAPTER 14

While Eadwig washed his face in the bathroom and tried to compose himself, I pulled Frank into Marcus's room and closed the door. "We're going to find Aurie," I said, gripping his hands. "Okay? Whatever it takes, we're going to find her."

His fear rolled toward me like hurricane-strengthened breakers speeding for the beach. "How? You heard the kid, he doesn't know where the grail is."

"You remember that Toula knows blood magic, right? The target of a trace doesn't have to be human, just a lineal relative. We'll get a sample from you, let her do her work, and hunt the bastard down. Aurie's going to be just fine."

"Unless the hole grows first..."

"Dr. Powell said it wasn't urgent yet."

"Maybe," he muttered, "but don't you think Toula's going to be *slightly* preoccupied in the next days? Simon Magus is falling to pieces in your den, and that's a fire she can't leave unattended—"

"I promise you, we're going to get her back. If Toula can't do it, then we'll find another wizard who can. It's not like we're hard-pressed for talent around here. Maria could probably name half a dozen magi who could run the spell." I hesitated, then hugged him, and was relieved to feel him squeeze me back. "Hang in there, okay?" I mumbled into his T-shirt. "If you and I could survive the damn Gray Lands, then we can track down one lousy wizard."

"If he's running the Archives, he's probably a halfway

decent wizard."

"Or just *really* anal."

Frank's chest hitched, but I wasn't sure if it was from weak laughter or a choked-down sob.

A moment later, Marcus cracked the door open and slipped inside. "Eadwig's calmer. Want to come out? Maybe there's something about the blasted cup that he *didn't* put in the diary."

"Yeah, sure," said Frank, breaking his hold on me. I glanced up in time to catch him wiping away the moisture beneath his dark glasses, then took his hand again and led him out to rejoin the crowd around the couch.

We found Eadwig sitting in the middle of the cushions, his face still splotchy and damp from the sink, his blue eyes haunted. "Better?" asked Toula, pulling back the coffee table to take a seat opposite him.

"Somewhat," he mumbled.

"Good, because I'm going to need some answers. Eadwig...or Simon, is it?"

The boy cringed. "Simon was *his* name," he replied, pronouncing it almost in the French style. "Not mine."

"All a matter of semantics, though, isn't it?" Maria interjected from her spot beside the window. "You have Simon's memories, his linguistic abilities, his talent—a novice wouldn't be able to cast wandlessly like you did at the Games."

"You know, we can argue over this later," said Toula before Eadwig could protest. "But where *did* 'Simon' come from, anyway?"

He sighed and looked past her, as if reading the answer over her shoulder. "For safety. All of the wizards in the order did it. Take a new name, leave their home, move far away. If anyone ever suspected what they truly were, at least their families would be safe." He paused, then added, "Simon...when he became a priest, one of the senior members of the order came from across the sea. He suggested the name."

"So Simon left home, moved…south? To the seaside?"
Eadwig nodded.

"That town was slaughtered, wasn't it?"

"Must we go through this?" he muttered.

"Just trying to compare against what we've been told,"
Toula replied. "I know it's not pleasant—"

"*Pleasant?* Fifty years of war, woman!" His color rose,
and his hands tightened into fists beside him. "Shall I tell
you of the dead? I can't count the ones he killed. The
slaughter in his dreams…or would you prefer to hear of
how he was tortured? Would you like to know what it feels
like to have a part of you amputated? He was frozen, but
they made certain that he felt *everything*." He turned to his
left, where Eleanor had taken a chair. "The queen and the
king. They *laughed* as he tried to scream. Not you, but—"

"My father," she said simply. "And Coileán's mother."

"They'd kicked my mother out by then," Toula added.
Eadwig swung back to her, and she shrugged at his
surprise. "Witch-blood, babe."

"*You?*"

"Wonders never cease. Now, I don't mean to be crass,
but you're supposed to be dead. What the hell happened?"

"A mistake." Eadwig's fists unclenched, and he
steepled his fingers beneath his chin. "It's all to do with
your precious grail."

"Enlighten me."

Perhaps some part of Eadwig had once been the most
powerful wizard in the world, but the part of him at the
controls that day was sixteen, and the grand magus had a
superb brook-no-argument stare. "He wanted it. He'd
found references to it in the books the order loaned him
for his studies, and he kept finding hints. To the east, the
north, the south, always hints. The bloody chalice that
gives life. He didn't know why blood was required—or
whose blood—but he didn't care. He was going to live
forever."

"It's not entirely terrible, but immortality *can* be

overrated," Eleanor said with a wry twitch of her mouth.

"Tell that to a man going gray and losing the strength in his limbs," Eadwig retorted. "He saw the end approaching. He could barely—" he began, then cut himself short, snapping his mouth shut as a furious blush rose in his face.

Three guesses as to what was failing Simon in his later years, Marcus thought.

I met his knowing gaze and grimaced.

"But he never found the grail," Eadwig continued. "And thank God and all the saints for that."

"Why?" asked Toula.

"Because the life the grail brings is no true life, and the cost is abhorrent. He didn't know until he went to Faerie."

"Don't look at me," said Eleanor as a few of us glanced her way. "I haven't got an evil cup collection."

"The two of them mentioned it on occasion while they were torturing him. A joke between them," said Eadwig. "He was too weakened to maintain his defenses, you see, and they pried for whatever they liked. There he was, an old, broken shell of a man, and the prize he'd sought for so long was a curse. It *amused* them. The grail was in Padova in those days—"

"Padua," Maria offered the room.

Patavium, if you wish to be correct about it, Marcus silently amended.

I realized he'd included Maria in the thought when she quietly snorted.

Eadwig continued, oblivious to the peanut gallery. "It was held by a prominent family. Several faeries frequented the area and reported on its state from time to time."

"But what does it *do*?" Ted pressed.

"It offers a sort of living death," he replied. "Created centuries before my time to punish a wizard of Egypt who made his name by killing faeries. The three of them forged it, the king and the queens, and placed it in his path. A temptation to his own doom. He should have destroyed it as soon as he understood its power, but men being men, its lure proved too great, and it was stolen from him and passed around before he had the chance. When he finally tried to reclaim it and break it, he was killed for his efforts." He smiled grimly at Ted. "Jude's drawing, the one made in blood, is rather appropriate."

"How so?"

"What I...*he*...gleaned from its architects is that the grail is the product of powerful enchantment. Any liquid poured into it turns to blood—or something bloodlike, rather. Drinking it thrusts one into an augmented form of stasis...like a bind, I suppose, but only those portions of it that stop aging. One can still walk and speak as before, though everything within the body ceases to move. No breathing, no heartbeat, the stomach and bowels go still. But to *maintain* this state, the enchantment is structured to require regular infusions of fresh blood—"

"From the grail?" Ted interrupted.

"No, that's only for the first drink. Mortal blood is necessary after that—fae blood will not work, they saw to that, and neither will the blood of cattle or wild beasts. A curse, you understand. To preserve one's own life, one must take the lives of others, then sleep to allow the fresh blood time to permeate. This they do during the day. The enchantment prevents them from walking about in sunlight, apparently. So yes, they have their immortality, but they're cut off from most of the facets of normal life, from their families—"

"Holy *shit*," said Quinn, "are you talking about vampires?"

Eadwig frowned. "About what?"

"Vampires. You know, like in folktales and...well, in movies and stuff, but I guess that's all still on your to-watch list. The undead, right? Drink a vampire's blood, and you basically die but grow fangs and keep going. They feed on blood. Sunlight's lethal, crosses and garlic ward them off, you can kill them with a stake through the heart or by beheading…sound familiar?"

"Somewhat," he allowed. "Though I never heard that crosses have any effect, and *garlic*? How is that supposed to work?"

She shrugged. "Like I said, folktales. But staking kills them, yeah?"

"I've never seen it attempted. Perhaps it would kill the cursed, or perhaps it would merely annoy them. *Sunlight*, now, yes. That's how the enchantment was designed."

"Hold on," Toula cut in, and turned to Eleanor. "What do you think? Possible?"

The queen chuckled dryly. "What, that my predecessors worked together, or that they created vampires on a lark?"

"Pretend they were speaking to each other. Vampires, yea or nay?"

She scowled into space as she considered the matter. "Seems like the sort of matter better accomplished with spellcraft, but the power necessary…honestly, I don't know if *I* could do it, but could Oberon and the others? Possibly. Difficult to say—I barely knew the old bastard."

"He was no slouch," said Toula, and focused on Eadwig once more. "All right. Evil grail on the loose. Where does Ireland come into the mix?"

Eadwig leaned back into the cushions and rubbed his eyes with the heels of his hands. "When they released him from Faerie, he was eighty-four years old and felt about twice that. He'd had time to reflect upon his…career," he said with distaste. "He knew his remaining days were few—"

"For a wizard of *his* ability?" Daphne asked incredulously. "I'd have expected him to make at least a hundred ten, a hundred twenty."

He opened his eyes again and stared at her until she glanced away. "You cannot imagine what they did to him in Faerie. Hell could take lessons."

Eleanor coughed into her fist. "Correct me if I'm mistaken, but my understanding was that Simon sneaked into the realm to kill the Three."

"Correct."

"You can't blame them for a lack of hospitality, then."

"They could have killed him at the start," said Eadwig. "I wish they had. *He* prayed for death every day, but they were having too much fun to let him die." When Eleanor didn't contest that, he continued. "He was broken when he returned to this realm, but he resolved to find that grail and destroy it. A small weight on the scales against everything else he had done, but he was determined. He renounced his Arcanum, broke his wand, and went west to a monastery."

Mal's face scrunched, and he folded his arms. "He had the *Arcanum* at his disposal, and he gave it up?"

"Presumably, he could trust no one," Artur murmured. "Yes?"

"He couldn't be sure of their loyalties. So many of them hated him already," said Eadwig, "and the Council were loath to lose the power they had seized in his absence. But he had faith in one of his grandsons, Ælfræd." A strain of tenderness crept into his voice. "He told Ælfræd his plan. The boy said he was willing to help…"

"He put those spells together?" Maria asked.

Eadwig's eyes widened. "Heavens, no. Ælfræd was barely more than a witch. That's why he was chosen—no one would suspect. To make this brief, Simon ensorcelled his diary and gave it to a friar who was journeying to Normandy. He put protections on it so that no one who sought it to use it would be able to find it—"

"Yeah, those spells fell apart forty-eight years ago," Toula interrupted. "Friend of mine bought your diary at an estate sale."

He seemed pained at the news. "They broke down?"

"No, Faerie was cut off for a few days, long story, but anything without a sufficient reservoir of raw magic crumbled."

"How the hell was *Faerie* cut off?"

"Tell you later," she replied. "Ireland?"

The boy rubbed his neck and nodded. "Right, yes. Simon knew he was in no physical condition to pursue the grail—he was too weak. Over the following two years, he perfected a complex system of spells that would restore his youth. Or so he thought," he muttered. "His mind would be held in deep sleep while his body gradually rejuvenated, returning to its earlier state. But the process would be slow—by his calculations, to roll back a single year, he would need to sleep for about fourteen. So his best option was to hide by faking his death. The order he had joined was comprised of genuine monks, not wizards in disguise, so no one saw the spells he wrapped around himself. And he'd brought a small fortune to the monastery, so when he decided that he wanted a particular tomb, the abbot said nothing. He prepared the spells, summoned Ælfræd for a visit, then created an illusion of death long enough to withstand a funeral mass and entombment. Once inside, he powered the spells around the tomb, then the set around himself." He paused, his gaze vacant. "The next thing he knew, he was me, and I was here. He was only meant to sleep for fifty years. That wouldn't have been long enough to restore him to a point before his time in Faerie, but it would undo some of the damage, make him stronger. He didn't risk sleeping longer for fear that Ælfræd would die in the interim. Ælfræd promised to return and free him, but I suppose he changed his mind—"

"Never had the chance," said Bob. "I made a study of the Magus's grandchildren when I was a young archivist. All had fairly illustrious careers but for Ælfræd, the footnote of the lot."

"How so? He came to harm?"

"He didn't suffer," Bob reassured him. "Lightning bolt, direct hit. He was probably dead before he hit the ground. Only about twenty years old."

"Then that must have occurred shortly after he left Ireland," Eadwig murmured. "Poor boy…"

Toula let that sink in for a moment, then said, "What I'm hearing, then, is that Simon grossly overslept. Baked too long. And instead of, say, eighty-three…"

"Sixteen." He stared back at her, his face taut. "And now carrying another man's memories, none of which reveal the location of the grail. Before you ask," he added as Toula's mouth opened, "the spell wasn't designed to alter his memory. He wanted a younger body with more experience. I suppose he missed this side effect in his calculations."

"But you've got *no* idea where the grail might be?" Lakshmi pressed.

He shook his head. "Not exactly, but…" Searching the crowd, his eyes landed on Ted. "You studied the grail, yes? As Jude did?"

"Sure," he replied. "I'd say there's at least a ninety percent overlap in our reading lists by now."

"You've got notes? Movement over time?"

Ted made a face. "They're not in order—"

"No matter. Bring them," he said brusquely, and rose from the couch. "You'll forgive me, but I'll need quiet if I'm to make any progress."

"Hang on, I still have questions," said Toula.

Eadwig brushed past her toward the kitchen. "As do I, but I trust you would prefer the child alive."

She seemed poised to argue, then bit it back and stood. "Frank, hon, come with me. Let's get a blood trace started."

Within five minutes, the flat was empty but for the six of us who called it home. "Going down to the hole," said Marcus, and kissed my cheek as Artur headed for the door. "When Frank comes back to work, someone should be there to sit with him."

"I'll be along soon," I said, and beckoned to Quinn, who loitered near the stairs, hugging herself. "Why don't you go, too? If there's any grail research to be done, more eyes mean better results."

Artur and Marcus nodded, and Quinn slunk after them out of the flat. When the door latched, I looked from Eadwig's makeshift office at the kitchen table—he'd gone up to his room for a moment—to Beth, who had said nothing for at least half an hour and was skulking by the kitchen sink. "Come on," I told her, "let's grab a bite. Want to go to town?"

"I'm staying in," she replied.

"To do what? Watch him read? Really, you can hang out in the subbasement today—"

"I'm staying," she insisted, and slowly turned to look toward the open window. "Guess someone needs to keep the coffee going."

When I came home that evening, Eadwig was sitting in front of Quinn's borrowed computer and a two-foot stack of Ted's old spiral notebooks, looking between Ted's research and an online world map—an addition from Beth, I trusted. A large wipe-off board had appeared on one wall of the dining nook, three-quarters covered over in neat purple marker. I said hello, Eadwig grunted something that might have been a response, and Beth looked up from the couch and her well-loved T.S. White to flash a small smile. "I offered. He doesn't want help," she whispered.

"Got it. Better put *that* away before Artur gets home," I murmured, ruffling her hair in passing, and she obliged by shoving the paperback under the furniture.

My other sister and Marcus arrived shortly thereafter with Quinn, the three of them having made a run into town for Indian takeout. We spread the bounty across the coffee table, but Eadwig never left his spot, and the rest of us ate in near silence, as if we were intruders in our own flat. Artur offered Beth a sparring session in the courtyard after dinner, but Beth declined and took over the couch once again, playing silently on her computer and keeping watch while the rest of us drifted to our rooms.

I woke around two, carefully untangled myself from Marcus, and slipped out of bed to check on my baby sister. When I cracked open my door, to my surprise, I found that Eadwig had at last taken a break—he and Beth had pulled up chairs to either end of the coffee table, and the Monopoly board was laid out between them. They played by the light of Beth's black Halloween candles, and from what I could smell over the artificial pumpkin spice, the coffeemaker had only just finished its drip.

The dice fell from Eadwig's hand, and his dog token skipped five spots. "Aw, Whitehall again," said Beth through a yawn, "and with the lovely hotel…"

"We can stop," said Eadwig, one hand hovering over his grubby cash.

Having grown up with my dad's old pre-2000 Monopoly set, I'd refused to switch to an electronic banking version, though all I'd been able to find in the charity shops were boards with London place names. From what I could see of the players' financial situation, Eadwig was having a rough night of it.

"Nonsense. No free hotel stays," said Beth, extending her palm. "Thank you for your patronage. Tip the housekeeping staff."

He slapped a few bills into her hand. "I'll concede. Go to bed."

"Nope."

"You're exhausted, you're awake only because of the caffy, and—"

"*Caffeine*," she corrected, "and so are you. Going to sleep?"

I couldn't see Beth's face from my room, but judging by Eadwig's narrowed eyes, I could imagine her smirk.

"I've got work to do," he replied.

"And you were going cross-eyed two hours ago. Sleep

on it, you'll focus better. At least nap."

"Rather not."

Beth shrugged and scooped up the dice, dropping them with a flick of her wrist. "Oh, would you look at that! Eleven. Let me just pop around here to Free Parking, and I'll take *that*…"

"Yes, because you're destitute right now," he muttered as she scooped up the pot. "This is just a slow death. Congratulations, you win again. Now go to bed."

"You're not the boss of me," she said with artificial cheer as she sorted the colored bills.

"Beth—"

"We agreed that we were friends, yeah?"

"Yes," Eadwig cautiously concurred.

"Well, as far as I'm concerned, friends don't let friends brood alone in the dark."

"I'm not *brooding*—"

"You would be. And friends especially don't leave suicidal friends alone." She finished her sorting and raised her head. "As long as you're sitting up, I'm sitting up. Won't be my first all-nighter, bub."

His reply was a short, frustrated sigh. "What if I promise to stay away from the windows? It was a moment of weakness, really."

"No dice," said Beth. "Speaking of which, it's your turn."

Snake eyes landed him on one of her four railroads and brought about the mercy of bankruptcy. "If you're not going to sleep, want to try a different game?" she offered as they packed the pieces away. "Kitty's got a stash in the hall closet. Checkers, chess, Scrabble, Yahtzee…" She paused, then added, "Maybe not Risk."

"What is it?" he asked.

"Another boardgame. The goal's to conquer the world, and Artur is *scarily* good at it."

Eadwig shuddered. "I've seen quite enough world conquering for one lifetime, don't you think?"

"Yahtzee it is, then," she replied, carrying the Monopoly box away. "You'll like this one, it's basically addition and multiplication. Top up the drinks, will you?"

He did as she instructed, but when she returned to the den with the new game, another charity shop special, he stopped her before she could lift the lid. "You needn't do this. I swear to you on whatever you like that I'll do what I can to help find the baby, and that necessarily means no long falls from windows."

Beth's head tilted in query. "Is that what you think I'm concerned about? You flaking out on us before we get Aurie back?"

"You're not worried about her?"

"No. I mean, *yes*, of course I'm worried about her, but right now, I'm worried about you, and I can only deal with so much at one time, so let's play."

"Why?"

"I mean, since you're too tired to keep working but won't do the logical thing and go to sleep, it's either play or stare at each other until dawn—"

"Why do you care?" he amended.

"Because we're friends," she said simply. "And I don't ever want to have to do again what I did today. Got it?"

He slumped in his chair as she set up the game. "I appreciate your sympathy," he murmured after a moment, "but it's unnecessary. I earned this."

The dice slid into the leather-wrapped cup in a rattling stream. "No, you didn't," Beth replied. "*Simon* earned all of it, not you. Here's your scorecard."

"You, ehm…you understand that I *am* Simon, yes? Or part of me is…" He took the paper from her and put it aside without reading the chart. "And if you'd seen in your future what…what *evil* I saw in mine, then you might join me at the window."

"Except it's not your future," said Beth, putting the cup aside. "It's his past."

"And we are—"

"No, you're *not* the same person. Look." Flipping her scorecard to its blank side, she began sketching with a golf pencil, then thrust the drawing across the table. "For the sake of argument, let's say that time is linear, okay?"

The boy suddenly seemed out of his depth. "If you say so…"

"Just work with me. Here's where you start," she said, jabbing her pencil at the left side of the page, "and then you follow this nice line all the way to the point of Simon faking his death, see? Straightforward. But you heard what Dr. Powell said—those memories that you have of things that happened after you went to bed in York are different, yeah? They don't feel like regular memories, do they?"

"No."

"Because—and correct me if I'm wrong, here—the spell Simon put together didn't just make him younger. If that were the case, those memories would feel normal…and, uh, did I hear something about Simon getting castrated in Faerie?"

"Please don't remind me," he muttered, hunching in his chair.

"So you're intact down below—"

"*Yes*! I beg you, can we talk about something else?"

It was difficult to tell with the flickering candlelight, but I could practically hear the blush in his voice.

"It's okay," said Beth, "you proved my point. What the spell did was this." She took the paper back and added to her drawing. "This other line is the spell. See, it loops back from the time it was activated to here, your last real memories."

"A circle, then," said Eadwig.

"Nope. Because *this* little bit here is you." I couldn't see what she was drawing, but she sounded proud of her work. "Here's where you and Simon split. So now we have the Eadwig on his way to being Simon, who woke up the next morning in York with his sick brothers and sisters and kept on living his life, and the Eadwig who woke up in

Glastonbury a thousand years after he went to sleep. Physically, I guess you're the same person—you must have the same aura if the grand magus was able to match you. But *you* aren't the guy who went to war for fifty years and…you know…had that sleepwalking incident with the wizards."

"I massacred them," he mumbled.

"*Simon* did. You've never killed anyone, have you?"

"I'm obviously capable of it! *Children*, Beth!"

My sister drank her coffee in silence for a few moments while Eadwig rubbed his face. "You know," she said after a time, "I told you that my mom's locked up, remember? Three years ago, she tried to kill Magus Corelli, and she was helping the Conclave…doesn't matter. The important thing is that I moved in with my sister. Eventually," she muttered. "Before that, when it was just Mom and me, I *hated* Kitty."

"Why?"

"Because Mom lied to me all my life, and I was too stupid to realize it. But I moved in here, made some friends in my class—my last year in Montana was *not* fun—and I started working with Artur. She's been kicking my ass for two years, and that's the only reason I did as well as I did at the Games. I had to keep my grades up to get lessons from her, see? And, like, I've been to Faerie. I went to the friggin' *Gray Lands* for a royal wedding. Next summer, Ted's promised to let me officially intern with the Team."

"Congratulations."

"Thanks, but I'm not bragging. My point is that if Mom hadn't gotten involved with the Conclave, none of that would have happened to me. I'd probably still be in Montana, feeling like shit every time I wasn't wizard enough to make her happy—I mean, let's be honest, you aren't looking at a future magus."

"You fought well at the Games," he protested.

"Again, because Artur has been kicking my ass. I'm

competent, not a superstar. But imagine that the spell Simon cooked up was on me and took me back to, say, thirteen, and dropped me here. I'd be a different person because I'd be missing three years of experiences. And since Simon had about seventy years of experiences that you haven't had—"

"But I have his memories," Eadwig pointed out.

"Okay. So you have an idea of what your life could be like under very specific conditions. Simon spent most of his time trying to put the Arcanum together, yeah?"

"Simplification, but that's fair."

"Well, that part's done. The Arcanum's been around for a millennium, so that's one thing off your list. Unless you're hell-bent on destroying the Minor Arcanum…"

"What's that?"

"Alternative organization," Beth explained. "Some of them don't like bureaucracy, and a lot of them are descended from wizards Simon killed in their sleep."

He groaned and reached for his mug. "Should have left them alone to begin with. Grivam warned me…"

"The merrow king?"

Eadwig's head shot up. "He lives? You know of him?"

"I don't rate an audience or anything, but yeah, he's still around. Friend of yours?"

He hesitated briefly. "And more. He saved my life…Simon's life, I mean. And Simon saved his. I'm sorry, the memories jumble—"

"Don't worry about it," she soothed. "Especially not now. Way too early in the morning for that." She picked up the dice cup and gave it a shake. "Want to play?"

"Are you sure you won't go to bed?"

"Mm. No. And I should warn you, I've been told I can be stubborn."

"I'd never have guessed." He held his scorecard to a candle and peered at the blanks, then looked back at Beth. "What if I become Simon anyway?"

"I don't know," she replied. "But if you can remember

how you feel right now about killing people in their sleep, then I'd say you have a good chance of not turning into him. Okay, so pay attention. The bottom half the card is where things get a little tricky."

I slipped out of my room shortly after five-thirty that morning to find that sleep had eventually triumphed. Eadwig was curled up in his chair, head back and softly snoring, while Beth had moved her chair in front of the window and grabbed an afghan. Their mugs had long gone cold, and Artur was carefully blowing out the candles to avoid a spray of black wax on the furniture.

"Hey," I whispered, snuffing the last with wet fingertips. "They were up all night—"

"I know. Saw you peeking," she replied, and grinned. Giving Beth a lingering glance, she added, "Baby sister's growing up, isn't she?"

"Could be. She makes a decent amateur counselor. Waffles?"

"Ooh, yes. I'll supervise."

The two in the den didn't stir even as I donned protective grill mitts and wrangled the steel waffle maker from its cabinet, and in the end, Marcus had to shake them awake and promise sustenance before they shuffled to the table. Given their grogginess, the meal was a quiet affair. Marcus and I did our best to keep a conversation going, and Artur added reinforcement, but Quinn only picked at her food. As Marcus cleaned up, I announced that we'd be returning to the office to keep reading. Eadwig nodded his thanks as Beth almost nodded off on her placemat, and I asked Quinn if she'd like to join us again. The conference table had become the center of our makeshift war room, but there was still ample space for a computer or two. Though she agreed to come, she seemed withdrawn and excused herself upstairs almost immediately thereafter.

I traded glances with my sisters, then started up after

her.

Quinn hadn't closed her door, and I found her sitting on the edge of her bed, staring out the window at the morning. "Everything okay?" I asked. "Tired?"

She started at my voice, almost falling off the mattress, and recovered with a slight flush. "Sorry, uh…sorry. Didn't mean to—"

"Are you okay?" I stepped into the room and latched the door behind me. "You haven't been yourself all morning. What's wrong?" Catching her incredulous look, I clarified, "Beyond Aurora and Eadwig. Bad news from home? Did something happen with your family?"

"My family," she said with a mirthless chuckle, "is exactly why we're screwed, isn't it?"

"We're not *screwed* yet—"

"Come on! The baby's sick and starving, the grail's been missing for centuries, and whoever the hell Eadwig is, he doesn't have answers for us. *Jesus*," she muttered, and turned back to the window. "I really liked Jude. How could I have been so dumb?"

"To be fair, this is the first time he's ever kidnapped anyone," I replied, taking a seat beside her. "He has a track record of being a stick in the mud, not a baby snatcher. Honest mistake."

"The whole damn family's cursed," she muttered. "First Grandpa's brother, now Jude…"

"That's two out of how many? Three, if you want to add James's son," I allowed, "but I guess he followed in his father's footsteps."

"What about Grandpa's parents, who happily kicked him out and never saw him again? Or his grandparents— they stole his freaking memory!"

I smoothed a wrinkle between us in the duvet. "It sounds awful, I get that, but remember that what they did to him wasn't that uncommon for families with duds. It's not right, and I'm with you there, but it doesn't mean they were completely evil. Your grandpa's not horrible, is he?"

"No."

"Neither are you. Just because Jude's gone off the deep end doesn't mean you're damned to do likewise." Lowering my voice, I added, "I know I told you about my mother. Did I mention that my biological father is dead?"

"Yeah…"

"Did I tell you that he tried to kill Artur and me?" Her eyes widened, and I shrugged at her shock. "I've fought and I've killed, but I don't think I've turned out quite like either of my parents. And if I'm not cursed to follow in their footsteps, then you're not cursed to be like your distant relatives. Okay?"

Quinn kept her silence for a moment, then mumbled, "I thought my life was turning around. Everything was going to be great here with Jude and the Archives, and now…"

I squeezed her shoulder as I stood. "Ted's always on the lookout for talent. How about it? Want to go back to the subbasement and read until we figure this mess out?"

She didn't seem to be sold on my reassurance, but she took my hand and followed me downstairs.

Saturday ended with a headache from the hours I spent staring at a computer screen beneath the fluorescent lights of the Team's conference room. Mal had taken the initiative of taping a large world map to the wall and adding pins with dates for the grail's last known locations, and by the time we broke that night, a web of red string sprawled across Europe, Asia, and northern Africa. Barely satiated by the bags of chips we'd munched well away from any manuscripts but too tired to eat a real meal, we dragged ourselves to bed. Eadwig was still rereading the diary when we got home, and Beth shook her head before I could ask for an update.

I curled up against Marcus that night, willing my brain to shut off but unable to stop my thoughts from cycling back to Frank, who'd locked himself in his office so that his pacing wouldn't disturb the rest of us. Maria had quietly slipped me the bad news: the blood trace had failed. Toula was tweaking the spell, but so far, there was no sign of Aurora. She'd started a second one on Jude, using an amplification spell on his sample on file, but she didn't hold out much hope. "It's possible that he's hiding her in the Gray Lands," Maria concluded, "but unlikely. Mulligan's people were able to block blood traces, and Toula's using what she knows of that spell to craft a workaround, but these things take time."

Neither of us mentioned the third possibility: blood traces only work on living targets. Surely Jude wouldn't have let her die, I told myself. Surely he wouldn't have dumped her as a burden and tried to trade on a false promise of her safe return.

The thought nauseated me, making me regret even the chips I'd eaten.

"It's been less than two days," Marcus murmured beside me. "There's no reason to assume the worst yet." I stiffened in surprise, and he rubbed my back to calm me. "You're not broadcasting, don't worry. But you're too tense to have anything else on your mind." Pulling me closer, he whispered, "Let it go for a few hours. You need to sleep."

"I'm sure Frank's not."

"We can't help that tonight. Want me to knock you out?"

Almost as soon as the words slipped free, both of us began to laugh, having reached the point of exhaustion where almost anything can be funny. "That's the most romantic thing anyone has ever said to me," I managed, then buried my face in the pillow to muffle the giggles.

The shaking from Marcus's side of the bed wasn't helping the situation. "Flowers, jewelry, and forced unconsciousness," he said. "Sorry, that…that came out wrong…"

"Forget it. I love you."

"I love you, too." He brushed my hair from my face in the darkness as we calmed, and I let myself enjoy the sensation of touch, grateful for a moment's distraction.

"You know," he began after a moment, "if you truly can't sleep, I might be able to think of a more enjoyable alternative."

"Mm. Remember that part about how Beth and Eadwig are still up?"

"I'll sound-proof the door," he offered.

"Thanks, but with them there, on top of everything else…"

"Not in the mood?"

"I'm sorry. Don't mean to disappoint you."

The blankets shifted as he sat up in bed, and I squinted when he motioned his nightstand lamp on. "Kitty, we're tired, there's an active kidnapping, and the way Simon Magus looks at your sister is not at all platonic. Don't let me make things *worse*."

Unsure of how much might be overheard in the den, I kept my voice low. "I just feel like I've been neglecting you, hon. With Quinn and Eadwig, and with Frank, and with Beth getting concussed…" I sat up as well, my bare arms chilling beneath the ceiling fan. "You've been pushing for a long weekend away for a month, now, and I've barely taken a *day*, and I'm sorry…"

He cupped my face and kissed me. "Tennessee will be there when we're ready, yes? I'm in no hurry. Don't feel guilty."

"We haven't even had a real date night in weeks—"

"And we will have *centuries* to make up for lost time. The last thing I want right now is for you to feel more stressed because of me, okay?"

"Okay," I mumbled, and flopped back onto my pillow.

Marcus cut the light and rejoined me. "You bear so much of the weight here already," he said as he pulled the duvet over my shoulder. "You're the axis around which this flat turns."

"I wouldn't go that far…"

"*I* would. You keep Beth in school and mostly out of trouble. Quinn trusts you more than anyone here. Eadwig listens to you when he won't listen to Beth. And as for Artur and me, nothing need be said. We've leaned on you for years."

"Y'all just needed a hand."

"And you provided it. We can't be the easiest of flatmates. Throw in Maria, and that's six people under your watch. Oh, and let's not forget Frank—you've been looking after him all summer. No wonder you're exhausted, my love." He kissed me again, and we lay together in the center of the bed. "I'm not leaving, and I'm not *disappointed*, of all things. What I want is for you to tell me either how to help or how to stay out of your way."

"You've been wonderful," I told him. "I don't know what more either of us could be doing tonight, to be honest."

"I could take Eadwig aside and warn him that if he pursues Beth—"

"What, you'll come after him?" I teased.

"Of course not. I'll alert Artur, and she'll convince him to change his ways."

I laughed softly and felt him reach for my waist. "We make a weird family, don't we?"

"Yes," he admitted, "but everything I want is right here, so…a little weirdness isn't too bad, is it?"

"Not at all." I closed my eyes and sighed as he hugged me. "Hey, remember that time you asked me what penguin tastes like?"

"Fine, a lot of weirdness," he mumbled, and held me until I fell asleep.

CHAPTER 15

By Sunday night, we agreed that we'd reached a dead end. Eadwig, ignoring the fact that Dr. Powell had yet to officially clear him, joined Beth, Quinn, and the Team in our conference room to inspect Mal's string map. "And here's where it disappears," Mal concluded, tapping a spot near the Belgian coast as he presented the timeline. "We know it was in Antwerp by 1700, but 1702 is the last confirmed sighting. The merchant who bought it reported in his log that he hired a fisherman he trusted to go down the river to the North Sea and drop it in a weighted sack. And since no one's seen it since, the odds are good that it's still on the sea floor."

Bob rubbed his chin. "If we had a part of the grail to work with, I know of a technique that would call the rest of it forth, but assuming it's intact…"

"We could dredge," said Daphne, "but that would take months, at least."

"We don't *have* months," Frank snapped.

"Try years," Ted muttered from the far end of the table. "Three and a half centuries of silt, currents, and whatnot—hell, at least you can take a magnet and find a needle in a haystack. We've got nothing to go on."

Daphne nodded. "Assuming it's even there. What's to say the fisherman didn't keep it or sell it? Or perhaps the merchant wrote that note to stop grail hunters from bothering him—a ruse of sorts, yeah?"

Eadwig, who had remained silent throughout the presentation, cleared his throat. "Have you considered the possibility that it went to the merrow?"

"What, intentionally?" said Mal.

"No. I recall Grivam being something of a collector, and he said it was not uncommon among his people. Perhaps one of them has seen it—if, that is, it landed in the sea."

For the first time that evening, I saw a glimmer of hope in Frank's eyes, unshaded as they were in the safety of our suite. "You think he'd give it up?"

"I think he would *trade*," Eadwig replied. "If we could present something more enticing…"

"Than an immortality-granting cup?"

The boy shrugged. "It could be that he doesn't know of its properties. The merrow have no skill with magic, remember. They're merely shifters."

"*Merely*?"

He looked back at Mal, who was bristling with indignation, and frowned. "Have I offended?" Beth leaned over and whispered in his ear, and his face colored. "I meant no disrespect," he hastily told Mal, "I was only saying that—"

"Yeah, yeah, whatever," Mal replied, cutting him off with a wave. "Just watch it with the 'high and mighty wizard' crap. And where do we find Grivam, anyway?"

Antony lifted a finger. "They've got a presence in the Florida Keys—the Fringe database covers that much. Hang on…" He tapped at his computer for a moment, then nodded. "Coordinates are in the system. Looks like Badger Parsons and Seamus Malone had a sit-down with him at some point."

Producing his phone from his pocket, Mal said, "They're in the settlement—want me to call my parents for their number?"

"I've got a better idea," I interjected before he could start dialing. "The merrow go back and forth between the realms, right? Why don't we just ask Ros? If anyone can get a message to Grivam, surely she can."

"Seconded," said Ted, and pushed himself to his feet. "Does anyone know what time it is in Faerie before we go barging over?"

I traded looks with Marcus, Mal, and Frank, all of whom appeared to be searching for an answer to a tricky riddle. Though it was seldom easy to keep track of the time difference when Faerie's end kept shifting, I'd been over enough in recent weeks to have an idea. "Say morning, but it's not like Ros sleeps."

"*Sam* does," Frank mumbled.

"Sam will understand," I replied, and opened a gate to the meadow outside of Val's mountain villa. I doubted that the king would have minded had we shown up in his courtyard—Marcus and I had standing invitations, after all—but protocol dictated that an Arcanum group not drop by uninvited, and common sense insisted that pissing off Val's guards wouldn't do me any favors. "We'll be back as soon as we have answers," I told Frank, and headed through, followed by Ted, Marcus, both of my sisters, and, to my surprise, Eadwig. Sealing the gate behind him, I said, "I thought you might want to avoid this place. Bad memories, yeah?"

"Horrible," he agreed, "but if it means locating Grivam—"

The rest of that thought ended abruptly as Ros materialized a few feet away and marched toward us, her radiance golden against the cloudless sky. "I *thought* you seemed familiar!" she exclaimed, pointing to Eadwig. "Wow. Uh..." She paused, cocking her head as she considered him. "You're kind of messed up, aren't you?"

His eyes widened in alarm, though whether at her greeting or her manifestation, I couldn't be sure. "Have, ehm...have we met?"

"Ros Bolin. Hi," she said, extending a glowing hand, which he shook with faint trepidation. "You know how Faerie has a consciousness?"

"So I'd heard..."

"Well, that would be me. My *predecessor* remembers you—or the other version of you—from the 1060s." She grimaced and hissed through her teeth. "Not pretty."

"Understatement," he muttered.

"Quite. That's a neat trick you pulled—oh, don't bother trying to put up a block, you can't keep me out of your head," she added with a grin. "*Nice* crafting. You should really go over that with Toula, she's great on the theoretical end—"

"If you're in my head, then why didn't you say something when I was here weeks ago?" he blurted.

Ros folded her arms. "Your memories were locked up tight, and honestly, I was preoccupied. I'm omniscient in this realm, but that doesn't mean I always pay attention to every detail as it happens. Since I was doing everything in my power to keep Frank's kids alive, you were interesting but not a priority. Don't take it personally."

Glancing toward the villa, I caught the motion of an opening door and waved at the guard. "Any chance that Grivam's around?" I asked Ros.

She shook her head. "Not here. Several of his children are, and I've asked them to find him and bring him back while we've been talking, but that could take time." Gesturing toward the villa, she added, "I also took the liberty of telling Val you'd stopped by, and you're expected for lunch...well, brunch, I guess," she said, considering the ascending sun. "Eleanor and Coileán are on their way."

"That's nice of y'all, but you know it's, like, ten p.m. in Glastonbury."

"Uh-huh. Which is also why Bonnie is heading off to have your rooms and a few guest rooms freshened. Any other questions?"

The guard seemed to be beckoning us closer, and Ted, who'd been to Faerie far too often for a respectable wizard, took it all in with a shrug. "Are we talking mimosas?"

The other two of the Three weren't the only ones on Val's impromptu guest list. Ted and I had just finished recapping the path of the grail when Bonnie, Val's chief of staff, opened the dining room door. "Found these two miscreants lurking in the courtyard," she announced, and stepped aside to admit Badger and Seamus.

I'd known the Fringe settlement's two-person security force since I was a kid, but even if we'd never met, their reputations preceded them: the coordinator who'd returned to the mortal realm following the Mulligan purge to search for the missing and held off an invasion from the Gray Lands, and the unwitting faerie lord who'd joined the cause and remained by her side. I'd seldom seen them so much as agitated—settlement policing was a cushy retirement gig—but that afternoon, they gaped at Eadwig from the doorway.

"Come in, come in," Val insisted, pointing to a pair of empty chairs. "I thought this might be of interest to you."

"That's a word for it," Badger murmured, her dark eyes fixed on the boy.

Although almost a thousand years separated them, Eadwig and Badger shared a certain commonality of appearance, subtle but for their strikingly similar hair: black and thick, with a white forelock over the left eye. Perhaps it was chance, or perhaps it was the product of a millennium's worth of genetic shuffling, but I wasn't imagining the hint of familial resemblance. Dr. Powell looked nothing like Eadwig, nor did Magus Lowe or any of the other descendants I could name off the top of my head, but there was no mistaking his echo in Badger's face. True, I mused, she was glamoured—having moved to Faerie in her late sixties, Badger hadn't minded returning to an appearance matching her husband's perpetual youth—but the glamour was natural, a version of what had been instead of an enchantment-based redesign.

Nor did it escape me that Badger, though a loyal Fringer, possessed a magus-level talent. Had she been raised Arcanum, she'd almost certainly have merited a seat on the Council alongside her less gifted cousin, Arnold Lowe. It was no secret to those of us with Fringe database credentials that Badger was a sleepwalker, able to access the mortal realm's dream space and connect with other sleeping talents—and that she was the first known sleepwalker since Simon Magus who could cast in there, a terrifying power. But Badger had used it sparingly, producing food and other supplies as needed to help hiding Fringers get to rendezvous points, while Simon had used it to horrifically different ends.

She stared at him as if taking his measure, then softly said, "You clever bastard."

"I…I apologize," Eadwig stammered, shrinking under her gaze, "have we met?"

"Simon *fucking* Magus," she said, drawing out each word. "Bloody hell."

"It's all right," Seamus murmured, clamping a hand on her shoulder, "steady, love—"

Badger shook him off and advanced toward the table. "I've got a lot of friends in the Minor Arcanum. Friends who told me *loads* about you, you sick fuck," she continued, her lip curling into a snarl. "And Grivam told me the rest. So give me one reason why I shouldn't end you here and now."

Before she could close the distance, Ros materialized between them. "Because he's not the genocidal version of Simon," she said, holding up her hands to stay Badger's march. "Call that one Simon Prime. This is pre-Simon Eadwig, carrying around Prime's memories. He's *sixteen*, more or less."

Badger scowled at them both. "Then how—"

"A spell with side effects that Prime didn't anticipate. It didn't just restore his youth—it turned back the clock, erased what had happened. Physically, emotionally, he's a kid," Ros explained, thumbing one hand over her shoulder toward Eadwig. "He's much stronger than he should be, and he's got a lot of Prime's accumulated knowledge—the spell wasn't perfect."

"He designed it that way," Eadwig mumbled.

"There you have it," said Ros. "So yeah, biologically, aurally, they're the same guy. But we almost have a dual timeline situation...you're right about that," she added, nodding to Beth. "Good way of conceptualizing the problem."

Though exhausted, Beth faintly smiled with the praise.

"To answer your question, Eadwig," Ros continued, "no, you haven't met. This is Badger Parsons, and she's never been thrilled with the knowledge that the Parsons clan descends from...how many of them?" she asked Badger. "Three, four?"

"Arnie says it's four proven," she grumbled, letting Seamus wrap an arm around her shoulders. "Dol, Guillaume, Amice, and Berthe."

Eadwig's eyebrows rose with comprehension. "You..."

"Old Arcanum family, at least up my father's side, and since everyone wants the prestige of a bloodline to the Magus, that's a lot of intermarrying cousins. It's possible that we've got links to other children of yours, but those four are known. Good old Simon and Béatrix," she said, her voice dripping with sarcasm. "And if you're actually *Eadwig,*" she added with an odd look, "then I assume she was the French one."

He nodded slowly. "Her father was powerful in Normandy. When Simon made peace with him, one of the conditions was that he marry Béatrix. She would have preferred a convent, but when that option was taken from her...she was a dutiful wife."

Badger's mouth twitched. "Not a love match, then?"

"Not at all. I would not disparage her," he hastened to explain, "she was beautiful and clever, and quite talented, but the marriage was political." He paused, then made a face. "*Four* children, you say?"

"Over a thousand years," Eleanor interjected. "That's

not indicative of a problem."

Badger spread her hands. "As I said, the Parsons are old-blooded, and those family trees get twisty."

While she didn't smile, her face softened a degree as Seamus led her to an empty chair. "We heard you're waiting for an audience with Grivam," he said, glancing around my end of the table.

"Grail quest," Artur muttered. "Finally, I get one."

"He never mentioned a grail when we spoke to him"—his wife nodded her agreement—"but everything I've heard of Grivam suggests he's a hoarder. Have you anything to trade in case he's got this grail?"

Ted broke a roll in half and reached for the herbed butter, Val's cook's perfected recipe. "Not yet," he said. "But since it's Frank's kid on the line, I'll give him just about anything he wants for the damn thing. Suggestions?"

Seamus looked to Badger as he sat. "What did we do last time? There was a fair amount of wine, and—"

"Bathrobe," she replied.

"*Right*. You think he still has it?"

"It's been forty-odd years. I can't imagine it's intact if he's kept it in salt water all this time."

"So, new bathrobe," said Ted. "Booze…"

"I gave him a walking stick once," Coileán offered, "and, uh…"

When he left the thought unfinished, Ros looked mildly ill. "Keep Dad out of this."

"I'm just saying that *favors* aren't off the table," the king protested.

"I know, and I would sincerely appreciate it if you didn't remind me." When he smirked in reply, Ros leaned over the table to glower at him. "I know in unfortunately intimate detail what happened that night because Dad and Ilunna have both spent time here, okay? I could also give you the play-by-play of my own conception, but *let's not go there*." Glancing up at the rest of us, she muttered, "Near omniscience has its awkward moments. Leave it at that.

And unless Ilunna has a little sibling they've all somehow managed to hide from me, I don't think anyone's going to be called upon for that sort of bargaining. She's in her sixties by now."

Vague as Ros had been, I caught her drift, and judging by the expression on my baby sister's face, she was right with me. My boss, however, was slower on the uptake. "Could you be a little more specific?" he began. "Sorry, I'm—"

"Sex," Artur snapped, cutting him off. "And not to be cruel, Ted, but if anyone's services prove to be necessary, I would think it'd be someone other than you."

"That's, uh…reassuring," he replied, though his face suggested otherwise. "Maybe we can stick to booze, eh?"

While the Three had questions—and I'm sure Badger had more than a few strong words left for Eadwig—those of us on Glastonbury time were wiped and bleary-eyed after a long few days of research, and Val had mercy. That afternoon, I put Beth in my old room while I crashed with Marcus next door. I'd just settled into bed when I heard her door click open and soft footsteps pad down the breezeway, heading toward the other guestrooms.

"Damn it," I groaned, and was about to get up and hunt her down when my phone beeped with a message from Artur: *She's protecting him. Leave her be.*

Or they're up to no good, I tapped back.

His room is between mine and Ted's, she responded. *I took the liberty of splitting his bed in two before he saw otherwise. Go to sleep. I have the watch.*

But weary though we were, no one slept well or long. Artur and I ended up in the dining room for a midnight snack that felt more like breakfast, while Beth and Eadwig surrendered to insomnia and emerged hours before dawn. By sunrise, Ted was on his third espresso of the morning and pacing the central courtyard, wandering among the flowers and fountains as we waited for news.

"Perhaps I should remove the caffeine from his next refill," Val mused, watching Ted from the threshold of the dining room. "Do you suppose he would notice?"

"He once called decaf an abomination unto God, so yeah, probably," I replied. "Better not make a bad morning worse."

He grunted noncommittally and shut the door, giving the two of us a moment's privacy while the rest of my party either dressed or stalked around the villa. "What does this mean for Toula?" he asked, taking the chair beside me as his drink topped itself up.

"Well, for starters, she's going to need a new head archivist—"

"Beyond that," he said, waving the matter aside. "The boy is more or less Simon Magus. If I heard you correctly yesterday, he retains…" Val frowned. "What would you call it, his predecessor? Former self?"

"Simon?"

"Sure. He retains Simon's knowledge and skill. And one must assume that his talent will continue to grow as he matures again. Simon was a legend in his time—how much more powerful will Eadwig be?"

"Honestly, I've been trying not to think that far ahead. Got enough fires to put out as it stands." I drained my teacup and nodded my thanks as it refilled. "There's no telling right now exactly what he remembers, or even if he can put everything he recalls to use. Toula mentioned sending him to Magus Popova for evaluation, but that's a matter for another day."

"And perhaps another magus."

"Popova knows her stuff. She was Maria's tutor, remember?"

"Maria wasn't *him*." He paused to sip his coffee—like Ted, Val never bothered with decaf. "When Toula took office, the understanding was that she would step aside if a more *acceptable* wizard with a talent like hers arose. The boy has yet to be tested, of course, but I wouldn't be surprised if he's a contender. Add to that the fact that he is or was Simon Magus, and..." His mouth tightened. "I worry about her in that place," he said, lowering his voice. "Once the Council learns of his existence, how many seconds do you think it will be before they call for her resignation?"

"No one's said anything, as far as I know," I replied. "Magus Lowe probably has some idea, and Quinn might have mentioned him to Magus Popova, but it's not like there's been a formal announcement."

"Only a matter of time," said Val. "The Magus has returned to his Arcanum."

"Except for that part where Eadwig wants nothing to do with him."

Val shrugged. "He is young yet, and he may not be given the choice," he said, pointedly clearing his throat at the last—a message for Ros, I had no doubt, considering how she had forced him onto a throne. "Even if he objects, that would still unsettle Toula's position, and we both know what happens when the Council gets crazy ideas." Finishing his drink, he returned the cup to the ether and patted my arm. "Do me a favor and keep this conversation between us, yes? My sister takes offense when I treat her as anything less than untouchable."

I smiled. "They're a pain sometimes, aren't they?"

"Trust me, brothers are no better," he said as he rose. "By the way, is my son treating you well?"

"*Val.*"

"I worry about you two," he protested. "You spend so much time in Glastonbury these days..."

"And you can't spy?"

"*Observe* is a better word. Toula tells me nothing."

"Good," I said, rolling my eyes. "Don't worry, I'm sure my dad's checking up on us as it is."

"But I can't talk to your father, so what use is that to me?"

"Maria would probably say something if there were an

emergency," I replied, pushing in my chair. "Or Ted."

Val nodded. "Mm, yes. He's not shy."

"See? Plenty of intel."

"Put my mind at ease and visit more often."

I couldn't be upset with him for caring—Val was the closest thing I'd had to a father since Daddy died. I seldom even removed his graduation gift, a pendant of tiny colored diamonds worked into the shape of a sunflower like the ones I'd loved back in Tennessee.

Before I quite knew what I was doing, I stepped closer and kissed his cheek. "Marcus is still treating me like gold. You have nothing to worry about."

"Hardly," he replied, but sounded pleased. "And I mean it—you need to come for dinner."

"Once the times realign—"

Before I could finish, Ros appeared by the door. "Grivam just crossed into the realm. Should be ashore in half an hour. Rally the others, and I'll make the gate."

When one thinks of watching a person rise from the sea, one's mind might go to *The Birth of Venus*, or perhaps to Bo Derek. The naked, youthful woman who emerged in the shallows fit the mold: thin and toned, with large, dark eyes and black hair that fell over her breasts and halfway down her back, she almost sashayed to shore, stumbling only once on her unfamiliar legs. She had the sort of attributes that would give a nearby swimsuit model self-doubt, but her smile was quick and warm. "Hello!" she called in Fae, taking in the small crowd gathered on the beach: the six of us from Glastonbury, the Three, and Ros, who'd gone corporeal for the occasion. "Father is behind me…" She glanced over her shoulder at the unmarred sea, then hurried up the slope and said, "We came quickly, and he's not as young as he was. Would a seat be possible?"

"Of course," said Eleanor, waving a shaded wooden bench into being in the sand. "May I offer you refreshments? A towel, perhaps?" she asked, pulling a fluffy blue bath sheet from the ether.

Pity, Marcus thought, and yelped when Artur stomped on his foot.

The merrow woman wrapped herself against the chilling breeze, nodded to the Three, then regarded Ros with unhidden surprise. "My lady, I've not had the honor."

"At ease, Ilunna," Ros replied, sounding perfectly pleasant to anyone who didn't know her well. "He wasn't invited. Sorry to disappoint."

Her smile dimmed. "That's too bad. How *is* Joey? I haven't seen him in years, and—"

"He and Mom are doing well."

"He and...oh. *Oh*," she said, wincing as comprehension registered. "He's your..."

"Mm-hmm."

Ilunna held up her hands and took a step back. "I meant no disrespect, my lady."

"I know," said Ros. "And he remembers you fondly."

"Likewise—*ah*." A splash behind her saved her from continuing the awkward conversation. "Father. Excuse me while I assist—"

"He would prefer to do it alone," Ros murmured, and Ilunna stood back while Grivam swam the final yards to shore.

His emergence was somewhat less graceful than his daughter's had been. While the merrow are long-lived, they do age, and if the Fringe reports were accurate, Grivam had seen over two millennia. The man who limped from the surf, leaning on a gold-topped, barnacle-encrusted cane, was wizened and stooped. His wispy white hair clung to his wet scalp above deep-set eyes, and his pale skin seemed to drape from his too-thin limbs. As he climbed up the hard-packed sand, he nodded first to his peers. "Valerius. Young Coileán. Young Eleanor." Spotting Ros standing with his daughter, he paused and cocked his head. "My lady. You called?"

"I apologize for troubling you, Grivam, but this is a time-sensitive matter," she said, and gestured toward my clump. "The Arcanum would like a word."

"Indeed?" He glanced at the bench prepared for him, then pivoted toward us. "I would have expected young Tou..." He fell silent, his mouth hanging slack, then hobbled two steps closer. "Moon and stars," he whispered. "*Eadwig?*"

"You know his name," Coileán remarked.

"As well I should. He gave it to me, but that was an age ago..." Grivam's lips moved soundlessly for a moment, and then he managed, "How can this be? You're *human*. You died, I visited your tomb, I..."

"Hello, old friend," Eadwig murmured, slowly closing the distance between them. "Perhaps you should sit."

"Perhaps," Grivam agreed, and sank onto the bench with clear relief when it slid behind him. Clutching his cane, he peered at Eadwig, then shook his head in disbelief. "How?" he asked again. "The last time we met—"

"Simon was old and weak. He feigned his death. The spell was only meant to rejuvenate him for fifty years. Ælfræd was supposed to free him—"

"*Ælfræd?*" Grivam interrupted with a bark of incredulous laughter. "You entrusted yourself to *him?*"

"He was a good boy," Eadwig protested. "Died in a freak accident, I was told."

"On a boat, in the middle of a storm. He couldn't shield himself from the lightning, and he knew it." The old merrow sighed and shook his head. "Why not Osric? Wasn't he your favorite once?"

"Compromised. The Arcanum refused to select a new leader until Simon's death, and Osric's father made no secret of his plans for the succession...but that's immaterial now. Simon used the spell so that he could seek out and destroy a cursed cup, a grail. Every record suggests it was cast into the sea three and a half centuries ago," he continued, gesturing to the Team, "and so we've come to ask if you know of its whereabouts."

Grivam's eyes narrowed. "*Simon* did these things, you say? What manner of address is this?"

Ros lifted a finger to draw his attention. "The spell didn't just restore his body—it spun his mind back as well, presumably to a point before he took on the alias. He still has Simon's memories, but they're not *his* memories, if you follow. Short version, Eadwig is and isn't Simon."

He stroked his chin. "A strange magic, this."

"An accident," Eadwig muttered.

"Only one as talented as you could have caused such a spectacular accident," Grivam replied. "Now, what sort of grail could have convinced you to attempt…*this*?" he asked, waving one hand toward Eadwig's much-rejuvenated body.

The boy cut his eyes toward Ted. "Created by the Three to torture a wizard. It brings immortality to those who drink of it…"

"Made the rounds across three continents for centuries," Ted continued, "and was allegedly dumped into the North Sea in 1702."

Grivam's head tilted in query. "Where?"

"Uh…does Antwerp ring a bell?"

To my surprise, he nodded vigorously. "Antwerpen? Yes, but it has been a time since I traveled its river. Tell me of the grail you seek…" He paused, his eyes widening, then turned back to Eadwig. "Immortality, you said? *That* grail?"

"You know of it?" he asked.

"I do. A gift was made." He coughed, and a glass of white wine appeared on the bench beside him. Lifting it in salute to Ros, he downed half. "My thanks. As for the grail, my son Pilp was injured and found by a fisherman, who, much as you or your predecessor did for me," he said, tilting his glass toward Eadwig, "took him home and bound up his wounds. He asked nothing in return, nor would he accept payment from me when Pilp introduced us—I could not speak his language, but my son knew enough to make his meaning clear," he explained. "Boudewijn, he was called. A rare man, advanced in years and wanting nothing but a good catch. His wife was dead, his children grown, and still he worked long hours on the river—and he was content. Pilp was quite fond of him. A few years later, Pilp brought me a strange cup. A beautiful thing it was, fashioned all of gold, with rubies set in the base—"

"A nine-pointed star motif?" Eadwig asked.

"Yes. Pilp told me that Boudewijn had been asked to throw it into the sea. The man requested that it be taken somewhere it would never be discovered, and it was no trouble for me to grant such a simple request. He died the next winter," Grivam continued, looking into the distance. "The grail remains safe in my keeping. And you would destroy it?" he enquired, turning once more to Eadwig. "The reason you yet live is this grail?"

"I would not lie to you," he replied. "But there's been an unexpected complication."

"How so?"

"One of their number has a newborn," said Eadwig, sweeping his hand toward our huddle. "The child is sick, starving, and at risk of death. She was taken by a wizard to be held in trade for the grail."

Grivam's dark eyes flicked toward Ros, who nodded. "He's telling the truth," she confirmed. "Ilunna, do you remember Georgie?"

"Of course, my lady," she replied, inching closer. "I've not seen her in years…"

"The child is her son's daughter. I am *deeply* concerned for her safety," said Ros, holding Grivam's stare. "The man who took her seeks immortality, and based on what I've seen from that one," she continued, pointing to Ted, "the grail is his ultimate prize. I doubt he'd be satisfied with anything less."

Eadwig cleared his throat. "Name your price, Grivam. What will you take for the grail?"

The merrow considered Eadwig for a long, silent moment as he finished his wine, then slowly blinked. "Nothing."

"You'll give it to us, then?" asked the boy.

"You misunderstand me. That grail is not for you." As Eadwig sputtered his protestation, Grivam spoke over him, his voice gravelly but strong. "You say you will give it away in trade. You won't drink of it first? *You?*"

"Its gift is a curse," said Eadwig. "No, I want nothing but destruction for the grail."

"You could live forever."

"Not like that."

A small smile played at the corners of his pale lips. "I cannot take that risk, Eadwig. Whoever you think you are now, I knew Simon all too well. He burned his path around the world once, and I won't give him a chance to do it again."

"I wouldn't do that," Eadwig mumbled, though he didn't sound entirely convinced.

"Really, it's not for him," said Ros. "They just want it to get the baby back, and once they've made the trade—"

"Then this wizard who would steal a sickly child to gain immortality will have it, and what's to stop him?" Grivam finished. "Again, a poor outcome."

"And I'm sure that the full resources of the Arcanum will be directed toward apprehending him and meting out whatever punishment is necessary. *Please.*"

"My lady," he replied, folding and unfolding his hands—I supposed his missing webbing was bothering him—"I appreciate your position, and I am certain that you would do whatever you could. But you can't make guarantees on behalf of the Arcanum, and once the grail leaves this realm, you will have no power over it. I can't imagine that the wizard would be so foolish as to agree to make the trade in Faerie, after all."

"He's an archivist," she tried again. "Not even a great wizard. Once the baby's safe…hell, Eadwig could probably take him now."

His quick smile, accompanied by a hint of teeth, didn't meet his eyes. "Assuredly so. But Eadwig is my greater concern. I *cannot* allow him access to such power." Turning to the Glastonbury cluster, he said, "Simon was a mighty man in his day. Do you know how many he killed?"

Artur chuckled softly beside me. "Come, now," she said to Grivam, "neither of us has clean hands. I've killed my share, and if the Fringe is to be believed, so have you."

"I don't deny it," he replied, placid as ever. "Artur of Afallon, yes?"

"I am."

"If I have heard truly, you killed to protect your people. Creatures from the Gray Lands."

"And ordinary men from the east."

"Again, in defense. I killed to finish a war I didn't start. *Simon* killed men, women, and children in their sleep."

Eadwig's shoulders hunched as Grivam spoke. "What can I do to convince you of my intentions?" he demanded. "Name it. What safeguards would you have?"

"Ros obviously thinks he's sincere. If we can do something to put your mind at ease, say so," Coileán added, and Eleanor and Val nodded.

But Grivam had eyes only for Eadwig. His fingers locked and unlocked as he considered the matter, until finally, he gripped his cane and stood. "You would prove your sincerity?"

"I would," said Eadwig, holding his stare.

"Go to the ones who call themselves the Minor Arcanum. My understanding is that some of the distant children of the people you slaughtered without cause are among their number. Turn yourself over to them and accept their justice, and when they're satisfied, send word for the grail. Ilunna will accompany you to ensure that all is as it should be."

"You can't do that!" Beth cried. "They'll kill him!"

Eadwig glanced back and gave her a brief, sad smile. "That would be the point. Nothing else will satisfy you, Grivam?"

The old merrow shook his head. "I've set the bargain."

"Then we're wasting time here," he said, and whispered open a gate back to the Team's conference room. He only took three steps before he turned back and fixed Grivam with an inquisitive look. "You warned them, didn't you? Titania and Oberon, I mean. Before Simon went across. They would never give him a straight answer, but he assumed they were forewarned." A faint flush rose in Grivam's face, and Eadwig smirked. "You did the right thing, old friend," he murmured, and walked out of Faerie without another backward glance.

CHAPTER 16

That evening, half an hour after our inglorious return, Ted stood at the head of the table, looking at the faces in the packed conference room—all of the Team, the grand magus, Maria, Quinn, Beth, and Eadwig, who sat alone in the corner, contemplating the middle distance. Ilunna, who'd been given a basic command of English and then whisked into Lakshmi's office on arrival, lurked against the wall behind Ted with her arms folded over the new T-shirt she'd been persuaded to don. Lakshmi, our resident mother, had fussed over her, using a bit of spellcraft to clean, dry, and style her black hair into a French braid, but Ilunna seemed ill at ease. Whether she disliked her assignment, her distance from the sea, or her new wardrobe remained unspoken. She'd greeted Toula warmly enough, though, and when I'd pried, the grand magus had silently explained to me that they'd met during the '13 closure. I knew that Ilunna had to be close to Lakshmi's age, but I'd spent precious little time around the merrow, and Ilunna's apparent youth surprised me—though they aged, it was at a glacial pace. Grivam, Toula had informed me with faint amusement, was only a couple centuries younger than Val, and though he was past his prime, he remained ambulatory and sharp.

Ted had a few choice words for Grivam—I could sense them at the top of his thoughts if I concentrated—though he remained civil in front of the king's daughter while he summarized the previous twenty hours' excursion. "And *that* is why we're screwed on the grail front," he said as he wrapped up. "Plan B. Grand Magus, any luck with the blood trace?"

Toula's mouth tightened to a thin line. "Unfortunately, no. I've tried a few techniques, but I suspect he's using the same blocking spell that Mulligan's people employed to hide the Fringe hostages."

"That was a diary spell, yes?" asked Bob, and pointed to Eadwig. "Can't he get around it?"

The table turned as one, but Eadwig didn't flinch under our stares. "If I'm correct about which spell you are referring to, then yes, there's a way to work through it and pick up the trail...and if I begin now," he added before Bob could reply, "I should have results for you in five or six days."

"Another five *days*?" Frank cried. "Aurie's starving! Is there nothing faster?"

"No, and we've wasted enough time." The boy sighed as he stood. "Where can I find the Minor Arcanum?"

Beth yanked on his arm to pull him back to his seat. "Are you nuts? Sit down! We'll figure something out!"

Shaking his head, he gently extricated himself from her grasp. "I don't want more blood on my hands than Simon already put there. I go to these people, they do what they like, Ilunna makes a favorable report to her father, and you get the grail for trade."

"But what if they want to kill you?" she pressed.

"If that's what they decide...well, Simon earned that and more a long time ago."

"*You* didn't! Listen to me, Ed, you don't have to—"

"That's enough," Toula interrupted, though she looked about as displeased as Ilunna after Eadwig's announcement. "We're running out of time. I'll make arrangements for the handover."

Around eleven that night, the grand magus arrived at our flat with guests. I wasn't entirely surprised to see

Dr. Powell with her, nor Magus Lowe, Toula's predecessor in office and the closest thing she had to a true ally on the Council beside Maria, who entered on his heels. The fourth person I didn't know as well, but Beth jumped out of her chair with hope in her eyes. "Carey, hi!" she called, waving as Toula led her entourage in.

Even Frank, who'd been morosely watching TV with us for the last hour, turned and flashed a brief, polite smile. "Dragged you into this, did they?"

Though the Minor Arcanum had no official leader, Carey Jones had become its representative to the other magical factions because her peers realized she could be trusted to be sensible. A short, sinewy woman approaching ninety, with a dark tan, a snow-white bob, and deep-set brown eyes, she rehabilitated horses and worked as a veterinarian in New Mexico. She had also been instrumental in the long Fringe recovery and evacuation process during the Mulligan era, which was the source of her connections beyond the Minor Arcanum. I'd made her acquaintance two years before during one of Toula's war councils, and I'd heard from Artur, Beth, and Frank how helpful she'd been the previous summer when Hope and Arik went on the run. Of all the Minor Arcanum members to turn up at my door, Carey was far from the worst option.

Still, she was there in her official capacity, and her greetings were perfunctory. "Where is he?" she asked, glancing around our crowded den.

Eadwig stood and nodded, and Carey stiffened in surprise. "*You?*"

"I assume you're not searching for Marcus," he replied.

Frowning, she turned to Toula and Dr. Powell. "He's just a kid. Are you sure?"

"Would you like me to describe what it felt like to kill several thousand wizards in one night?" said Eadwig, his tone flat. "I will, if that's necessary to convince you. I won't say I'd be pleased to do it, but it's an option."

Suddenly, I heard Artur in my head: *Look at his hands.*

Eadwig had balled his fists at his sides, not in a threatening manner, but rather as if he were in need of pockets. As still as he was standing, I could just make out the tremor in his arms.

Glancing across the den, I locked eyes with her. *Terrified.*

Though Carey wasn't a natural telepath, she seemed to pick up on his fear without our help. "Tough talker, aren't you?" she said, folding her arms. "You're really Simon Magus?"

"As I said, he is and he isn't," Dr. Powell cut in. "He's a walking gray area."

"And what do you think?" she asked Eadwig.

"I have his aural signature, apparently, and his memories," he replied. "He is, in a way, my past and my future. So if you would bring him to justice…" He shrugged. "I'm close enough, I would suppose."

"You've got a good stiff upper lip, I'll give you that," said Carey. "And for all intents and purposes, you're a teenager with someone else's life already installed." She studied him for a moment in silence, then muttered, "*Shit.*"

"If you've decided to kill me," Eadwig managed, a wobble creeping into his voice, "would you please do it quickly? Your people didn't suffer."

"I'm not killing you," she said with a slight sigh, but before Beth could get too excited, Carey added, "Not here, at least. This isn't a decision I can unilaterally make."

The temporary respite didn't improve Eadwig's mood. "Time is short. The sooner you decide, the sooner *she* can bring word to her father," he said, pointing to Ilunna, "who will then surrender the grail so that *he*"—his arm swept toward Frank—"can get his daughter back. We need to act quickly."

"Believe me, I appreciate that," Carey replied, "and Frank, honey, I'm so sorry to hear about Ione and the baby. But I'm just one wizard, and this isn't my call. Give me a few hours to summon the others," she told Toula, "and bring him out to me. Arnold, you remember the way to the ranch, right?"

"Not senile yet," Magus Lowe told her. "How long would you like, three hours? Four?"

"Three should do it, and he's going to need an escort. Someone to keep him under control."

Eadwig spoke up at that. "You have my word, I won't fight back—"

"Not to be rude, but that's no guarantee. Toula?"

"I'll accompany him," said the grand magus, rubbing her elbow, "and I'm sure I can convince Coileán to come along. Worst-case scenario, we can take him down together."

"That'll work. Hey, one of you do me a favor and make the gate back, huh? Sooner I'm home, sooner I start on the phone tree."

Magus Lowe did the honors, then sealed the gate behind her. After giving Eadwig a long, searching look, he said, "She's not a bad woman, son. I wouldn't give up hope just yet. But while we're waiting, why don't you come over here with me and talk about that diary of yours? I have *loads* of questions about the theory."

The gesture was a blatant distraction, a fact made undeniable when two pints of beer appeared on the kitchen table with a flick of the magus's hand, but Eadwig joined him all the same.

"That's got to be so weird," Quinn murmured, standing with Maria and me on the other side of the flat. "He's a descendant, right? Like, you grow up hearing about this famous ancestor, and out of nowhere, he's there and willing to go over his work with you…"

"Meh," said Maria, and tilted her head toward the couch, where Marcus and Frank were zoning out with a documentary on marine life once again. "That's my ancestor over there. The novelty wears off."

"But he's not *famous*. I mean, look at them. The magus

is practically fanboying."

"He's being kind," I said, "and I'd venture to say that Eadwig's not the weirdest thing he's ever encountered..." Looking up at the sound of a door slamming into the wall, I saw Artur emerge from her room with full leather armor on and a practice sword at her side, half-dragging Beth along. "Going somewhere?" I asked.

"Courtyard. Could do with a bout," Artur replied.

I started to protest—we were well on our way to midnight, and much of the castle was surely sleeping—but the look in my sister's eyes made me think better of it. "Got enough light?"

She called forth a white orb and tossed it into the air as proof, then beckoned to Ilunna, who had commandeered a chair near the television. "You, girl—you're a merrow, yes?"

Ilunna's dark eyes narrowed. "Yes..."

"Then there's nothing in that program you've not seen. Come with us." When she wavered, Artur added, "We won't tell your father, and Eadwig's not going anywhere. Unless you want to stare at fish all night..."

She hopped out of the chair and followed them, and I shared a knowing look with Maria as the door latched behind them. "I'm all for distraction," she said, a glass of wine manifesting in her hand. "Who else is drinking?"

When the time came to venture to New Mexico, I wasn't drunk, but my edges felt somewhat rounded off. Toula had agreed that Marcus, Maria, and I could go along—if these were to be Eadwig's last moments, he could have at least a few familiar faces present—and Beth, still flushed from her practice fight and shower, refused to be denied. Rounding out our party were the grand magus, Magus Lowe, Ilunna, and Coileán, who said little aloud but, judging by the looks he and Toula exchanged, seemed to be carrying on an involved conversation. At the appointed hour, Magus Lowe reopened the gate, and Eadwig, with a nod to Quinn and Artur, took his leave. I glanced back before I slipped through, but Frank, who'd finally crashed around midnight, remained snoring on the couch, unaware of our departure.

The wave of dry heat that greeted us was a marked change from Glastonbury but not oppressive, especially not with the hour nearing sunset. I stepped out of my flat onto a gravel parking lot of sorts and surveyed my surroundings: a pair of pickup trucks, an SUV, a rust-flecked flatbed trailer, abandoned in the short grass, and nearby, a two-story brick house with white shutters, nicely maintained but for the overgrown flowerbeds. Past that stood several large outbuildings—barns, I guessed, thinking of the farm where I'd grown up. Daddy had raised sunflowers, not livestock, but the trappings were similar enough to translate: warm summer nights, well-used trucks, and the familiar scent of grass and manure, albeit somewhat fresher on the Joneses' ranch.

The house's front door opened, and a tall, elderly man sporting a black T-shirt and faded jeans stepped onto the stoop. Like Carey, he was bronzed and weathered with age, but his hair was gray to her white and pulled back into a long ponytail. "Right on time," he called, waving in welcome. "Arnie, man, good to see you!"

Despite our late hour and the circumstances, Magus Lowe beamed. "Hello, Zeb!" he called, hurrying across the gravel to greet him. "Sorry to drop in like this—"

"Hell, you know you're welcome." As he surveyed our group, he spotted my sister and grinned. "Beth! Hey, honey, how are you?"

She reciprocated with a weak, nervous smile. "Been better."

"I can imagine," he replied, sobering. "How's Frank holding up? Carey filled me in."

"Sleeping, bless him," said Magus Lowe, and began the introductions. "You remember Toula, I trust, and Lord

Coileán—"

"Been a while," said Zeb, nodding to them both. "Welcome. The horses are either in the far pasture or *that* barn," he added, pointing to the nearest of the outbuildings, "so if anyone on the fae side wouldn't mind steering clear, I think we'd all appreciate it."

Coileán smirked. "Not your first rodeo, huh?"

"We had Seamus and Kip out here simultaneously. Want to talk about spooked horses?"

"Speaking of Seamus," said Magus Lowe, "I believe you've met his cousin, Marcus—"

"Also avoiding the barn," Marcus interjected.

"—my colleague, Maria, and Beth's sister, Kitty—"

"No barns," I added in turn.

Zeb nodded to us. "The wedding, yes. Nice to see you all."

Magus Lowe grunted at the continued interruptions. "And Ilunna of the merrow."

She bit her lip as Zeb's eyes widened. "I do not know my status concerning the…barn?"

"Better safe than sorry," said Zeb. "Got to admit, I was never expecting to meet one of you."

Ilunna turned her head, taking in the wide fields and snaking wooden fences. "We are far from the sea?"

"Landlocked," he confirmed.

"Mm. This could be a substantial part of the problem."

Magus Lowe cleared his throat and slung an arm around Eadwig's shoulders. "Last but not least, Zeb, this is—"

"*That's* Simon Magus?" Zeb interrupted, peering at the pair. "Him?" Eadwig nodded miserably, and the old wizard rubbed one hand over his face. "You really are just a kid," he muttered. "Fuck."

Seizing her opening, Beth piped up. "So maybe you guys could, like, *not* kill him? Eadwig hasn't hurt anyone, Simon did all of that, and you'd be punishing the wrong guy—"

Zeb lifted a hand to stop her. "Carey told me, hon. This isn't my call."

"But you get a vote or something, right?" she pressed.

"Not this time…" He paused as the front door squealed open a crack, then turned and motioned for the person inside to emerge. "Coast is clear! Come on out, you two."

After the week I'd had, I shouldn't have been so shocked to see Hope and Arik slip out of the house. Neither had bothered glamouring for the occasion—this was to be a gathering of wizards, after all, not mundanes—and their striking cynaeli coloration was on full display: black hair, blue eyes, and unmistakably purple skin. Hope skewed toward a deep violet, while Arik—who looked cynaeli only because his father, the Gray Lands' consciousness, thought it would be a good idea—was paler. Both were of slight build and dressed all in blue, he in a loose tunic and trousers, she in a more fitted gown that dipped low over her flat chest.

"Howdy!" Hope called, her natural accent giving way to a touch of her mother's Oklahoma twang. "Did y'all just arrive?"

"Oh, my God, Hope! What are you doing here?" I began, my spirits momentarily lifted by the happy surprise of seeing her again…and then it hit me.

Zeb wouldn't have a say in Eadwig's fate because the Minor Arcanum was leaving the decision to others.

Almost all cynaeli, even those like Hope of the half-human persuasion, are natural mediums. A cynaeli sufficiently grown and trained can temporarily empower a spirit, making it visible and audible to those like me who could walk through a crowd of ghosts without the first clue that I wasn't alone. One with particular age or talent might raise multiple spirits simultaneously. And then there was Hope, possessed of a freakish talent leagues beyond the average cynaeli's. When Hope put her mind to it, she could raise an *army* of the dead.

Carey hadn't just been working the phone tree to bring the rest of the Minor Arcanum out to the ranch. She wanted Simon's victims to have a say in his punishment—and considering the thousands he had killed, who better for the task than Hope?

As my face worked, she must have overheard the direction of my thoughts, and she nodded. "The Joneses called two hours ago and asked an emergency favor. I couldn't very well say no."

"And I'm along to see that she does not kill herself," Arik explained. "Especially in this realm, with less ambient magic…"

She patted her husband's arm. "I feel *fine*. Are we ready to begin?" she asked Zeb.

"Just about, I'd think." Pointing to Eadwig, he said, "That kid over there is the reason we're here."

Hope flashed a taut smile. "Believe me, I'm hearing plenty already. I…oh, hi, Orson," she said, waving at a patch of empty space on the outskirts of our clump. "Came along with them, huh?" She paused for a moment, apparently listening. "I think that's a conversation we could save for later, don't you? Zeb, which way to the meeting place?"

I felt her reaching for my mind as we followed our host around the house and toward the pastures. *What did my dad want?* I asked as I admitted her.

He's not thrilled about Beth's choice in men.

She swears they're just friends.

Sure, she does, Hope replied, her thought shaded by incredulity. *But seeing as the next hours might put an end to Orson's perceived problem, I thought we could put it aside for now.*

With that unpleasant idea knotting my guts, I reached the back of the house and saw the place the Joneses had prepared. Beyond a training ring, the nearest pasture was almost entirely covered with an out-of-place parquet floor, which rested just above the grass. Half the floor was full of identical white wooden folding chairs, most occupied, and above the seated guests, attached to nothing, unlit chandeliers hung at the ready in case the proceedings outlasted the daylight. As I stepped into the makeshift room, the temperature dropped about ten degrees, and the buzzing of gnats ceased. The Joneses might not have had an Arcanum education, I mused, admiring their handiwork, but they certainly weren't witches.

A wave of agitated murmuring rolled around the room at our arrival—hardly surprising, all things considered. That the grand magus would have been invited to a Minor Arcanum function would have been unthinkable only a few decades before, that she would bring along one of the Three would have been ludicrous, and that he would be quietly chatting with his Gray Lands counterpart while they took their seats beside a merrow would have been a fever dream. That *any* wizard would willingly use a direct line to the Gray Lands would have been so far beyond the absurd that it wouldn't have been worth mentioning. Yet there they were—and with a variant of Simon Magus, no less, who stood awkwardly by while the rest of us made ourselves as comfortable as we could. There was no chair left for Eadwig, an oversight that escaped no one's notice.

With a nod to Zeb, Carey walked to the middle of the open half of the floor, where a simple wooden podium waited on a small dais. She held her wand to her throat and whispered, and I saw the flash in the magical spectrum as the spell coalesced. "Thank you all for coming on such short notice," she said, her voice amplified, then nodded to our section of chairs. "And our guests."

She paused, and I heard what sounded like a few seconds of jumbled mumbling from several points in the crowd—translators, I realized, repeating Carey's remarks in half a dozen other languages.

When the noise subsided, she beckoned to Eadwig with two fingers, and he slunk his way toward the dais, his shoulders hunched. She gestured a chair from the ether at the edge of the platform, and he took his seat in front of the waiting wizards, his face blank but his mind radiating fear. Holding her hand to her neck, she said, "If you would."

Though wandless, Eadwig easily repeated the amplification spell and waited.

Pulling a folded piece of paper from her back pocket, Carey smoothed it on the podium, cleared her throat, and began. "State your name, please."

His voice was almost monotonic, as if he were gripping his vocal cords to keep them from shaking. "Eadwig, son of Oswald."

"Alias?"

I saw his Adam's apple bob when he hesitated. "Simon."

"You are the wizard known as Simon Magus?"

"I was. I will be. It's…muddled."

I cut my eyes to Hope, who seemed to be staring into space. Listening for her thoughts, I could just make out their tenor: she, too, was translating, repeating the conversation for the audience I couldn't see, and I didn't disturb her.

Slowly, methodically, Carey continued her questioning, guiding Eadwig through his version of events and pausing only when the rumbling of the crowd grew too loud to go unchecked. Throughout the long hour of his confession, he refused to look at his interrogator or at the assembled, instead studying a point on the parquet with his hands in his lap. Only once Carey asked why he'd surrendered himself did he turn to her. "A sick child was taken and is being starved. The man who took her demands a certain cup in trade. Grivam holds the cup and said he would not relinquish it unless I submitted to your judgment."

Carey held his gaze, her face a blank. "There are presumably some in this organization who would see you die for your crimes."

"I understand." Pointing to our group, he added, "They've come only to ensure that I don't harm you. They won't save me."

The murmuring rose again, and Carey waited until it quieted. "Do you regret what you did? What Simon did?"

He nodded. "Yes, and he regretted it in his last days. His time in Faerie gave him an opportunity to reevaluate his actions," he said. "He regretted much of what he did. His legacy is built on blood, and that..."—Eadwig's voice cracked—"that isn't who I want to be. I never asked for talent. I didn't want to leave my family. When Simon went south, he never saw them again. Too risky. He didn't want to be a priest, he didn't want that loneliness, he didn't want the threats and the politics and the fighting. But innocent people died because some damn wizards who thought themselves to be petty kings wanted to send him a warning, and he fought back. And in the end, he became something that I...I can barely imagine. Something awful. That's not what I want. That's not what I *ever* wanted. I don't know when he stopped being me, but...God have mercy, I'm sorry," he said through tears. "For him, for us, for...whoever I am, for what he did, I'm sorry. And if blood is the only thing that will satisfy you, he has more than earned it."

Carey waited for a moment, then turned to Hope. "I believe we've heard enough. What say you?"

"Be careful, darling. I'm here," Arik murmured to his wife in Cynaeli. "If there's insufficient magic, they'll understand—"

"I can do it," she replied in kind, then closed her eyes, took a deep breath, and exhaled.

I'd seen Hope pull off that particular bit of sorcery once before, when she raised an army outside of Arc 2 at Artur's behest, but I'd been too worked up in that moment to really pay attention to the forces at play. The ether itself seemed to vibrate with the power flowing and focusing through her, and as a wrinkle of concentration formed between her eyebrows, the dead began to appear in droves. They remained translucent, but I could make out the details of their appearance. Before us, almost covering the empty half of the floor, was a throng of men and women whose faces spoke of a geographic spread from Australia and the South Pacific to the Americas. They sported a variety of styles of dress, from simple loincloths to elaborate robes and feathered capes. A few wore more substantial worked furs; others were laden with jewelry. Their sheer number was heart-wrenching, but the glimpses of children in their midst made me ill. Judging by the rumbling from the living half of the crowd, which had resumed at a more panicked pitch, I wasn't alone.

"Hope," said Carey, seemingly unfazed by the milling dead, "please ask them to stand to my left if they believe Eadwig should suffer their fate or to my right if they would prefer a different outcome."

"A moment," she replied through gritted teeth. "They want to discuss this."

We watched for a long five minutes as Simon's victims spoke to each other, moving among small groups like participants in an unfathomable dance. Finally, they began to drift to either side of the floor, forming two tight clumps in judgment.

I let out the breath I hadn't known I'd been holding when I saw how much larger the right-hand group was.

Carey nodded to both factions, then addressed Hope again. "Please convey our thanks. I'm sure this can't be easy—"

"There is a...suggestion," she interrupted, and looked imploringly at the nearest of the dead, who nodded. With a groan of relief, she cut the connection, and the spirits vanished from our sight. "Bear with me," she mumbled, rubbing her head, and Arik pulled her close in protection.

As we waited, Eadwig kept his seat near the podium. He'd slumped, perhaps in relief, though his face had turned red and blotchy.

The assembled were talking among themselves by the time Hope recovered enough to pass the message. "Those who voted for a lesser punishment felt it unfair to hold the boy entirely responsible for the man," she explained, still leaning against her husband. "Whatever he is now, he is not completely Simon."

"What do they suggest?" Carey's mouth tightened with distaste. "A bind, I take it?"

"No. He's talented—that shouldn't be wasted. They suggest a binding oath in two parts. First, he will swear to never seek or hold power over the Arcanum. Simon Magus must never rule them again."

I cut my eyes toward Toula, whose fingers had entwined with Coileán's.

"Second, he will swear that if the Minor Arcanum has need of him, he will come to their aid...even against the Arcanum." Hope straightened in her chair and gave Arik's knee a reassuring pat. "Does that seem agreeable?"

"If that's agreeable to the dead, then I don't think we have room to argue," said Carey, and turned to the crowd, waiting for a response. When no one protested, she motioned for Eadwig to stand. "You understand what this entails, right?" she asked him. "You're not just making a pinkie promise."

"I'm familiar with oaths," he replied, and looked her in the eye. "I accept your terms and swear to them. Should I break this oath, let the penalty come upon me."

Behind me, Ilunna leaned closer and whispered in my ear, "I do not understand."

"An oath like that isn't easily broken," I whispered back. "When an adept makes that sort of promise, it binds him in a more physical sense. If he breaks it, he could have any number of problems, from pain all the way to sudden death. An oath like that kept Nath from invading this realm."

Carey stared back at Eadwig for a moment in silence, then extended her hand. "You've been given a second chance, young man. Don't make us regret it."

He clasped it with due solemnity. "I won't."

"Good. You know how to sleepwalk?"

"I...yes, I think so."

"All right. So do I." Her grip on his hand tightened as she leaned toward him. "If I *ever* catch you in the dream space, I'll call in every favor I have to kick your ass so hard that you'll wish the vote had gone the other way. Got it?"

"Yes," he squeaked.

She released him with a curt nod. "He's all yours, folks," she said to our group. "Take him back to Grivam with...well, I won't say our blessing, but you can have him."

Within minutes, we'd said our goodbyes to the Joneses, Arik, and Hope, and Toula opened a gate back to my flat. It wasn't quite four in the morning, and the place was quiet but for Frank's snoring. I flipped on the dim stovetop light so as not to disturb him and waited for the others to join me in the kitchen. "What now?" I asked. "Back to Faerie?"

"Just a minute," said Beth, opening her arms. Trembling, Eadwig fell into her embrace, and she held him tightly, letting him cling to her until his shaking stilled.

The old merrow stood at the edge of the sea, leaning on his cane, and gaped as we approached. When he recovered his voice, he managed, "I, uh...I did not expect to see you again."

"Nor I you," said Eadwig, his face freshly washed and losing its splotchy color, "but here we are."

Grivam turned to his daughter, who spoke before he could utter the query. "He did as you asked, Father. They released him with an oath."

"An oath," Grivam repeated incredulously. "Do they not know what he—"

"Simon's victims decided the penalty," Eadwig interjected, "so yes, I would think they were informed. Are you satisfied?"

He considered the matter briefly, then sighed. "I

suppose I must be."

"You always were a man of your word. The grail, then?"

"I sent a messenger for it after you left, but it should be some time yet until his return…" He squinted at the afternoon sun. "Nightfall, I would imagine."

"At least another four hours," Coileán murmured to Toula. "Do you have a number for Jude? Want to call him, set up a handoff meeting?"

She pulled her phone from her pocket. "That was my thought."

"You could have it here, if you like."

The suggestion was met with a snort. "He's not *that* stupid. Excuse me," she said, and wandered down the beach to make the arrangements.

Grivam still seemed uncertain, and Eadwig stepped closer, scuffing his loafers in the sand. "You have my word that I'll not drink of it. As soon as the child's returned, the hunt to recapture the grail begins, and when I find it, I'll destroy it."

The king cupped his damp, bony hand against the boy's cheek. "You say that now, but you're in the bloom of youth once again. How tempting it must be to never grow old, never tire…"

Eadwig covered Grivam's hand with his own. "All of Simon's family are dead—Béatrix, the children, the grandchildren…"

"Cuthbert."

"Long dead. And it feels as though I lost *my* family only weeks ago. Do you realize that you are the only person Simon knew who still lives?"

His mouth twisted toward a wry smile. "I'm too old to give you a proper welcome back."

"My point precisely. Why would I want to live forever, only to watch my loved ones grow old and die?"

My throat clenched at his words, and I forced myself not to look at Beth.

"If this is my second life," Eadwig continued, "it will be my last."

Before Grivam could reply, I heard the crack of an opening gate and turned to see Coileán's brother, Aiden, still wearing the protective flannel shirt he used when working around steel and sliding a pair of plastic goggles atop his head. "What's up?" he asked, shoving his gloves into the back pocket of his jeans. "Ros said you wanted to see me—"

"*Aiden?*"

He spun at Ilunna's voice, saw her standing near her father, and beamed. "*Hey!*" he cried, jogging over to meet her. "What are you doing here?"

"Official business," she replied, then wrapped her arms around his neck and kissed him so deeply, I wouldn't have been surprised had his ponytail stuck straight out with shock.

While they explored each other's tonsils, Ros manifested and gave Coileán a sour look. "Happy?"

"He's spoken fondly of her," the king protested, "and the last time he saw her, he was Eadwig's age. No harm in letting them have a little fun now, eh?"

I glanced at Grivam, who seemed utterly unbothered by Ilunna's too-friendly greeting, then wrapped my arm around Marcus's and leaned close. "I know," he said, "long night. Or, uh…day? I've lost track."

"Long friggin' summer," I mumbled.

"Perhaps they should find a room."

I watched as Aiden ripped off his goggles and flung them into the sand. "Perhaps."

CHAPTER 17

We might have held the grail, but Jude held the cards, and he refused to be hasty in the trade.

"It's smaller than I imagined," said Toula, standing at the head of the Team's conference room table. The coffeemaker sputtered in the corner as it finished its drip—a second round, as the grand magus had pulled plenty of tea and coffee from the ether, plus a tray of slightly questionable Danishes. Enchantment-made food was an art, and while Toula's output was respectable and welcome at our morning meeting, it wasn't Michelin-quality.

Ted, who'd scooted his chair aside to give her room, regarded the cup in the center of the table as a starving man might a stare at a T-bone just plucked from the grill. "It's *beautiful*," he declared.

"Oh, granted, but…I don't know, I was thinking it'd be bigger."

"What," said Mal, "like one of those novelty glasses that holds a liter of wine?"

She shrugged. "Maybe? I mean, you hear *grail*, and you get…well, that."

The vessel—the Antwerp Grail, the blodig calic, whatever it was—stood roughly the size of a Burgundy glass, though it had far greater heft. The cup was made of gold, and having been rinsed clean of sand and salt, it shone like a museum piece, no worse for its long journey. The thick foot was set with nine ruby cabochons, each connected to its neighbors by delicate swirls etched into the metal, and just as Jude's drawing had shown, the bowl was decorated with the curious nine-pointed star, which repeated at regular intervals around the circumference. All in all, it seemed harmless, the kind of relic one might find behind glass and softly lit with an explanatory plaque beside it.

"Touch it, if you like," said Eadwig, who'd snagged a chair opposite Ted. "You'll not harm it." Ted still seemed unsure, and Eadwig added, "Or damn yourself. The curse only takes effect if one drinks from it."

My boss reached across the table and grazed his fingertips over the inlaid foot, then gently pulled the grail toward him and cradled it like a priceless relic. "Beautiful," he repeated. "I never thought...all that searching, all those dead ends, and I never imagined..."

"Congratulations," Artur interrupted, thumping him on the back, "grail quest accomplished. How long until we're rid of it?" she asked Toula.

She rolled her eyes and sipped her tea. "Jude's meeting us tonight at eleven."

"Here?" asked Frank. "He's bringing Aurie here?"

"I wish. I suggested Arc 2 or any of the other installations, even offered him free passage, but he didn't bite. Hell, I volunteered Afallon—figured you wouldn't mind," she told Artur—"but *someone* is slightly paranoid, and he's given this thought. He says he'll meet us atop Arthur's Seat at eleven tonight."

Bob's face screwed up in bemusement. "What, Edinburgh?"

"I'm sorry, *where*?" Artur interjected.

"Decently accessible, not too close to Glastonbury, and sufficiently public that no one's going to risk any large-scale magic. And it's a hill up in Scotland," she explained to my sister. "I don't know where the name came from, but maybe someone figured you wandered through."

"I never went to bloody *Scotland*! Honestly," she muttered. The following string of profanity was intelligible only to the two of us, but no one requested a direct translation. Having passed into legend in a fashion with little relation to reality, to her great chagrin, Artur grumbled whenever she found her name affixed to a place she'd never seen in some far-flung corner of the island.

"I thought we'd go up today and scout while we have light," Toula continued. "Look for traps. He took pains to warn me against tricks—not that I was going to try anything," she hastened, looking at Frank. "Not until Aurie is safe."

"How do you want to play this, then?" asked Magus Lowe, who'd stuck around at her request.

Toula sucked her teeth. "That's the thing. Jude didn't just specify where and when—he specified who was to make the drop. Just you," she said, and pointed down the table at Quinn.

Her gray eyes widened in alarm. "*Me?* Why me?"

"That doesn't seem wise," said Magus Lowe, frowning. "One person, not even a magus…" He peered at her briefly, then glanced back at Toula. "Is that, ehm…"

"Ms. Dellucci," she finished. "Yeah."

"I was afraid you'd say that." Turning back to Quinn, he continued, "I mean no disrespect, young lady, but you've only just begun your education, and Jude is certainly a…*credentialed* wizard."

"Out of my league, you mean," said Quinn.

"Exactly. If he were to pull a wand on you—"

"Magus Popova has been working on my shields."

"And I'm sure they're quite good for a beginner. You're still outclassed. All he'd have to do would be to grab you, and he'd have two hostages, plus the grail."

"But he doesn't need two hostages," said Toula. "The cup's the prize. So here's my thought." To Maria, she said, "Get Aiden on the phone. If he's not otherwise occupied, I want a discreet earpiece and a tracker. Range on the earpiece should be at least a mile, and I want that tracker broadcasting its coordinates at all times. Tell him I need them ASAP."

She scribbled the instructions on a scrap of notepaper. "We're putting the tracker on the grail?"

"No, on Quinn. Jude's no fool—he'll check the grail for tampering, and it wouldn't take much to fry a tracker hidden on it."

"You could put it under one of the rubies."

"Still risky, and I don't want to jeopardize Aurie's safe return. The tracker is in case he snatches Quinn."

"Or we could set up a blood trace on her now," Magus Lowe offered.

"Sure, unless Jude uses the same blocking spell on her that he's got going on himself and the baby, and I'd really rather not waste time trying to break through it. So here's the plan: Quinn, you'll make the drop tonight with the tracker hidden on you and the earpiece in. We'll be there to guide you if you need us." She paused, then said, "If you're willing, that is. If you're not comfortable with this, no one's going to force you."

Though she appeared a bit queasy, Quinn nodded. "Sure. I'll get the baby back."

Toula gave her a tight smile of gratitude and finished her drink in one sip. "Right. Give me a couple of hours to prep, and we'll head over. Maria, tell Aiden this is more important than Ilunna, and, uh…" She looked to her right and patted Ted's shoulder. "I'm sorry, hon, but you're going to have to let the grail go at some point tonight."

The problem with surveilling a meeting on top of a hill is that one tends to lack decent cover. Arthur's Seat was the highest point in Edinburgh, a bald knob atop a grassy slope that gave way to thick gorse and brambles before descending to the ringing road. I'd made the easy walk to the top once before, partly for the panoramic view of the city and the distant fields, and partly because I enjoyed the sort of summitting that didn't require crampons. But the hill and its surrounding park, while lovely and green in the warmth of August, were virtually useless for our purpose; the hill itself offered no good hiding places, and there was barely a camouflaging tree above road level. There was, however, a partial wall of a ruined church situated within the park, overlooking a modest lake. It wouldn't offer much shelter, but seeing as the ducks and geese started hissing and causing a ruckus whenever our party came too close to the water, it would have to do. The little brown rabbits that emerged at twilight just gave us a wide berth—fortunate, that, as the last thing I wanted to deal with while trying to be stealthy was attack bunnies.

Small wonder that Jude set the meeting so late in the evening. The sun didn't set until around nine-fifteen, and the evening walkers took their time in vacating the park. The eight of us in the retrieval party—Toula and Maria, our magi; Artur and Marcus, our additional firepower; Eadwig, who carried the grail in a canvas satchel; Quinn, the delivery girl; Frank, who refused to be left behind; and I, running tech—grabbed dinner in a pub at the base of the mountain, but even with all the walking we'd done throughout the day as we scouted for hiding spots, no one did more than pick at the food. Quinn in particular was antsy, draining her Coke and running off to the bathroom three times before Toula paid the check, though Frank, whose dinner was a Heineken with a liberal dash of Tabasco, was little better. He played with his silverware, shredded a paper napkin beneath the table, and stared around the pub as if expecting to see Jude emerge from the restroom at any moment.

With night—or the closest thing to it in the Scottish summer—having fallen, we emerged and made our way back toward the ring road. Just before we reached it, I called a halt behind a thin screen of trees and brush to outfit Quinn for the evening. Aiden had come through for us—Ilunna, it appeared, wasn't the sort to hang around and make small talk after having her fun—and I carefully inserted a beige plastic device, a combination microphone and speaker, into Quinn's right ear by the light of Maria's pocket flashlight. "Comfortable?" I asked as Quinn made the fine adjustments.

"Close enough."

I gave her what I hoped was a reassuring smile, focused my will, and concentrated on the earpiece, which Aiden had shielded with a preliminary enchantment to protect from my fumbling. The small glamour I wove hid the earpiece from view, and Maria pronounced my work suitable before tweaking it to hide the enchantment deeper in Quinn's aura. I stepped a few yards away and tested the earpiece using what appeared to be a cheap mobile phone, and Quinn gave me a thumbs-up.

"Okay," said Toula, taking hold of Quinn's shoulders, "breathe. You're going to do great up there." Eadwig passed her the satchel with the grail, which Toula slung over Quinn's body. "Straight up the slope. Got a light?" Quinn lit her keychain flashlight, and Toula nodded. "Good girl. Remember, don't antagonize him, don't get cute, and don't pull out your wand unless it's a matter of life and death. We'll be at the ruins if you need us."

Gripping the satchel's strap, Quinn started her trek through the night wind, and I watched until her light was a speck in the darkness. "Want to follow now?" I asked Toula.

"No."

I glanced at my phone's readout and saw we only had twenty minutes until the rendezvous. "It's not a long hike, but in the dark—"

"We're not going up there."

"What? *Why?*"

"Because," said Toula, folding her arms as she contemplated the hill, "Quinn can't shield her thoughts, can she?"

That gave me pause. "You think Jude—"

"I think Jude may not be the world's most talented

mind reader, but Quinn's scared to death, and what do you suppose is going to be at the top of her thoughts? She's got you in her ear and us waiting at the ruins. If Jude can look, he won't have to work hard to see that."

"What's the plan, then?"

"As far as Quinn knows, she's going to be on her own." Beckoning to Frank, Marcus, and Artur, Toula said, "You three go mess with the ducks. Eadwig, go with them and keep a lookout for police."

He frowned. "What do police look like?"

"You'll know them. Marcus, can I trust you with communications?"

"I suppose," he said uncertainly, taking the controller from me. "What am I to do with this?"

"Convince Quinn that there's been an emergency down here, we can't go up the hill after all, and the earpiece is malfunctioning. *Sell* it. And make sure *that* stays lit," she said, pointing to a small amber light on the controller.

"What is it?"

"Shows that the tracker is powered up."

"Tracker?" he repeated, bemused. "I thought Aiden didn't have time—"

"We didn't want to risk leaks," Eadwig explained. "It's sewn into the bag with the grail."

Though he seemed put-out by this development, Marcus stepped away to impart the bad news to Quinn, and Toula asked me, "How's your invisibility?"

"Decent?"

"Mm. Maria, cover her if she starts wavering. Come on, girls."

"Where are we going?" Maria asked as we jogged after Toula.

"Up the other side, of course. I'm not leaving that kid alone on the mountain."

While it would have been far simpler to create a gate to our destination, the flash might have given us away to Quinn. Instead, Maria and I scrambled to keep up with

Toula as she picked a path around the hill in the darkness, only occasionally sending a dim red orb ahead to reveal the way. Two-thirds of the way up, Toula stopped and vanished, and Maria and I did likewise, creating a glamour of invisibility to shield us from Jude's prying eyes. With virtually no light on the hill, there was little chance of the faint heat mirage effect being noticed.

Quinn had already topped the hill when I arrived, holding Maria's hand to follow her and Toula to a quiet spot. I couldn't see Quinn's face, but her nervousness rolled off her like fog from a lake, presumably amplified by the "problems" with our prearranged plan. She hugged herself, patted the satchel to check on the grail, and pulled out her phone every so often to check the time.

At eleven on the dot, my eyes smarted with the lightning flash of an opening gate, and Quinn jumped away in alarm as the hole opened. Out stepped Jude—emptyhanded.

Where's the baby? I heard Maria think.

Shit, Toula replied.

Want me to check?

Stay out of his head, she warned. *Don't risk him feeling a probe.*

"Quinn," said Jude, sealing the gate behind him. "Glad to see you again. You came alone?"

She spread her arms. "See anyone else?"

"No," he replied, a smile in his voice, "and if that ruckus down the mountain is any indication…your ride's back at the lake, eh?"

"I don't know. I'm alone up here. Now where's the baby?"

He *tsk*ed. "Patience, girl. Did you bring the grail?"

"For the baby. That's the deal."

"And you'll have the tyke, safe and sound, once I'm satisfied that you've held up your end of the bargain. Let's see it."

Quinn's hand went to the bag's clasp but stopped.

"I'm not trying to deceive you, Quinn," said Jude. "I'll have no use for the lizard once I get the grail. Do with her as you like. Now show me."

Her jaw tightened, but she undid the buckle and pulled the cup from its padded resting place. "Ta-da."

Jude whispered an orb to life and floated it between them, bathing Quinn and the golden chalice in its white glow. "Beautiful," he murmured as she turned it for his inspection. "Absolutely breathtaking. Where on earth did you find it?"

"The merrow had it."

"Greedy bastards," he replied with a snort. "You're certain that's the Antwerp Grail? The Magus was convinced?"

"Yeah, and so was...what's her name, Ros? She's over in Faerie. I wasn't there when they got the grail from Grivam, but they said Ros was sure it's the cup you're looking for."

"Ah," said Jude, "the mongrel formerly known as Roslyn Carver. She's still around, is she? Have you met her?"

Quinn shook her head "Can't say that I have. Why?"

In the orb's light, I could just make out Jude's smirk. "She's the reason your granduncle is dead. Oh," he continued with a faint chuckle, "you didn't know that I knew? Toula dove into my family's records shortly after you arrived, and I put two and two together. You're James's dud brother's...granddaughter, yes?"

"My grandpa's name is John," said Quinn, her voice like ice.

"That makes us cousins, you know. Third once removed, if my tree is accurate. Last of the American Mulligans—my, my."

"The name's Dellucci."

"Call yourself whatever you like, but the blood's there. Diluted, in your case, but that's a wizard's talent you've got." He paused to once again stare longingly at the grail.

"That's why I took you on, you know. I was curious to see how far the family had fallen. I mean, your degree was a perk, and no mistake," he said as her carefully composed face twitched. "You're qualified for Archives work. But I had my own reasons, you understand—and you exceeded all expectations."

Even from a distance, I could tell that Quinn was struggling to respond. "I'm…sorry?"

"I'd assumed a new-blooded Mulligan would be nothing special, but my dear, you're *quite* talented. With the proper tutelage, a few years' remedial work…you'll make the family proud."

"I'm not interested in genocide," she snapped.

"Who said anything about that?" Jude replied, taken aback. "Heavens, girl, what *have* they been telling you?"

"Enough. And since *you're* letting the baby starve in her sleep, I tend to believe them."

He sighed and rubbed his arm. "Quinn…James was far from perfect, but he did have a vision and the courage to pursue it, which is more than most can say. Do I agree with his methods? No, not entirely. Mass murder is usually a bridge too far. But you've got to admit that what he accomplished was remarkable. He held *Faerie* at bay. And what do we have now in his stead? Faerie's puppet," he said with disgust. "That's all our so-called grand magus is, you know. There are faeries working in the bowels of the Archives, in Arc 2 itself, and no one bats an eye! What's next, a permanent delegation from the Gray Lands with a suite in the executive wing? An ambassador to the damn Minor Arcanum?" He shook his head as if to dispel the thought, then focused on Quinn once more. "Do you know why I chose you to meet me here?"

"Because I'm not fully qualified with a wand?" she retorted.

"No. If I wanted someone ill-adept at magic, there's a shifter…well, *mongrel* shifter, whatever the hell he is, on the Away Team I could have requested. But we're family, you and I, and I want to give you an opportunity. Come with me."

Quinn took a step back, almost lost her footing on the uneven stone, but righted herself before tumbling. "I didn't agree to do this to run away with you. I'm here for the baby, and that's it."

"Don't be so short-sighted," said Jude. "I'm creating a new arcanum. A *true* arcanum. And with that grail, I can offer immortality to the finest wizards in the world. Don't you see the possibilities, Quinn?" he continued, warming to his subject. "The research, the training, the study, all without the time constraints of the human lifespan. Our talent only grows stronger as we age, you know. My God, can you imagine a wizard of three centuries? A millennium? Think of what we could accomplish with *time*!"

She held the grail up to the light. "Look, I get it. You're going through a midlife crisis. But I'm warning you, this thing is cursed—"

"Says who? Simon Magus?"

"Actually, yeah. And since it's his diary that's full of warnings—"

Jude laughed aloud. "My dear girl, surely you know what a smokescreen looks like? 'Oh, no, don't touch it,'" he minced, "'it's horrible. Just help me find it so I can make sure it doesn't fall into the wrong hands.' You would think that after a thousand years, the old boy could come up with a better story than that."

"He's telling the truth! He wants to destroy this!"

"So he says. But tell me, if he were willing to be buried alive for all those centuries to have a second chance at youth, why *wouldn't* he want that grail?" Smiling smugly, he asked, "You've had eyes on it all day?"

"No," she admitted. "The grand magus kept it safe."

"Ah. So you can't say that Simon didn't sneak off with it for a quick sip." As her face worked, Jude said, "He's not stupid. Why else would he be willing to surrender it now if he hadn't already received its benefits?" Lowering his voice to a conspiratorial murmur, he added, "If you want to talk genocide, dear, he's worse than cousin James ever dreamed of becoming."

"Eadwig's not a killer," she replied, though she sounded uncertain. "You didn't see how he reacted to the diary."

"I saw plenty," said Jude. Pointing to the grail, he asked, "You're sure that's the real thing? They didn't switch the true grail for a pretty copy?"

"I'm sure."

"You have proof?"

"I'm *sure*," she muttered.

"Mm." He studied it for a moment longer, his graying blond hair whipping in the hilltop breeze. "Convince me."

"*How?*" asked Quinn. "Look, this is the cup I was given to trade, and you didn't even bring the baby—"

"Test it." His smile hid an edge. "If I'm to have immortality, then surely my little cousin should as well. Unless, of course, that grail is a fake designed to kill me, in which case..." He shrugged. "Can't be too careful. You understand, don't you? And if you're being honest with me, then I'm giving you the greatest gift of all: immortality *and* perpetual youth." Reaching into his jacket pocket, he extracted a leather-wrapped flask and held it up for inspection. "What do you say, Quinn?"

You don't have to do this. Maria's voice echoed in my mind, and I assumed she'd looped Toula in to make it a four-woman conversation. *Walk away, just put the grail back in the bag and give it to him, we'll find the child—*

Quinn had a pro's poker face. While she couldn't broadcast her reply, Maria saw and shared it: *It's okay.*

It's not okay, Toula insisted. *We can break through the spell hiding the baby, it'll just take a few more days—*

She may not have a few more days, and you heard what he said, thought Quinn. *Last American Mulligan. This goddamned family is going to do something good.*

Quinn!

But she was already extending the grail. Jude emptied the contents of the flask into the cup—"Just water, I assure you," he said—and Quinn peered at the liquid. Dipping a finger inside, she held it to the orb and watched it drip red onto the stone.

Don't do this, Toula pleaded.

Closing her eyes, Quinn lifted the grail to her lips, hesitated, then sipped.

As soon as she swallowed, she cried out and fell to her knees, the grail slipping from her grasp and bouncing off a stone. Clutching at the bare rock, she screamed like she'd been set on fire—and then, a few seconds later, the fit passed. She remained on her hands and knees, shaking under the orb and regaining her composure as Jude retrieved the grail.

"Well, now, that sounded pleasant," he said, grabbing her arm and pulling her back to her feet. "How're we feeling, hmm?"

"It burned," she whispered, a hitch in her voice. "Oh *God*, it burned…"

"There, there, dear, the worst is over," he soothed as he helped her brush off and straighten her satchel. "All we need do now is test it."

"Test—"

Before she could complete the question, he reached into his pants pocket, flipped open a large knife, and plunged the blade into her stomach. He gave it a twist for good measure before yanking it free, and Quinn screamed again as her hands rushed to hold the wound. Blood wicked through her shirt, a blossoming red flower against the gray cotton, and she sobbed with the pain.

No one move, Toula thought to Maria and me, even as my muscles tensed to spring for the summit.

As Quinn cried and covered her stomach, Jude observed her from just out of her reach with a clinical air, waiting until her tears slowed and she began to sniffle before making his approach. Grabbing her hands, he forced them aside, then peeled her shirt off the sticky wound to see the damage. "Let's clean this," he murmured, whispering a wet rag from the ether, and dabbed at Quinn until both of them—and the three of us in hiding—could see the result.

Yes, Quinn still had a gash in her abdomen, but it had ceased to bleed—not clotted, but *stopped*—and the hole was closing more by the second.

Jude released her and smiled. "You're welcome."

"You sick fuck…"

Chuckling, he cast his flask full again, poured its contents into the grail, and then, with a mocking, "Cheers," he braced himself and took a swig. Having observed Quinn's reaction, Jude was better prepared, and he managed not to fall off the rocks while the enchantment went to work on his body. I wanted to push him down the hill—hell, there were some lovely cliffs nearby—but Toula's occasional warnings not to intervene held me at bay.

When Jude finally staggered to his feet, a wild look of triumph in his eyes, Quinn had recovered the grail and tucked it into her bag. "You got what you want," she said. "Give me the baby *now*."

"Manners, Quinn," he said, and tutted as he opened a new gate. "Come with me, and you'll have her." When she didn't budge, he eyed her over his glasses. "My word is good. She's unharmed, and you can take her with you…for *that*, of course," he added, pointing to her satchel.

Quinn glared at Jude, but she sighed and marched through the hole, and Jude extinguished the orb as he made his retreat. As soon as the gate sealed, Toula threw off her glamour and waved open her own gate to the lake, and Maria and I scrambled after her. She'd barely stepped onto the level path before she was calling for Marcus. "The tracker?" she demanded. "Is it working?"

He held out the controller, revealing the amber light

and a set of coordinates on the readout. "It's growing more specific…"

"Cannes," she announced. "Son of a bitch went to the Riviera. Come on, let's get out of here."

"Why are we leaving?" Eadwig demanded. "She can't make gates, she'll be stranded here—"

"That's assuming he lets her go, and with all the screaming, I wouldn't be surprised if the cops are on their way. So we're taking this show back to Arc 2," she said, ripping open a fresh gate to her office, "and I'll give her an hour before I hit France. Are the coordinates still narrowing?"

"Yes," said Marcus, "and he doesn't appear to be moving—"

"Good. Pack it up, we're out," she ordered, and we left the agitated ducks in peace.

Half an hour later, we sat around Toula's office as she talked to Aiden with the speakerphone on, trying to pinpoint Jude's hiding place. The coordinates continued to grow digits after the decimal point, and by then, the two of them had plotted him to within a one-mile radius. He had gone to ground not in Cannes, but rather in Théoule-sur-Mer, a smaller coastal town to the southwest. Judging by the conversation from Toula's desk, there were only a handful of potential properties, searchable with a sufficiently large security team.

I'd risen to grab a Coke from the Council's breakroom when Toula's intercom chimed. "Yes?" she said, depressing the button.

"Sorry, Grand Magus," came a man's voice, "there's someone outside the gate, doesn't have credentials…" He paused, listening to what sounded like muffled mutterings to us, then resumed. "Quinn Dellucci? She asked me to buzz you, but—"

"On my way," Toula interrupted as Frank rushed for

the door.

I made it out the front gate several lengths behind him—there was no catching Frank on a straightaway—and while I couldn't see Quinn, I heard his joy. By the time the rest of us arrived, he was clutching his unconscious child, who was unclothed but for what appeared to be a soiled diaper. Toula put two fingers to the baby's neck, then held up her phone. "Got to go, Aiden," she said, unceremoniously cutting the call short, and dialed. "Bee? Baby's back. I need you outside *now*." Turning then to Quinn, who remaining standing in the middle of the drive, she beckoned her toward the guard shack and created a chair. "Hang in there for a few minutes, okay?" she said. "He let you go?"

Quinn looked dazed. "Invited me to come back once I got rid of Aurie. I told him I'd consider it…"

"Where *is* he?"

"Looked like a hotel room, I think. He had the drapes pulled, and I didn't see any signs…I wasn't there long enough. I'm sorry, I should have been better at this—"

"Honey." Toula took a knee and gripped Quinn's hands. "You listen to me. You did well. We're going to take care of you, and then we're going to find him, yeah? So let's get the baby checked out, and then I'm siccing Dr. Powell on you. Sit tight."

A few minutes later, the doctor came running out of the castle, bathrobe flapping, her similarly clad wife on her heels. She took one look at Aurora, felt for a pulse, then said, "Infirmary, go. Daisy, call Pritam Bhat, he's in my contacts. I'll need a gate to pick him up."

"On it," I said, pulling out my own phone.

"Oh—good," said Dr. Powell, seemingly noticing the small crowd for the first time. "Ehm…fine. Love, why don't you wake the medics instead?" she asked Daisy. "We'll need all hands tonight." She nodded to Toula when a gate into the infirmary manifested, then hustled Frank through and began barking orders to the poor medic on duty.

Dr. Powell was Arc 2's only licensed doctor, a medical jack of all trades who augmented mundane procedures and remedies with a healthy dose of spellcraft. Beneath her in the infirmary were a cadre of medics, wizards with a knack for healing magic and training in at least field medicine. Soon, the duty medic was joined by her five colleagues in their nightclothes; one young man had reached the infirmary before realizing that he'd thrown a T-shirt on over his boxers but had neglected to complete the ensemble, and he'd hastily grabbed a clean set of scrubs. I arrived with Pritam, whom I'd pulled from his predawn treadmill session, to see a flurry of medics running around the infirmary at Bee's barked orders.

Spotting Daisy and Frank sitting in a corner of the room, I left Pritam to wash off and joined them. "What's going on?" I asked.

Frank's face was drawn, and Daisy held his hand as they waited together. "Underweight and dehydrated are the eyeballed findings," she murmured. "She's in a growth spurt, but she's had nothing to sustain it. When did she last eat or drink?" she asked Frank.

"Friday morning," he mumbled. "Took a bottle before her checkup."

"Not quite four days, then," said Daisy. "They started an IV, and I think I heard Bee mention an NG tube, but I'm staying out of the way." Seeing Frank's unspoken query, she explained, "Easier to feed her. She won't have to do any of the work, and since she'll probably be lethargic when she wakes…"

"She's not awake yet?" I asked.

"No, Bee's kept her under. I don't know what they're planning…is that the herpetologist you brought?"

"Pritam, yeah." I took the chair beside them, saying little while the infirmary unit did its work. Half an hour later, Pritam—still sweaty but gloved up—slipped over to deliver an update. "She's stable," he told Frank. "Vitals are

weaker than we'd like, but part of that is due to the spell.
Bee's put her on a feeding pump—nondairy formula with
added protein powder. It's the best we can do at the
moment. I know she'd had more meat-based feeds, but
those tubes are tiny, and we'd rather not risk a clog."

"When will she wake?" he asked.

"We think it'd be best to keep her under for now.
Don't want to make her uncomfortable. And with your
permission, we want to go ahead and repair the hole in the
next day or two, just to be safe. We'll need the bind off for
that, so—"

"She sleeps through the whole thing," Frank finished.
"Whatever you think best."

Pritam patted Frank's slumped shoulder. "Go home,
rest. She's in good hands."

"I'm not leaving her."

As the look in Frank's eyes forbade argument, Pritam
offered him an open infirmary bed. This suggestion was
also rejected until Bee came over, learned of the problem,
and jabbed a finger toward the mattress. "If you're staying,
you're sleeping. You're no use to her if you can't see
straight."

"I slept last night—"

"*Stop*. You can't have slept well all weekend, and when
was the last time you ate a real meal?" She folded her arms,
daring him to defend himself. "You're in objectively bad
shape, and that's not doing Aurie any favors. Bed, and I'll
wake you for breakfast."

He grunted but surrendered. "You know, Bee, I'm not
actually your patient."

"No, but since Ros can't be here, *someone* has got to
look after you." She watched until he was horizontal, then
nodded. "Right, then. Kitty, was there something you
needed, or are you just cramping my space?"

"Actually," I replied, "yeah. It's Quinn."

She frowned. "The new girl? What about her?"

"Drank from the cursed grail. Would you mind taking a

look? I think she was down by the guard shack…"

Dr. Powell's eyes opened wide behind her glasses, and she ran from the room in a cloud of red curls.

While the medical team was rushing about with Aurora, Toula had done her best to keep Quinn comfortable, or at least calm. Easier said than done—Quinn teetered on the edge of a breakdown, and the soothing cup of Assam that Toula had encouraged her to drink had been regurgitated in *spectacular* fashion shortly after its consumption, along with the rest of Quinn's stomach contents. She'd managed to keep down a few sips of lukewarm water, but no one wanted to risk anything more substantial than that.

As Dr. Powell poked and listened and measured, Eadwig offered her the condensed version of his former self's findings concerning the grail and its effects. The doctor used a modified imaging spell to produce a visual of the enchantment at play, pulling its tangled channels from deep within Quinn's aura, and then, with a sigh, she said, "Toula, make this easy on me and open a gate to Faerie."

The grand magus started to comply, then paused and glanced uncertainly at the patient. "Uh…does anyone know what time it is in Faerie?"

I tried to run the numbers. "Daytime, I'm almost certain. Maybe noonish?"

"Yeah, that's what I was afraid of." When she opened the gate, it revealed nothing but blackness beyond its lightning rim. "Just in case, uh…*photosensitivity* is an issue," she explained, and stepped aside.

Dr. Powell stood in front of the hole in the fabric of the realm, waiting until Ros manifested on the other end and her glow brought the stone walls of the windowless dungeon into view. Most wizards exhibited extreme politeness, if not a little fear, when confronted by Faerie's consciousness. Then again, most wizards hadn't precipitated the fall of the Mulligan regime as fifth graders.

"Hiya," said the doctor. "Got a mess on my hands. You busy?"

A chair appeared behind Ros, who sat back and crossed her legs. "Shoot. Just tell me it's not Maria again—"

"Oh, she's fine. Do you know anything about the Antwerp Grail?"

"Too much of late. Did the exchange go off?"

"Yeah, the baby's in the infirmary. Unfortunately, Jude wouldn't make the handoff unless Quinn here tested the cup first…"

Ros groaned as her eyes squeezed shut. "*Shit.*"

"Vomit, actually. She claims she hasn't voided or defecated since drinking, but given her body's reaction to *tea*, I imagine we'll see something from that end soon."

The patient, who remained sitting beside the guard shack, looked like she wanted to crawl into a hole at that.

"Vitals are nonexistent," Dr. Powell continued, oblivious to Quinn's mortification. "No pulse, no respiration, and body temp is at thirty and falling. She's not chilling—no gooseflesh, no shivering, nothing like that. I mean, these are the strangest symptoms I've ever seen," she continued with more than a little frustration. "She only takes in air when she wants to say something—"

"*Vampire*, okay?" Quinn interrupted. "You can stop dancing around it."

"Maybe this is just the scientist in me, but I'd rather avoid the V-word," Dr. Powell told her, then turned to Ros again. "It's a stasis bind of some sort, but this is enchantment-made, and I haven't the faintest idea how to safely unravel it. Do we overload it? Have her step through to you for a minute?"

"No, and *no*," Ros replied, massaging her forehead. "That one's a doozy, and to be frank, Quinn's not too far off. Your teeth haven't sharpened or anything, have they?" she asked, looking past Dr. Powell toward the guard shack.

Quinn ran her tongue around her mouth and shook her

head. "Not that I can tell. Is that next?"

"Shouldn't be—just making sure. Here's the problem: drinking from that damn cup is deadly. What you're seeing," she told the doctor, "is Quinn paused at the moment of death, more or less. By all metrics, she's not alive."

"Except for the fact that we're having this conversation," Quinn muttered.

"*Magic*," said Ros, emphasizing the declaration with jazz hands. "Yeah, you can think, talk, move…and eat a *very* particular diet…but you're heading for room temperature, kid. Can you still cast?"

She pulled her wand from the back of her waistband, focused, and cocked an eyebrow at the gate as a small shield appeared.

"Good. Get used to that talent," said Ros, "because it ain't getting any stronger. Talent grows throughout life, but technically, you're past that point. Now, she's not going full zombie," Ros said to the doctor. "You shouldn't see bits dropping off. The enchantment is keeping her ambulatory and *intact*—it's trying to preserve her as she was at the moment it took effect. So she won't age, and she should heal from any injuries pretty quickly—"

"Jude fucking stabbed me," mumbled Quinn.

Dr. Powell winced in sympathy. "I'd wondered about that stain. Was it, ehm…deep?"

"*Yeah.*" She lifted her blood-soaked shirt to reveal her smooth, unblemished abdomen. "Hurt like a bitch, but it closed up."

"As expected," said Ros. "Whatever you break or tear should put itself back together, assuming the enchantment remains intact. I wouldn't try amputation, but anything short of that is probably reparable."

Quinn rolled her wand between her palms, fidgeting as Ros and Dr. Powell studied her. "So, uh…about that photosensitivity thing. And blood …"

Ros's expression shifted toward pained. "Hate to tell

you, but he's right about those," she said, gesturing to Eadwig. "Light in general's not the problem. The Three were intending to make daylight lethal, and I think what they actually accomplished was an overreaction to strong UV. That's my educated guess, so stay inside and away from blacklight for now. As for food…well, yeah, you're on a liquid diet from here on out. The way the enchantment is designed, blood is what'll keep you going. If you don't tank up on occasion, the enchantment falls apart, and you drop dead. On that note, don't leave the realm. If you try to go to the Gray Lands, the lack of magic will break the enchantment. If you come here, there's a protection on the border that breaks spells and enchantments on living things. You're close enough to be caught in it."

"Walt?" Toula murmured.

"Yeah," she said, looking pained. "My predecessor remembered that *all* too well. You didn't actually see the head when it was alive, did—"

But Quinn cut her off. "*Human* blood? I can't drink that! I'm not going to kill anyone, I…shit, I can't—"

"You know, dear," Dr. Powell calmly interjected, "you *are* at an Arcanum installation. It's possible to reproduce most things with the proper application of spellcraft. I hold quarterly blood drives for the infirmary's stocks only because I don't like replicating blood more than a few times, just in case I make a bad batch. But say we put a bag or two aside for you, copy as needed…it should be doable."

"Or I could just kill myself now and save us all the trouble."

Toula's voice rose to the top during the outburst of protest. "No. *No,*" she insisted, standing over Quinn's chair until its occupant was forced to look up at her. "You did something foolish but brave, okay? You acted quickly, and the baby's alive for it."

"I'll second that," said the doctor. "Even with the

systemic slowdown from that bind, I doubt she would have lasted another twenty-four hours. She's badly dehydrated."

Still, Quinn's eyes began to well up. "I don't want to live like this. What if I hurt someone? I don't want to be just another Mulligan…"

"*Honey*," said Toula, squeezing Quinn's shoulders until she fell silent but for a sniffle. "There are bad and good in every family, and I'm not worried about you. Let's not do anything rash." Sweeping one arm toward the castle, she said, "There are *loads* of windowless rooms in there. You've spent time in the Archives—you know how little natural light there is."

"Bad for inks," she mumbled.

"Exactly. And since our head archivist is on the lam and won't be getting his job back, I'm going to have to appoint someone to replace him, which will make a vacancy, and with your training…hell, the job's yours if you want it. You can keep working with Anna Popova, but let's get a proper office for you instead of a cubicle."

"Just be aware that her circadian rhythms have flipped," Ros pointed out. "She's going to be drowsy during the day."

"Remarkably, books don't sleep." Toula released Quinn and offered her a hand out of the chair. "Come on, Ms. Dellucci. You've had one hell of a night. Let me walk you home."

Though she seemed hesitant, Quinn accepted and set off with her. "There's a window in my room," I heard her say to Toula. "Do you think blackout curtains are enough?"

"Why don't I just treat the glass to block most radiation for now? We'll dial it back until we figure out your tolerance."

"You can do that?"

"Quinn," she replied, opening a gate to my flat, "you remember that part about how I'm grand magus?"

"Yes…"

"It's not because I give a good stump speech," she said, and closed the hole behind them.

CHAPTER 18

Three a.m. rolled around, and to the general relief of the crowd gathered behind the protective wards of Toula's office, the coordinates from the tracker in the grail's satchel hadn't budged. "Either he's dumped the bag or he's made camp," said Magus Lowe as he circled Toula's sitting area, refreshing teas. "And if we wait for dawn to make our move, we'll have the advantage. There's no sense in spooking him quite yet…"

His voice faded when a rapping sounded outside the door. Putting a finger to her lips, Toula rose and cracked it open, then relaxed and widened the gap. "Can't sleep, huh?"

"Nope," said Quinn—who, fortunately, had changed out of her bloody T-shirt. Extending her cell phone to Toula, she announced, "I called Chicago. Grandpa wants to talk to you."

"I'm sorry, *what*?"

"Come on, it's not like he doesn't know about the Arcanum. Oh, and this is on speaker, so if you wouldn't mind…"

Toula motioned Quinn into the room and latched the door, resetting the privacy wards before she took the phone. "Hi, Dr. Dellucci? This is Toula Pavli."

Distorted as it was, I recognized the old man's voice on the other end. "Grand Magus?"

"Yes, sir," she said, tensing.

He grunted. "Heard you people might be in need of a cardiologist."

She cocked her head as if the phone had suddenly switched to Esperanto. "I…beg your pardon?"

"I mean, I'm retired. Hands aren't are great as they once were. But if you need someone who knows his way around the vascular system, I might be able to help."

After a brief pause to digest that unexpected offer, she said, "That's very generous of you, but you should be aware that the patient is—"

"A neonate?"

"And a dragon."

"Quinnie mentioned that. I'm no pro in that area, of course, but unless you have a herpetologist who specializes in cardiology on hand, you might want to let me take a crack at it."

"Hold that thought, please," she said, and searched the assembled until her eyes fell on Maria. "Get Bee up here, okay? Doctor, would you mind coming over?"

"What, to England?"

"I know it's getting late over there—"

"Hell, woman, bridge night just ended. I'm up and dressed. Can you make one of those gate thingies? Or those kids who stopped by with Quinnie, they could do it."

Pulling an image of Dr. Dellucci's apartment from my memory, I opened a gate into his kitchen, and his voice suddenly grew clearer. "*Ah*, good. Hold that there, I'm coming…"

Toula hung up and handed the phone back to Quinn as he shuffled through the gate, leaning heavily on his wooden cane. "Hi, honey," he said, smiling at his granddaughter. "Good to see you again."

She met him with a hug around the neck, and he patted her back with his free hand, then let her help him to Maria's vacated chair. He looked far more dapper than he had the first time we'd met, sporting a navy blazer, pleated chinos, and a green silk necktie with a tiny print of scattered playing cards. Even his fine white hair had been tamed with a dollop of gel. Other than his too-white tennis shoes, a necessity for the aged and unsteady set, he seemed ready for a night on the town.

"Our doctor is on her way," said Toula, resealing the gate, then paused and gave him a long once-over. "Got to admit, this isn't what I expected you'd want to talk about."

"Oh," he replied with a flash of yellowed teeth, "we're going to have a *nice* long talk about whatever the hell you maniacs have done to my grandbaby, but since Quinnie's not bleeding, let's deal with the infant first. Consider this triage."

A few awkward minutes later, Maria returned with Dr. Powell and Pritam, and Dr. Dellucci pushed himself back to his feet with a groan. "You're the medical team here, I take it?" he asked.

Dr. Powell chuckled with incredulity. "*I'm* the resident GP. Dr. Bhat is a herpetologist on loan."

"What were we thinking, cath or surgery?"

"Cath would be great," she replied, "but since this isn't my specialty, I'll let you be the judge. She's got scans back in the infirmary. I don't know if I have an appropriate catheter on hand, but if you can show me what we need online, someone here can replicate it."

"*Is* there an appropriate catheter for a juvenile dragon?" he retorted. "Well, won't be the first time I've made do. Procedure in the morning?"

"Assuming she remains stable," said Pritam. "And her father clears it, of course."

One of Dr. Dellucci's eyebrows inched upward. "Her father?"

"He's asleep in the infirmary, if you want to chat now."

At that, the first eyebrow's mate joined it. "Good God, man, how large *is* this infirmary of yours?"

"We'll explain," said Dr. Powell, offering him her arm as Maria waved open a gate.

He accepted, shifting his weight between her and the cane, but gave Quinn a last look before heading out.

"You're next, baby girl," he promised, and limped off to work.

Closing the hole behind them, Maria said, "He might be able to fix you, Quinn. If we overload the enchantment, then, say, get the defibrillator—"

"Won't work," she said glumly.

"Dr. Powell shocked the hell out of me and saved my life," she protested. "Believe me, they work."

Quinn shook her head. "You're thinking of a Hollywood defib, which is right up there with Hollywood crime labs that magically zoom and enhance pictures. A defib's only useful if your heart's beating arrhythmically— if you flatline, it's not going to do you any good, and your only hope is drugs and CPR. Watching medical dramas with Grandpa is...*educational* would be the nice word." Patting her chest, she said, "No pulse, no heartbeat, nothing to shock. And since I assume my heart stopped back in Scotland...I mean, it's been hours. CPR at *this* point? May as well give mouth-to-mouth to a cadaver, you know?"

As she slumped in her chair, Maria looked to Eadwig, who'd been brooding for much of the night. "What about the spell Simon Magus used in Ireland? She would only need to be rewound by a day...what would that be, a fortnight in stasis?"

"Yes," said Eadwig, "but it wouldn't break the enchantment on her, and it only works on living subjects. I doubt it would do anything for Quinn." Turning to her, he said, "I will find a solution. If we can recover the grail, then I'll make a study of it. A proper study this time, not mere theorizing from afar."

"That's nice of you to offer," Quinn replied, "but Ros seemed pretty down on the idea of fixing me—"

"She doesn't know everything. *Much*, yes," he admitted, "but not everything. Besides, what else am I meant to do with myself?" He spread his hands and shrugged. "Simon became me by accident, and only because he sought to destroy the grail. If we accomplish that, then what other purpose do I serve?"

"Okay, first, that's still an *if*," I cut in. "It ain't over until we have the damn cup back, and for all we know, Jude dumped the bag and bolted. Second, you don't need some grand purpose to justify your existence. Whatever else Simon did, he gave *you* a fresh start."

"A start, yes, but with the weight of his sins on me." He lifted his empty mug and headed for the teapot on the sideboard. "The spell that led to me was intended as a step toward atonement. I exist to even the scales."

I caught his arm as he passed my chair and pulled him to a stop. "You exist because you exist. You're not bound to try to make up for someone else's misdeeds."

"Yeah, seriously," Quinn interjected, "don't turn me into your raison d'être. I made my choice—this isn't your fault."

At that, Magus Lowe pointedly cleared his throat. "Let's not be hasty. Kitty, I trust you recall that bit from your studies about how almost every fundamental casting technique in use today has roots in the Magus's work. I know it wasn't my class, but I'm sure you were tested on that matter at *some* point."

Eadwig twitched in surprise, then regarded him with a bemused frown. "Truly?"

The old magus nodded. "And that's not counting the diary and what we've pulled from it in the last forty-odd years. Simon's work is *foundational*. The Minor Arcanum, whether they admit it or not, use variations on those techniques. There's never been a theoretical wizard his equal...perhaps close," he offered, nodding to Toula, "but I'd say he remains in a class unto himself."

"And you're too generous, Arnie," said Toula, though she seemed pleased. "No one asks to see my notes."

"All I'm suggesting is that if Ros thinks Quinn's condition is incurable by means of enchantment and Eadwig wants a crack at the problem, I don't think he should be dissuaded. But that's a matter for daylight," he added, wincing as he shifted in his seat. "Speaking of which, how long until we go after the blasted thing?"

"About two and a half hours," said Ted, who sat in a corner of the room with his computer in his lap. "The sun will be up by then, but not much. France is an hour ahead, remember." Glancing at Quinn, he said, "I'm still shocked that he let you go. You saw his hiding place."

"Not much, and not for long," she said. "Anyway, he knows I can't make gates."

"No, but a fair number of people in this room can, and at least the fae contingent could pull your memories and use them to get close. Jude's not an idiot, so why risk himself like that?"

"Maybe there's a trap," said Daphne, who'd parked herself near the tea and was passing the long night working on paper revisions. "I'm sure the room's warded half a dozen ways. Or what if he's warded it to prevent gates in unless he makes them?"

"That's possible," Toula replied, "but unlikely under these time constraints. I spent *days* with the Arc 1 ward system when Harrison decided to lock the place down—difficult to manipulate alone, impossible to rush. Honestly, I don't think Jude's wizard enough to pull it off." She sipped her drink and frowned into space. "Just careless, maybe? Drunk on his own power?"

"Actually," Quinn murmured, "he threatened me."

The grand magus straightened. "How so?"

Her voice remained soft but measured. "He said that if I helped you pursue him, he'd kill my family. Showed me a printout with names and addresses for my parents, my brother, my aunts and uncles, some of my cousins…he's been busy, I guess. And seeing as I'm the only wizard of the bunch…"

As Quinn smiled tightly, Toula said, "If we don't get him at first light, we're moving your entire clan here for safekeeping. That's a promise. Now, who wants to go bag him? I'm in, and…Maria, Kitty, Marcus?"

"I'll go," Artur offered.

"Sure, just understand that I want him taken alive if possible."

"And me," said Eadwig.

She held up a hand to stop Magus Lowe as he began to protest. "Remember that Simon wasn't just a *theoretical* wizard," she said with a little smirk. "That's six, then. Anyone else? I'd like to keep this reasonable."

I lifted a finger for her attention. "Shouldn't we save a spot for Frank?"

"Ooh. Maybe. He might prefer to be here with the baby, but yeah, I'd say that's fair if he wants to tag along. Of course, he's sleeping right now…"

I felt the eyes of the room turn on me, and I rose with a groan. "Y'all want me to wake the dragon, don't you?"

"Only if it's no trouble, dear," the grand magus replied, and I saw myself out to a chorus of admonitions from the more senior Team members to stand *behind* him. I was still a kid when Frank had almost roasted Antony in a moment of disoriented midnight panic, but institutional memory endured.

In the end, only the six of us went. Frank wanted Jude dead, but when he woke to find Dr. Dellucci in the infirmary, going over a plan of attack for Aurora and eager to attempt the repair, he decided to stay behind. "I have my daughter back," he told me, "and I intend to keep her. Give the son of a bitch hell for me."

Toula seemed relieved at the news—Frank could be as reasonable as they came, but the situation was far too personal to ask him to keep a cool head.

We made our final preparations at quarter of six that morning, the rest of the Team and Beth having been sent home to sleep. I'd seen Quinn back to the flat and double-checked the opacity of her windows before nudging my little sister, wired from the all-nighter and the grand magus's infinite caffeine supply, toward her room. Only Magus Lowe remained in Toula's office, waiting on standby to summon Arcanum security and whatever magi he could rouse if she made the call.

Marcus, who'd babysat the tracker all night, provided the reference photos we needed for the gate. For a guy who predated Arabic numerals, he'd proven surprisingly adept at Internet research, and he'd cross-referenced the tracker's coordinates to a high-end spa resort on the beach—judging by the photographs, a modern property decorated in rich tones, the sort of place that would offer exotic salt-based therapies and decorate the desserts with edible gold. Whatever else could be said of him, Jude's taste wasn't terrible.

"Here's hoping there's no morning seaside yoga," said Toula, studying a photograph of a wide marble terrace with a lovely view of the blue Med, then stretched out her free hand and created a tiny gate, a floating hole barely as large as a fist. She peered through the opening, muttered, "Pool boy," then twitched a finger by her side, as if she were changing her view on a screen. "Okay," she said after a moment, "I've got us back by the pool shower, and the coast is clear. Let's do it." With that, she widened the hole just enough to allow our group passage, then quickly sealed it behind us.

The trick to navigating a place where one has no business being is to project confidence. A purposeful stride and a relaxed face can throw off all but the most perceptive, particularly if one otherwise looks the part. I'd practiced the technique many times since joining the Team, weaseling my way into restricted library collections and onto protected sites with nary a spell—a useful life skill, since I'd been almost untalented until my surprise augmentation two years prior. But Toula was in no mood to fool with disguises or sweet-talking desk attendants. A flicker of will rendered her invisible, and the rest of us followed suit. In seconds, the shower once again seemed empty, the only clue as to our presence being the faint atmospheric disturbance at the edges of our glamours. Eadwig's had been the last to coalesce—glamour came more easily to the fae, after all—but his was as complete as any of ours, no small feat for a wizard.

Wait, Marcus thought, broadcasting to the rest of the group. *Let the tracker catch up.*

We stood around in silence until a slight beep sounded near the place where I last recalled seeing my boyfriend. *It's back*, he informed us. *Head inland.*

Does it suggest altitude? asked Maria.

A pause. *Eighteen meters above us.*

Unless you plan to climb the balconies, I suggest we find a door, thought Artur. *Follow me.*

Remember that part about how you're invisible? I replied, then stifled a yelp as an elbow jabbed into my side.

Can you locate me now? she retorted as her footsteps sounded on the tile, moving toward the main building and its brightly lit lobby.

We crept after her, taking care to muffle our footfalls, and paused outside an automatic glass door. After only a moment's wait, a pair of housekeepers emerged with a cart of folded white towels, and we slipped through the gap, unseen by the staff or the small black security cameras.

After gauging the height of the ground floor's soaring ceiling and doing a rough guesstimate, Toula punched the button for the elevator—a large one, by European standards—and the six of us squeezed inside for the ride to the fourth floor of guest rooms. When we disembarked, we stood near the elevator and waited for the tracker to confirm that we'd reached the right level. *This is it*, thought Marcus after a few seconds.

Left or right? came a voice I recognized as Eadwig's. *Twenty rooms on this floor, according to the sign.*

Just listen, Toula replied.

I closed my eyes, held my breath, and opened my mind,

feeling for the ones around me. The five minds of the rest of our party were prominent, but I pushed past them, expanding my range and trying to pick out details of the minds behind the closed doors. A man standing before the bathroom mirror had just nicked his neck with his razor. A woman in the next room was pondering the thread count of the smooth sheets. A little boy was hungry and ready to go to the beach. His sister was telling herself a fantastic story involving the two dolls she'd brought along on holiday…

Pain. Pain and confusion and fear.

Left, I told the others, and followed the signal from the strange mind. This wasn't the pain of a sunburn or a shaving cut—this was red and raw, and its owner was cowering like a wounded animal in its burrow.

On I ran to the end of the hall and the last beach-facing door, its steel handle decorated with a NE PAS DÉRANGER sign in an elegant script. *This is the place*, I thought. *Hear him?*

Stand aside, Toula ordered, and as I slid toward the neighboring room, I saw a spark around the latch. The handle depressed beneath the touch of an unseen hand, and I heard Toula mentally count to three before she pushed it open and stormed into the darkened room.

I followed on her heels and wished I hadn't. The place was night-black, the only light a sliver falling through the gap in the ornamental curtains. The room reeked of alcohol and vomit, a bouquet more common to the gutter outside a nightclub than a posh resort, and I quickly surmised the cause once Toula sent a white orb floating toward the ceiling to illuminate the scene: a bottle of Dom Pérignon sitting on the dresser, half empty, beside the grail.

And Jude…dear God, *Jude*.

I'd expected him to have taken on something like Quinn's pallor, perhaps, or maybe to appear a little green from his celebratory drinking. Instead, his face, hands, and bare chest were the color of flesh after a week in the Sahara without sunscreen, mottled with blisters and blackened patches. He cowered in the wide bed with its expensive white linens, a charred wreck staring with terror in his eyes at the door that seemed to open of its own volition.

As soon as the latch clicked behind the last of us, we dropped our glamour. "Jude, you idiot," said Toula with a sigh, then snapped, "*Ah.* Don't bother," as his hand fumbled toward the wand on the far nightstand. "We've got you outnumbered. Will you come quietly, or do we have to make this difficult?"

He cringed at the suggestion of further pain. "How…how did you…"

Marcus lifted the tracker's controller as I plucked the satchel from the rug. "You've been broadcasting your location all night," he said with an unfriendly smile. "No need for Quinn to say a word."

I marched over to the curtains and peeked through the gap at the climbing sun. "Let me guess—stayed up to watch the sunrise?" I asked Jude. "Stood a little too close to the window?"

"What did you do to me?" he demanded, sounding far more like a petulant child than the all-powerful being he'd intended to be.

"Nothing," Eadwig replied, slipping between Toula and Artur to confront him. "You did this to yourself."

"The grail—"

"I warned you it was cursed, as did Quinn. You didn't listen."

"But…but you…*you* drank of it!" he sputtered. "You must have—"

"I've done nothing of the sort," said Eadwig. "I am"—he paused to briefly glance around our group—"yes, I am the only mortal man in this room."

"But you—"

"Simon cheated death, but only temporarily. He knew

the grail was evil."

"Quinn—"

"Knew what it would do and drank of it anyway to save the child," he said, an edge creeping into his otherwise placid voice. "The baby lives yet, no thanks to you, and Quinn is safe for now…away from the light," he added, cutting his eyes to the curtains. "She had a term for the effects of the grail, I don't recall it—"

"Vampirism," I offered. "Or something similar."

Jude's eyes bulged in his burned face. "What do you mean—"

"No pulse," I began, counting off on my fingers, "can't eat or drink normal things without throwing them all up— guess you found that out the hard way—and extreme sensitivity to sunlight. On the plus side, as long as you consume enough human blood, you'll exist like this indefinitely."

"Though you'll never be any stronger," said Toula. "As far as your talent's concerned, you're already dead."

Jude's lips moved soundlessly as he grappled with the terms of his damnation, and I couldn't help but notice the grand magus's nearly imperceptible smirk.

"You kidnapped a child, held her for ransom, and recklessly endangered her life," she continued. "Moreover, you're not safe out in the open, and you're on a *highly* specialized diet. So I'll give you a choice. One, return with us to Glastonbury. You'll be bound and imprisoned until I've decided you're no longer a threat to yourself or anyone else, but you'll be fed and protected from the sun. Two, I'll bind you and leave you alone with Frank for five minutes, and you can try to explain to him why you snatched his little girl. Whether he keeps *his* bind on during those five minutes is entirely up to him."

Neither was a great option, especially not for someone who'd had dreams of heading his own arcanum: a long incarceration in the dungeon or a quick trip down a dragon's throat. But Jude had no chance of fighting his way out of that hotel room. Though talented, he was no bruiser—he wouldn't have won in a fair fight against Toula, much less against the six of us.

He was, however, wizard enough to do a slight bit of wandless casting.

Jude stretched his blistered hand toward the window and whispered a single word. I saw the tendrils of the spell coalesce almost instantly, channels of magic that latticed in the gap between the curtains before splitting violently apart...and taking the curtains with them. The protective covering fell to either side, bathing the room in bright morning light, and Jude jumped off the bed to throw himself into his own inferno.

"No, wait!" Toula yelled, jumping to save him, but Artur caught her wrist, holding her back as Jude burned. He only screamed once, a high-pitched wail that ended as his neck burst into flame. Within a minute, all that remained of the head archivist was a pile of ash atop a few scraps of burned clothing, a wide scorch mark on the rug, and the unpleasant aroma of grilled meat overlaying the vomit and booze.

"Fucking *hell*," Toula muttered, pale and visibly shaken, as the last of the flames licked themselves out. "That...wasn't part of the plan."

"Would *you* want to spend decades in the dungeon with my mother?" I retorted, then plucked the grail off the dresser and considered the mess on the floor, trying to think of it as only ashes so as not to be sick. Jude had gone out in a blaze of dishonor, and he'd never been better than prickly toward the Team, but at the end of the day, he was still a person with a family, and I couldn't just leave him there to be swept up by housekeeping. "Hey, hon?"

"Yes?" said Marcus, a note of queasy uncertainty in his tone.

"Do me a favor and make a lid for this thing, won't you?"

By the time I'd whisked Jude's earthly remains into the

grail, Marcus had produced a flat golden cap, which he sealed across the mouth of the cup. With the makeshift urn secure, Artur willed the rug clean and whole, Toula and Maria tackled the bathroom and the problematic funk, and as Marcus gathered up Jude's few belonging, I turned to Eadwig, who eyed the grail in my hand as if it might have been an open bottle of hydrochloric acid. "Let's get this back to the castle, and I'll transfer the, uh...*cremains* into another vessel. You can melt down the damn grail as soon as it's clean."

"No, I can't," he said with distaste.

"Huh?"

"I can't," he repeated. "Not until I understand its construction—if I'm to have any hope of fixing Quinn, that is." He folded his arms with a short, frustrated huff. "Now, how do we keep the damn thing secure? I'm not turning it over to the Archives—*anyone* could walk through that cup room Jude showed us." He paused, reconsidering. "Then again, they've kept the diary secure, have they not?"

"Conclave," Maria called from the bathroom.

"That would be a 'no,'" I translated. "Grand Magus?"

"Hmm?" she replied.

"How secure is Coileán's library?"

She emerged in short order, still green around the gills, but at least she hadn't added to the mess Jude left behind. "Secure enough. Why?"

I held up the grail. "Eadwig needs to study this. Where can we keep it that no one's going to be tempted to take a swig?"

"Where did that cap come from—"

"Temporary resting place," I said, giving the grail a light shake, and Toula's mouth moved in a silent *Oh*. "So...what would you say the odds are that we could take this damn thing back where it came from?"

"Decent. Let me talk to him." She gave the room a final inspection, then opened a gate back to her office. "Come on, before someone reports screaming to security.

I hope Jude paid in cash."

As we hurried across, Magus Lowe pushed himself from the couch. "Where is he?" he asked, scanning our group for the missing seventh person. "Don't tell me he ran—"

"There," said Eadwig, pointing to the grail I carried. "Or what remains of him. He chose to avoid a dungeon."

The old magus warily eyed the grail, then met Toula's weary gaze. "Funny how Mulligans seldom last long in your custody."

"Coincidence, I assure you," she replied, and put her phone to her ear. "And if you'll excuse me…" She leaned against her desk as the line opened. "Hey, Gramps. Got the cup. Jude fried himself in front of us…" She paused as a gate cracked open near the door, then put the phone down as Coileán jogged through. "That wasn't me begging you to come over. Not my first guy on fire."

"You never beg, and those don't get easier," he replied, and folded her into his arms. "Crisis averted?"

"Mostly," she said as he loosened his hold. "Eadwig wants to study the grail and try to fix Quinn, but given the security situation here—"

"Or lack thereof," the king interrupted.

"Glass half-full, glass half-empty. Mind putting it in storage for now? Once, uh…once we take Jude out of it?"

Realization dawned, and disgust crossed his face as he considered the grail. A simple brass box appeared on Toula's blotter. "Would one of you like to do the honors?"

"Not particularly, but sure," I said, too tired to watch my manners. With Marcus holding a piece of paper steady beneath the new urn to catch anything that missed the target, I carefully transferred the ashes, then willed the grail clean as Marcus sealed the box. As I gave the cup a final check for debris, I noticed the faint stain around the bottom, like strong tea mixed with red wine left on cheap porcelain. Shuddering, I handed over the grail, and Coileán turned to Eadwig.

"You think you know more than Ros, eh?" he said, a dark eyebrow arching in challenge.

Eadwig didn't leap into a fight. "Overall, no. As to the application of spellcraft, quite probably."

"I mean, those few months of formal Arcanum education I had were *helpful*," said Ros, manifesting on the far side of the gate, "but Simon Magus has a point."

Eadwig tensed at the moniker, but Coileán didn't press him. "Do you want to come over now?" he asked. "You've seen the guestroom situation—it's no trouble to move you closer to the library."

The boy started to answer, then hesitated, visibly conflicted. "I…I suppose I—"

"He needs training, does he not?" said Artur, meeting Toula's and Coileán's eyes in turn. "Toula, you were going to send him to Popova, I believe. Assessment, any missing basics…"

"Sure," she replied, "but Helen Carver could do that just as well in Faerie. Heck, stick him with Helen and Badger, and they'd have him in shape in no time."

"But what of his mundane education?" my sister pressed. "He's missed the last thousand years."

The thought she shot my way was intended for Marcus as well, and he seamlessly picked up the argument, a party to our conspiracy. "Artur and I should work with him. This is ground we've trod, you know."

"And it's no trouble keeping him in our spare room," I added. "Eadwig's been working ever since he arrived. A little time to catch his breath wouldn't be a bad idea."

The grand magus and the king shared a look suggesting that we weren't as subtle as we'd hoped. "Do you really think it wise to keep *him* on the premises?" Coileán countered. "We know what he's capable of, and if memory serves, the dream space is accessible in this realm…"

"He's a kid," I said. "I don't care whose memories he's housing, he needs to be around other kids."

"We can't just slot him into regular classes," Magus

Lowe protested. "He'd either be leagues behind or leagues ahead, depending on the subject. And how would we explain him?"

Toula rubbed her chin as she considered the issue, and then, with a long look at Eadwig, she said, "Tutoring is an option. Arnie, I trust that you can acquaint Eadwig with the essentials of a remedial mundane education. A computer, a few textbooks…you could supervise, couldn't you?"

"Well…yes," he said, taken aback, "but I'm no expert in—"

"I'm not asking for calculus and Romantic poetry. History, geography, political science, maybe a little cultural appreciation. Basics." Turning to Maria, she said, "I'll leave it to you to explain to Ted why there's a new provisional member on the Team. You guys work together and decide on a cover story that in no way suggests *that* kid is anything like an incarnation of Simon Magus, got it?"

A slow smile creased Maria's face. "Capisco."

"And as for you three," she concluded, sweeping one finger down the line of my flatmates, "I'm tasking you with keeping him alive and fed."

"We've managed thus far," I replied.

"Then keep it up. Okay, people, get out of my office. *Shoo.* Get some rest, and Coileán, if you'd please take that thing with you…"

He rubbed her shoulder. "Come with me. You need sleep, Glinda."

"I've got James Mulligan's big brother doing a cardiac procedure on a hatchling this morning. No rest for the wicked, I'm afraid."

We vacated the room, giving them a moment's privacy, and Eadwig slumped past the Council offices beside Artur, his expression unreadable. As we reached the staircase, she put an arm around his shoulders and pulled him toward the landing. "You did well, boy," she murmured. "Jude's death wasn't your fault."

His eyes narrowed in suspicion. "That's...decent of you."

"It's the truth."

"I thought you disliked me on principle."

"You're tolerable," she replied, and leaned closer. "That being said, if you play with Beth's affections, I will *hurt* you." The boy swallowed hard, and Artur released him with a hearty pat on the back. "Glad we had this talk," she said, and led the way home.

All told, it took two MDs, a PhD, and a fair amount of wizardry to fix Aurora, but the procedure was an unqualified success. By Wednesday night, as those of us who'd been going for days finally dragged ourselves from bed, Toula had restored the baby's transformation bind, and Aurora woke in her father's arms, no worse for her ordeal or for the nearly six days she'd missed. Frank brought her with him to the Team meeting Thursday morning, and she sat happily in his lap, pink-cheeked and grabbing at the dry-erase markers, as Ted and Maria explained that Eadwig had been assigned to their keeping.

The boy had taken a chair in the corner, away from the table, and shifted in his seat as my colleagues studied him. Once Ted sheepishly admitted to Lakshmi, our overworked logistics guru, that "put him in the storage closet and move the boxes around" was the extent of the planning he'd accomplished, he turned to the nervous subject of his discourse and grinned. "Come on over here, Eadwig. No one's going to bite."

"Aurie might," Frank interjected, jiggling one knee to make the baby bounce.

"Eh, she doesn't count. Not even provisional yet. Pull up, son," he said as my side of the table scooted our chairs around to make room.

Eadwig slid his chair into the gap, his eyes darting back and forth as he took in the array of computers on the table. "I…I apologize, Quinn has been teaching me to use one of those devices, but—"

"Aw, hell, don't worry about that," Antony interrupted, and pointed to Artur and Marcus. "We got those two up to speed. You'll be fine in a few months."

Still, Eadwig remained uneasy. "I would have studied your reports and familiarized myself with your work, had I been given more time, but—"

"Hold it," said Mal. "Can you cast as well as Simon Magus could?"

His brow knit. "I…yes, I remember the techniques. I still have his strength—"

"Then the rest is gravy."

"Let me put it like this," said Daphne, leaning across the table toward him. "Currently, I'm the strongest wizard on the Team, and I use a maple wand."

Eadwig looked at her blankly.

"I'm not a magus-level talent," she clarified. "And since it's always nice to have someone around who can stop rockslides, manage gates, *and* pick up a steel carabiner without making a production of it…you know, welcome aboard, Eadwig. Or, ehm…are we going with Ed or something? No offense, but *Eadwig* is the sort of name that raises the questions we're trying to avoid."

For the first time that morning, he smiled. "Ed, then," he replied. "I could be Ed."

But even with Eadwig sorted, there remained the matter of Quinn.

For a twenty-eight-year-old woman suddenly finding herself among the ranks of the ambulatory dead, she proved to be a trooper. She'd awakened shortly before sunset Wednesday evening, safe behind her magically smoked windows and unsure of what to do with herself. By the time the rest of us arose, she'd showered, fixed her curls, and brushed her teeth, and was sitting at the kitchen table, playing solitaire on her phone.

Around nine, Dr. Powell knocked, carrying a white cooler the size of a lunchbox, and Quinn watched with unease as she opened it in the kitchen. "This is the original stuff," said the doctor as she rummaged through the lower cabinets. "Type O, to be precise. I'll switch you to a homemade copy soon enough, but while you're still adjusting, let's not get too experimental. And where do you—*ah*, there," she said, pulling out a copper saucepan. "Quinn, dear, I know this is uncomfortable, but you should pay attention."

Reluctantly, Quinn stood by as Dr. Powell heated a pot of water on the range, then dropped in a translucent bag of blood once it reached a simmer. "The silicone shouldn't melt, and it's reusable," she explained, prodding it with a spatula. "Now, give it a few minutes in the bath—it'll probably go down more easily if it's not the temperature of gazpacho." When she was satisfied with her gruesome cookery, Dr. Powell removed the bag with a pair of tongs, let it drip over the sink, then pulled a large steel tumbler from her cooler and plunked it onto the counter. "No need to use a clear glass," she said, pouring the bag's contents into the tumbler, "and the odds are decent that your cup's not going to walk away in *this* flat." She screwed on the lid, which came with a steel straw, and handed the tumbler to Quinn. "Bottoms up."

Quinn squared her shoulders, drew an unnecessary deep breath, then took a test sip. She swished the liquid around her mouth as if she were tasting a fine wine and swallowed it without gagging.

"Passable?" the doctor asked.

Her response was a longer sip, punctuated only by the movement in her throat. Unhindered by a pesky need for oxygen, Quinn drained the tumbler within a minute, then licked her lips and chuckled weakly to find Dr. Powell still watching her. "Better than I thought it'd be," she confessed.

"Good. Your color's returning."

Quinn raced into Beth's bathroom to see the effect: a faint blush beneath her skin as the enchantment carried her meal throughout her body. Though it subsided within the hour, Quinn was almost chipper after her dinner, and she promised to be in her room well before sunrise. We didn't share with her the details of Jude's demise, and to my relief, she didn't ask us to paint her a picture.

The next morning, while the Team met, Dr. Dellucci joined Dr. Powell for breakfast in the castle's massive dining hall, a properly Gothic space filled with wooden tables and lined with paintings of dead wizards I couldn't name. Their meeting wasn't about Quinn, as she later told me—Dr. Powell had already filled him in on the contours of the curse, and he'd been mollified by Toula's post-surgery news that someone would be working on a way to break the enchantment. Rather, Dr. Powell came to the table with a job offer. Sure, Dr. Dellucci was almost ninety-five, but his mind remained sharp, and the spell she'd cast on him the day before had eased some of the pain in his joints. Wizards tended to be longer-lived than mundane humans, and while there were no data as to the relative longevity of duds, Dr. Dellucci surely stood a better chance of passing his centennial with magical assistance than he did in a mundane facility. While Dr. Powell could handle most of the installation's illnesses and injuries, she had little time to train her underlings in more than the basics of medicine, and having another qualified physician on hand could help her on both counts. He wouldn't carry an equal load, and he'd always have a medic with him to handle any spellcraft, but the thought of coming out of retirement sat well with the old doctor— and he'd be near his little Quinnie, to boot. In the end, Dr. Dellucci had requested only three things: a bachelor pad with handrails and a walk-in tub, an invitation to the senior wizards' weekly bridge night festivities, and a promise that he would never be introduced by his birthname. He didn't care who knew about his little brother, but he didn't want Quinn saddled with that sort of baggage.

But the elderly Dellucci patriarch couldn't just disappear from Chicago without telling his children any more than Quinn could extend her "internship" indefinitely. And so, on Friday morning, Toula brought Dr. Dellucci to Quinn's parents' house in the wee hours. His panicked son, Zachary, who was passing a sleepless night because the assisted-living facility had *misplaced* his father, took one look at the hole in space that had appeared in his kitchen and fainted. Once he came to and his father cleared him to sit up, Dr. Dellucci asked if Zach could get his siblings on a group chat, then sat in front of Zach's computer with his five bleary-eyed children and slowly explained where he'd been and why. He told them about recovering his memory when the eldest of them were still teenagers and why he'd kept the secret, and then he turned the floor over to Toula to fill them in on the rest of the family. The four joining remotely were skeptical until Zach, still a little woozy from his faint, told them about the lightning-wrapped gate he'd seen, and Toula called up a few fireballs for emphasis.

It must come as a shock to learn that you've got wizards in the family, and I imagine it was a massive disappointment to the Dellucci siblings to hear that only Zach's daughter had any talent. But Toula insisted that they could come for a visit, since their father would be in residence...and once the others signed off, she and Dr. Dellucci told Zach and his wife, Farah, who'd finally woken with the noise, about what had befallen Quinn. Putting it mildly, her parents were displeased with this development, but Dr. Dellucci insisted that he'd talked with Quinn, and she was coping. He called her to let her know he'd broken the news, and she sat up past her bedtime in her blacked-out room, reassuring them by the light of her reading lamp as her mother choked back tears.

"I'm *fine*," I heard her say from my position in the corner of the room, well away from the phone's camera. "They're working on a way to fix me, and until then, you've *got* to see the library in this place. Oh, and I got a job, did Grandpa tell you?"

Her cheerful façade fell when she hung up, and I hugged her, having been waiting with her as moral support for the inevitable call that morning. "What if Ed doesn't figure it out?" she mumbled, flopping onto her bed. "What if I'm stuck like this until…you know…I get sick of it all?"

I squeezed her cold hand. "We're talking about the guy who managed to turn back his own clock just to go after a stupid cup. I still have faith."

Leaving Quinn to rest, I returned to the den and collapsed onto the couch, weary to my bones. By then, the last solid sleep I'd gotten had been upon our return from France two days prior. I'd gone to bed at a reasonable hour the previous night—Ted certainly wasn't demanding anything of the Team that week—but I'd screamed myself awake an hour after I closed my eyes, haunted by my mind's detailed replay of Jude's last moments.

"You're safe," Marcus had soothed as I'd cried in his arms. "I've got you, Kitty, you're safe now."

Eventually, I'd drifted off again, only to wake well before dawn when Marcus had his own nightmare. We'd held each other until the windows lightened behind their shades, both of us afraid to attempt sleep and neither willing to admit it.

It was two weeks before we slept through the night again, long after Frank's enormous bouquet of thank-you roses had wilted. It was three weeks before I didn't find Artur nursing tea at the table, dressed and on alert, when I emerged from my room. I couldn't tell how Eadwig was coping—I'd soundproofed his and Quinn's adjoining rooms to accommodate their different schedules, and he was often gone when I awoke, having slipped across to Faerie and the corner of Coileán's library he'd claimed for his research. When he made an appearance in the subbasement, it was to access the Archives' scanned resources, a task made far simpler with Antony down the hall to walk him through the process. In the evenings, as Marcus and I made dinner, Quinn and Eadwig would pass each other in the kitchen, the one waking, the other ending the day. She never pressed him for an update, nor did he have good news to share, and as soon as he ate, he escaped upstairs to continue his work until late in the night.

But near the end of August, as the short summer holiday ran down, I saw Quinn corner him near Artur's room while I was setting the table for five—Quinn made her own meals and handled her steel tumbler, which she usually took as breakfast to go. "I appreciate all the work you're putting into this," she said softly. "Really, I do. But don't kill yourself on my behalf. At least take a night off."

He fidgeted as she squeezed his shoulder. "There must be a solution—"

"And it's driving you crazy, I get it. Try to stop obsessing, will you? It's not like I'm getting any worse." She glanced over her shoulder at the den, where Beth was cramming to finish her summer reading before the new term, then back at him. "She's been reading Dickens all day. Why don't you see if she wants to take a break?"

The answer to his awkward enquiry was an emphatic yes, and the dinner table gained elbow room that night, as Beth slopped a hearty portion of my lasagna into a plastic container and took Eadwig to the roof for al fresco dining. When I retired that night, Beth's book remained where she'd left it, dog-eared on the couch, but the old Monopoly board had returned to the coffee table.

"I sent them to bed around four," Quinn reported as I made coffee in the dark early the next morning. "Put Ed out of his misery. Tell him to take the day, huh?" she said, turning for the staircase to beat the sunrise.

"He wants to help."

She paused and looked down at me. "And I'm grateful.

But this was a decision I made, and…you know, I'd do it again. I can live with the consequences. Or, uh…well, whatever you call this. 'Living-adjacent,' maybe."

Though Quinn seemed more at peace than I'd seen her in days, the thought of her spending her waking hours alone as the castle slept sat poorly with me. "Want to go to the movies tonight? Marcus and I thought we might see what's playing after work."

She smiled, then—a warm, genuine smile. "Aw, thanks, but I'm booked. Grandpa's finally going to teach me to play bridge," she replied, and slipped upstairs to bed.

Since my time as a student at Arc 2, the more social-minded of the parents and teachers had prevailed upon Magus Lowe to authorize a start-of-term party for the older students. What had begun as a mixer with punch and bite-sized desserts had morphed into a Saturday night semiformal dance in the competition room, complete with a Council aide and his DJ equipment on the balcony. The lighting had grown more complex with each iteration, and the previous August had seen the introduction of a fog machine.

My little sister had designed her own dress, a strappy red number that nicely showed off her curves, especially as she teetered atop new black heels that she swore were more comfortable than they looked. She'd allowed Quinn to help her tease her blonde hair into an updo and curl the strands framing her face, and with her best smoky eye in full effect, Beth looked closer to twenty-six than sixteen.

"Don't worry about tonight," Artur insisted for the tenth time as Marcus and I gathered our luggage in the foyer. "I am chaperoning. No harm will come to her."

"And I'm hanging out with Artur," Quinn reminded me between slurps of her breakfast. "Rest assured, there will be no nonsense on the dance floor."

"Perhaps a little," Artur suggested.

"Okay, *reasonable* nonsense, but nothing…*ah*. Let's see," she called, turning at the sound of footsteps on the stairs.

I had to admit that Ed cleaned up nicely. He'd tamed his hair with Quinn's help and some styling gel, and she'd coaxed him into a black button-down and dark trousers, polished without being stuffy. She beckoned him close, undid his top two collar buttons, then stepped back and surveyed her handiwork. "Passable, yeah?"

Before we could give him a hard time, Beth emerged in a cloud of hairspray, her spike heels clicking against the floor. I glanced at Ed in time to see his face light up, and as Beth wobbled toward him, she grinned. "Well? What do we think?" she began, then caught her shoe on the rug and almost tumbled.

Ed steadied her as she righted herself, and she blushed as she took his arm. "Lovely," he said, looking up at her— in those heels, she was a good four inches taller than he was—but if he minded the height discrepancy, he gave no indication. "If you don't feel like dancing in those shoes, I don't know the dances at all, so—"

"Oh, I'll teach you," she said, tugging him toward the door. "Come on, I don't want to be the last to arrive. Bye!" she said, pausing in her exodus to give me a brief hug. "Have…fun?"

"I'll have you know that Winston, Tennessee, is an exciting destination with its very own Holiday Inn," I teased. "Behave yourself. Artur's in charge."

"What else is new?" she retorted, and socked Marcus in the arm before sweeping out the door with her date—a *friend* date, she'd assured us, though no one in the flat except the two of them seemed to believe it.

"Take your holiday," said Artur with a smirk. "I'm sure we'll manage somehow."

As Quinn stepped into Artur's room for safety, I envisioned the photos I'd found online and directed my gate into the abandoned parking lot behind the quiet motel. It opened with a rush of humid August air and a flash of afternoon sunlight, and Marcus and I hurried through, encumbered only by our well-used camping backpacks. Once I'd sealed the rift, he turned in a slow circle, taking in the cracked asphalt, the motel—which, truth be told, didn't seem to have been updated since I'd left town—and the field of weeds stretching toward the gas station in the distance. "This is it," I told him. "We could have gone back to the Riviera, remember."

"I've had quite enough of the Riviera for now, thank you," he replied, and followed me toward the entrance.

Officially, check-in wasn't until later in the afternoon, but business in my hometown was slow, and the clerk gave us a pair of keys without protest. Once we'd dumped our belongings in the clean but unremarkable room, I slipped my purse back over my chest and gestured toward the door. "I make no guarantees, but if you want to see it…"

"Ready when you are."

Fighting the butterflies in my stomach, I remembered my childhood home: the old farmhouse, Daddy's pickup truck, the endless field of sunflowers. Hoping that something remained of the place, I envisioned the stop sign at the four-way intersection half a mile away and opened a small gate. Seeing no traffic—not unusual for the roads out by our farm—I widened it enough to give us passage, then pointed up the dusty road, past the Nicholsons' fenced pasture. "That way."

Marcus stayed beside me as we walked along the edge of the road, dodging bits of litter and the occasional ant bed. "Mom sold the farm to the Andrews," I explained, kicking a plastic Coke bottle with a sun-faded label into the grass. "They were our next-door neighbors, relatively speaking. Nothing's exactly next door when you're talking about farms. But they were nice, they went to our church, Mrs. Andrews taught the children's choir—"

He caught my hand and gave it a gentle squeeze of reassurance.

"Sorry," I mumbled, "I just haven't been back since I

was ten, and I'm hoping…"

My voice faded as we rounded the curve. There, in the distance, was my old house, just as it had always been. There was the long driveway, still nothing but rutted dirt, a brown scar cutting through the tall grass. And there, beyond the house…

"They kept the sunflowers," I whispered, staring at the sprawling field of bobbing yellow heads. "Oh, they *kept* them."

I was almost running by the time I reached my old driveway, and I was in a full red-faced sweat as I clomped up the porch steps and knocked the dust off my tennis shoes. My heart in my throat, I rang the doorbell and waited until the blue inner door opened, revealing a middle-aged brunette on the other side of the screen. "Can I help you?" she asked warily—and with good reason, considering the disheveled state I was in.

"I'm so sorry to bother you, ma'am," I said, barely conscious of my long-suppressed drawl breaking free, "but I was passing through town, and I used to live here, and—"

Her jaw dropped. "*Kitty*? Kitty Connolly, is that you?" I nodded, and she pushed open the screen door. "I'm Mary Brooks Andrews, remember me?"

"Mary Brooks?" I echoed, a wide smile breaking across my face. I remembered the Andrews' gawky eldest daughter, who'd gone off to college only to come home to the family farm. She was gawky no longer, a grown woman in a loose green T-shirt and Levi's, and her hug was tight enough to threaten respiration.

"I never thought you'd be back!" she exclaimed. "And look at you, all grown up! Oh, and who's this?" she asked, spotting Marcus over my shoulder.

"My boyfriend," I replied. "We're on vacation."

"And you dragged him out *here*? You crazy, girl?" Sobering slightly, she continued, "Hope you don't mind what I've done with the place. Little fresh paint, redid the kitchen, but the bones are still here."

"It's perfect," I replied, taking in the wicker porch furniture and the half-depleted citronella candles along the railing. "Have you lived here long?"

"Since your mama sold it to my folks. They deeded me the place about a year later. I still can't believe she sold your family farm…"

"She wasn't in a great frame of mind," I said, which I thought was more than generous. "But you're still growing sunflowers?"

Mary Brooks's eyes crinkled as she smiled. "Mama let the flowers handle themselves the year they bought the farm. She was planning to switch crops the next year, but I guess enough seeds dropped, since the sunflowers came back, and…well, it was Mr. Orson's field, you know, and Mama decided they could stay. I don't know *what* he put in the soil out there," she added, lowering her voice. "Never seen sunflowers grow that well or bloom as long as those do. It's like that field was meant for them."

I could have told her—even from a distance, I could see the fine lines of the spell Daddy had woven around and through that field, a spell that remained unbroken years after his death—but I just smiled.

"They're not a bad crop," said Mary Brooks, "though really, it's the photo shoots I love. We get people from all around who want to take pictures out there, and I charge twenty bucks a session. Sell souvenir flowers for a buck a pop. *Stupid* easy money."

I chuckled along with her. "Would you mind terribly if I took a walk out there?"

"Not at all. And if you want some flowers, be my guest," she replied. "Lord knows I've got oodles. Great to see you again, hon," she said as she hugged me a second time. "Welcome home. Y'all staying long?"

"Passing through," I replied, and climbed down the porch steps. "I'm glad you got the place," I added, rejoining Marcus. "Daddy always said you had a knack for farming. He'd be happy to know you're taking such good care of the land."

"That's sweet of you to say," she replied, and waved us on toward the field. "Have fun out there. Don't get lost, now!"

I took Marcus's hand and led him down the grassy path toward the sunflowers, then pushed through a narrow row to reach the forest of green stalks and leaves. Weaving among the six-foot plants, I pulled him with me deeper and deeper into the field, until there was nothing around us but flowers and their patchy yellow canopy overhead. "They're a little shorter than I remember," I murmured, gazing up at the giant heads, "but I was a kid the last time I was out here…"

"This is beautiful," he said, and produced a knife from the ether. "Are we taking some with us?"

I thought of the little sunflowers my dad had ensorcelled long ago, that permanent bit of summer he'd given me when I cried to see the field harvested…the last thing I had of him, destroyed by teenage wizards with no shred of compassion for a grieving child. My fingers went to the diamond pendant in the hollow of my throat, Val's sunflower, as dear to me as Daddy's flowers in its own way.

"I'd like a few," I replied. "And I should take some to Beth. Daddy would want her to have them."

Marcus helped me pick out a dozen nearly perfect blooms and cut them for me until I looked like a pageant queen with a bouquet cradled in my arm. I worked a quick enchantment over them, preserving them from damage and decay, then looked up to find him smiling at me. "What?" I asked, grinning back at him.

"Are you glad we came?"

I nodded and kissed him. "This is better than I'd hoped. I mean, you still haven't seen the wonders of the Kroger," I joked, "but this…" I paused, drinking in the familiar flowers I thought I'd never see again. "This is almost home." I blinked away tears as my eyes pricked and laughed at myself. "Sheesh, getting sentimental over a field. Sorry." Shifting my armful of flowers, I teased, "Fancy city boy like you, bet you never thought you'd be dating a farmer's daughter, huh?"

I'd turned away to make an attempt at stealthy tear drying when he said, "No, but now I want to marry her."

I whirled around, almost dropping my flowers in my surprise, only to find Marcus on one knee. "What…are you…"

"If you'll have me," he murmured, his dark eyes hopeful. "I love you, Kitty."

I cried in earnest then, though I managed to tell him yes. He rose and pulled me close, being careful not to crush the sunflowers, and held me until I was laughing in his arms. "Did I do something wrong?" he mumbled into my tangled hair. "That was what Antony suggested, but—"

"No, no, that was just right," I assured him, my heart as light and full as it had ever been. "Perfect. Yes. I did say yes, didn't I?"

"Repeatedly."

"*This* is why you've been pushing for a holiday?"

"I wanted to do it somewhere that made you happy. Maria discovered that the sunflowers were still here months ago—it was her suggestion," he replied, then reached into his pocket and extracted a small cloth bag. "I hope you like this. If not, you won't hurt my feelings…"

The ring he extracted was an emerald, perfectly clear, round-cut, and set in gold. I held out my hand, and he slid it onto my finger, adjusting it ever so slightly to fit over my knuckle. Holding up my hand to examine it, I wiggled it back and forth in a shaft of light that slipped between two flowers, then kissed Marcus again and whispered, "I love you."

"Is it suitable?"

"Oh, yes. You did *good*."

The day was warm, the flowers awkward in my arms,

but we took the long way back to town, talking of everything and nothing and daring to make plans for the rest of our lives. The motel was almost in sight when a thought struck me: "Should we tell Val? What time is it over there?"

"What's the rush?" Marcus asked. "Don't you think he'll learn of this soon enough?"

I mulled that over, my mental list lengthening: my sisters, Maria, our flatmates, the Team, the grand magus, the Three, Hope and Arik, the Joneses, at least half the Fringe…

"Yeah, it can wait," I decided, and kissed him again.

All in all, forever didn't seem half bad.

ACKNOWLEDGEMENTS

Have I mentioned that *Stranger Magics* was meant to be a one-off book? But here we are now, at the back of the *thirteenth* title in the series…and it's not over yet. Thank you for joining me on this strange journey.

Once more, I thank the Novel Chicks for putting up with me. Adam Domby continues to provide his excellent feedback, for which I remain grateful.

And yes, here's to you, Mom and Dad.

ABOUT THE AUTHOR

When not writing fiction, Ash Fitzsimmons is an appellate attorney and an unrepentant car singer.

Find her online:
www.ashfitzsimmons.com

www.ingramcontent.com/pod-product-compliance
Lightning Source LLC
Chambersburg PA
CBHW020254030726
47499CB00001B/201